DARKLY ENCHANTED

Magic exists,
if you know
where to look

SPELL BOUND

Enjoy the fantasy!

STEPHANIE JULIAN

Steph J

Spell Bound, Copyright 2011 by Stephanie Julian
Published by Stephanie Julian

All rights reserved.

Layout by www.formatting4U.com

This ebook is licensed for your personal enjoyment only. This ebook may not be re-sold or given away to other people. If you would like to share this book with another person, please purchase an additional copy for each person. If you're reading this book and did not purchase it, or it was not purchased for your use only, then please return to Amazon and purchase your own copy.

Thank you for respecting the hard work of this author. To obtain permission to excerpt portions of the text, please contact the author at stephaniejulian@msn.com.

All characters in this book are fiction and figments of the author's imagination.
ISBN: 0984663118
ISBN-13: 978-0-9846631-1-8

*In the contemporary world, magic holds no sway.
But appearances can be deceiving.
Old gods remain, old ways continue and creatures of myth live among us.
If you know where to look...*

A centuries-old curse
Gabriel Borelli was born a warrior. He's dedicated to avenging his father's murder and protecting his mother, who's living under a centuries-old curse. He can't allow anything to distract him from his course... not even the one woman who may hold the key to all he desires.

A magical connection...
Shea Tedaldi and her young brother hold a powerful magic men will kill to possess. She needs a hero who won't falter in the face of danger. Gabriel is that hero, even if he refuses. But she won't take no for an answer.

A dangerous desire...
Neither of them expected such searing heat to explode between them. And if that heat consumes them, it could destroy the very things they've vowed to protect.

DEDICATION

To my guys. Love you always.

Glossary

Aitás – Underworld

Arus – magical power inherent in the races of Etruscan descent

Attonitum – looks like a cross between a revolver and an inoculation gun and would be useless in the hand of an *eteri*, a regular human. The iron grip warms to the touch, while the quartz crystal concentration chamber pulses with a pale pink light. The solid copper barrel focuses the magic.

Blood Bound – An ancient tradition tying two souls and their fates together for all eternity by mingling blood during sex.

Boschetta – a group of thirteen *streghe*

Enu – humans of magical Etruscan descent

Eteri – Etruscan for foreigner, used to describe regular humans

Fata – mythical beings of magical Etruscan descent such as folletti (fairies) and linchetti (night elves)

Goddess Gift – magical abilities including but not restricted to scrying, healing, far-seeing, affinities to herbs and crystals

Grigorio – a male born with enhanced senses and strength and an affinity to metal; in ancient times, the *grigori* were warrior priests and guardians of the Etruscan race; they were thought to have died out

Involuti – Founding gods of the Etruscans, those from whom all other Etruscan deities are descended

Lucani – Etruscan werewolves; they form the Etruscan army, based on the ancient Roman Legion

Priestesses of Menrva's – originally a group of thirteen unmarried women who pledged their lives to the Etruscan Menrva, Goddess of Wisdom, and kept safe her most sacred gift to the Etruscans, the twelve Nails of the Ages; through the centuries, they handed down their duties to their nearest living female relatives

Strega – (plural *streghe*) Female of Etruscan descent endowed with Goddess Gifts

Stregone – Male of Etruscan descent endowed with Goddess Gifts

Salvanelli – one of the races of the Etruscan Fata, thought to be extinct

Versipellis – literally "skin shifter," shapeshifters including Etruscan *lucani*, Norse *berkserkir* (bears) and French *loup garou* (wolves)

Prologue

Tuscany
1495

"You bitches." Brown eyes red-rimmed and blazing, Fabrizio Paganelli shook with grief and fury. "You killed him."

"No." Dafne, the *boschetta*'s leader, bowed her head, sorrow etched in every line of her normally placid expression. "We could do nothing for him. His illness was too advanced."

"You lie." Paganelli clutched his youngest son's body in his arms, Christo's beautiful face finally peaceful in death. Such a stark contrast to his father's madness. "I came to you for help."

From her position in the circle around the bed, Celeste's heart hurt for the grief in the man's voice. But her skin crawled at the evil underlying his tone.

Could the other twelve members of her *boschetta* not hear it? Or did they hear only their soft prayer to the Etruscan Great Goddess Uni for Christo's safe journey to Aitás? Celeste mouthed the words but watched the distraught father with wary eyes.

"I begged you to cure him," Paganelli raged. "Instead your magic killed him."

"I am so very sorry, Fabrizio." Daphne reached for him but Paganelli drew back, as if she might contaminate him somehow, his mouth twisted with a sneer of disgust and anguish.

"Sorry does not bring back my son!"

And neither could Paganelli's great wealth, though he had tried to buy Christo's health. Celeste knew he'd spent a fortune on modern physicians for cures that failed. By the time Fabrizio had begged the *streghe* to save Christo with their magic, the young man had been too ill.

She had been shocked when Dafne had gathered the women to attempt to heal him anyway. Though the *streghe* ministered to the villagers on a daily basis, the Paganellis, the largest and wealthiest landowners in the valley, had never approached them for anything.

Celeste had argued against it. She did not think it wise to reveal the *boschetta*'s true power to Paganelli. They were not like other *streghe*, women of Etruscan descent who used their Goddess Gifts to heal and make small spells and potions.

Their *boschetta* alone had a secret and sacred duty to Menrva, the Etruscan Goddess of Wisdom, handed down to them from their mothers and their mothers before them. As Menrva's priestesses, they protected her most sacred gift to the Etruscan people, the Nails of the Ages, and waited for the day she once again demanded their duty to her.

For more than a thousand years, her priestesses had waited.

Celeste's hand crept to the leather thong around her neck and the iron key hanging from it. They should have said no to Paganelli, but Celeste's younger sister, soft-hearted Andrea, had begged them to help Christo and no one could deny her anything. Even though Celeste, a healer, had sensed the black tumor in his stomach was too advanced to heal.

"No, Fabrizio," Dafne continued to try to calm the distraught father. "We tried—"

"Charlatans! Whores!" Paganelli's voice bounced off the walls of the lushly furnished bedroom in the Paganelli's huge manor. "I'll make you pay. You will all pay."

Celeste's bile rose at Fabrizio's fast-building fury. That angry emotion felt like black smoke in her lungs, nauseating her.

"Please, Fabrizio," Dafne pleaded. "I understand—"

"What do you understand?" he raged, one hand slashing out in front of him. "You understand nothing. Your children live. How can you understand my pain?"

Celeste felt a sliver of pain strike at the center of her heart. She and her mate had not yet been blessed with children. She sometimes wondered if they ever would be.

Great Goddess, please, grant us a child—

"Fabrizio, try to remain calm," Dafne said. "You'll cause yourself injury. I know your pain is intense but you must think of your remaining sons. They need you now."

The old man's mouth pulled back in a snarl, thick white hair shaking around his face in his fury. "Christo was the most precious, the most powerful of my sons. You have robbed me of him."

Rising from the bedside, Paganelli jerked a knife from the sheath on his belt and cut his dead son across the arm.

The thirteen women of the *boschetta* gasped as if with one body, several members stepping back, breaking the circle.

No, Celeste thought, he wouldn't dare…

As the knife dripped red, Paganelli slashed across his chest, mingling his blood with his son's.

"I, Fabrizio Paganelli, curse you to outlive your loved ones so that you, too, can feel this agony." He snarled the words, biting them off like a dog tears into meat. "So that you may know the pain of watching your children die while you stand helpless. And I demand Veive, God of Revenge, forbid you to bear another female child. You will produce no more *streghe*. No other father should fall prey to a *strega*'s lies. You'll pay. You'll all pay…"

Chapter One

Present Day

Blood. Everywhere. The floor, the walls.
Her dad.
Blessed Goddess, no...
Thick, dark. On her hands, her clothes. The metallic odor in her nose. Overpowering.
Her mother...oh, gods, what did they do to her mom? Can't breathe. No air...
Too late. She'd been too late.
Wait...Someone here? No, someone in her head, whispering. Her mother...
In the basement.
Sneakers sliding in—No, don't think. Move. Basement. Dad's workroom.
Beneath the workbench.
Her mother's voice. Her dead mother...Oh, Mom—
The spell.
Runes beneath the table. A spell of concealment. The ancient Etruscan language rolled off her tongue in fierce bites. Knife across her palm, her blood on the runes.
The workbench slid away from the wall.
And she screamed and screamed as blood poured out...

* * *

Shooting straight up in bed, Shea Tedaldi gasped for air in the semi-dark bedroom, tears in her eyes.

The bed creaked as her hand shot to her left. Warm, soft skin, rising and falling in the rhythm of sleep. Leo's small body huddled on his side under the covers.

She breathed a sigh of relief.

Just a dream. Another dream about that awful night that left her terrified and shaking.

Whoever was on their tail was getting closer. The voices in her head—those maddening, unintelligible, buzzing voices in the back of her mind—were frantic.

It was time. She and Leo needed help or they needed to leave this dingy apartment in Reading, Pennsylvania, and run like hell. Just like they'd done four months ago in Atlantic City.

The voices had put up a clamor then, too, so much so she'd decided to move here and finally look up the man her mother had believed she could entrust with Leo's life.

So why are you thinking about running again? Without even talking to the guy?

Well, that was easy. Because five years on her own had taught her that people screwed you all the time. Since running away from home at seventeen, she'd learned to rely only on herself.

Yeah, and how's that working for you so far?

"Oh, just shut up," she whispered as she slid her legs off the side of the bed and sat on the edge, willing the shakes and the tears to stop. No need for them. Leo was fine. At least, as fine as a six-year-old with monsters on his ass could be.

Turning, she watched her brother sleep, his too-long hair inky black against the stark white sheets.

Everything about him was growing fast. He needed a haircut. And, since shopping wasn't exactly on her to-do list, he needed new clothes. His ankles had started to show beneath his jeans. He'd need new shoes, too, and socks, because his were full of holes.

But mostly, Leo needed not to worry about boogeymen who wanted to cut out her heart and turn him into a monster. He needed his parents...

She took a deep breath and straightened her spine, twisting her neck back and forth until it cracked.

Time to get off your ass.

Because the men who'd killed their parents were getting close again. And the man who'd ordered their murders, Dario Paganelli...he wanted Leo.

Her stomach rolled and she rubbed it with her hand, trying to ease the ache. But nothing helped.

Dario Paganelli was the boogeyman her parents had whispered about behind closed doors, the monster who had forced them to live like hermits. He was the cause of Shea's every fear and heartache.

He'd made her life hell without ever meeting him. And now that monster wanted Leo, a little boy who looked like an angel but controlled enough power to burn a house to the ground.

Goose bumps danced on her skin. Paganelli was a cold-blooded monster who would break Leo, remake him in his own evil image. Then turn him loose on his own people.

Great Goddess, he's only six.

Sighing, her gaze shifted to the small round table in the corner.

The altar at their home in Wisconsin had been made from the base of a lightning-struck walnut tree from the dense woods enclosing their property. Nearly five feet in diameter, that altar had dominated the small clearing where her parents had held their rituals for the Great Goddess Uni. Passed down through the millennia, those rituals connected them to the Etruscan Mother Goddess, renewed their faith in Her and Her protection over them.

Shea prayed every day, just as her mother had. But so far, she'd gotten no guidance from the supposedly all-mighty Uni. No inspiration. No help.

Which was why she'd moved them here. To get help. And to hide.

The largest population of the once mighty Etruscan race, maybe five thousand or so, lived here in Reading and Berks County, conveniently located over a ley line of earth power and smack up against the Schuylkill River. A ley line and running water to power their magic must have seemed like a hole-in-one to the first Etruscans who'd moved here from the old country in the early 1800s.

They'd blended into the melting pot of nineteenth-century Reading but maintained their ancient culture. They lived outwardly normal lives but instead of adding to the collection of churches that stood on every other corner, they built hidden temples for their goddesses and gods.

The *eteri* who shoveled lasagna and rigatoni at Marelli's Trattoria on south Seventh Street would choke on their food if they discovered Uni's Temple was built into the back of the building.

Here, she and Leo were just another two faces in the Etruscan community. Two more bodies at temple where they sat in the back and kept their heads down. Until everyone lifted their faces toward the ceiling to ask for Uni's protection for the Etruscan race. Then she begged for Leo's safekeeping.

Spell Bound

But did Uni hear? Did She care?

Hell, after everything she'd seen in the world, after her parents' murders, Shea wasn't sure the Great Goddess existed anymore.

But monsters did exist. And for those, she had weapons.

She lifted the attonitum from its spot on the bedside table. It looked like a cross between a revolver and an inoculation gun and would be useless in the hand of an *eteri*.

But in hers... The iron grip warmed to her touch, while the quartz crystal concentration chamber pulsed with a pale pink light, responding to her *arus*, the magic inherent in the blood of all Etruscans. The solid copper barrel would focus that power wherever she pointed, strengthening it into a heated blast similar to a laser.

There was nothing sleek about the attonitum, nothing like the Beretta Px4 Storm her dad had taught her to shoot and that she always carried. But the gun didn't give her the headache the attonitum did.

Such a failure.

Using magic was always a lesson in pain. Her head pounded whenever she worked a spell or used her Goddess Gift to heal even a minor cut. And though she'd developed a mental shield to keep the voices to a dull buzz, a migraine was never far away.

But she'd use the weapon, to protect Leo. She'd made a promise. And she knew, even in death, her mom would hold her to it.

Like someone had twisted the volume dial, the voices grew louder, chattering over each other like angry hornets. Though she couldn't understand them, Shea knew they were warning her. She and Leo were out of time.

Reaching under the bed for the backpack always within arm's reach, she pulled out her mom's grimoire and a sheet of paper fluttered out from between the pages.

She didn't have to read it to know what it said. She'd memorized months ago what her mom had written before her death.

"Too much to say and not enough time. Know we love you and your brother. In time, we hope you can forgive us for all we hid from you. Please understand that we did what we thought was right.

The men who will kill us will come after Leo. These men work for Dario Paganelli. If Paganelli catches you, he'll kill you, Shea. He'll take your brother and pervert his powers to hunt the remaining Priestesses.

Neither you nor your brother can fall into Paganelli's hands. The consequences are unspeakable. Use the locator spell to find Mr. Brown in Reading, Pennsylvania. He's a grigorio and a friend. He'll protect you both. Tell him I sent you and that all is done in time.

And always remember we love you."

Tears filled her eyes but she blinked them back.

Their dad had been a *grigorio*, too, one of the legendary Etruscan warrior priests. Great warriors who could handle a sword as easily as a gun and who always had a ready smile. Her dad had seemed invincible.

And Dario had killed him.

The bed jostled and she turned to find Leo staring at her.

She smiled at the drowsy look on his sweet face and ran a hand through his soft dark hair.

"Hey, bud. How'd you sleep?"

He shrugged but said nothing.

Biting back a sigh, she leaned forward to lay a kiss on his forehead. "Think you're awake enough to give me a hand with something?"

Leo's eyes widened as he nodded, but he held out his arms for his morning hug first. She was already halfway there and wrapped his skinny little body against her.

So small. He was so small.

No, she couldn't let fear screw with her mind right now. They had a spell to perform.

"Okay, then." She opened the grimoire to the spell her mom had mentioned. "Let's see what we need."

She and Leo headed to the window. Since empathic healing was her only Goddess Gift, and headaches and migraines hampered her spell-working abilities, she needed Leo's unusual strength to feed most spells.

It used to scare the shit out of her, that sense of helplessness she got whenever she tried and failed to work a spell.

Her dad had always said, "It's all right, sweetheart. You'll get the hang of it eventually." He'd never given up on her. Her mom...

Since she couldn't think about that without getting depressed, she pushed it out of her mind and focused on the task ahead. Setting an unopened phone book on the window sill, where the sun shone directly through, she dropped a pinch of saffron, a pinch of cinnamon and a topaz stone to draw the light into the bottom of her moon bowl, which would capture and hold the spell's energy until she released it.

Lifting her face into the sun, she said, "Usil, Lord of the Amber Light, hear our humble plea. Illuminate the abode of Mr. Brown with your soft breath." She bit down on her bottom lips as a sharp pain knifed through her temples. "Okay, Leo, blow."

Leaning close, Leo blew the dry ingredients over the phone book, the scent of the spices strong in the morning air. When they'd settled on the book, Shea opened it somewhere near the middle.

Please, let me have done this right...

Shea breathed a sigh of relief when the soft breeze they'd called with the spell blew across the pages for several seconds. As quickly as it started, it stopped again.

Starting at the left, she ran her finger down the columns of names and numbers. And there, in the center of the left page, listed under appliance repair in the yellow pages, was a number for G. Brown. A number with eight digits and a street name but no building number.

It looked like a misprint, but Shea knew better. Since she couldn't use a regular phone to make this call, she'd have to wait until she got to Harry's to use the old black rotary phone in the dressing room. That phone was connected to the communication system only Etruscans could use.

More waiting.

Please don't let it be too late.

She turned to Leo with a smile, this one more natural. "Looks like it worked, babe. We'll give Mr. Brown a call later, okay? You and me, we're a great team, huh?"

Leo nodded but he didn't smile. He never smiled. He barely ever spoke.

And it broke her heart.

She took a deep breath. "Alright, then, how about some breakfast?"

Leo's big dark eyes, so like their dad's, just watched her. Silent. Waiting.

Shea wished she knew for what.

* * *

Another dead end.

Gabriel Borelli slammed the front door behind him and threw his coat at the nearest chair. It missed and fell to the floor with a heavy thud.

Fuck it. He'd check the weapons later.

Right now, he needed a drink. That bottle of Mezzaluna vodka in the cabinet didn't stand a chance. Not after the month he'd had.

Four fucking-endless weeks chasing a rumor that turned into a dead end. The *versipellis* Harry had put him in touch with had been positive she'd seen a man who fit Dario Paganelli's description in a restaurant in the Outer Banks. It'd been his first lead in more than a year, but it'd been a damn bust.

And now it was time to face the music for his absence.

Bottle in hand, he took a healthy swallow before he picked up the black handset from the 1940s-era phone and dialed the eight-number code to get Phil.

"May I help you?"

As always, that high-pitched female voice made him think of the old Lily Tomlin phone-operator skit on "Laugh In." His dad had loved that show.

"It's Brown. Messages?"

Phil's purely feminine sigh made his temples throb.

Damn, this is gonna suck.

"There are several, as you would know if you'd checked in every week, as you're supposed to. Not once a month, Gabriel."

Gods be damned. He was a *grigorio*, a lean, mean, Etruscan bad-ass whose enhanced senses made it damn-near impossible for anyone to get the drop on him. His affinity for all metals but iron gave him the power to slap bullets out of the air with a simple spell. And his unusual strength made him hard to kill and nearly impossible to beat in a fight.

And Phil was not his mother so why the hell did he, a twenty-eight-year-old man, feel like he had to apologize?

No way. He wasn't gonna do it. He didn't need to—

"Look, I'm sorry." *Shit, you're an idiot.* "I've been out of touch—"

"And where exactly have you been?"

Not in this lifetime, babe. "Personal business. What messages?"

Phil huffed and, for a few seconds, he was sure he was going to have to apologize again and that might just make him chug the rest of the bottle.

"Crimson Moon called three times."

Yeah, he'd figured his mom would call at least once while he was gone, even though she had his cell number.

"Lupe's Low End called twice."

Goddamn Quinn. His best friend needed to get over his distrust of cell phones, too.

"And one attempt was made to procure your services."

Fuck. For Phil to forward an outside call to him meant someone had asked for him by name. That usually only happened when another *grigorio* wanted his help.

"Who was it?"

"Unknown."

Huh? "What the hell does that mean?"

"That means," Phil huffed, "she didn't leave her name."

"And this female asked for me by name?"

Spell Bound

"Yes, she asked for Mr. Brown. When I told her you were unavailable, she hung up."

Well, shit. The existence of the *grigori* and the cursed *streghe* they protected was a carefully maintained secret, even among the Etruscans. The story of how the women had been cursed by Fabrizio Paganelli to unending life had become myth. How their sons were born *grigori*, the great warrior protectors thought to be extinct, a legend.

For someone to ask for him by his call name...

"Christ, Phil. Did you find out where she was calling from? Did you—"

"Do you think I don't know my job, Gabriel Borelli?"

Fuck. Second rule of being a *grigorio*—Don't piss off Phil.

"Of course you know your job. I'm sor—"

"Don't bother," she snapped. "I don't appreciate your language or your insinuations, Gabriel. You are expected at ritual in four nights. I suggest you get some sleep before you get your ass over there. And the next time this phone rings, I expect you to answer it."

Gabriel took another slug from the bottle as Phil hung up on him. Loudly. And not before shoving a tiny spell through the line to make his head ache. Damn, that woman was vindictive.

Still, he should have checked in. It was part of the deal. *Grigori* were to be available at all times, any time. His father, the former Mr. Brown, never would've missed a check-in.

No, Davis Borelli had been one of the best *grigori* ever.

Before he'd been murdered by Dario Paganelli.

No, Dario hadn't pulled the trigger. But the bastard

was responsible for his dad's death. Just as Dario's father Fabrizio had been responsible for the curse that had arrested the lives of the *streghe*.

Maybe Fabrizio would have been more careful if he'd known the curse would screw his son, too. The deities could be spiteful when they granted your wishes. Fabrizio had cursed the thirteen *streghe* but that curse had trapped his son Dario in eternal life, as well.

And now Dario hunted the *streghe* with a bloody vengeance. The bastard had a lot to answer for. And Gabriel would make sure he answered in blood.

Another few slugs and the bottle surrendered its last drop.

Gabriel's gaze slid to the cabinet. No more Mezzaluna. He had a bottle of Grey Goose, but on top of the Messaluna, it might be lethal.

He sat there for a few seconds, wondering just how drunk he needed to be to take his mind off the fact that he wasn't any closer to finding Dario and murdering him.

Pretty damn drunk.

He definitely needed a change of scenery.

Chapter Two

Gods be damned, there he was, Mr. Brown, their supposed savior, drinking himself into a stupor.

For the third night in a row.

Shea grabbed the pole in the center of the catwalk and gave the few men sitting in the Spyder Club's front row a good view of her naked breasts as she swung around a second time. She needed the tips.

While the midnight regulars lining the catwalk ogled her, Mr. Brown never glanced toward the stage from his table in the back corner. She didn't think he even realized there was a dancer up there.

The dark-haired man with the don't-fuck-with-me expression probably wouldn't recognize her if he fell over her on the street, which was a distinct possibility at the rate he was sucking down tequila.

Great. Just great. What the hell am I supposed to do now?

She barely heard the throbbing beat of the Black-Eyed Peas' "My Humps" as she went through her bump-and-grind. She knew it well enough not to trip over her four-inch, stiletto heels. But the chill spreading through her body scared her.

Four days ago, she'd called the number in the phone book, the one she and Leo had found using the locator spell.

A female voice had said hello but when Shea had asked for Mr. Brown, she'd been told he was unavailable and would she liked to talk to Mr. Blue?

Her mother's letter mentioned only one name. Mr. Brown. Not Mr. Blue. She'd hung up without answering.

That night after work, she and Leo had cased the street listed in the phone book. They'd scrutinized every building for ten blocks and she had known immediately which house was Mr. Brown's. The Etruscan runes carved around the door like decoration gave it away.

They'd parked and staked out the house, her '72 Dodge Dart blending in among the older Plymouths and Chevys on the street. Later that night, an unfamiliar dark-haired man had walked into the building.

They'd left without knocking on his door.

Tomorrow, she told herself. She'd approach him tomorrow.

But the next night, that man had taken up residence at that table and begun to drink. And drink. And he'd returned to that table every night since.

He hadn't said a word to anyone except Harry. Of course, "Give me the bottle" wasn't exactly conversation.

This was the man her mother wanted her to entrust with Leo's life?

Uh, no. She didn't think so. Not until she'd learned a lot more about him.

* * *

"Leo? Hey, hon, I'm back."

Shea shut the door to the dressing room behind her, walking through the cluttered space to throw the few scraps of material she'd stripped off on stage in her cubby.

"Shit, you done already?" Vibia groaned at the makeup mirror, outlining pale blue eyes with black liner, dark hair already teased and sprayed into carefully tousled waves. "Guess I better get a move on. You know how Marci gets when I'm late. What a bitch."

Shea just shrugged her shoulder. No way was she getting between the two *lucani versipelli*. Skin-shifter tempers were infamously short, particularly the Etruscan wolves, who had the whole Latin temperament going against them, too.

The fur would fly, literally, if the women shifted into their wolves and went after each other.

"Hey, Vi, is Leo in the bathroom?"

"No." The woman waved her hand toward the door. "Dilby came to take him DownBelow. Said the band wanted him to sit in on percussion. He's got a gift for music, your boy."

Cold fear swamped her before she could prepare, stealing her breath and crushing her stomach in its grip. She nearly ran for the door before she stopped and took a deep breath.

"Hey, sweetie," Vibia said, frowning at her. "He's fine. You know Dilby won't let anything happen to him."

"Yeah." She forced a smile. "Yeah, I'm sure he's fine."

Dilby had been the first person to befriend them after Shea had gotten the job here. Shea hadn't wanted to make friends, but Dilby had been relentless. In a good way. Always chatty but never nosy. The lead singer of DownBelow's house band, Dilby had been the first person to put a musical instrument in Leo's hands. She'd make sure nothing happened to him.

Still, these past few weeks, Shea had become terrified to let him out of her sight.

She refused to leave him alone in their apartment when she went to work. The kid was only six. But dragging him to a strip club nearly every night, even if he only sat in the dressing room, was no life for a kid. Hell, being on the run was no life for a kid.

He deserved more. He deserved to grow up in his own home with his parents, free from harm. Safe. Cocooned.

Suffocated.

Like she'd felt.

Oh, not at first. At first, it'd been heaven. Just her and her parents. A forest to play in. Books to read. Weapons to train with. Spells to learn. Not that she'd had much luck with that, but still…

Until she was twelve, she hadn't known there were living beings in the world other than her parents and the animals who roamed a forest so thick it blotted out the sky in spots.

Then a lost hiker had stumbled through her parents' strong perimeter wards and asked her to show him the way back to the road. Fear had frozen her vocal cords and she'd run home, barely able to for words to tell her dad about the hiker.

Until that moment, she'd never once questioned her parents about why they never left the forest surrounding their cozy log home.

"There are people out there who would hurt you if they knew about you," her mother had said. "It's for your own good, Shea."

As a stupid teenager, she'd believed her mom had wanted to control her life.

"You're special, Shea," her dad had claimed. "We can't trust anyone else. This was the only way."

Spell Bound

Yeah, she was really special. A special kind of screw-up.

Well... shit. She shook those thoughts out of her head.

She hadn't planned on going DownBelow tonight but no way would she make Leo leave. If he was going to sit in with the band, she didn't want to miss it. The kid was a musical prodigy. Put an instrument in his hands and he could play it. And not just play it, but make it sing. Percussion, guitar, bass, violin. Anything he could hit or had a string. He had some trouble with wind instruments but she was pretty sure that had to do more with lung capacity than talent. Give him a few years and he'd master those, too.

If he had a few years.

No, none of that now.

If she was going DownBelow, she needed to change. The jeans and t-shirts she'd worn to work weren't gonna cut it. Not if she didn't want to stand out.

And she really didn't want to stand out.

"Hey, Vi. You got anything I can wear? I wasn't exactly planning to go tonight."

Vi gestured with the bright red lipstick she was applying. "Not really. Look in the closet, babe. Something'll jump out at you."

Hell, why hadn't she thought of that? Probably because she had too damn much on her mind.

The club had been built as headquarters for a beneficial society in the early 1800s, but in later life had been home to the Reading Communist Party, the Daughters of the American Revolution and, for a time in the 1920s, a burlesque theater.

Only the red velvet curtains over the stage and windows remained in view from those days, but the heart of that old theater lived in this closet. Along with clothes from just about every decade since.

Leo loved to hunt in the trunks for treasure like plastic swords and funny hats. He was too young to realize the treasure was the clothes. Growing up as she had, clothes had never been much of a concern. Jeans, t-shirts, sweaters.

But now…well, now she knew the difference between a basque and a corset. Black velvet on her skin made her shiver with lust. Leather molded to her body like a lover and the sheen of satin against her olive-toned skin and dark hair made her glow.

Ah, there it was, the cream satin basque, hanging from the pole on the side wall. She pushed aside two Victorian gowns to reach it then turned to one of several old steamer trunks on the other side of the room. She'd seen a whole trunk of black leather… Yeah, this was it.

She pulled out a couple of skirts that looked like they might fit her then headed back into the dressing room.

Vibia would need to help her with the basque and then she was going DownBelow.

There, at least for an hour or so, she could forget that the man she needed to save her brother was drinking himself into a coma.

* * *

"Hey, Harry. What's happening DownBelow?"

From behind the huge mahogany bar that dominated the north wall of the club, Harry gave him a once-over as he tapped a beer for a waitress.

Gabriel figured he didn't look too good, not after three steady days of drinking.

Fuck it. Tonight at ritual, he'd sober up fast.

"Since you've been drowning yourself in tequila for the past three nights, I guess you didn't have any luck?" Harry asked.

He met Harry's gaze head on. He'd managed to avoid this conversation until now. "Nothing there."

Harry nodded once and a brief flash of sympathy passed through his eyes. Anyone else, Gabriel would've told them off. He didn't need their sympathy.

But Harry was the only person Gabriel trusted with this part of his life. Harry wanted Dario dead, though he'd never explained why.

And Gabriel didn't really care. They wanted the same thing.

"Band's in," Harry said finally. "Gonna be full. You know the drill."

Yeah, he knew the drill. And no one, if they wanted to be allowed back into The Spyder or DownBelow, ignored Harry's drill. No weapons, no fighting. No excuses. You fucked up and you were banned. Forever.

Looking at the guy, you wouldn't think he was such a badass. Five-ten, short brown hair, brown eyes, average looks, the kind that would get him passed over in a lineup even if he was guilty.

But looks, as they so often were, were deceiving mothers.

Gabriel had been in Harry's office a few times, long enough to look at the photos on the walls. They chronicled the building's history from the time of its construction in the early 1800s through the next two-hundred years. In every single picture, Harry stood somewhere in the background, looking exactly as he did today.

Not such a shock, considering all Gabriel knew about

the world. Still, Gabriel didn't know what Harry was. He wasn't *Enu*, a human of magical Etruscan descent, like the *streghe* and the *versipelli*. And not Fata, an Etruscan elemental being such as the winged folletti and the goat-legged *salbinelli*.

Harry was something else. Someone you didn't want to fuck with. He was ancient, older even than the cursed *streghe*, though no one wanted to piss him off by asking just how old. Everyone who came through The Spyder's doors learned to get and stay on Harry's good side. And those who didn't…well, nobody had actually dared get on Harry's bad side since Jimmy Hoffa's disappearance.

Gabriel was no exception.

In the hallway outside the club, he entered the darkened alcove that held a perpetually out-of-order phone. At least, out of order for those who didn't know how to use it.

Without lifting the handset, Gabriel checked to make sure there were no *eteri* from the strip club wandering around then punched in four digits on the base. After a two-second lull, the rumble of well-oiled pistons warned him the back wall was about to swing open. When it did, a rush of air blew out and Gabriel stepped into the holding room, the wall shutting behind him as an overhead light came on. One by one, more lights clicked on down the descending hallway.

Sliding out of his leather duster, he hung it and the arsenal it held in one of the empty lockers lining the wall.

From his right boot, he pulled his pugio, the short silver dagger he'd inherited from his dad, and put it in his coat pocket. In his jeans and t-shirt, he'd stand out some. But everyone who came to DownBelow thought they knew who and what he was—just another Etruscan descendent with a little inherent power, an *Enu* who worked construction for an *eteri* firm out of Philadelphia.

Last, he took off his boots and socks and let his bare feet settle into the dirt floor, soaking in the undiluted power of the ley line running beneath the city. Above, in the concrete streets and brick buildings, magic still flowed strong enough to make Reading one of the most powerful old cities in North America.

But down here, in the earth itself...Goddess, it was like injecting pure heroin into his veins. And, yeah, he'd been there, done that, in that dark period after the deaths of his dad and brother.

But magic wouldn't give him the problems drugs would.

He stood for a few seconds, eyes closed, letting the power seep into his body, mingle with the *arus* in his blood. Let it cleanse some of the anger that'd been building the past week. Sweating out the alcohol would take a little more time, but it'd take a lot more than five or six liters over three days to seriously affect him.

The disappointment would take longer to dissipate and that was the real bitch. He'd thought for sure he'd had a decent lead this time. Dario, that bastard, had eluded him again.

He shook his head. He'd deal with that later.

Tonight, he'd let himself get blown away by the band, maybe get laid before going to ritual. Yeah, getting laid would go a long way toward clearing his head.

Opening his eyes, he realized he heard music. The steel door at the end of the tunnel muffled most of it, as did the dampening spells covering every inch of the ceiling, walls and floor.

Still, he could feel it in his bones, his blood beginning

to pound in rhythm. Queen, maybe, though it wasn't anything he recognized, and his dad had loved the band.

By the time he reached the door, they'd moved onto something else, something with a slower beat that made him think about sex. Now that he'd started thinking about it, he couldn't stop. And since he couldn't remember the last time he'd gotten laid, he figured it was too long.

There were bound to be a few willing female *lucani*. After a night at DownBelow with the band, they'd be aching for it and most knew he'd be good for a few hours, at least.

Laying his left hand against the bare steel, he gave a shove with more than just raw force. He put a little power in it, making the metal warm to the touch. A lock appeared in the center of the rectangular door. Pulling out the silver key he always wore around his neck, he inserted it in the keyhole. The key had been made by his mother and blessed by Laran, the Etruscan God of War. Laran would be at the ritual tonight. And He'd probably be pissed off at Gabriel for missing the last one.

Something else to worry about later.

Right now, he pushed through the door and into the dizzying rush of DownBelow.

* * *

"Leo, honey, you having a good time?" Shea asked.

Leo's head whipped around as he sat at the back of the wooden stage, mostly hidden from the crowd behind the drum kit. The band was between songs but gearing up to go again.

Though he never smiled—not once, not since she'd carried him out of their parents' house sobbing, before he'd set the entire place on fire with the touch of his hands—he did have one expression that indicated maybe, just maybe, he might smile one day.

His dark eyes widened as he nodded, excitement radiating from him like heat. A set of bongos lay on his lap. Probably Tessa's, the band's percussionist.

"Hey, Shea." A small brunette with bright green eyes bounced across the stage. She wore a short, pink dress that looked like a pair of baby doll pajamas Shea had had as a child. With her wavy, chestnut hair, pointed features and petite frame, Dilby managed to pull it off without looking like a pornographic Shirley Temple. "You're done for the night?"

"Hey, Dilby, thanks for bringing Leo down. I'm sure he was bored stiff in the dressing room."

The girl smiled, the expression making her look almost as young as Leo. Shea had no idea how old Dilby really was. Or what she was. She wasn't *Enu*. Or rather, she didn't feel *Enu* to Shea. She was probably *Fata*, though her ears weren't pointed like the linchetti and she didn't have a *folletta*'s wings. Her legs were regular human legs, unlike a *salbinelli*'s goat legs. She was probably *gianes*, a female wood elf.

Still, Shea never asked because she never wanted to answer the same question.

"No problem," Dilby said. "Tessa's out of town so we're hurting for percussion. And Leo, my man," she flashed a smile at the boy, who stared back with adoring eyes, "is a rock god, aren't you, hon?"

Leo nodded again and, for a few brief seconds, Shea held her breath. She willed him to speak, to say something. Anything. Blessed Goddess, the kid hadn't said more than a hundred words since he'd seen their parents lying in pools of blood. His screams for them still reverberated in her nightmares.

Of course, he didn't say a word, and she and Dilby sighed in unison. When they left, Dilby was the person Shea would miss most.

As if she'd read her mind, Dilby flashed a rueful smile, ruffled Leo's inky black hair and headed back to center stage. The guitarist, a guy named Caeles who looked to be about twenty and had the pointed ears of a *linchetto* peaking out from beneath curly brown hair, started to pick out the opening notes to My Chemical Romance's "Dead," and the crowd began to writhe.

Leo picked up the beat without hesitation, little hands smacking the skins. He nodded to Shea before closing his eyes to concentrate.

"I'll be right up here," she said, though he probably hadn't heard her. That was okay. He knew she'd be there if he needed her.

Walking up a few rows into the mostly empty seats facing the back of the band, Shea sat on the warm stone, heated from below. From her vantage point, she could see the entire club.

Who would ever guess that beneath this city was a perfectly formed amphitheater? Though tiny in comparison to the architectural wonders built by the ancient Romans in Europe, Africa and Asia, just the fact of its existence was amazing.

Ten circular rows of stone seating encompassed the arena where the band played and the audience danced. Some nights, especially during the spring and summer, the arena held the circensis, the games. She and Leo had actually attended a couple since moving here.

Though she'd been careful to keep to the fringes of

society, only occasionally going to temple and making no friends with the exception of Dilby, she couldn't resist the circensis.

As a kid, she'd loved to listen to her dad talk about the times he'd taken part in the Reading games as a teenager. Right here, on this floor, their dad had won many times, whether he'd fought with his bare knuckles or weapons. He'd lost a few times, too, and Shea thanked the Gods they no longer fought to the death, as they had in ancient times.

Still, the Etruscans maintained their hunger for blood and violence. Shea believed that appetite worked in their favor, gave them an edge to survive.

Even though they'd hidden their culture to protect themselves, the Etruscans worshipped in temple every week. They made sacrifices to their flesh-and-blood deities, like Nortia, Goddess of the Fate, and Tivr, God of the Moon. Those deities lived among them, their existence a carefully guarded secret from the *eteri*.

But as much as the Etruscans liked a good fight, good sex ranked above it.

The band's *strega*, Gemma, stood on the opposite end of the stage from Leo. Another tiny brunette with pixie features and hair straight to her ass, Gemma chanted in Etruscan, weaving a strong euphoria spell that had enticed a few couples into the stands already. Bodies pressed tight, the couples' hands roamed, mouths locked. No embarrassment at their public display.

Though Shea had never gotten down and dirty with anyone, she considered sex a natural part of life. Most *eteri* had a skewed sense of sex, considered it dirty or immoral, to be hidden away in dark rooms.

She didn't understand that, especially as the beat of the

music and the spell encouraged her body to move. She was halfway to the arena floor before she realized she'd gotten up.

One dance, she reasoned. If she stayed to the left of the stage, she'd be able to keep an eye on Leo and dance out some of her frustration.

Just as she hit the floor, Dilby and the band lit into "Love to Love You, Baby," and the trancelike beat seduced her. Since she didn't want to stand out, she approached a group of single females she'd seen here before. Though she didn't know their names, they welcomed her into their circle with nods and quick smiles.

But the women's attentions immediately refocused on the single men watching the action from the perimeter. Waiting. Everyone was looking for a partner tonight, someone to connect with, someone to make magic with.

Behind her, a male body pressed against hers. Hard and hot, he plastered himself to her, hands on her hips as he picked up her rhythm. He was fully aroused, his sex a stiff rod rubbing against her ass.

Goddess, his hands made her blood heat as they cruised from her hips up her sides to her breasts, cupping them, testing their weight. So firm. So hot. He wanted her. She felt his desire in the pulsing of his cock, in the thrust of his hips against her ass.

Damn, it'd be so easy to turn, to wrap her arms around his shoulders and her legs around his waist and let him carry her off into the stands. Let him take her mind off everything and—

The voices buzzed through her mental barrier, making her temples ache with the effort to ignore them. But she lost her rhythm and stepped out of the man's hold. Damn it, she had to get off the dance floor before she embarrassed herself.

Without saying a word, she stumbled away, back up the risers, sinking into a seat, wanting to sink into the stone and away. Just away from this all.

Not fair. So not fair.

Tears threatened but she'd be damned if she'd let them fall. Couldn't give in because she was afraid if she started, she wouldn't stop. The fucking voices. Sure, they provided an early warning system for danger, but obviously they didn't want her to have any fun. They wanted to keep her alone. A virgin.

With a shiver, she forced her attention back to Leo, still seated at the back, little hands hitting the drums. So small. So vulnerable.

Vaffanculo, was she nuts? Of course she couldn't hook up with anyone. Who would protect Leo while she went off and got laid?

She let her gaze travel the room, looking for anyone who might be looking at him a little too long, who paid a little too much attention to him. All she saw were people having a good time.

Several more couples and one, no, two threesomes had joined the others in the stands. Luckily all were still clothed, but she and Leo needed to leave at the next break. The rest of the band would play for at least another hour, possibly two. Until those audience members who'd stayed reached their climaxes.

Sex magic fueled the wards that kept DownBelow concealed from the outside world. Harry considered it a fair trade since he charged no admission fee to see the band.

While the band members made decent livings as session musicians for the *eteri*, they were bigger than The Beatles to the Etruscans. She often wondered how they managed to balance those two worlds and keep their sanity and their secrets.

She nearly hadn't. She'd almost run back to her parents after the first disastrous six months she'd spent on her own. Sneaking away from her home had been easier than she'd expected. After her encounter with the hiker, she'd been determined to see what other secrets the rest of the world held.

Her mom had refused to discuss even the possibility of her leaving. Her dad…well, her dad had stepped up her training. As if he'd known she'd found a way to sneak past the perimeter wards and walk to the town she'd discovered in the neighboring valley. As if he'd known, one night, after a particularly bitter fight with her mom when she was seventeen, she'd pack a bag, steal some money and run.

At the town, she'd gone to the bus depot and bought a ticket, headed for Philadelphia.

She was going to be a ballerina. She would dance on famous stages around the world and fall madly in love with a man who would not want to lock her in a home in a forest.

She would not give up her life to be a member of an ancient *boschetta* dedicated to the Goddess Menrva. Hell, she couldn't even work a spell without her brother's help and the constant threat of a migraine.

Heart pounding as she sat in that smelly bus, her eyes had widened as the cities became bigger and dirtier. When she'd finally stepped off the bus in Philadelphia, she'd cowered in the bus station bathroom for an hour. There were too many people, too many cars, too much noise. And in her head, the voices whimpered in fear.

Goddess save her, she'd been an idiot. She should've

Spell Bound

gone home then. Maybe if she had, things would be different. Maybe her parents would be alive.

And she and Leo definitely wouldn't need the dubious services of the man who'd just walked into the club through the front entrance.

She'd seen Mr. Brown from the stage, but now that he was this close... Damn, he was gorgeous—if you liked guys who looked like they spent the better part of their lives bench-pressing cars.

Obviously she did, because her libido came to life on a wave of heat that flooded her body from scalp to toes and every place in between. Her breasts tightened, the nipples pebbling into hard points, and her sex clenched with a ferocity that shook her.

What was wrong with her? She hadn't had such a strong reaction to the guy she'd been dancing with earlier. Was this a belated reaction to that? Or a reaction to the euphoria spell Gemma wove to lure the patrons into sex?

Unlike everyone else here, Mr. Brown—she really doubted that was his name—wore jeans and a black t-shirt, though he was barefoot like everyone else. His dark hair hung in thick, layered lengths past wide shoulders. His broad brow, high cheekbones and square jaw covered by a closely trimmed beard proclaimed his Mediterranean heritage.

And those dark eyes constantly scanned the crowd. From his intent expression, she got the sense he never let his guard down. That was a good thing. In that way, Mr. Brown reminded her of her dad.

Still... she wasn't ready to hand over Leo's safety to a man she didn't know enough about. Even if he was *grigori*.

Chapter Three

Someone was watching him and it was getting fucking annoying.

Through his enhanced perception of the environment around him, Gabriel felt the attention like a feather brushing against his skin. But he couldn't pinpoint where it was coming from.

Gabriel shook his head, trying to think through the euphoria spell Gemma had cast. Combined with the alcohol in his system, it was making him fuzzy.

And that was unacceptable.

His dad would've kicked his ass for impairing his senses like this. And he deserved it. But gods damn it to hell, he was still pissed off. He wanted that bastard Dario to bleed before he cut out his black heart and burned what was left of his body.

Just the thought gave him a warm glow inside.

"Hello, Gabriel," a woman's husky voice broke through the bloody little daydream he had going. "Haven't seen you for a few weeks."

He looked over his shoulder, leveling his gaze on the beautiful woman running her fingers through the ends of his hair. "Connie. How you been?"

Her lithe *versipellis* body swayed to the music as she moved in front of him. "Bored. What about you, Gabe? Wanna make a little magic?"

As she brushed long mahogany hair over her shoulder, he let his gaze drop to her breasts. They were great breasts. He'd held them, tasted them, rubbed his cock between them. Knew he could again tonight.

Yeah, but do you want to?

Hell, even his body was undecided. He was half hard from the combination of her proximity and the euphoria spell. A few minutes with Connie's talented hand wrapped around him and he'd be ready to perform.

But do you want to?

Connie lifted one perfectly arched eyebrow at him, swinging her hips to the music. But her expression never changed. If he told her no, she'd move on. He was just another body to her. Which is all she'd be to him.

When the hell had he become such an asshole?

He shook his head. "Thanks for the offer, Connie, but not tonight. Don't think I'll be much fun."

She shrugged. "Your loss, big guy."

And swayed off toward a pair of male *versipelli*, who welcomed her with big grins.

Fuck. He was so fucking off his game tonight—

"Hey, Gabriel. That face would give a serial killer nightmares. What's new, man?"

Not one damn thing. "Hey, Digger. Got any new toys?"

Douglass Alfieri flipped him off. He hated the nickname but had been stuck with it ever since he'd taken over his father's work as the *grigori armafictor*. Digger's Goddess Gift of enhanced affinity for metal gave him one kick-ass ability for making weapons.

"Yeah, I have, actually," Digger said. "I've been working on the Titus-4. I think I have the malfunction in the directional mechanism figured out. You know how the steam was getting caught in the concentration chamber? Well, I think..."

Gabriel let the guy talk, though he didn't understand half of what he was saying. That's why Digger made the weapons and Gabriel used them. The guy was a certified genius when it came to combining metals and crystals into killing machines.

Digger didn't look like a genius. The guy was too...damn, the guy was too damn pretty for it. Somewhere in his ancestry lurked a Fata. Or three. All those chiseled angles in his cheekbones and nose, the pointed chin, the deep-set eyes and broad forehead...had to be a little linchetti or folletti in his genes.

"...so I adjusted the amount of pressure needed to run the pistons and..."

Gabriel let Digger ramble, listening with half an ear, while he tried to pinpoint who the hell continued to watch him. He didn't get the sense that he was in any danger. Just that she—it was definitely a she—was curious. And intent.

"...then I shot the guy in the head, ripped his heart out with my bare hands and rubbed his blood all over my naked body."

Gabriel's head shot around. "What the hell are you talking about?"

Digger wore a wry smile. "Huh. Guess you were listening. Amazing how you can hear exactly what I'm saying and still be a million miles away. I never learned to do that. Save me a world of hurt when my mother's in town."

Guilt knocked him upside the head but Gabriel didn't have the time for it. Still, he couldn't help feeling like an ass. "Yeah, sorry. Got a lot on my mind."

"No luck this time?"

Beside Quinn, his brother in everything but blood, and Harry, Digger was the only other person who knew Gabriel hunted Dario. "Nothing."

Digger clapped him on the shoulder once. "Sorry."

And that was enough of that. Time to get the hell out of here. "You going to ritual tonight?"

Digger nodded. "Of course. You ready?"

"Might as well."

As he turned for the exit, he caught a glimpse of something out of the corner of his eye. A woman alone, sitting on the risers behind the band. She was far enough away that he had trouble making out more than long dark hair and a small frame in the low light.

There was something about her...something that snagged his attention. Had she been the one staring at him? She wasn't now. Her attention seemed to be fixed on the stage. Probably one of Caeles' groupies, a shy one.

Just his luck.

* * *

And there he went. Out the door with another guy.

A really pretty guy, Shea thought. Maybe the *grigorio* was gay.

Which would be too freaking bad because the guy was hot.

Still, that didn't explain why the voices wanted her to follow him. Their urgent buzzing as he disappeared left her with no doubt that she should go after him.

And yes, she knew how truly weird that would sound to anyone but... Well, probably to everyone else.

When the door closed behind their supposed savior,

she returned her attention to the stage, where the band was playing a funky version of Suicidal Tendencies' "Institutionalized."

And, wow, how fitting was that? If she were an *eteri*, she'd probably be in a mental institution right now, eating vanilla pudding and weaving baskets.

She'd been almost eight before she'd realized the constant drone that'd always been present in her head were voices, voices she couldn't understand. She'd lived with them for so long, she'd figured everyone had them. But the horrified look on her mom's face when she'd finally grown old enough to explain had made it clear not everyone heard voices.

She'd tried to talk about it with her mom a few times but each time her mom had gotten tears in her eyes. What little girl wanted to make her mom cry? So for several years, she hadn't asked.

Then, shortly after the hiker incident, she'd asked again.

"So, Mom. Are we ever gonna talk about these voices in my head? Or are they just something else you're not going to tell me about?"

Jesus, she'd been such a smart ass, so righteously indignant. Such a jerk.

"Everything we've done has been in your best interest, Shea. Everything we do is for your protection. The voices…they're your curse to bear, Shea. Great Goddess protect you, but I wish they weren't."

And that was all she'd said.

Thanks for that, Mom.

At least her mom had taught her how to set up the mental wall to dim the voices when they began to grow in intensity as she'd gotten older.

"Hey, Shea. You okay? You look a little pale."

Dilby stood in front of her, holding Leo's hand. The kid looked content but tired.

Damn, she'd zoned out for a few minutes. Dangerous. "I'm fine. Ready to hit the road, bud?"

Leo darted a quick glance at Dilby before nodding. Shea figured, if he had his way, he'd stay all night. But he never complained, never objected, not to anything.

She held out her hand and he tucked his much smaller one in it.

"Then let's go. We've just got to make one stop on the way."

* * *

To look at the building, you'd think it was just another empty brick monstrosity south of Penn Street.

No *eteri* would ever believe it hid the sanctuary of an Etruscan deity.

Hell, just saying that in casual conversation would make any *eteri* cross the street to avoid you. Then again, most people didn't believe in things like curses or *streghe* or magic. They didn't examine lightning for predictions of future events or make predictions about their lives by which direction birds flew overhead.

They certainly didn't slash their forearms and offer their blood in sacrifice to Laran, God of War. And they'd never believe the dark-haired man standing before Gabriel was an actual God.

"You wanna tell me where you've been?"

Laran stared at him with hard, gunmetal grey eyes, his sharp expression set in stone cold lines. The god didn't look much older than thirty, but he had strands of pure white in his black hair. He stood just a few inches taller than Gabriel, but it was amazing how much bigger he seemed. His presence overpowered everyone in the vicinity.

Guess godhood did that to you.

For a brief second, Gabriel thought about not answering Laran's question. And decided he didn't want to take his life in his hands.

"I was checking a tip in South Carolina."

Gabriel held his breath waiting for the next question. He figured Laran knew he hunted Dario. He was a god, after all. But he'd never said a word about it to Gabriel.

Serena had forbidden the *grigori* to hunt Dario. Something about Dario's destiny being tied to breaking the curse.

Well, fuck that. He wanted to kill the bastard. Laran had to know that.

Gabriel stared back into the god's eyes, deep-set in a face full of sharp angles and broad planes. If Gabriel swung that way, he'd say Laran was attractive. In a compelling, Tommy Lee Jones' kind of way. Not a man you wanted to fuck with.

And if Laran decided he'd overstepped his boundaries, Gabriel would pay a price. The God of War suffered no fools or dissenters.

But after a few seconds of silence, during which Gabriel heard worry in the hushed voices of the other six *grigori* gathered for the ritual, Laran nodded once and turned toward the altar.

Dodged that bullet.

Gabriel released the breath he must have been holding and joined the other men at the altar as Laran began the ritual.

"Great Tinia, Father of all Etruscans." Laran's deep voice carried through the open space, reverberating off the brick walls enclosing the courtyard filled with a small forest of oak, pine and birch trees. "Accept the sacrifice of my blood and the blood of your mortal sons as tribute for our gratitude. Give your sons the strength to fight against those who would harm your children."

"Accept our offering," Gabriel and the *grigori* chanted as Laran drew the dagger he held in his right hand from his left elbow to wrist. "Bless us with your strength."

Laran extended his arm and let his blood drip onto the breasts of the red-headed woman splayed on the altar. Though he vaguely recognized the woman's face, Gabriel didn't know her name. He'd never seen the same woman here twice.

In ancient times, Laran would've had a temple full of priestesses as well as a cadre of priests who attended his every need and performed this ritual. But over the past two millennia, as the Etruscan civilization dwindled, the old ways had adapted.

Today, Laran performed his own rituals. Which didn't exactly look like a hardship to Gabriel, considering. A little blood for sex.

The combination was so important to the Etruscans, it fueled most of their power.

"Great Father," Laran moved to the base of the altar, where the woman's body was positioned at exactly the right height for Laran, "feel the strength and power I offer to You on our behalf."

A soft breeze blew through the space, rustling the leaves and ruffling the woman's hair, sending red strands dancing. Laran grabbed her hip in one hand and his cock in the other and fitted their bodies together with one lunge.

The woman gasped in ecstasy as Laran sank deep and closed his eyes.

"Let our offering please You as it pleases us."

Laran's hips began to move, thrusting and retreating, never faltering in his recitation of the ritual. The *grigori* continued the accompanying chant as the air in the temple thickened, the spell increasing in intensity. Laran's voice deepened, as well, until he was nearly growling. The woman's ecstatic cries lent potency to the spell and when she finally broken into orgasm, Laran came, as well.

Their combined climaxes infused the air with a heady power that blasted into the *grigori* like a nuclear wave. It drenched them in magic, seeped into their bodies, into that part the Great God Tinia had given them that made them *grigori*.

Closing his eyes, Gabriel breathed through the almost overwhelming sensation as the power sank deeper, clawing its way into his blood and his bones and his mind. So much power. Almost too much. Never too much.

When he could manage, Gabriel opened his eyes and looked around, his enhanced vision picking out the distinctive blue auras surrounding his fellow *grigori*. In addition to detecting emotions in auras, *grigori* identified the type of magic user by the underlying color of their aura. Blue for *grigori*, purple for *streghe*, yellow for *versipelli*.

The black tinge around Larth's aura told Gabriel he needed to get laid. Diego was worried about something according to his maroon-ringed aura. And Aulus lusted after either the woman or Laran, Gabriel couldn't tell which and didn't care either way.

Lucumo and Joseph's auras were untainted by any hint of stress. He'd never actually seen the brothers pissed off about anything, but they were relentless machines when it came to protecting their charges.

And Digger... Well, Digger sought redemption with the same intensity Gabriel wanted revenge. Not that any of the other *grigori* would see that in his aura. He'd gotten damn good at submerging his true feelings.

The other *grigori* would only be able to tell that he was pissed off, which was no surprise to anyone. Only Laran might see more, and probably had, but he'd never interfered, never questioned.

Of course, what God of War would question a man's right to revenge?

"Hey, Gabe. You want to stop at The Cellar?" Aulus called to him as the *grigori* broke the circle and headed through the courtyard to the exit, allowing the woman and Laran a little private time to get cleaned up. Or go again, if he interpreted those moans correctly. "These other pansies are wimping out on me."

Gabriel considered hitting the local banquet hall, run by the small tribe of monacielli who made their own wine and cooked like gourmet chefs. They looked like smaller, rounder versions of that Food Network guy his mom loved to watch and cooked even better.

Sounded good but he shook his head. "Not tonight, wiped out. Maybe next time."

Tonight, he needed a few hours of sleep.

Tomorrow, he'd start over. And when he finally found that bastard Dario, he'd rip out his heart and burn him into a little pile of ash.

Chapter Four

"I am in need of a *grigorio*."

The voice, husky and feminine, made Gabriel's libido jump up and beg her to do him, even through the pounding hangover.

But her use of the word *grigorio* rang all his warning bells, even through the headache from the combination of ritual and the amount of alcohol he'd consumed over the past few days. Add in the fact that he'd only just gotten to sleep a half hour ago, and he'd actually thought about ignoring the damn door. But the knocking had been too loud and he didn't want to attract the neighbors' attention.

Who the hell was this woman who knew what a *grigorio* was?

Eyes narrowed, he checked out his visitor from head to toe, though there wasn't much to see. Baggy jeans, good running sneakers and a gray hooded sweatshirt that concealed her face and most of the rest of her. She had something to hide. Hell, didn't they all?

She couldn't hide the fact that she was *strega*, though. Her purple aura pulsed around her, tinged with neon green. Stress. She was tiny, no taller than five-three, but he'd been deceived by size before. And was smarter for it.

Crossing his arms over his chest, trying to ignore the

ice pick digging into his temples, he leaned against the doorjamb, paint flaking to the ground in a snowfall.

"What the hell's a *grigorio*? Some new sex act? Since when do hookers go door to door?"

She didn't flinch but her body stiffened. "I was told you would help."

He snorted. "Help what? And by who?"

"Celeste."

Holy fuck.

He had to work at keeping his expression blank. Celeste was one of the cursed *streghe*. She'd disappeared more than twenty years ago and no one had seen her since.

Still…"I don't know anyone named Celeste—"

"She said all is done in time."

Fucking hell. She had the correct code words. Was this the female who'd called Phil to speak to him earlier this week? How the hell had she known his call name and how had she gotten his address?

And what did she know about the *grigori*?

"What's your name?" He flicked an impatient hand toward her hood. "And take that down. I don't deal with people I can't see."

After a split-second hesitation, her hands emerged from the front pocket of the sweatshirt. Slim and pale, they trembled slightly. Not as calm as she pretended.

His eyes narrowed as the hood fell, revealing dark, rumpled waves that disappeared into the sweatshirt. With her head bowed, he still couldn't see her face.

Annoyed, he placed a rough finger under her chin to tilt her head back. And pulled back as if burned.

Shit. *Arus* coursed through her like water in a fast-moving stream. And her face…she looked familiar. She wasn't one of the cursed *streghe*. He'd memorized all their faces as part of his training. Still…

"Who the hell are you?"

She lifted her pointed chin and flashed flat brown eyes at him. Colored contacts. What the hell?

The woman's long black lashes snapped down and her pink tongue emerged to lick full lips. "I need a *grigorio*. I was told you would help. I have... There are complications."

No shit. "Honey, there're always complications and you still didn't tell me your name."

Her lashes flickered again and her lips quivered. *Vaffanculo*, he really didn't want to have to deal with a weeper. Not that it would've swayed him. He actually had more respect for her when, after a few seconds, her mouth firmed and she looked him straight in the eyes.

"I have a child. We need your protection."

Oh, fuck no. Pushing away from the doorjamb, he backed through the door, ready to close it in her face. "I don't do kids, babe. Whoever Celeste is, she wasted your time."

He caught a quick glimpse of the shock in her eyes before her arm shot out to grip his forearm for one brief second before letting go. "Please." Her voice sounded strangled, as if she didn't use that word much. "My...child needs protection. If you really are a *grigorio*, you have to help. He's *grigori*, too."

Holy shit. How the hell had she gotten her hands on a *grigori* child? He knew every *grigorio* in the Americas. Had one of them been stupid enough to father a child without knowing?

Someone had screwed up big time. But even though he had a sworn duty to protect this kid, there was no fucking way he could.

He stepped back, his heart as cold as winter ice and

his expression probably the same, if the look on her face was any indication.

She took a step away from him, her heel catching on a crack. She reached for the wall to steady herself but missed and his reflexes kicked in. He grabbed her arm before she hit the sidewalk.

A small body streaked from the darkness of the doorway to the girl's side and a pair of dark eyes flashed up to his.

Fuck. His heart froze and the cold extended through his veins.

The woman's mouth parted but no words emerged.

"*Figlio di puttana.*" Gabriel realized he was about to crush the bones in her arm and released her.

This time she did fall on her ass.

Gabriel barely noticed, his gaze locked on the child. He could have been Nino's twin. Nino, who'd been only nine when that bastard Dario had killed him.

"How old is he?" His voice menaced like the low growl of a Harley.

The woman rose, dusting off her ass, then gathered the wide-eyed child to her side and dropped a light kiss on his midnight-black hair.

"Six."

He cursed again, this time in Romanian and nasty enough to strip paint from the side of a building.

In a flash, the woman's expression went blank, but the boiling-hot look in her eyes told him he'd crossed a line. She'd translated.

"I don't appreciate your language, Mr. Brown." Her frigid tone made his balls try to crawl back into his body. "You're right. We'll find someone else."

Wrapping the boy's small hand in hers, she turned

and picked their way down the broken sidewalk to a muddy green Dodge two-door on the next block.

She never looked back. The boy did, just once, pinning him in place.

Air rasping in his throat, Gabriel drew in a huge breath. Then he cursed in three languages, one long dead, and slammed the door.

* * *

Hands trembling, Shea got Leo in the back seat, made sure he fastened his seatbelt then kissed his dark head before locking and closing the door.

Walking to the driver's side, she made sure to check their surroundings, look for danger. Fear settled into her stomach, making her slightly nauseous.

In the car, her hands started to shake like leaves in a hurricane. It took four tries to get the key in the ignition and two twists for the car to start.

When the engine caught, she winced as the sound shattered the pre-dawn silence in this rundown neighborhood south of Penn Street. Potholes lined streets littered with trash. The air hung stale in mid-July, smelling like Leo's sneakers when he wore them without socks.

Gods-damn son-of-a-bitch. That mother-fucking bastard.

Tears threatened to fall but she bit her tongue until they retreated. Couldn't let Leo see them. Didn't want to scare him more than he already was.

Damn, she'd been so stupid. But what the hell had she expected? That the man she'd watched drown in alcohol the past three nights would turn out to be their savior? What kind of imbecile was she?

How had she screwed up so badly? That *ceffo* knew

what they looked like now. They'd have to leave Reading. Whoever had killed their parents and was looking for Leo was close. She could feel them, like a malevolent shadow creeping closer.

She would not let those fiends get Leo. But she was so tired of being alone, of being Leo's sole protector. Icy talons of fear gripped her stomach.

What now?

Leo, bless him, sat in the back seat, staring out the window at the early morning shadows. How much of the conversation had he heard? Had he understood what that man had said?

That alcohol-soaked bastard was a disgrace to all *grigori*, men of unquestionable dignity. The asshole wasn't supposed to turn them down.

They needed to get out the city. Needed to go far away. Needed—

Wait, deep breath. One thing at a time. First, they needed to get back to the apartment. Taking a deep breath, Shea put the car in gear then pulled a wide u-turn. Pink tinged the edges of the horizon. They'd go back to the apartment, get some sleep. Then she'd have to—

She slammed on the brakes as Mr. Brown stepped into the street half a block in front of them, a muscle-bound gorilla in worn jeans and a black T-shirt that stretched over his massive chest. He looked pissed off.

Join the club, buddy.

Why the hell had she been so attracted to him earlier tonight? Must have been the euphoria spell.

She'd either have to go around him or through him. *Grigori* had superior strength, which made them extremely hard to kill. Right now, she'd love to test that fact by introducing him to the bumper of her car. At sixty miles an hour.

"Thinks he's Superman," she muttered under her breath. "Arrogant *ceffo*."

She slid a quick look over her shoulder at Leo, now staring out the front window. She really had to watch her language or the kid would be swearing like a sailor before his next birthday. If he were still alive.

No, none of that.

Her foot twitched on the gas pedal then she pushed it to the floor.

Mr. Brown just stood there, arms across his chest as if he played chicken with cars all the time. Maybe he did.

At the last second, she flipped the steering wheel to the left, feeling the car want to slide. She kept her foot on the gas and passed within inches of him. A hard grin pulled at the corners of her mouth. Her father hadn't taught her how to drive their old Jeep through the forest for nothing.

In the rearview, she found Leo, his eyes so wide she could have drowned in them. Then she looked through the back window. Mr. Brown still stood in the middle of the street, hands now on his hips.

"Don't worry, sweetie, he's still in one piece." Lucky bastard. "We don't need him anyway."

She didn't add "because he's an asshole who turned us away." Leo probably knew understood exactly what had happened back there.

Glancing into the rearview again as she navigated out of this armpit of the city, she tried to gauge Leo's response from his expression. It was like trying to scry in a muddy creek. Did he realize that she was all he had and, if she couldn't protect him, he could end up like their parents or worse?

Okay, deep breath.

"Leo, you okay?"

He met her gaze in the rearview and nodded.

He was fine. For now.

But what about later?

* * *

Gabriel stood in the middle of the road for a good two minutes, staring after them.

The girl was gutsy. Terrified, but not wanting to show it. Willing to stand up to him, and, by the Gods, he could be a scary son-of-a-bitch.

The kid... *Vaffanculo*. The kid was so damn young.

What connection did they have to Celeste?

The sharp blast of a car horn tore through his thoughts and he sidestepped the cherry-red vintage Mustang bearing down on him, passing close enough for him to feel the engine's heat.

Someone in the car shouted something foul in Spanish and a hand emerged from the window to give him the finger. Stupid kids.

With a wave of his hand, Gabriel directed a quick spell and a small stream of power at the car's metal bumper, loosening the bolts that held it to the frame. That bumper would fall off in a couple of blocks. His affinity for metal wouldn't have done a damn thing to a newer car with a fiberglass bumper. Guess it was his lucky night.

Then again, not really.

His concentration shot, he walked back to the deceptively dilapidated building that had been in his father's family since the late 1800s. He closed the door behind him and set the state-of-the-art security system as well as binding the protection wards again. In the kitchen, he picked up the rotary phone hanging on the wall and dialed.

"Crimson Moon Productions. Please hold."

He heard a click then silence. Thank the Gods, no Phil and no Muzak. The last time he'd called, some idiot had decided New Age elevator tunes were appropriate hold music.

"Hello?" The voice on the other end was husky with sleep and wariness. Good for her.

"Serena. It's me."

A soft sigh escaped the woman on the other end of the phone line. "Hello, sweetheart. Is everything alright?"

"Yeah. Had some visitors tonight."

She paused. "Nothing serious, I hope."

"No. A young woman and a boy. Said Celeste sent them."

She gasped. "Oh sweet Goddess. Who was she?"

"I don't have any idea. But she knew what to say."

"Describe her."

He paused, taking time to choose his words. "Long, dark hair. Five-three. Had a kid with her. Said he was six. Didn't get names."

"But they mentioned Celeste?"

"Yeah."

Serena fell silent and Gabriel knew what was coming. It's what he should've done in the first place, if he wasn't such a screwed-up ass.

"Do you think you could—"

"I'll bring them up to you."

He hesitated a split second too long to hang up and heard her say, "Gabriel?"

"Yeah?"

Another pause, this time on her end.

"Will you bring them? Will you come yourself?"

He heard the longing in those words and ruthlessly squashed the small flare of warmth it lit in him. He didn't have time for it.

"Yeah, when I find them."

He heard the smile in her voice. "Good. It's been too long."

"Goodbye, Serena."

"Goodnight, sweetheart."

He depressed the cut-off then lifted his finger to dial again.

* * *

Serena set the phone in the hook, letting one hand linger on the silver handset while the other clutched the iron key hanging from the leather thong around her neck.

Her heart pounded furiously, making it hard to breathe.

She'd last seen Celeste twenty-five years ago. A year after that, her best friend had disappeared off the face of the earth.

And a year ago, Celeste had died.

Serena vividly recalled the night she'd woken from sleep, screaming in agony, knowing Celeste was gone. The psychic tie that bound their *boschetta* was strong. A death among them felt like death for all.

Serena still missed her with a nagging ache.

Which made the appearance of this girl and her child such a mystery.

Why would they approach Gabriel with Celeste's name as a calling card? Who was this girl and how had she known Celeste? Why did she have a *grigori* child and why had she specifically asked for Gabriel?

What had happened to Celeste?

Now there are only nine.

There had been thirteen at first, thirteen women with a sacred duty to the Etruscan Goddess Menrva to protect her most precious treasure. Today, the remaining nine were scattered around the world, living in fear for their lives, under assumed names. Or hiding in luxurious holes.

Because that bastard Fabrizio Paganelli had screwed them six ways to Sunday. Cursed them to this never-ending life, removed them from the natural order of life. Condemned them to wait hundreds of years for the rebirth of their blood-bound mates.

And set his son Dario on them like a rabid dog.

Rage rose like a storm-fed creek, boiled in her chest like the old friend it was until the force of it nearly buckled the floor beneath her feet. Five hundred years she and her fellow *streghe* had lived—cursed by a distraught father over the death of his beloved son.

With the floorboards still shaking beneath her, she released a scream that would have leveled trees in the forest if the house wasn't warded to deny the passage of sound. She screamed until she was hoarse, *arus* swirling around her, threatening to suck everything in the room into a vortex.

Damn it, she didn't want to have to buy new furniture. Not again. With a final sob, she fell into a heap on the floor, trying to catch her breath.

"Idiot," she chided herself. "You need to get a grip."

It was time to get off her ass and break this damn curse.

Her first attempt had failed nearly thirty years ago, when she'd made herself a whore for one night to seduce her most hated enemy.

She'd debased herself because the Goddess Menrva had promised, despite Fabrizio's curse forbidding the *streghe* to ever bear another female, that one of the thirteen would indeed have a daughter who would end the curse.

The Goddess Menrva had sent a vision to the *boschetta*'s seer, Dafne, just before her death. Dafne hadn't cried or screamed or begged for mercy when the villagers the *streghe* had cared for all of their lives had tied her to the stake at Fabrizio's urging.

Instead, she'd lifted her face to the sky and closed her eyes. And when the flames licked at her feet, Dafne had looked straight at Serena and said, "Do not despair. The Goddess has promised there will be a daughter. Menrva has not abandoned us completely."

Then Dafne had thankfully passed out before the flames consumed her.

Burning flesh of any kind still made Serena nauseous.

Rising from the floor, she dusted off her skirt and bowed her head. She wrapped her hand around the key again and fed just a bit of *arus* into it until she felt it return to its natural state. An iron nail.

"Great Goddess Menrva, She who guides us with her wisdom and entrusts us with Her most sacred possession," she said. "I'm holding You to that promise. Please don't let us down."

Chapter Five

The alarm rang at four p.m.

Shea tossed her hand toward the bedside table to swat the clock into submission. The little black box emitted a sharp, bat-like squeak then went silent.

Without opening her eyes, she reached across the bed and laid a hand on Leo's chest. Still asleep. She swore the kid would sleep through an earthquake.

Sighing, she rolled out of bed to a chorus of squeaky springs, walked the few steps to the bathroom and closed the door behind her. Dropping her boxer shorts and tank top on the floor, she set the shower several degrees beyond hot to ease the dull ache in her temples.

Damn, she wished she could stay in here forever. Let the water wash over her skin, washing away her... what? Her sins?

To hell with that. She didn't believe in sin. Only right and wrong. She didn't steal, she didn't cheat. She'd never taken another life.

But she would. To protect Leo.

Would that be so wrong?

Sighing, she dropped her head down and let the water soak her head, work some of the tension from her neck. It hurt like a bitch, but she couldn't afford to call off work.

They needed the money, especially if they were going to be on the road for a while. Especially after last night—

No. She shook her head and reached for the shampoo. She refused to think about last night. Or about what might happen today. She couldn't change the outcome of one and worrying about the other would make her sloppy. And that could be deadly.

Leo needed her to be on her toes. She couldn't bear to let him down more than she already had.

With a sigh, she raced the hot water heater to the end of her shower then walked back to the bedroom. Wet hair cool against her back, she pulled on jeans and a T-shirt, not bothering with underwear. Just have to take them off when she got to work anyway.

She hated to do it, but she was going to have to give notice tonight. Harry had been good to her these past four months and she'd been able to put aside some money. Not a lot. But it might be a while before she found a job that paid as well.

If you find one at all.

Yeah, probably not something she wanted to think about right now.

Instead, she dropped to her knees in front of the altar, opened the circle and began her daily devotional. Holding her mother's lead athame across her palms, Shea lifted it to the sky and bowed her head.

"Uni, Mother Goddess, give me the strength to fight should I be called on to do so. Menrva, Vessel of all Wisdom, grant me the knowledge I need to defeat our enemies.

"Great Goddesses, let me not falter in my duty."

Please don't let me get my brother killed.

With that cheerful thought, she felt eyes on her and turned to find Leo watching her from the bed.

She dredged up a smile for him. "Hey, bud. Did I wake you?"

He tilted his head to the side. "You look like Mom."

Her mouth dropped open but nothing emerged.

Those four little words were so sweet and so devastating. Like he'd taken the athame and stuck it in her heart.

She forced herself to hold the smile, wanting him to continue but almost afraid of what he'd say next. "I'm taking that as a compliment, babe." She tried to keep her tone light, but it was so hard. They never talked about their parents. It was just too difficult for both of them. "Hungry?"

Those wide, dark eyes regarded her with...what? Anger? Fear? Despair? She waited for him to say something else. Anything. But after a silent minute, she caught back a sigh.

"Leo, come here."

She opened her arms and he bounced off the bed, throwing his arms around her waist and squeezing tight. She hugged him back just as hard.

Her heart pounded almost painfully. Goddess bless her, she loved this little boy with all her heart. He was all she had left of family and she was terrified of losing him. Terrified of screwing up and losing him to the monsters that chased them. Of getting herself killed trying to protect him and leaving him alone.

Without help, how long did they have until the men who'd killed their parents—who'd been so much stronger and had still gotten caught—found them?

They had to run.

"I love you, Leo."

He squeezed tighter but didn't say another word, his small body warm against her own.

Damn that bastard Brown for refusing them. They needed to get the hell out of Reading. Tonight. After one more night of work to get her last check.

Then they'd go. And maybe...maybe there was something she could do to help them get away.

"Hey, Leo. You want to help me with a spell?"

Pulling out of her arms, he looked up at her, eyes bright as he nodded.

She smiled, trying to look excited. And confident. Yeah, right. "Alright, bud. You sit here for a sec." She pointed to the space in front of the altar then grabbed her backpack from beside the bed and pulled out their mom's grimoire.

She paged past spells to cure warts and heartburn, spells to induce comas and even one titled Love Potion. She'd had a few private laughs over that one.

But now... There it was, near the back. Concealment Spell.

Glancing through, it didn't look that difficult, and she had all of the ingredients they needed on the altar. Of course, nothing ever looked difficult until you were ass-deep in frogs, as her dad used to say.

Oh, Daddy...

Shaking off those thoughts, she grabbed what she needed and sat in front of Leo, placing the abalone moon bowl between them.

"Okay, bud. Let's do this."

In the bottom of the bowl, she placed the bloodstone and sprinkled dried heliotrope over it.

With the grimoire on her lap, she held out her hands and waited for Leo to place his in hers. She'd been teaching Leo as much as she could about spell casting. Which wasn't as much as it should have been.

She'd been a lousy student, which was why she hadn't attempted this spell before. It took a lot of power and an equal amount of control. And she didn't have much of either.

She closed her eyes, knowing Leo would follow her lead.

"Great Goddess Uni, Mother of all, protector of the Etruscans. We, your children, beseech Your aid."

Their hands warmed as power built between them, causing goosebumps to coat her arms. Lowering their hands, she wrapped Leo's around the edge of the bowl, then did the same with her own, funneling the power into the bowl and the bloodstone.

"Danger follows us. Evil tracks us. Bless us, Great Goddess, with a veil to hide us from those who seek us and mean us harm. We beg You to answer our plea."

The bowl shook beneath their hands, rattling against the floor, making the moonstone dance like a Mexican jumping bean in the bottom.

Shit, that was so not good. They were drawing too much power. She wouldn't be able to contain it for much longer.

Please, Goddess, just long enough to charge the stone.

"For your aid, we thank you, Uni, Lady of the Sky, the Earth and the Water."

Okay, time to release the spell into the stone.

"Leo, let go of the bowl. Slowly, bud."

He did it perfectly, sliding his palms then his fingertips from the lip of the bowl until he was no longer touching. As if he'd been casting for years. He probably had been. Her mom had started her training when she was four.

The bowl continued to rattle.

Shit, this is gonna hurt no matter what—

Sharp pain sliced into her temples right before the power blew her across the room. Pain shot up her spine as her back hit the wall, milliseconds before her head connected.

Yeah, that was going to leave a mark.

"Sissy!" Leo scrambled across the floor after her, eyes wide.

She held up her hands. "I'm okay, bud. I'm fine." Except…scorch marks covered her hands, making pain shoot up her arms and into her head. Her palms felt like she'd dragged them through a bed of red-hot coals. She dredged up a smile. "You and me together, kinda like Mentos and Diet Pepsi, huh?"

Leo never looked away from her hands, teeth latched into his bottom lip as his dark head tilted to the side. Before she could react, he placed his small hands over her burns. She drew in a sharp breath, steeling herself against the pain—that never came. Instead, she felt heat, not burning red heat but cool white—

Shit. "No, Leo, don't—"

He wrapped his hands around hers, holding on so she couldn't get away without possibly hurting him, his grip was that tight.

And then she felt the tingle of Leo's *arus* working against her own. The relief was immediate as her burns disappeared. Fear rose close on its heels.

Great Goddess, please let him be okay. "Leo, let me see your hands."

She braced herself for the sight of burns on his small hands. *With empathic healing, you took the injury on yourself—*

No burns. His hands were perfectly soft and smooth.

She took a deep breath. Only six and he healed with no side-effects.

Such a special little boy.

"Leo," she looked straight into his eyes. "How long have you been able to do that?" She couldn't heal without retaining some of the original injury on herself for a certain period of time, depending on the severity.

He just stared at here, as if he didn't know the answer to her question. Or he just didn't want to answer.

With a sigh, she gathered him onto her lap and held him, until she remembered the spell they'd been trying to work.

Looking down, she saw the bloodstone at the bottom of the moon bowl. It looked like a charred piece of wood. Her chest contracted like someone had punched her.

So much for that. Failed again.

Why her mother had ever thought she was special was beyond her.

Leo followed her gaze, little shoulders drooping as he caught a glimpse of the stone.

"It's okay, bud." She hugged him tight. "We'll be okay without it."

But she swore she felt those damn frogs biting her ass.

* * *

They left the building at seven.

Gabriel had to hand it to the girl. She'd hidden them well. She'd only screwed up once. But once was all it took.

He'd called in a favor with the local police and ran down her license plate. The registered name and address were bogus but she'd gotten a parking ticket two months ago on this block.

He'd been staked out since early afternoon and it'd finally paid off.

Her apartment was in an older building in center city. It had character but wasn't rundown. Her neighbors appeared to be young and single, coming and going at all hours. Probably never even realized there was a kid living there.

He was pretty sure no one saw her or the boy leave the building. In her baggy jeans, grey sweatshirt and red ball cap with her hair tucked under, she looked like every other city kid with a backpack slung over her shoulder. The boy walked at her side, dressed exactly the same, though his hat and sweatshirt were blue.

From a few blocks behind, his enhanced sight allowed him to track them in the fast-falling dusk. He was careful, but obviously not careful enough.

She realized she had a tail after five minutes. She didn't stop or look around, but she stiffened and her feet faltered for two steps. Then she continued on as if nothing had happened. It wrung a reluctant grin out of him.

He followed them easily for five blocks. Then they turned down an alley off Chestnut Street. And vanished.

"Fuck."

"Sure, buddy, but it'll cost ya."

A glassy-eyed teen stood on the corner. Gabriel would have ignored him but his dad's ingrained habits kicked in. He pulled a couple bills from his pocket and shoved them at the boy.

"Eat." With a small spell, he planted a mental picture of the Chinese restaurant up the street in the kid's head. "No drugs."

Stephanie Julian

Staring at the two twenties in his hand, the kid nodded.

"Yeah. Sure."

Gabriel didn't wait to see if the kid obeyed. He ran into the alley, searching the dark shadows and hidden spaces for any trace of the girl and the kid. And found nothing.

Well, hell. It'd been a damn long time since anyone had gotten the better of him. That it was a girl... Hell. That just made it worse.

When the alley dumped him onto Spruce, he stopped, eyes narrowed.

Where the hell was she headed?

She wasn't dressed like a waitress but there were a few restaurants in the area. There were also a couple of funeral homes, one manufacturing operation, a few bars, a few—

Shit. Shit. He knew why she'd looked familiar.

She was one of Harry's girls.

* * *

Like much of the rest of the city, The Spyder had seen better days.

Once the lodge of some benevolent order of animal, the building retained its original stone façade, but the grand arched windows had been boarded over and painted black. Only the decorative wrought-iron grills remained. The front door was arched, as well, and wouldn't have looked out of place on an English castle—thick-planked and iron-studded.

Only the Etruscans knew the oak door and iron studs were natural spell repellants.

A bas-relief border of trees and deer and rabbits cut the building between the second and third floors. If you looked closely enough, you could see the toothy creatures that lurked behind those trees.

After returning to the girl's apartment to retrieve his Audi, Gabriel parked the car close to the alley at the back of the building then walked to the front door.

"Dan, how's it going?"

"Hey, Gabe. How's it hangin'?" Shaved head gleaming, ebony skin shining in the dusk, Dan Ferryman gave him the once-over before letting his gaze slide back to the street. "Not planning on using any of that hardware tonight, are you?"

"Not unless I need to."

Dan's normally grim face split in a toothy grin, showing the elongated incisors that marked him hereditary *versipellis*. Harry employed mostly skin-shifters, from bouncers to bartenders to dancers. With their superhuman strength, they gave him an edge on any *eteri* who might want to pick a fight. "That's what I like about you, Gabe. You know how to sling the shit. You wanna talk to Harry?"

"Just here for the show."

Dan's snort could be heard through the thick door.

Pausing in the hall, Gabriel gave his olfactory sense time to adjust to the smell. How the hell the *lucani* dealt with it, he'd never understand. Their sense of smell was a hundred times better than his and his was three times better than a regular human's. The amount of alcohol, cigarettes and sex in the air could be a lethal combination.

Shaking his head, he stepped into the main room.

At one time, the club's public space had been a grand meeting hall with high ceilings, stained glass windows and rich wood paneling fit for an English manor.

But years of hard living had decayed the interior until it resembled a whore who'd stood on her corner too long.

Paint peeled from the paneling in rainbow flakes. Faded red velvet curtains covered the gaping holes where the windows had been, dust clinging to the folds like lint in a fat man's gut.

Heading for the bar on the left wall, he avoided the tables on the floor and the dozen or so men who watched three dancers gyrating on the catwalk. None was the girl he was looking for.

He took a deep breath of stale air thick with smoke from substances legal and others not so much.

"Gabe." Harry set a shot of tequila in front of him, slim white hands working fast, pale gray eyes never wavering.

Gabriel downed the alcohol before saying, "I need one of your girls."

Harry's bland features tightened infinitesimally. "Nothing kinky and no marks. A C-note for the first fifteen minutes. Which one?"

Gabriel let his gaze roam the murky room. "I'll let you know."

He tossed a twenty on the bar for the drink and the info and moved to the table farthest from the stage. After a few minutes of lazy pole-dancing, the three strippers left, and the girl he'd followed appeared.

Holy shit.

Dressed in black leather shorts made for a five-year-old and a couple strips of red leather that barely covered her nipples, she slinked onstage to some music he didn't recognize. The heavy bass thudded low in his gut and lust grabbed him by the balls as she rubbed her body against the silver pole in the middle of the stage.

Heat drenched him as she tossed her thick mane of hair over her shoulders and bent backward until it swept the floor. Breasts straining against the straps, she rubbed her crotch against the pole then swung around it.

And then she began dancing in earnest.

Holy fucking hell. Gabriel's mouth dropped open, allowing him to drag in a little more air so his lungs didn't quit on him.

How the hell had he not noticed the girl was damn hot last night?

Oh yeah, hangover.

Shit, he must have been further gone than he'd thought.

She wasn't tall, but she had a natural grace that should have looked out of place in a hole like this. Her hair, a silky brown-black curtain, veiled her face, hinting at secrets. But those flat brown eyes stared straight ahead, making no eye contact with anyone as she gyrated down the catwalk with the lazy stride of a porn star.

He wanted to watch her eyes but couldn't tear his gaze from her breasts, jiggling beneath the constraint of leather. Oh yeah, he was a breast man.

Not that he didn't appreciate her firm ass. The strip of material between her legs wasn't wide enough to completely cover the lips of her sex when she bent at the waist and shook her ass at the crowd. The move elicited a few whistles from the men and made Gabriel shift in the hard wooden chair to alleviate the binding pressure of his jeans on his stiffening erection.

He had the insane, caveman urge to jump onstage, grab her and run.

At that moment, her gaze locked with his. Shock froze her in mid-move, her mouth—damn, what he could

Stephanie Julian

do with that mouth—fell open then closed tight. A second later, she whipped around, hair flying out behind her, and walked off stage.

Gabriel walked back to the bar and threw five hundred-dollar bills in front of Harry.

"I want her."

Harry made the bills disappear and nodded to the door at the end of the bar.

"Room three."

* * *

Shea fidgeted on one of the room's two wooden chairs, foot tapping, listening for the sound of his footsteps.

She thought she'd lost him on the street earlier. How had he found them? Had he finally remembered her from the past nights he'd drunk himself stupid?

And why the hell had he followed her in the first place?

His response last night had been crystal clear. He wouldn't help them.

Had he changed his mind? Hell, did she even want his help after last night?

She sighed and heard despair in the sound. She couldn't afford to say no if he offered. There was too much at stake. Leo's life was worth any aggravation he could dish out.

Especially after that spell she and Leo had attempted today.

She needed this man and, boy, did that piss her off.

Down the hall, a door opened then closed, footsteps approaching.

Spell Bound

"Okay, deep breath, relax." She breathed in. "You can do this."

Her back tightened as the door opened, and she lifted her head to meet his eyes straight on. His dark gaze, however, slid all over her, from her unbound hair to the tips of her red toenails, visible in her open-toed black-leather stilettos.

Heat burned over her like an open flame. Which didn't make any damn sense because he wasn't looking at her with any kind of sexual intent.

Which just frosted her cookies.

Vaffanculo, what the hell is wrong with you?

He was just a guy. And she so did not need a guy. But she did need a *grigorio* and this one exuded strength as some men reeked of cologne. He wore his confidence as casually as he did the black coat and dark, tight jeans. The combination drew her like a cat to cream.

Her stomach clenched and her fingers itched to run through his ink-black hair and over his broad shoulders. She had the completely foreign urge to curl her legs around his waist and cling, let those huge hands run up and down her body and—

And, boy, did that piss her off. She hadn't had to sell herself to survive. Not yet.

She would sell herself to this man if he agreed to protect Leo. From the look on his face, he realized that and she hated him for it. But her body certainly didn't.

After what seemed like forever, his gaze locked on hers. Closing the door behind him, he took the seat across from her. A grin ghosted around the corners of his mouth. Waiting.

Ceffo. Did he think she was going to run screaming? If the bastard wanted a lap dance, she'd give him one that left him with a hard-on for a week.

Standing, she forced herself to relax, to treat him as just another guy who saw her as an object, not a person.

Stopping two feet in front of him, she met his gaze.

"I assume you know the rules," she said. "No touching. If you do, I leave and you are removed and banned. Don't bother to offer me money for anything other than the dance. I'm not for sale."

She didn't wait for him to say anything, just looked away and started to dance.

* * *

Damn, she was actually going through with it.

Gabriel hadn't come to talk, and he certainly hadn't come for a lap dance. But when he'd seen her in that skimpy outfit, with those beautiful tits and toned legs and long, dark hair…well, he was a guy.

A guy who'd been impressed as hell by her backbone yesterday. She'd told him off then walked away. In her position, he would have done the same.

Tonight, he'd come to take her to Serena, to find out who the hell she was. He wouldn't put up with any shit, but that didn't mean he couldn't have a little fun first.

Well, maybe fun wasn't the right word.

Because a hard-on the size of his was not fun unless he was naked and the woman was willing.

And from the expression on her face, that wasn't the case.

She began facing him, gyrating her hips then letting her upper body get into the motion. She moved in perfect rhythm to the piped-in music, every inch of her body a sinuous delight.

Her legs—long and sleek in four-inch stilettos—

looked strong enough to break his neck, but not overly muscled. Her hips and ass curved in a way only women should and her stomach, though flat, wasn't hollow. She was no cocaine-starved junkie who weighed ninety pounds and had breast implants.

No, her tits were her own. Firm and high, with just enough jiggle to prove their authenticity.

His gaze caught and held on her chest as she raised her arms over her head and did a slow turn. When she faced away from him, she bent at the waist, wrapped her arms around her legs and wiggled her ass at him.

His cock, already hard, began to throb as painfully as if she'd reached out and grabbed him. Hell, he was as close to coming without physical contact as he'd been since he was a teen.

And that made this woman dangerous.

When she straightened, throwing her hair over her shoulders, he'd had enough.

He snaked one arm around her waist and pulled her onto his lap, clapping his hand over her mouth before she screamed.

He trapped her easily, but her desperate squirming made his cock kick in his jeans. He took a deep breath, which didn't help because it was filled with her scent, spicy and clean, and whispered in her ear.

"I'm not going to hurt you. I'm here to protect you. And take you to talk to someone. I'll let you go when you stop struggling, then you're going to come quietly."

* * *

Shea finally made sense of the words the dirty, rotten *ceffo* had whispered in her ear, and anger replaced her fear.

Her heart still beat at heart-attack pace, but she forced herself to relax and he released her the second she stopped trying to get away.

Instinct took over and she jabbed her spike heel into his combat boot as she stood and faced him. The guy didn't even flinch.

"*Vaffanculo.* You are a Grade-A bastard. What makes you think I'm going anywhere with you?"

Crossing her arms under her breasts, forcing them tighter against the straps, she watched his gaze dip for a few brief seconds, making her nipples ache against the leather.

Son-of-a-bitch.

He smiled as if he'd read her mind. "You came to me for help, babe. Either you take it or they take the kid. I've seen what's after him."

Damn him. Her stomach rolled and, for a minute, she thought she might throw up. He was deliberately trying to scare her.

And since she'd seen first-hand what those men would do…she was terrified.

They could be anywhere. Sitting in the audience. Next to her on the street. They were close. She could practically feel them, like a dark presence that lingered on the outer edges of her consciousness. They'd killed her parents. There was no way she'd let them have Leo. But if something happened to her, Leo would have no one.

Unless she trusted this man with the steady dark stare and rock-solid jaw under a finely trimmed beard that covered his chin and continued up to meet his sideburns.

She sighed. "Why are you here now? You made yourself perfectly clear last night."

He shook his head. "No, I didn't. Look…last night…

I wasn't expecting you. I was tired and..." He sighed. "I didn't mean to offend you. So, may I please offer you my protection?"

Her lips twitched at his apology during which he never apologized and at his purely male look of exasperation. He had to know she wouldn't say no. There was too much at stake.

"Can you at least tell me your name? And who wants to talk to us?"

His head inclined the slightest bit. "Gabriel Borelli. And all your questions will be answered when we get where we're going. But we gotta go now."

"Fine. Just let me change—"

Borelli held up one hand to silence her as his eyes narrowed. He turned toward the door, revealing, for a brief second, the armory beneath his coat.

A brief flash of memory sparked as she recognized a few of the weapons under that coat. Her father had had many of the same in his own collection. Gabriel Borelli was a warrior, exactly who she needed to keep Leo safe.

His intense concentration as he listened to something outside the room actually calmed her. She didn't hear anything but he obviously did. Something that set him on edge.

After a few seconds, Borelli made a sharp motion with his head for her to follow him.

Slipping off her heels, she watched as he opened the door and looked both ways. Then he waved her into the hallway that connected these small rooms to the dressing room at the end.

Where Leo waited.

Borelli dogged her heels, a gun the size of a small cannon in his hand. They reached the dressing room in seconds. No one appeared in the hall as they slipped inside.

"Leo," she whispered. "Come on, we've got to go."

His dark head popped up from under the vanity table where he'd probably been playing his PSP. His eyes widened when he saw Borelli and he looked back at her with fear in his eyes.

"It's okay, bud." She smiled at him as she shrugged into her hoodie and pulled on her sneakers. No time to change the shorts. "He's here to help."

Leo looked again at Borelli, who swiped a quick look at Leo before returning his intent gaze to the dressing room door. Her brother took a second to make up his mind before he moved to her side.

She grabbed his hand and her backpack…

And froze as her skin tingled. Someone was using a spell to search for them. Someone powerful.

Oh, shit. They'd been found—

Borelli grabbed her shoulder and shook her, breaking through the fear that'd nearly paralyzed her. He didn't say a word, just motioned toward the door at the rear that led to the back alley.

She didn't need to be told twice. Holding tight to Leo's hand, she'd barely pulled him through the door when the shooting started.

Chapter Six

The dressing room door muffled the first few blasts. But as the wood splintered under a barrage of bullets, the sound of the gunshots pounded her ears.

"Get to the end of the alley and wait for me there," Borelli hissed before he turned back into the room.

He fired twice, the sound reverberating off the walls of the narrow alley, making rats scurry from their hiding places. Leo flinched but never hesitated as Shea forced him to run faster down the alley.

Stopping where he'd told her, she put Leo between herself and the brick wall of the building and watched Borrelli.

Walking backward to keep an eye on the door, the *grigorio* continued to shoot. Gunsmoke hung in the air, the stench thick and choking.

When he reached them, Borelli slung Leo over his shoulder like a sack of flour and grabbed her arm. Then he ran like hell.

She had a hard time keeping up, but she kept her mouth shut. Her heart flooded with adrenaline and fear made her stomach roll. Afraid to slow them down, she concentrated on not stumbling. As a kid, she'd learned to run on deer trails in the forest in her bare feet, her dad right behind her, ready to catch her if she stumbled.

"Shit." Her foot snagged on something and she nearly fell. Gabriel dragged her until she had her feet under her again.

"Concentrate or we're dead," he hissed. "I can't carry you both."

He was right, damn him.

They didn't run long, but it was a flat-out sprint up the alley. Shea's lungs burned and her calves sang with pain.

But when Borelli skidded to a halt, she wanted to scream at him to keep going.

Until she saw the three men at the end of the alley.

Borelli nearly dropped Leo in his haste to put the boy behind him and against the wall of the building. Then he grabbed Shea's arm and pulled her behind him, as well.

He kept his gun leveled at the men, two of whom had guns aimed at them.

The other was a boy, tall for his age, but still only a child. Maybe fourteen or fifteen. He looked like an angel with strawberry-blond hair and a face full of curves instead of angles, though his body was almost painfully thin, at that awkward stage between teen and man.

He smiled then, sweet and innocent. His expression sent a chill through her entire body. Goddess, the vibe she got from him slithered on her skin like slick black oil. He was anything but innocent.

Borelli's voice hissed between his teeth. "We need to get to the tan car behind them. When I tell you, grab the kid and follow me."

"Hello, *grigorio*." His voice just beginning to deepen with age, the teen made the title sound like a curse.

Gabriel never looked away from the two men with the guns. "Don't even try it." Borelli stared straight at them. "You'll both be dead before you pull the trigger."

Spell Bound

The teen laughed, a weirdly young sound. "You wouldn't dare shoot that thing in my vicinity, would you, *grigorio*? A bullet is such a small thing to alter. One tiny flick of the air and it can land somewhere you didn't expect."

As if to demonstrate, one of the men squeezed off a round, straight at Borelli's head. Shea gasped, but the teen waved his hand in the air and the bullet veered away and lodged in the building.

Goddess, the boy was *grigori*, like Gabriel. Cold terror spread through her body. This is what Dario wanted to turn Leo into. Oh, Goddess, please—

"You know, you're right about bullets." Borelli's gun didn't so much as waver. "But then, I never was much for machinery."

Faster than her brain could process, Borelli's hand, still holding the gun, shot out and connected with one of the men's chins before tossing a left hook at the other.

As the men fought, Shea kept her eyes on the teen. He stood to the side, his unwavering gaze stuck on Leo. Waiting.

Shea hated waiting. Damn it, she wanted him to make a move so she could do something. Not only had her dad taught her how to drive, but he'd taught her how to take care of herself, too.

Finally, the teen's eyes narrowed and he began to inch forward, seeing a tiny gap in the fighting between Borelli and the other two men.

Come on, bastard. Come on.

He came at her first with magic. His *arus* brushed against her and she braced herself against it. It was so cold, it burned. A fierce hatred fueled it, one she couldn't fully grasp. She only knew it hurt, and her head began to pound.

Steady.

When he was close enough, her fist swung out and clipped him on the jaw. Pain radiated up her arm at the force of the blow and the kid rocked back on his heels. But a second later, he smiled and slugged her back.

She saw it coming, knew it would hurt like hell, but she took it like her father had taught her. And when it didn't drop her, the boy's smile finally faded.

And hers spread.

"Hey, kid. Didn't your mom tell you it isn't nice to hit girls?"

She grabbed his shoulders, catching him off guard. Then she pulled him forward and kneed him in the groin with everything she had.

He hadn't been expecting it, stupid kid, and he fell to the ground with a strangled screech, clutching his balls.

"Run, now," Borelli yelled as he finally knocked one of the men to the ground and kicked the other away. "The car."

Shea obeyed mindlessly. She picked up Leo, her brother's arms wrapping around her neck, the warmth of his body sinking into her skin. Hugging him tight, she ran.

They were nearly to the car when the men caught up to them. One grabbed for Leo, the other hit Borelli with enough force to knock him into her.

She stumbled against the car and hit her hip hard. Still, she twisted, struggling. She had to get Leo away. Had to—

Someone began to scream, someone close.

A shaft of pain shot through her head, nearly blinding her, but she struggled toward the car, holding onto Leo as tightly as she could.

She didn't realize until the man grabbing for Leo fell away that he'd been the one screaming. He dropped to the ground, writhing and waving his burning arms, the flames quickly spreading.

Spell Bound

"Get in the car!" Borelli shouted at them. "Get in the car!"

Her mouth hanging open, she stood there, motionless. Blessed Goddess. Leo. Leo had done that.

"Sissy."

Startled by the sound of his voice, she turned to look into her brother's deep brown eyes. She saw his fear so clearly, it jumpstarted her body. She turned to wrestle open the front passenger door and slid in with Leo.

Boosting him over the backseat, she said, "Stay down and don't move."

She watched while he did that then turned to see Borelli slide into the driver's seat.

The car came to life with barely a sound, a fact that struck her as funny. With all the rest of the drama, there should be roaring engines.

The thought didn't last long as Borelli pulled a tight U-turn and peeled out in the opposite direction. Turning to look through the back window, she saw one of the men lift his arm, point the gun and shoot.

"God damn it, get down." Borelli palmed her head and shoved it onto the leather seat, even as he turned the next corner one-handed and at nearly fifty miles an hour. "I don't want you to get fucking shot."

He took another turn without braking, his hand still on her head, and she heard a small "oof" from the backseat. Habit made her say, "Watch your language."

His fingers tightened in her hair. He wanted to respond. She could practically hear the words on the tip of his tongue.

He didn't. Instead, he released her, replacing both hands on the wheel.

Sitting up, she let her gaze roam over their foul-mouthed savior. Except for a split lip, a decent-sized bruise on his cheekbone and a bloody tear in his pants at the knee, Borelli looked okay.

She felt awful. Her jaw throbbed from the right hook the teen had landed and her head throbbed with the onset of a migraine. She wanted to curl into a ball and pass out.

Closing her eyes slowly, she tried to suck in a few deep breaths but the pain wouldn't let her.

No, can't afford this now. Leo…

With a force of will she didn't realize she possessed, she pushed the pain back into a tiny corner of her brain until it was manageable…or at least simmered below agonizing.

When she felt she could, she shot a look at Borelli. He was focusing an enormous amount of concentration on his driving. It was a palpable force that didn't encourage conversation.

Fine by her. She needed a few minutes to regroup. With a grimace, she muttered the pain-blocking spell her mother had taught her years ago, knowing it would only delay the inevitable.

They drove for at least fifteen minutes, winding around the city streets before Borelli broke his silence to speak to Leo.

"You okay, kid?"

Gingerly, she moved her head to see Leo nod. He looked steady, as if he hadn't just made a grown man cry in agony.

Then Borelli glanced at her and lowered his voice. "You okay?"

And here she thought she'd been hiding it well.

"I'm fine."

"You took a pretty good shot to the jaw." He raised a hand. "Did you—"

Spell Bound

"No!" Hell, no. If he touched her, it'd be like throwing gasoline on the fire of her impending migraine. "No, it's fine. I just need to eat."

Hopefully that would help hold back the gnawing pain in her head. She refused to take one of the pills in her pack. She couldn't afford to be knocked out right now.

"Check the glove compartment," Borelli said. "There's usually something in there."

Pushing her hair out of her eyes, she sat up cautiously, checking the back window first to see if anyone was following them, seeing Leo, huddled on the seat behind Borelli.

He looked up at her at the same moment and she no longer saw fear in his eyes. Questions, yes. Even a little excitement.

"You okay?" she asked.

He nodded once then looked at Borelli. She knew exactly what he was thinking.

Head still throbbing, even through the pain-blocking spell, she turned to Borelli. "Where are we going?"

Late-night traffic was nearly non-existent, but the man didn't spare her a glance as he pushed the car even faster. "We're gonna find a hole to crawl into for a while."

Now, why didn't she like the sound of that? "Where?"

"Somewhere safe."

* * *

"What do you mean, you lost them?"

Peter's chin shot up, a wild look of fear in his eyes. "They've got a powerful *grigorio* with them now. And the boy's strong. He killed Phillips, made him burn with his hand."

Dario Paganelli raised his eyebrows, surprised. Not something he felt every day. "What do you mean? He lit a match and set him on fire?"

Peter shook his head. "The kid touched him and he burst into flame. I've never seen anything like it."

Now, that was interesting. The boy had la tocadura de bruja. And how convenient was that, considering?

Rising from behind the desk in his St. Pete Beach home, Dario went to the window to look out at the warm Florida sunshine. "Do you at least know which way they went?"

"Yes. Yes, we do. They headed north."

Dario nodded, though he wasn't condoning Peter's actions. His men had been chasing this boy for a year, ever since Kelsey, his latest *grigori* protégé, had felt his very strong energy from halfway across the continent.

The deaths of Kyle and Celeste Tedaldi, a *grigorio* and one of the original thirteen *streghe*, had been an unexpected bonus, but they'd hidden their son too well. His men hadn't been able to find the child at their home in Wisconsin and, with her dying breath, Celeste led him to believe the boy was on the west coast. His men had spent a few fruitless weeks chasing down that tidbit of information.

Now, they'd lost him again.

Dario hated setbacks. The boy was more valuable than even he'd thought and would make his mission, the mission with which his father had cursed him, that much easier.

All of the boys he had stolen from the *streghe* over the centuries had served their purpose well. Kelsey, especially, had been most helpful. But Celeste's son could prove to be the strongest of all.

"Why would they return north when we believe the *grigori* stronghold is somewhere in the west?"

"I don't know," Peter said. "Possibly to throw us off."

Dario nodded. "That could be. But it could also mean he's taking them to the women. I've long thought they were holed up somewhere in the northeast, but they've concealed themselves well."

He paused, knowing Peter hung on his every word. The other man remembered what had happened to the man who'd filled the position before him. That man had allowed Kyle and Celeste to escape almost twenty-five years ago. He had to have the carpets and wallpaper replaced after he'd freed the man's head from his body.

"You know, I've always wanted to say this. Too many movies, I guess." Dario turned and let his gaze linger on Peter. "Find them. Find him and bring him to me. I want the boy alive."

Peter swallowed audibly. "Yes, sir."

"Kill the girl and the *grigorio*. They're unimportant."

* * *

Gabriel didn't speak as he drove over the Bingaman Street Bridge then east on Route 422 before turning left onto Shelbourne Road.

The urban sprawl of Exeter Township soon gave way to the farmland of Oley Township. Frequent checks in the rearview revealed no tail, but he wanted to be sure before he took them to the safe house.

He still couldn't quite believe what he'd seen. The kid had the tocadura de bruja, the touch of the witch. It was rare, even among *grigori*.

No wonder Dario wanted the kid so badly. The kid had power, more than he should at his age, but he didn't look any worse for wear for using it.

Shea, however, hadn't opened her mouth since she'd asked where they were going. He slid a glance at her. Her skin shone ashen in the faint light of the dashboard. She looked ready to faint.

"Hey, are you okay? You weren't hit, were you?"

Taking a deep, shuddering breath, the girl shook her head. "No, I'm…I'm fine. Just a headache. I'm fine."

Headache, his ass. She didn't look fine. Far from it. Maybe some food would help. There hadn't been anything in the glove compartment when she'd checked. He'd have to resupply his stash of granola bars.

"Hey, kid." He waited until the boy looked at him in the rearview. "Spread out for a while, take a nap. You're tired."

He flicked a tiny sleep spell at the kid, just enough to make him yawn before nodding.

"Please," Shea spoke so softly he almost didn't hear her, "don't do that. Not to me, either. We're not…" She paused. "Just don't."

"He needs to sleep. We need to talk."

She sighed and those gorgeous lips pursed, but he was right and she knew it.

A few minutes later, she stole a look over her shoulder. The kid had already gone lights out.

"So where are we going?" she asked.

He deliberately didn't answer. It was guaranteed to piss her off and that's exactly why he did it. She looked a little too shocky. He figured pissed off was better than terrified.

Shea gave a disgusted hmph. "Where. Are. We. Going?"

He glanced at her and watched the lines in her forehead deepen. Not at all detracting from the exotic beauty of her face.

Which he really didn't need to be thinking about right now.

Shit.

"I want to make sure we don't have a tail before we double back and head to a safe house. When I think it's safe, then I'll take you to talk to Serena."

"Who's Serena?"

Could she really not know who Serena was? Especially if she knew Celeste, it seemed really fucking unlikely that she wouldn't know who Serena was. Still... "Someone you're going to want to talk to."

Out of the corner of his eye, he saw her lift one hand to her head. She rubbed her temple, as if trying to ease a headache.

Join the club, babe.

"What's your real name?" he asked.

"My real name is Shea. Shea Jones."

"Yeah, right."

"Listen, Mr. Borrelli—"

"Back to mister, huh? What? Asshole's not working for you anymore?"

For a second, he thought she might actually laugh. He'd really like to hear that. Then she shook her head. "Watch your language, please."

"The kid's asleep."

She glanced over her shoulder and the tough exterior she'd been holding on to seemed to melt away. Making her look years younger. And exhausted. "I know, it's just... He's so young. I..." She frowned. "I need to thank you. For...back there. I don't know what I—"

"Don't." He cut her off before she said anything about undying gratitude. This was his job. Hell, it was a sworn duty, and he still felt like shit for turning them away last night. "Everybody's fine. Just answer my questions. I need to know who sent you to me. Start with your parents. Who are they?"

Shea hesitated, torn between her parents' deeply ingrained admonitions against revealing anything personal and the need for answers from her only source of information.

That source was scowling at her, and he had a perfectly gorgeous scowl. It made his sharply defined features even more handsome, from the straight slope of his nose to his high cheekbones.

She frowned in return but said, "My parents are Celeste and Kyle Tedaldi."

She bounced against the door as the car hit the shoulder. Borelli jerked the wheel back to the left as he steadied the car. Then he shot her a long glance that took her in from head to toe.

"You're lying."

Her mouth dropped open. Of all possible responses, that hadn't been one she'd imagined. "Why would you say that?"

He snorted, making her more angry and confused by the second. "I don't know what game you're playing but you can't be Celeste's daughter. Is the kid your son?"

Completely confused by his belligerent attitude, she rubbed a hand over her throbbing left temple. "Leo is my brother. Our mother ca—sent for me to get him a year ago. I'd... been away from home."

"Bullshit."

Her temple gave a short, sharp tug and she rubbed it

with one finger. "It's the truth. Why would I lie about something like that?"

"Where did they live?"

"Wisconsin."

She could see him thinking about that, processing the information.

"Look—"

"Listen—"

They broke off.

Gabriel took another look out the rearview then sighed. "Alright, something's off here and I need to know what it is if I'm going to protect you. I'll give you the benefit of the doubt that you're Kyle's daughter, but you aren't Celeste's."

Shea's temples began to pound in unison. "Why would I lie about that? What would I have to gain?"

"You can't be Celeste's daughter. If you were, you'd know why."

What the hell was he talking about? He wasn't making any sense.

Then again, maybe she didn't want to know. "Well, I am but I don't."

He snorted. "Come on, Shea. You're smart enough to have gotten this far, but don't think I'm gonna believe you're the answer to everyone's prayers."

Confusion bit into her headache, trying to breach the wall the spell had erected against the pain. Surprisingly, the voices were a barely perceptible buzz in the background. "What does that mean?"

Gabriel stole another look at Shea, taking careful note of the purple aura that marked her *strega*. He searched for the black streaks that would identify her as one of the thirteen women he was sworn to protect. He didn't find a trace of black. Just a whole lot of jagged red lines. Pain.

She managed to keep that pain out of her expression, her beautiful face unmarked by it. She was a true beauty and, from the photo he'd seen of Celeste, she had been, too. Still, there were a lot of beautiful, dark-haired women in the world.

And none, as far as he knew, had yet been born to break a five-hundred-year-old curse.

"Borelli, if you have something to tell me, just spit it out."

He shot her another quick glance, found her staring straight at him through those lifeless brown contacts, her expression a mix of fear and confusion. Without stopping to think, he released the wheel with his right hand and grabbed her arm.

At first, he felt nothing and that was shocking. Then, as if a wall had fallen, thoughts that weren't his own flooded his brain, whispered bits and pieces of conversations he couldn't understand. He could make out nothing coherent, but the intensity of the link began to grow.

He knew he was driving, but, suddenly, it didn't matter. The voices were speaking to him and he had to listen harder, had to understand—

The voices cut off as Shea ripped her hand out of his with an agonized cry.

Holy shit.

The car veered to the left this time as his hand twitched, jerking the wheel and nearly taking out the car coming toward them. The driver laid on the horn and shot him the finger as Gabriel fought to get the car and his body under control. His muscles shook against the unreasonable urge to grab her hand again and listen to the voices. They needed him.

"What the hell was that?"

He heard fear in his voice and hated it. Hated that she'd done this to him.

"*Vaffanculo*, what the hell just happened?"

"Don't touch me."

No shit. "Yeah, I got that much. Just tell me what the hell that was."

She made a sound low in her throat, somewhere between a moan and a sob. "My own private hell. Did you find out what you needed to know?"

"No. Explain."

She shook her head. "I can't." She paused and he wasn't sure she was going to continue. Then she sighed. "The voices have always been there. My mother used to call them my guardians. As I got older, I learned to ignore them. To build a mental wall and keep them to a manageable hum."

Well, shit. Whatever was wrong with this girl, it was major. She'd managed to keep her and the kid one step ahead of Dario's men for a year, and that took a fair amount of brains, so he ruled out just plain crazy. Schizophrenia was a possibility, and he was sure there were a dozen other mental illnesses she might have that could account for the voices.

But whatever it was, it was scary. And she lived with it daily.

"Did Celeste ever tell you why you hear voices?"

Shea shook her head and let her gaze meet his. He really hated those contacts.

"She just said it was my curse to bear. I've learned to live with them, to mentally wall them up most of the time, but they're never truly gone."

Oh, no. No way. No fucking way. He didn't believe

it. He couldn't believe. "You really want me to believe you're the one, after all these years?"

She shook her head again. "What are you talking about? The one what?"

She looked dead serious, confused as all hell and terrified. He had the unbelievable urge to take her in his arms and tell her everything would be okay.

Could it be possible?

Hell, after the life he'd lived and the things he'd seen, he would have admitted that anything was possible. But to think this girl was finally the one, after five hundred years? And she didn't know?

He wasn't sure he could accept that.

"Borelli. The one what?"

He wasn't going there yet. "Did your… Did Celeste ever talk about her family, her *boschetta*?"

She paused again, this time longer. Then she asked, "Are you telling me she had family?"

"Did she tell you about her past?"

Shea sighed and he heard disgust in the sound. "My mother didn't talk much." At least not to her. Her mom just looked at her with those sad eyes, her disappointment so clear in the flat line of her mouth. "My dad…"

"What about your dad?"

A small smile tried to lift the corners of her mouth. "I never doubted his love. He taught me how to fight, how to read, how to write. How to think. I could handle a knife long before I knew how to add. He was a school teacher before he met my mother. He was older than her—"

Borelli snorted as he navigated the dark back roads.

"What the hell's that supposed to mean?" she asked.

"Oh, come on. If you really are Celeste's daughter—and I'm not saying you are—then you know how old your

Spell Bound

mother really is. You know the history. And if you don't, then it just proves my point that you're not her daughter."

Shea didn't know what to say to that. Well, she had a few things, but telling the man who'd saved Leo from certain death that he could stick his head in his ass probably wasn't a good choice.

Still, his denial of her parentage was starting to grate. Even she could see the resemblance between her and her mother. More than she wanted.

But if Borelli wanted to play twenty questions then she'd play along. But she wanted some answers of her own.

"Tell me why you're so sure I'm not...Celeste's daughter."

"What did Celeste tell you about the curse?"

She frowned. "You mean the voices?"

"No, I mean the curse."

A cold shiver made its way up her spine. That one word sound so... ominous. She really didn't want to ask but knew she had to. And she knew she wasn't going to like the answer. "What curse?"

He fell silent again, eyes checking the rearview every so often.

Something too much like terror started to creep through the agony of her building migraine. "Borelli, what the hell's going on?"

The minute the question left her lips, she wished she could take it back. She didn't want to know.

Blessed Goddess, she was so screwed up. Which should be expected from someone who'd been twelve years old before she'd seen another person other than her parents. Before she knew there were things like telephones, televisions and radios.

This curse he kept talking about…something else her parents had failed to mention. But Borelli would, if she had to pester, sweet talk or bully him all the way to wherever the hell they were going.

She took a deep breath and started on her second option. "Please. I need to know."

He shot her another look, his eyes narrowing. "When we get where we're going. Rest until then. You don't look too good."

That's because the blocking spell was wearing off and the migraine was gaining strength.

For a brief second, she considered badgering him until he gave her the answers she wanted. But her head hurt too much.

With a huff, she turned to look out the passenger side window. A few crowded developments gave way to open fields filled with waist-high corn on both sides of the two-lane road. They passed a few old stone farmhouses and brick churches and drove through a covered bridge to more fields.

At the edge of the fields, a forest reared up as they climbed a hill.

Her lids grew heavy and she must have fallen asleep because when she opened her eyes, the car was bumping along an unpaved road, shooting spikes of pain through her head. After what seemed like hours, Gabriel pulled the car to a stop.

Nauseous, she looked out the window, barely able to make out the outline of a two-story house. Gods-be-damned, her head felt like someone was trying to cut a path out from the inside with a dull spoon.

Vaguely, she realized Gabriel was rounding the front of the car, heading toward her door. Behind her, she heard zippers opening and closing as Leo searched for something in the backpack.

A few seconds later, Leo's hand appeared over the seat, clutching her brown prescription bottle.

She turned to give him as much of a smile as she could. "It's not that bad."

"What's not that bad?"

Borelli's low-pitched voice sounded just beside her. He'd opened her door, ready to reach in and pull her out.

She flinched away. If he touched her now, it'd feel like nails driving into her temples.

Before she could say anything, Leo grabbed Borelli's arm. "Don't."

Borelli glanced from Leo to her and back again. His jaw clenched, but he nodded and backed away, leaving the door open for her.

Okay, she could do this. She could. She just needed to get out of the car, walk into the house and get horizontal. Surely there'd be a bed somewhere. She just needed to lie down for a little while.

Sliding off the seat, she had to grab the car door as a wave of nausea rolled through her. She barely avoided throwing up at the *grigorio*'s feet. And how embarrassing would that have been? "Where are we?"

"Safe." Borelli grabbed her bag from the back seat and waved Leo up the short flight of stone stairs looming ahead of them. He waited for her to move before following.

With every step, the pain in her head intensified. She couldn't let it take her down. Not yet. Alone, she could dissolve, but not now. Not in front of Borelli. She didn't want him to think she was weak.

Grabbing the metal railing to the side of the stairs,

she pulled herself up each step. When she reached the top, she felt like she'd climbed Mount Everest. And was about to die from exposure.

Leo stood before the large front door, waiting.

"Hey, kid," Borelli said. "Never stand in front of a door if you can help it. Leaves you vulnerable."

Borelli stepped to the side of the door as he reached for a string around his neck. Pulling it from beneath his shirt, he revealed an antique silver key that he slipped into the lock. The door opened without a sound, and he stuck his head inside for just a second before he waved them through.

Goddess, please, just a few more steps.

The nails in her temples became railroad spikes, crushing against her brain. Her knees started to buckle and she stumbled and nearly fell. Only Leo's small body by her side kept her from hitting the ground.

"Through the atrium and dining room, the bedrooms are at the back on the left." Borelli's voice rumbled in her ear. "Lay down."

Barely able to see, her eyes squeezed nearly shut, she wasn't sure she was going to make it until Leo took her hand, guiding her.

She stumbled ahead, agony increasing with every step.

Chapter Seven

Gabriel watched them make their way through the rooms, watched Shea take every step as if it were killing her.

He felt useless and he abso-fucking-lutely hated that. He was *grigorio*. He'd been raised to believe he could find a way to fix or fight anything.

He wanted to pick her up, tuck her in bed and make her better simply by the force of his will.

Which was really stupid. He could only perform rudimentary healing spells. And the kid had told him not to touch her. Probably aggravated the migraine.

What he should do is check the house, tucked into a forest in the southeastern Berks County hills. The wards had been in place when they'd arrived but that didn't mean he should let his guard down.

His gaze tracked to the back of the house. Or maybe he should follow Shea and Leo to make sure they found the right room.

Yeah, it was a lame-ass excuse, but he needed to make sure she was okay. And maybe the kid would need his help with something.

The door to the first room was open, and Leo knelt beside the bed, his back to the door.

Shea lay on the bed, curled into a ball, arms over her

head, as if warding off blows. Her eyes were squeezed tight but she looked to be asleep.

He'd seen this woman take a right hook to the chin and smile. The pain had to be excruciating if it had her laid out like this.

"Leo."

The kid spared him a quick glance over his shoulder but immediately went back to staring at Shea. Leo looked almost as pale as his sister, and Gabriel spent several gut-wrenching seconds debating what he should do.

What would he do if it that was Nino sitting there, looking like his heart was bleeding?

Walking over to the bed, he shut off his internal critic and let instinct take over. Bending, he picked up the kid and held him. Little arms twined around his neck as Leo started to cry. The sound made his chest ache so badly, he wondered if he'd broken a rib during the fight.

Bullshit. You know you didn't.

He walked out of the room, the boy now wrapped around his body and clinging like a monkey. If he loosened his arms, Leo wouldn't have fallen. But Gabriel didn't let go. When they got back to the atrium, he sat on the couch in the living room and let the kid cry himself to sleep.

* * *

After he'd put the kid in the room next to Shea's, Gabriel picked up the phone and dialed.

"Serena."

"Hello, Gabriel. Is everything alright?"

Not by a long shot. "Tell me about Kyle and Celeste. Everything you know."

Spell Bound

He heard Serena take a deep breath, caught off guard by his unexpected demand.

As a *grigorio*, he'd been taught the history of the *boschetta*, had had it drummed into his brain until he could recite it in his sleep. He knew Celeste had been Serena's best friend. That Celeste and her husband Antonio had been blood-bound before Antonio's death five-hundred years ago. The ancient rite of mixing their blood together during sex had enabled Celeste and Antonio to find one another each time they were reborn. Like a magical homing beacon. He knew that Kyle had been born with Antonio's soul.

He knew that they'd disappeared, seemingly off the face of the earth, more than twenty years ago.

"What exactly are you looking for?" she asked.

His heavy sigh reverberated through the phone line. "Just... Do you know if Kyle had any children before he met Celeste?"

"Gabriel," Serena's voice held a breathless quality he'd never heard from such a pragmatic woman before. "What are you saying?"

"I don't know." Great Goddess, he didn't even want to think about what he was trying to say. What it would mean to this woman. "Just answer the question. Could he have had other children?"

Serena went silent for several longs seconds. "Celeste found Kyle when he was fifteen but did not take him for her own until he was twenty-one. I suppose there could have been other children. But not after he and Celeste were together. They were devoted to each other."

Yeah, that's what he'd thought. Still, he'd had to ask.

"Gabriel, the girl. Is she... Does she say she's..."

Hell, even Serena couldn't finish the thought. Not out loud.

So he did it for her. "Yeah. She claims she's Celeste and Kyle's daughter."

Another pause. "Do you believe she is?"

That was the million-dollar question, wasn't it? After all these years—

"Gabriel, what do you think?"

His sigh made the phone line crackle. "I don't know what to think yet. We'll be there as soon as we can. I want to make sure we don't have a tail."

* * *

"Quinn, I believe Gabriel may need your help."

Quinn Kennett ignored the familiar tug Serena's husky voice always gave his libido and flopped onto the sofa in his apartment in Philadelphia.

"Hello to you, too, babe. How's it going? I'm fine, by the way."

He heard her sigh, heard her disappointment. And couldn't care less.

"Quinn, please. I know things haven't been good between us—"

He snorted, his upper lip curling back in a snarl. "Yeah, well, considering the fact that you only call when you need something, I think I pretty much deserve to be pissed off."

Shit. Shit, that sounded so damn whiny. Why did he let this woman do this to him?

Because he was an idiot, that's why. A gods-damned reincarnated, blood-bound idiot.

And wasn't that a cosmic fucking joke?

For seven years now, since he was seventeen, he'd been pining after this woman. The woman who was supposed to be his. The woman who, five-hundred years ago, had bound herself by blood and love to his soul.

And the woman who, today, wouldn't allow herself to love him back.

"Quinn, please." Her persuasive voice floated over the phone lines. "We don't have time for this now. Gabriel needs you."

"And you don't, do you, babe?"

She didn't answer right away and he held his breath waiting for her reply.

Gods, you're such an idiot.

"Quinn—"

He sighed, knowing he couldn't refuse her anything. "What do you want me to do?"

"Go to him. Keep him safe. And Quinn?"

"Yeah?"

"You stay safe, too."

Then she was gone and he sat there, staring at the black plastic receiver in his hand until it began to beep.

Anger built until he hurled the receiver across the room. Reaching the end of the cord, it snapped back and nearly clipped him on the shoulder. He growled at it then dropped his head back to stare at the ceiling.

Damn. He had no back bone. No matter what Serena asked him to do, he did. Why didn't he just hand the woman a leash and a collar to put on him? He was already whipped.

Well, at least he'd get to see Gabe. They hadn't been in the same place at the same time in at least six months. He missed his best friend, though he'd never say that to Gabe. Gabe would shake his head and shrug him off. It wasn't that Gabe didn't care. He just wasn't into public displays of emotion. Hell, Gabe had been trained not to show emotion at any time.

That's okay. Quinn usually had enough emotion for both of them. And they were in an uproar now.

Serena tied him in so many damn knots every time they talked, he'd been avoiding her for months. Which was pretty fucking easy since she never left her home. And *lucani* business kept him so damn busy he didn't have the time to camp out on her doorstep. Not that he would.

Fuck no. He was sick of chasing her.

Yeah, and what a load of shit that is.

It was nearly two a.m., the nearly full moon a pale disc hanging in the sky, calling to him. He pulled on his sneakers.

He'd walk as far as he could then change and let his wolf run to its heart's content. Or at least until he wore himself out.

* * *

The world slowly came back into semi-focus.

Shea reached for the glass of water Leo always set by the bed after she slept off a migraine.

It wasn't there.

Groaning, she sank back into the firm mattress. She didn't want to open her eyes yet. She knew she had to get her contacts out but she was going to enjoy the blessed calm for a few minutes more. She hated to take the prescription pills because they knocked her unconscious, but, oh blessed Goddess, it felt wonderful to wake to complete silence in her head, even if it would be short-lived.

She reached for the opposite side of the bed.

Leo wasn't there.

Spell Bound

Her eyes flew open and she sat straight up, the previous hours coming back to her in a rush. The drive, the fight, Leo's power.

"Hey. Take it easy."

Gabriel sat in a chair next to the bed, a glass of water in one hand. "Drink this." He placed the glass in her hand before she could reach for it. "Leo's fine."

Jeez, could the guy read her mind now? She hoped not. She had way too much to hide.

She sipped, eyes still closed. Yes, she was in high-avoidance mode but she figured she was entitled for a few minutes.

After placing the empty glass on the bedside table, she looked around the room, noting its bare walls, plain wooden dresser and short bedside table. She looked anywhere but at Gabriel, who stared straight at her.

"Where are we?" She nodded at the room in general. "This doesn't look like a hotel."

"It's not. It's a safe house built by the *lucani*."

Her eyebrows raised, she met his dark eyes, but his expression showed nothing.

"It's been here for years," he continued, motioning toward her neck. "Available to anyone with the right key. Yours would work. It was your mother's, right?"

She reached for the iron key on the leather strap around her neck, feeling the metal warm in her hand. She released it before it transformed itself into its natural shape. Her gaze narrowed as she digested his words. "So you're saying you believe me now? To what do I owe your sudden change of heart?" She threw back the covers—and grabbed them back again when she realized she was naked. "Hey! Where are my clothes?"

He smiled, and her breath stopped in her throat as

heat pooled between her legs. Those lips, framed by that dark scruff, drew her gaze. She wanted to lean in and put her mouth over his, feel the rough scratch of his beard against her skin. She wanted him to kiss her, to wipe her mind of everything but her desire for him.

And that was really not good. Not now, on top of everything else.

Forcing herself to drop her gaze, she hoped he never realized what she was thinking.

"Pick new ones out of the chest," he said. "There'll be something in there to fit you. Meet me in the atrium and we'll talk. Don't wake the kid. He's next door."

Then he walked out, leaving her sitting there with her thighs clenched and an ache low in her gut.

* * *

Before Gabriel headed to the front of the house, he stuck his head into the neighboring bedroom to check on the kid.

Sound asleep and looking even younger than he was.

Too damn young.

Hell, they were all too young when they started.

Gabriel had been three. He still had the wooden practice knife his dad had made for him. He'd gotten the real deal when he was a year older than Leo. The following year, he'd gotten a gun.

Leo hadn't said anything about training. Hell, the kid hadn't said anything at all. But, Christ, the kid had power. Too much. Maybe Kyle had been killed before he could start Leo's training. Then again, maybe Kyle had never intended to train him.

So many maybes. His eyes burned and he felt like he

Spell Bound

could sleep for days. But there was no time. Shea was on her way. They definitely needed to talk.

He headed for the atrium, the main gathering space in the house, and dropped into the sofa, willing his body not to fall asleep as his thoughts raced through the information he had. And more importantly, what he didn't.

After a few minutes, he heard her footsteps on the wooden floor, measured steps, as if she were taking her time, looking around.

Cautious. Good. That he could handle. Pissed off was okay, too.

The way she'd looked at him in the bedroom, when he'd smiled at her... That was a complication he didn't need.

Gods' balls, the woman hit all his buttons. And when he'd undressed her earlier, every single one of those buttons felt like they'd been pressed, fondled and hung out to dry.

He'd realized after he'd pulled her shorts down those long, smooth legs that he shouldn't have started on her clothes. Shouldn't have even thought about it.

But he'd tried to be a nice guy.

Oh, yeah. You're a real prince. Just admit you wanted to see her naked.

No, that wasn't exactly true. He'd wanted her to be comfortable. Which was completely out of character for him. He was a damn good fighter. A damn good *grigorio*. But he was, by no stretch of the imagination, a humanitarian. He didn't play well with others.

But he couldn't stand to see her uncomfortable.

So he'd undressed her. And stared, hard and aching, at her naked body as she lay passed out on the bed.

Pervert.

Maybe he was.

"In here," he called, cutting off that train of thought.

She came through the dining room, skirting the upholstered chaise lounges and low side tables that replaced a typical table and chairs, her expression showing every ounce of her wariness. That he'd expected. The clothes she'd chosen to wear...not so much.

She'd picked a dress. And not a slinky, sexy dress, but an honest-to-Gods girly dress. Soft pink fabric dotted with tiny purple flowers draped over her slim body while the neckline only hinted at the generous curves of her breasts. The high waistline began right under her breasts and the skirt fell below her knees but the sleeves ended high on her arms.

Hell. She looked young. Girl-next-door college student, not the prophesied savior of the women he'd sworn to protect. One of whom he loved more than his own life.

Shea claimed to have never heard of the curse. If that was true, she probably didn't know how to break it either. And that was the real bitch of the situation.

No one knew how to break the curse.

And he had to tell her. The weight of that responsibility settled on his shoulders like ten tons of bricks.

"What?" She frowned and her hands landed on her hips, eyes narrowing. "Never seen a dress before?"

He swallowed a smile and nodded toward the couch across from him. He really was starting to like this girl more than he should. Especially when she was pissed off.

"I've got questions you're gonna answer. Now. And," he added when she started to object, "I've got some answers. But no more bullshit, Shea. I need to know how much you know about the curse."

Spell Bound

She moved closer to the couch, continuing to stare straight into his eyes, and he realized she'd taken out the brown contacts she'd been wearing.

Oh holy shit. Her eyes.

He swore his heart stopped for a full five seconds before it started beating again like he'd just jumped off a cliff. Blessed Goddess, it was true. The answer to a five-hundred-year-old curse stood in front of him, staring at him through eyes he'd only seen on the thirteen cursed *streghe*.

Anyone catching a quick glimpse of them would think they were hazel, that indiscriminate mix of colors that could range from blue to green to brown and any variation in between.

But when you looked into a cursed *strega*'s eyes, you saw how truly odd they were, like someone had shattered a stained glass window then set the shards in a round frame. It was so unusual, most of the women wore contacts when they went out among the *eteri*.

As if his intent scrutiny embarrassed her, she looked away as she sank into the chair across from him. "I don't have a clue what you're talking about."

Christ, this was a nightmare waiting to happen. One he wasn't prepared for. One he needed to get prepared for right now. "Your mother never mentioned a curse? Did she ever talk about Italy? About the time she spent there? How long ago it was?"

She shook her head. "No."

"She never mentioned Serena or Andrea? Tullia or Madrona or Furia?"

Again, she shook her head but a tiny flicker of her expression told him she knew the names.

"Don't lie to me," he said. "You know the names,

don't you?"

Her chin lifted slightly. "Yes, I know the names of the Priestesses. I have to. It was part of my training."

Holy freaking hell. Celeste had trained her to take her place as a Priestess of Menrva and, after her death, the nail, hidden in the shape of a key, had passed to Shea. He'd seen it hanging around her neck when he'd undressed her. He just hadn't wanted to believe.

"And Celeste never said anything about a curse?"

"No." Then she frowned. "But I always knew there was something she wasn't telling me. Something to do with the voices, something I didn't realize until I'd left. But I couldn't go back, not then."

"What do you mean, when you left?"

Swallowing, she dropped her gaze and let it rest on her hands in her lap. "Until I was twelve, I didn't realize there was a world outside the boundaries of my home in Wisconsin. There was only my mom and my dad and me."

Damn. Kyle had hidden them good. But that wasn't anything they needed to discuss right now. "Do you know how old your mother was?"

Now she returned his gaze steadily. "I'm assuming not forty-three like she told me."

"Try five-hundred-and-forty-seven."

He thought for a second she was going to faint. Her mouth parted and she started to draw in fast, shallow breaths. When her eyes glazed over, he reached for her and pressed her head down between her knees. She didn't fight him.

"Slow, deep breaths, Shea." Leaving his hand on her nape, he rubbed, trying to comfort. "Come on, don't pass out on me now."

Because there's more.

Spell Bound

If it had been anyone else, he would've continued to hammer away, try to trip her up. But he had to respect a woman who smiled when she took one on the chin.

And that did not bode well for his future.

"Not...going...to pass...out."

It took her a minute, but she finally caught her breath. When she sat up, the look she gave him burned. "What aren't you telling me?"

He leaned back into his chair, squashing a smile. "What makes you think there's more?"

She waved a slim hand in the air, her skin still pale. "Oh, please. There's always more. There's probably more you don't know."

Smart ass. He liked that about her. "You sure you're ready to hear the rest?"

She swallowed and blinked. She looked ready to say no.

Then she nodded.

"In 1495," Gabriel began, recalling the tale every *grigorio* memorized as a child, "Fabrizio Paganelli cursed the thirteen Priestesses of Menrva, living as simple *streghe* in a Tuscan village, to outlive their loved ones and to never produce another *strega*. He blamed them for the death of his youngest son. And because he was a powerful *Malandante*, the curse worked."

From the shocked look on her face, he could tell Shea knew what that meant. The *Mal*, like *streghe*, were born with the ability to work magic. But the *Mal* used that power in dark ways. An ancient secret society of Etruscan descent, the *Mal* orchestrated much of the chaos in the world, benefiting from death and destruction.

"The women didn't know that right away," he continued. "At first, they dismissed Paganelli's ravings.

He was distraught with grief, and no one in the village believed the *streghe* had killed his son. But years passed and the women didn't age.

"Eventually, the town turned on the *streghe*, burned their seer at the stake and murdered their families. They attempted to kill the remaining *streghe* by slitting their throats." The thought made blood lust boil in his veins. "But their bodies healed and they left the village, scattering across Europe, hiding wherever they could, eventually making their way to America.

"At the time, the *streghe* didn't know Paganelli's curse had also trapped his three remaining sons in never-ending life. Paganelli's son, Dario, made it his mission to kill every one of the women. That's why he wants Leo. To use his powers to hunt the *streghe*."

Gabriel took a deep breath, trying to rein in the fierce anger he felt whenever he thought about Dario. "Any of this ring a bell?"

She nodded, her expression shell-shocked. "Mom told me that Dario is trying to find and kill the Priestesses, that he wants Leo to use against them. But she never... Mom never..." She took a deep breath and lowered her gaze to the floor. "This is the first time I've heard anything about a curse."

Gabriel shook his head. Why the hell had Celeste not told her?

Then again, how do you start that conversation?

Surprise! You're the key to breaking a five-hundred-year-old curse. Welcome to the world. Now all you have to figure out is how to do it.

After a few moments of silence, she looked up. "What did they do? After they found out they'd been cursed."

"They begged the Goddesses, Uni and Menrva, to release them. No go. Then, before the villagers burned her, Dafne foresaw the birth of a daughter to one of the original thirteen to end the curse."

Shea blinked and swallowed, the only outward sign to give away her fear. He wanted to reach for her hand but stopped before he touched her, remembering what had happened the last time. The voices and how they had aggravated her migraine. He didn't want her to repeat that.

So he waited for her to make some signal that she was ready.

Shea's eyelids fluttered then she drew in a deep breath. "Do you know how she's supposed to do that exactly?"

Gabriel shook his head. "Neither do the women."

Her eyes narrowed. "Dafne didn't tell them?"

He shook his head.

And waited. He expected more questions. Hell, he expected anger, fear, maybe tears.

Instead, she sat there, staring at her hands. Finally, after what had to be at least two minutes, she drew in another breath, but didn't lift her gaze. "Do you think Dario knows…about me?"

She sounded exhausted. Defeated. Lost. The urge to grab her out of her chair and set her on his lap, put his arms around her and hold her, made his muscles twitch.

Instead, his fingers curled into the arms of his chair, anchoring him in place. "We didn't know about you. We're not sure Paganelli even knows about the prophecy. He was away at school when the townspeople burned Daphne and tried to kill the others.

"I figure your mother discovered fairly early in her pregnancy that she was having a girl and she and Kyle disappeared before anyone could find out. Your father was a damn good *grigorio*, descended from Dafne's line. He's probably the one who realized your mother was carrying a girl. From everything I've heard, Kyle was damn good with the sight."

Gabriel was right, Shea thought. Her dad had been the best. A well of sadness hit her chest and tears burned in her eyes. An image of her dad popped into her mind, his brown curly hair always in need of a trim, his quick smile and steady dark eyes. Blessed Goddess, she missed him.

She took a deep breath, pushing down sadness. "He was. He always managed to be wherever I needed him, right before I fell out of a tree or tripped over rock." She took another breath, trying to steady herself against an encroaching dizziness. "Is your mother one of the thirteen?"

He nodded. "But I can't tell you which."

"Why not?"

"Safety precaution."

She figured that seemed logical. "What about your father?"

"Davis Borelli."

"Is he still—"

"He died several years ago."

"What aren't you telling me?"

He smiled again and her eyes widened. Damn, the man was gorgeous when he did that. Luckily, he didn't do it often because it made her want to lean in and taste him. "Nothing you need to know right now. Look, Shea, I know this has been a lot to take in. But now you've got to think. Did your mother ever say anything about the curse? Something you might not have thought was important at the time, something that might make sense now but didn't then."

Muscles twitching with nervous energy, Shea stood and began to pace. "My mother taught me how to draw the circle and work spells. She taught me what I needed to do as a Priestess. To protect the nail at all times."

Her hand grabbed and held onto the key again. Without conscious thought on her part, the key drew on the *arus* in her blood and transformed into the nail. One of Menrva's twelve Nails of the Ages.

From the time she'd been old enough to understand, her mother had drilled her on the ancient spells and rituals the priestesses would need when they were called on by Menrva to resume their duties.

Every day they'd studied a new spell or reviewed an old one. She'd grown to hate it. The spells made her head hurt, so much so she constantly screwed them up. And her mom had looked so sad.

Over time, she'd come to dread the day her mom would hand over the nail to her. She didn't want it. She couldn't do the spells, she couldn't protect it. She was defective.

Not once had her mom mentioned anything about a curse. Her five-hundred-year-old mother. Something else she couldn't wrap her mind around.

Still, she'd known there was something her mom wasn't telling her. She'd sensed it, like a current between them.

That old pain, the one she'd gotten whenever she and her mom argued, was back, lodged in her chest like a dagger she couldn't pull out.

Mom, why didn't you say anything?

But the feeling of betrayal by her dad was worse.

"Shea. Did your mom ever say anything about a curse?"

Gabriel's repeated question cut through her thoughts and she turned to face him, anger beginning to replace shock.

"My mom was difficult to talk to. And she never, ever said anything about a curse."

Gabriel's expression remained unreadable. "I guess she felt she had good reason."

Fuck that. No reason would ever have been good enough to keep this from her.

Jesus, Mom—

"So why'd you leave?" he asked.

Gabriel watched as her mouth tightened as Shea's gaze disconnected.

"I didn't know there was a world beyond the forest we lived in until I was twelve." The bitterness in her tone cut through the air like tiny knives. "A lost hiker somehow found his way through the wards on our property. My dad hustled him away pretty fast, but it was too late. The secret was out."

She met his gaze then. "Ballet was the one thing my mom and I actually enjoyed doing together. She'd taught me since I was three or four. It was the best part of the day, when my mom and I would go into the studio to dance."

Her smile turned bittersweet. "When I was twelve, my dad introduced me to the wonders of TV and movies. I must have watched 'The Red Shoes' and 'A Chorus Line' and 'Center Stage' hundreds of times. And I decided I wanted to be a ballerina.

"When I was fifteen, my mom told me I'd never be a ballerina. That I would live the rest of my life alone because no one could be trusted. That's when I started to plan."

"Plan what?"

Her hands did that wavy thing again. "My great escape. I was fifteen, after all, and I wanted to see the world. My mom was just as determined to keep me away from it. I started exploring past the boundaries my parents had set. I found out we lived several miles from a small town and I used to sneak there. I was fascinated to see so many people in one place.

"My dad used to leave the door to the communications room open sometimes and I could watch whatever I wanted. I had the biggest crush on David Boreanez from 'Buffy the Vampire Slayer.' Until I realized he wasn't a real vampire. You know that whole cross deal is a hoax, right? And the sunlight death?"

Her lopsided smile reached inside his chest and grabbed the air right out of his lungs. Holy shit, he didn't need this now.

Her smile faded fast. "Anyway, I heard my parents fighting sometimes. About me. I think my mom wanted to lock me in my room and never let me out. I couldn't understand why she didn't lo—why she wanted to keep me hidden."

She stopped pacing to stare at an abstract painting on the wall, her expression tight. What was she thinking? Hell, at this point he didn't have a clue—

Leo's terrified scream reverberated through the house and they ran for the bedroom.

Chapter Eight

Lea Tulane's eyes flashed open, immediately awake from a deep sleep.

She reached out and laid her hand on Brian's back, sleeping beside her, listening for the sound of his breathing. She released a relieved sigh at his slight wheeze. He was okay.

Brian was only seventy. Not old. Not really.

Oh, hell. Who was she trying to kid? Every morning she woke, she thanked the Great Goddess he was still here.

They'd been lucky. They'd had a good fifty-five years together. This time. But life had started to take its toll. Brian's blood pressure was too high. His knees creaked and he didn't recover from their lovemaking as fast as he used to. Not that it wasn't good.

Alright, at least she could be honest with herself. There hadn't been enough of it lately to be good. Brian wasn't as interested in her sexually as he had been. Some of it had to do with the way his body had changed over the years. And some of it had to with the way hers hadn't.

And there went her chances of getting back to sleep tonight.

Sliding out of bed, she walked to the window, drawn by the light of the almost full moon. Summer treguenda was approaching and she'd thought about returning east to celebrate.

She enjoyed southern California, possibly the only place on earth where she, stuck at twenty-eight, and Brian, at seventy, could live without being stared at. Much. But she wanted to see her sister—

An odd shadow shifted across the grass. Just a palm frond moving in the ocean breeze? Or someone sneaking onto the property?

She shivered, straining to distinguish two a.m. shadows from potential intruders. Brian always told her she worried too much. But after five-hundred years on the run, she figured she could cut herself a little slack.

The shadow moved again, and now she could see it was a palm, one of the large ones flanking the patio—

A floorboard creaked on the first floor.

Adrenaline pumped through her bloodstream, covering her skin in goose bumps.

Her hand crept to the silver chain around her neck and the iron key hanging from it. Someone was in the house. The housekeeper had left hours ago and they didn't have a security guard, although many who lived in this gated community did.

Brian wouldn't hear of it. He'd protected her on his own for years. Why would he need help now?

She glanced back at the bed. Brian still slept soundly.

Had Dario's men finally found her? Should she run? Wake Brian? Draw them away?

Or...was she ready?

Even if it meant death the way Dario dealt it, maybe it was worth it. Brian would soon be taken from her again. She'd spent more than fifty years alone before they'd reunited. Before that, it had been more than a century.

Time was a bitch she couldn't escape.

Concentrating on the open door to their room, she

could just barely hear the scrape of soft-soled shoes on the wool carpet covering the stairs.

If she gave herself to them without a fight, would they leave Brian alone?

No, she knew that was too much to ask. But maybe Dario would make it quick...

She wondered if it would hurt.

Footsteps in the hall now.

Slipping the key from around her neck, she dropped it into her wooden jewelry box. Her sister would find it there. She had to believe that.

* * *

Shea was closer to the bedroom but Gabriel was faster.

He burst through the door, gun in his hand. The room was dark, even with his enhanced sight.

Shea tried to move past him but he barred her way. How the hell could someone have slipped past the wards without him knowing?

He flipped on the light switch, trying to see everything at once. Leo huddled on the bed, pillow clutched to his chest, rocking back and forth.

"Borelli, let me in." Shea insisted.

"Stay back," he hissed. "Leo, are you okay?"

"Dark," Leo whimpered.

"Gabriel, move your ass now."

Shea's tone nearly singed his eyebrows. But his given name coming out of her mouth... Well, that singed other, lower places. Since he didn't sense anyone else in the room, he let her by. She ran for the bed as Leo launched himself at her and clung like a baby monkey as she sat on the side.

"Shh, it's okay," she whispered. "I'm sorry. It's my fault."

"Dark," Leo wimpered.

"I know. I'm sorry. Calm down, bud. Deep breaths."

Gabriel took a couple of deep breaths to calm his own runaway heartbeat.

Shit, the kid wasn't being kidnapped or murdered. He was afraid of the dark. And Gabriel had put him in the darkest room of the house.

Fuck.

He caught Shea's glance, expecting to see condemnation there, but she only shook her head.

"My fault," she said. "I'm sorry. I should have checked on him. I always leave a light on for him if I'm not here. You didn't know."

Because he hadn't asked.

As Leo clung and drew in deep breaths while Shea held him and rubbed his back, Gabriel complicated the situation by sitting on the bed next to them. He should keep his distance. It was one of the first things his dad had taught him. It was why Davis hadn't been his mother's true mate, merely her companion.

"Hey, kid. Wanna know what scares the shit out of me?"

Shea and Leo looked at him. Shea's mouth tightened at his language, Leo's eyes still wide and terrified. But after a couple of hitched-in breaths, he nodded.

"Spiders. They freak me out. All those legs and some of them bite. I know they're tiny and I could crush them before they get to me, but I had to learn how to overcome that fear because sometimes there's gonna be spiders."

The terror in Leo's eyes began to fade as curiosity settled in. He released his death grip from around Shea's neck and moved a little closer to Gabriel. "How?"

Shea's indrawn breath drew his gaze for a second before concentrating again on Leo.

"By studying them, learning everything I could. Then they weren't so scary anymore. If you want, I can teach you some stuff. Maybe then the dark wouldn't freak you out so much. The dark can be good. We can hide in the dark. And you and me, we can see things in the dark other people can't."

Leo's eyes widened even further.

"Some are kind of cool," Gabriel continued. "Come here."

Gabriel stood and held out his hand. Leo stared at him for a second before slipping his small hand in Gabriel's larger one and sliding off Shea's lap. Surprise lit her expression for just a second before her eyes narrowed. She watched from the bed as he took Leo to the window but didn't open the blackout shade.

"Now, I'm going to have your sister turn off the lights, but I'm not going anywhere, okay?"

Leo's hand tightened on his and he drew in a sharp breath. But he didn't say no.

"When she does that, we'll be able to see things only a few people in the world can see, okay? *Grigori* are born with special powers. These powers make us protectors."

"I'm a *grigorio*. Daddy told me."

"Yeah, you are. Shea, hit the switch and close the door."

He knelt down beside the kid, still holding his hand. Shea hesitated only a second before she rose and the room went dark.

"Leo, hey, look at me, bud. I know you think you can't see me, but you can. You just have to know what you're looking for."

"Dark."

"No, it's not. Not really. Focus on the sound of my voice and I'll help you see."

* * *

Dario stood at the top of the stairs, watching the *strega* walk into the hall and close the door behind her. Her calm expression told him she was not surprised to see him.

His eyebrows lifted. Did she think she could defeat him? By herself? From the reports he'd gotten, her *grigorio* was old, slow. Not a threat to him or the three men he'd brought with him.

"Dario." Her voice was steady, her gaze locked on his.

"Tullia." One of his men stepped forward but Dario made a swift motion with his hand, ordering him to stop. "You're not surprised to see me."

The *strega* smiled and he had a flash of another life, the life he'd had before…all this. He'd known Tullia from the village, one of only two members of the *boschetta* he'd known personally. He hadn't seen her in more than four centuries, but, of course, neither of them had changed. At all.

"No, not surprised," she said. "It's been a while, hasn't it?"

He saw no fear in her eyes. Curiosity, something he hadn't experienced in years, made him continue the conversation when he should finish this. "Yes, it has. Are you ready to stop running?"

Tullia's chin lifted, and her eyes, those strange, shattered-glass eyes he and the cursed *streghe* shared, blinked back tears. "Yes. But I have a request."

Now, this was new. The *streghe* he'd dispatched before had fought him with all their power. They hadn't wanted to die. And still, he'd defeated them because his cause was right. Still... "And that is?"

"I don't want Brian to suffer."

Understandable. "If he does not put up a fight, I can honor that request."

"I'll make sure he doesn't."

Even more interesting. "And what about you, Tullia? Don't you want me to spare your life?"

She smiled, a bittersweet twist of her lips. "I am not a fighter. But do you honestly believe killing us will release you from the curse, Dario? Will murdering thirteen women ensure entrance into your heaven?"

Yes, that's exactly what he believed. "This is not murder, Tullia. I'm releasing you. Don't you see? You, too, will benefit from this. We'll all be free."

Tullia's smile was sad as she shook her head. "I'm tired. And I'd like to believe you're right, that my soul will be free to be return in another body. But nothing is ever simple, is it?"

No, of course not. But nothing would be right until the *streghe* were all dead. "I'll make it fast, Tullia. And Brian will not suffer."

Pulling the dagger from his jacket pocket, he motioned two of the men into the bedroom and held out his hand to the *strega*.

"Then let's finish this," Tullia said and took his hand.

* * *

Shea leaned against the door and held her breath, one hand on the light switch in case Leo freaked again. She was willing to give Gabriel a little leeway here, but not at her brother's expense.

"Don't focus too hard," Gabriel said. "Don't try to force yourself to see what's in front of you. Relax."

Oh, man, that voice. Shea felt tension ease out of her at Gabriel's tone. It was mesmerizing. Deep and raspy, it should sound rough. Instead, it made her shiver. And boy, was that a huge, Fatal hole just waiting to swallow her.

And when the hell had she made the switch from Borelli to Gabriel? It seemed so much more...intimate.

"Now, look for the outline of my face. Use your eyes but also use your inner sight. Do you know what I mean?"

When Leo shook his head, Gabriel said. "Use your *arus* as well as your eyes. Relax and let that power seep out of your body a little, then look around. Now look at me. What do you see?"

Leo paused then gasped. "A cloud around you. It's...blue."

"That's right. Now, look around, see if you can see your sister."

Leo turned toward her. "She's not blue."

Shea frowned.

"That's right, she's not." Gabriel didn't sound surprised or worried. "What color is she?"

Leo looked at her for a few more seconds. "Purple."

"Good, now I'm going to open the curtains and we're going to look outside."

"Okay."

Leo's excitement rang loud and clear in his voice as Gabriel opened the curtains and introduced him to his heritage.

She'd been kidding herself for too long. She'd believed that once they were safe, after she'd found someone to help them get rid of the men on their trail, she and Leo would be home free. They could set up house somewhere. Leo would go to school. She'd get a real job, although what that would have been, she didn't know.

They'd live a normal life, one without magic she couldn't work or monsters who wanted to take Leo from her. No sacred duties to Etruscan goddesses who abandoned their priestesses.

All a stupid dream.

She had a counterfeit high school diploma from a defunct Colorado school, but she didn't have the knowledge to go with it. She could read Latin and ancient Etruscan and knew her multiplication tables, but she'd never had to balance a checkbook. Or use a bank, for that matter.

Her father had taught her to protect herself with her hands but she didn't have enough magic to keep Leo safe. And she didn't know the first thing about getting a real job that didn't involve taking off her clothes.

"What's that? A dog?"

Leo's excited voice drew her back to the present. "It's a fox. See the color around it. Wild animals have a different color than pets."

And the curse. That big freaking curse her parents had never told her about. The one she'd been born to break.

What the hell did she have to do for that? She was pretty sure she didn't want to know.

"What about the bears?"

"Where do you see bears, Leo?"

"In the trees."

Gabriel paused. "I don't see anything there, Leo, but maybe I'm not looking in the right place. Are they close to the house?"

Leo shook his head. "They're walking away."

Another pause. "Do they look like the other animals?"

"No, they're kinda...foggy."

"Okay, Leo. You did really well. Bet you're hungry, huh? Let's see if we can find something to eat."

When Gabriel closed the curtains, Shea turned on the light. And found Gabriel staring at her.

A chill shivered down her spine. Something was wrong. She could tell from his expression. And she was pretty sure she didn't want to hear what he had to say.

* * *

After a quick, silent snack in the kitchen, Shea told Gabriel she was taking Leo back to bed.

Since the little boy could barely keep his eyes open, he figured she was right. But when she didn't come back, Gabriel headed to Leo's room and found them both asleep on the bed—Shea on her side, Leo curled into the curve of her body.

They looked damn near angelic—for a girl who held the key to a five-hundred-year-old curse and a boy who had powers greater than his own.

Leo had been able to see trace energy left behind by the *versipelli* who took care of this house. Gabriel couldn't. He wasn't that good.

Back downstairs, he picked up the phone in the living room and dialed the one man he trusted most in the world.

"This better be fucking good," Quinn growled into the phone. "It's six o'clock in the fucking morning."

Gabriel smiled. "Good morning to you, too, *ceffo*. Gettin' your beauty sleep or just gettin' old?"

"Gabe." Quinn sounded wide awake now. "You okay? Serena called earlier. Said you might need help."

"We ran into a little trouble—"

"Hey, you alright?"

Gabriel's lips curved at the worry in Quinn's voice. "We're fine. We're holed up in the safe house in Oley."

"What's up?"

"You need to see it to believe it. Just get up here."

"Gabe, what—"

"Just get here. I need back up because if anything happens to me, I know I can trust you to take care of them."

"Them who?"

"Leave soon, Quinn."

"Whoa, Gabe, you're really freaked out, aren't you?"

Yeah, he was. "And Quinn? No chasing cars."

"You bast—"

Gabriel hung up, feeling a little better.

Chapter Nine

Gasping for air, Serena woke from a restless sleep.
Gone. Another one gone.
Hands shaking, she reached for the light on her bedside table, knocking over her glass in the process. As water dripped onto the thick carpet by her feet, tears she couldn't control ran down her cheeks.

Tullia.

Her gaze flew to the photos on the built-in bookcases on the far wall. The last time they'd had their photo taken, only six had been here. Pretty, round-faced Tullia—or Lea Tulane as she called herself now—with her brown hair and sweet disposition hadn't said much, but Serena could tell she'd been tired.

Hell, weren't they all tired?

Unable to go back to sleep, she left her room and headed for the basement.

As she was the only one in residence at the moment, the house was silent except for the tick of the clock in the front room. She bypassed the lights on her way to the back. She could see as well as a cat in the dark, and she knew this building like she knew the lines of her face.

Everything had a place.

Perhaps, if Gabriel had the girl, her *boschetta* might have a place in the world again.

Down the west hall, she bypassed the main atrium and the dining room, a study and two bedrooms. At the end of the hall, she pushed through the door and headed into the basement.

At the bottom of the circular, iron stairwell, she flicked a switch and blinked until her eyes adjusted to the light.

The pinball table pinged and the Pac-Man game beeped as they came to life in the cavernous room. The pool table Davis had loved gleamed to her left. A widescreen, plasma TV dominated the wall to the rear along with a sectional couch big enough to fit twelve. A library of DVDs filled shelves on either side of the screen.

Picking up the remote from a table by the bottom of the steps, she turned on the television, hitting the favorites button until Cartoon Network appeared. Typically, this early in the morning, they showed old Tex Avery and Chuck Jones cartoons.

She was in luck. Bugs Bunny. Thank God it wasn't that stupid "Ed, Edd and Eddy."

Next she headed for the bar and poured herself a double shot of Jack Daniels, enjoying the burn as it sank into her gut and warmed her from the inside. Never too early for Jack.

Several Road Runner cartoons and five double shots of Jack later, she felt sufficiently warm and pleasantly buzzed.

When the phone rang, she knew she shouldn't answer it. Not in her state. But she had to. Others would have felt what she'd felt. They would call to commiserate. The *grigori* would have questions. She'd have to alert those who didn't know.

"Hello." Oh, dear, she sounded a little tipsy.

"Serena? Hey, are you okay?"

Quinn.

Oh, Sweet Uni, not now. Not while she felt so alone, so…desolate.

She covered the bottom of the ancient black receiver and took a deep, shaky breath, trying to calm her racing pulse.

"Serena, is something wrong?"

"No, Quinn. Nothing's wrong. What do you need?"

Quinn paused and she could practically hear him thinking through the phone lines. He'd never known her to drink. And since it wasn't a pretty sight, she didn't want him to even suspect.

"Gabe called," he said finally. "I'm meeting him at the safe house in Oley." He paused, but she knew he wasn't finished. "Then we'll be up to the compound. You gonna be glad to see me?"

He didn't expect an answer. He was merely yanking her chain. But the words escaped before she could stop them. "More than you know."

The silence from the other end of the phone was deafening.

"Serena—"

"No." She took a deep breath. "No, don't say anything. Just hear me out."

She paused, listening to the nearly tangible silence on the line.

"It's been hard, so hard, to stay away from you. But you've got to understand, I've lost you twice before. The first time nearly killed me."

Quinn huffed at the old argument. "I'm. Not. Them. I'm not your other husbands—"

"No. No, I understand that. I know you want me to

love you for who you are. And I do, Quinn. I really do. But I can't separate the past and present anymore. It's been so long. Too long."

She felt tears threatening, but she'd be damned if she broke down now.

"Christ, Serena—"

But she couldn't shut herself off, either. "I ache for you, Quinn, and I can't have you. It would be the death of me this time. When you die, I'll walk straight to Dario and let him cut out my heart, cut off my head and burn my body."

"No!" Quinn's voice sounded strangled. "No, Serena, what if—"

"There is no 'what if'!" Oh Goddess, now she was yelling. She drew in a deep breath, trying to calm herself. "I can't let myself consider 'what if.' You need someone, Quinn, someone who can love you. Someone—"

"Oh, fuck that! Damn it, you listen to me now." Quinn's voice took on a tone she'd never heard before. Hard and forceful, and Goddess forgive her, it made her thighs clench.

"There is no one else for me. There won't be, not ever. From the first moment I saw you, I knew. That's the way blood-binding works, right? There will never be another woman and if I die a virgin, then, fuck it, I will." She could hear him breathing now. Sharp, shallow breaths that sounded harsh over the phone line. "I'm through giving you time. If you want to ignore me, you'd better get fucking good at avoidance, baby. 'Cause I'm gonna shadow your every footstep until I die."

Now their silence held another kind of power. If Quinn had been standing in front of her right now, she would have grabbed him and dragged him to her bed. Instead, he was safely out of reach.

Spell Bound

Damn.

After what seemed like an hour, Quinn broke the silence as she knew he would.

"Shit." He let out a heavy sigh. "I'm sorry. Damn, I'm sorry. That wasn't right."

She loved the hint of South in his voice that came from being raised in Maryland for several years. She loved the deep tone and she wanted to hear him whisper that he loved her while he stripped her naked and threw her on a bed, on the floor, up against a wall. Hell, she didn't care where.

She just wanted him. And he would be here soon.

"Serena, you still there? Hey, I'm sorry, babe. I got carried away. It's late and I'm tired and—"

"No, Quinn. It's my fault. It's all my fault. I'll see you when you get here. Stay safe."

She hung up before he could say anything else and make her break down in tears.

Which she did anyway.

* * *

Gabriel couldn't wait any longer.

He'd let Shea sleep for four hours while he sat and flipped through more than two hundred channels in the TV room off the atrium, finally settling on Cartoon Network. He had a thing for old Bugs Bunny cartoons.

But now, they had to talk. He eased open the door to the bedroom and looked around.

Shock gripped him by the throat when he realized she wasn't there. Only Leo slept on the bed.

Where the hell was she?

Not caring if he woke the kid, he turned and began

pushing open the rest of the doors on that side of the house. She had to be here somewhere. She wouldn't abandon Leo. But she wasn't in any of the other rooms.

He pushed open the last door and got a blast of flower-scented steam.

"Hey, don't let all my hot air out, Leo. Shut the door."

Shit. This was not good.

He should leave. He knew he should close the door with him on the other side, putting solid wood between them. Instead, he stepped into the bathroom and enclosed them in the warmth together.

The bathroom didn't have a tub, but it did have an enclosed shower stall in the far corner opposite the toilet. On the sink to his right sat a small bag.

"Hey, Leo, I want you to take a shower when I'm done, okay? I know you hate the idea, but it's been two days and you're starting to smell a little ripe, buddy."

Come to think of it, he hadn't a shower in, oh, a couple hours, at least. What would she do if he shed his clothes and stepped in there with her? His balls tightened and his cock began to harden.

He could just make out her silhouette through the heavily frosted glass, twisting muscles low in his gut. What was it about this woman that made him feel like a teenager with raging hormones? Yeah, she was beautiful, but hell, he'd been with beautiful women before, and it'd been easy to walk away every time.

He'd learned to control his base emotions, but when they became overwhelming, he took care of them with one-night stands and forgettable women.

He'd never met his soul mate. Was pretty damn sure he didn't want one. His dad had taught him you couldn't

Spell Bound

have ties, not real emotional ties, to a woman and still function efficiently. You couldn't split your concentration. Something or someone always suffered for it.

After Nino and his dad had been murdered, it'd been easy for Gabriel to shut off his emotions. Easy not to let anyone in, get too close.

Now, he wanted to get close to this woman, get inside her.

"Leo, come on. I'm done."

Before he could respond, she opened the shower door and stepped out. Naked.

She paused when she saw him and her eyes widened, but she didn't scream. Or hurry to cover herself.

In fact, she acted like men stared at her naked body all the time.

Shit, he really was losing it. He'd forgotten how she'd made a living. Thousands of men had stared at her smooth, olive-toned skin, full breasts and long, toned legs.

"Sorry, I thought you were Leo." She reached back into the shower to turn off the water then reached for a towel on the rack next to the shower. He watched the sway of wet, dark hair on her back, drawing his gaze to her perfect, heart-shaped ass.

Then she wrapped a towel around her body.

He drew in a deep breath and forced himself to speak. "We need to talk. I'll meet you in the atrium—"

"What?" She tossed him a glance over her still-damp shoulder. "The sight of a little naked flesh makes you just another stupid male? You're here now. Talk."

He straightened at the challenge in her raised eyebrows. Fine. He could do this.

"I called for backup. I've got a man coming. When he gets here, we're going to head to the compound."

Pulling a small bottle from the bag on the counter, she squeezed some of the contents onto her palm. "Where is this compound?"

"Outside the city limits." He watched her rub her hands together then smooth the cream onto her arms. Heat spread over him and he swore he felt her hands running over her skin, along his own skin.

Hell, it was just hot in here. Probably all he felt was the steam from the shower.

"And what is this compound?"

She lifted her right leg and rested her foot on the sink so she could rub cream into her thighs and calves. The towel shifted enough for him to catch a glimpse of dark curls between her legs.

He shifted his gaze to the window. "After the *streghe* came to America, Serena built a home here. The area was mostly forest, rocky, hard to farm. Today, it's been preserved as woodlands and provides good cover. There aren't many neighbors and it's difficult to get to the house without a four-wheel-drive. And there're some pretty serious wards surrounding the property. It's built on a convergence."

She frowned at him over her bare shoulder. "A what?"

Damn, didn't she know anything? "A ley line. Like Stonehenge."

She nodded, her confusion clearing. "So, Serena's the leader of the *boschetta* now?"

Out of the corner of his eyes, he saw her switch legs and his body temperature rose another five degrees. He couldn't tell whether she was tormenting him or truly didn't have a clue.

"Not really. After Dafne was killed, the remaining

streghe scattered across Europe. Serena attempts to keep in touch with the others but there are a few who haven't been in contact for decades. One hasn't been heard from in a couple of centuries. Serena lost touch with Celeste more than twenty years ago."

She fell silent as she finished her legs and reached for her clothes sitting on the sink. Finally, she was going to put him out of his misery.

Instead, she moved the clothes so she could open the doors under the sink. Then she bent over to check the contents of the vanity and that was the last straw. He turned away.

"Shea, put your damn clothes on and then we'll continue this conversation."

He couldn't see her, but he knew she'd straightened and was staring at him.

"You're kidding, right?"

He drew in a deep breath and closed his eyes. "No, I'm not kidding. I'm not a eunuch and you're parading around—"

"Parading?" She choked out a laugh. "You're kidding, right? Are you really that much of a prude, Gabriel? You're the one who came in here in the first place."

No, he wasn't a prude. And yeah, he'd consciously closed the door behind. But he was fast losing the grip on his control around her and he didn't like it.

"Look, just come downstairs when you're dressed and we'll finish this."

She went quiet for a few seconds. Then she sighed. "Do you really think this is ever going to be finished?"

She wasn't talking about their conversation now.

He turned and found her sitting on the lid of the

toilet, her head bowed, dark wavy hair draped around her face, shielding her.

Christ, he was an asshole.

"Shea." He reached for her shoulder and she flinched away.

"Don't touch me."

Fuck tha— Oh, wait. Those damn voices. He didn't want to hurt her. Instead of resting his hand on her shoulder like he wanted to, he dropped to his knees beside her. "Shea. Look at me."

Sighing, she lifted her head. Her mouth was set in a line and her eyes were dry. But despair lurked under the surface.

He fought the urge to take her in his arms. If he did, he was afraid he wouldn't let go, voices be damned.

"We'll find a way to finish this, Shea."

"I can't let anything happen to Leo."

"That's why you came to me. You're not in this alone anymore. I won't let anything happen to him. Or you."

She drew in a deep breath and blinked. "That's a far cry from three days ago when you didn't want anything to do with us."

Rub it in, babe. "Yeah, well, things change."

She snorted. "Tell me about it. Three days ago I was a stripper. Today, I'm the only hope of reversing a five-hundred-year-old curse. Guess I might just amount to something after all, huh?"

She smiled, just a crooked twist of her lips, but Gabriel swore he felt a crack in the wall of reserve he'd built over the years, the reserve that kept him from getting too close. The wall he'd built after Nino and Davis.

He nodded, afraid to do anything else. "I'd never count you out in a fight. Now, will you please get dressed so we can go downstairs?"

He should move. He should get up and walk out the door. But her gaze continued to hold his, her smile fading.

When she leaned forward and pressed her mouth against his, he froze.

God, her lips were soft and mobile against his, but her kiss wasn't sexual. It was sweet and hot and—

Oh holy hell, this was one big catastrophe waiting to happen.

Heat rushed through his blood and his heart pounded until he was sure she could hear it. He reached for her again, lacing his fingers through the wet strands of her hair.

He let her kiss him, just a light touch, a soft press, almost as if she didn't know what she was doing. But it was more than enough to completely scramble his circuits.

And make him want more.

With a softly indrawn breath, she pulled away and he forced his fingers to release her hair.

Her shell-shocked expression mirrored his feelings. He wanted to wrap his arms around her, pull her against his chest and kiss her until she gave him what he wanted.

Hell if he knew what that was right now.

Before he did something really stupid, he stood and walked out.

* * *

Shea watched Gabriel pull the door behind him, leaving her alone in the bathroom.

What the hell had she done?

The last two days had been a mess. Information overload and emotional turmoil.

And now she'd kissed Gabriel.

She hadn't thought about kissing him. She'd just moved in and pressed her mouth against his gorgeous lips. It'd been a surprise response to the strength she found in his words. To the way he'd protected Leo. She knew she didn't need to do everything anymore. She could transfer some of the burden she'd been carrying onto his broad shoulders.

Three days ago, she wouldn't have thought a man would enter into her life plans for the next, oh, ten years, at least. She hadn't met a man yet who could divert her attention away from the mess of her oh-so-screwed-up life.

Today, she couldn't imagine what she'd have done without Gabriel.

Whoever said they didn't make heroes the way they used to had never met Gabriel.

If he hadn't been at the club, those men would have killed her and taken Leo. He'd walked in at precisely the right moment, had gotten them out and away before Leo had fallen into the wrong hands. He'd gone from bastard to hero in hours and now she kept thinking about kissing him, about running her fingers through his hair and wondering how his beard would feel against her skin.

And yet it wasn't just his physical strength that drew her.

Whenever she looked at him—and she'd been looking a lot—she yearned for something she'd never wanted before.

An emotional connection.

Groaning, she dropped her head in her hands. How could she be so damned stupid?

Hell, he'd been embarrassed by her nudity, not turned on. He hadn't kissed her back, hadn't responded to her kiss in any way.

Could a person die of embarrassment?

Chapter Ten

Shea walked into the kitchen twenty minutes later—after forcing herself out of the bathroom—to find Gabriel at the table, steaming coffee mug in front of him, cleaning the barrel of a gun. A radio in the background played smooth jazz. Soothing. So at odds with the man himself.

He didn't look at her as he spoke. "We've got maybe fifteen minutes, half an hour before Quinn shows up. Then we're going to leave."

Gabriel sounded pissed off. Business as usual.

Good. That was good.

She didn't want to talk about that kiss anyway. Didn't want to want him.

Nodding, she walked to the counter to get a mug, filled it with water then set it in the microwave to heat. There had to be tea here somewhere. "For the compound."

"Yeah." He put down the barrel and picked up the stock. "I want to make sure we're not followed, so I don't think we'll get to the house until after midnight. Do you know how to shoot a gun?"

Ah-ha, a box of Lipton. She could deal. She snagged a bag and took her steaming mug out of the microwave. "I can shoot."

"Have you ever had to?"

Dipping her bag, she shook her head as she turned back to face him. "I will if I need to. For Leo."

"You might have to. They've seen what Leo can do and they'll want him even more now."

A chill ran through her that not even the hot tea could dispel. "What are we going to do?"

He caught and held her gaze. "That's what we need to decide. How far are you prepared to go, Shea? What are you willing to do to save your brother?"

She didn't have to think about that one. She owed Leo so much. "Whatever it takes."

"Sometimes that's not enough."

Although his expression showed no emotion, she heard something in his tone. "You know that for a fact, don't you?"

He nodded, his gaze never wavering. "What if I told you I could send you away, somewhere they'd never find either of you? But it'd mean you'd be in isolation for years. Could you do it? Would you be willing to give up your life to save his?"

Six years. She'd been out in the world six years. Had it been enough? Was she willing to give up the rest of her life to save Leo?

She blindly reached for a seat at the table and folded herself into it. Guilt and anguish settled on her chest with all the weight of a collapsing building.

She swallowed before speaking. "I was fifteen by the time I got truly pissed off at my parents, about the secrets they'd kept from me. When I was seventeen, I left. I was going to be a ballerina. I was so sure I'd land a spot in the Rock School in Philadelphia."

That had been just the first of so many misconceptions and mistakes on her part. The teachers had said "Thanks, but no thanks" at the open auditions.

And blown her every hope and dream out of the water.

A soft thunk brought her attention back to Gabriel. He'd set the gun on the table and she had his full attention.

"What happened?" he asked.

His gaze locked on hers, completely focused. Those dark eyes mesmerized, made her want to tell him everything. But after all this time, that rejection still stung like an entire nest of hornets.

She looked away, shrugging. "I didn't get in."

"Why?"

Damn him, why wouldn't he let this go? "Because I wasn't good enough."

He snorted and picked up the gun. "Yeah, right. I've seen you dance, Shea. You've got talent."

Sudden tears made her blink. What was she supposed to say to that?

He saved her from having to answer. "Why didn't you go home?"

Because I was too stubborn to admit defeat. "I thought about it after the first few nights on my own. There were too many people, too many buildings, too much of everything." She'd felt like a complete failure. And she'd wrongly blamed her parents for that. "I knew I'd have to get a job and waitressing looked easy, but you can't earn enough at a bar to pay the bills. So I started dancing. Clubs always need women willing to take their clothes off and I don't have much of a problem with that. About three years ago, I got lucky and found a job with a *lucani* businessman."

Gabriel's eyebrows rose. "Who?"

"James Riley. He was good to me, gave me a job in Trenton, found me a place to live."

"What'd you tell him? About yourself."

"That my parents kicked me out because I was different and I didn't have anywhere else to go."

Gabriel snorted. "Yeah, Jimmy can be a sucker for a pretty face and a sob story. Still, he can smell a lie before you open your mouth."

"I think…I think maybe my dad knew all along where I was and asked Riley to look out for me. He had me waitress for a while but I wanted to dance."

She'd often wondered what her father thought of that. Had he been horrified? Mortified?

Dad, I'm so sorry, for everything.

"How'd you end up with Leo?" Gabriel asked.

Sighing, she took a sip of her tea before answering. "My mother called to me, just before she was killed."

Gabriel frowned. "She knew where you were then?"

She shook her head. "I heard her voice in my head, telling me I needed to come home, that I needed to get something and keep it safe."

Gabriel paused for a few seconds and she couldn't tell whether he believed her or not. But he didn't push it. "You got there before Dario?"

"No, they'd already left by the time I arrived."

His eyebrows shot up. "How'd they miss the kid?"

"My parents put him in an enchanted sleep and hid him in a secret room in the basement. I never would have found him if my mom hadn't told me where to look."

And if she'd never shown up, her brother would have remained in that enchanted sleep until his body had withered away and died. She shuddered at the thought.

"After she was dead?"

She nodded.

Gabriel fell silent, staring at her. She didn't have a clue what he was thinking.

Spell Bound

"How'd you find me?" he finally asked.

"Mom left her grimoire and a letter with Leo, telling me how to find you, what to say."

"But she never said anything about the curse?"

She shook her head, tears starting to gather again. "She must have been pregnant with Leo when I left. Maybe they knew something like this would happen, that I'd be around to care for him if anything happened to them."

That made sense. What didn't make sense was why her mom hadn't told her about the curse. Maybe her mom had been disappointed when the simple fact of her birth hadn't broken the curse. But why hadn't she contacted the other *streghe* and tried to figure it out? Why had they gone into hiding?

"Shea." Gabriel's voice cut through her thoughts. "What are you thinking?"

"That none of this makes sense."

Goddess, that slow smile of his must make women fall at his feet. And she was halfway to the floor.

"Yeah, well, then we'd better start coming up with some answers," he said.

"And you know someone who should have some?"

"Yeah."

Gabriel rose and walked to the counter to rinse out his cup, glancing out the window as he did. "We need to get Leo up and—Shit."

Spinning away from the sink, he ran for the back door.

"What's wrong," she called, but he was already outside.

She got to the door just as he walked back into the house, carrying a huge grey wolf in his arms, blood dripping from its back leg.

"Close the door and lock it," he ordered. "And bring the first-aid kit. Damn it, Quinn. Don't do this to me, not now."

Shea grabbed the oversized kit from its spot on the kitchen counter before following Gabriel into the next room. He'd already laid the animal he'd called Quinn on its side on a soft rug by the stone fireplace and was examining the wound, cursing under his breath. Grabbing the kit out of her hands, he tore it open, reaching for a brown bottle.

"I know this is gonna hurt like hell, just don't bite me, buddy."

Gabriel ran an unsteady hand through the animal's fur and she heard the wolf's low whine. Then he turned to her, a grim look on his face.

"I'll hold him down. You need to pour this over the wound." He held out the liquid-filled bottle. "Just do it fast."

He wrapped his arms around the wolf, holding the animal's uninjured limbs close to the body. Then he nodded to Shea.

Without stopping to think, she did what he'd said.

The wolf howled loud enough to wake the dead and fought to get away, giving Gabriel nasty scratches on his cheeks, arms and legs. But Gabriel held on until the animal wore itself out.

When the wolf calmed, Gabriel released him and the animal turned toward her, his eyes blue and startlingly human. Then he closed them and went limp.

Gabriel sat there, hands on his thighs, eyes closed. He was working some kind of spell, she realized. She could feel the energy coming off of him, like heat off a stove.

She stayed silent, watching, until Gabriel opened his eyes and snagged her gaze.

"This is Quinn, *legatus* of the Eastern States Pack. Plans just changed."

* * *

Gabriel refused to leave Quinn's side and Shea would not leave him.

Funny thing was, he didn't mind having her near. She left once to check on Leo and, for the few minutes she was gone, he couldn't stop worrying. When she returned, the worry lightened and he could almost believe everything would be okay.

Gabriel wasn't worried that someone had followed Quinn. It was possible but unlikely. Quinn would have let himself die on the side of the road before he'd lead anyone here.

Quinn must have been hit by a car. At least that's what the damage looked like. It would've been funny if it hadn't been so damn bad. Both back legs were injured, one definitely broken. He'd lost a lot of blood, if the amount on his fur was any indication. Gabriel didn't know how long he'd spent dragging himself here.

He couldn't shift back to his human body, the damage was too great. He'd heal at a faster rate than a human or wolf, but until then…shit.

If anything happened to Quinn, he'd… Hell, he didn't have a clue.

Serena would be devastated.

He sat there staring at the beautiful fur he'd teased Quinn about endlessly as a teenager. They didn't need this. Not now.

"Your legs are going to cramp," Shea said. "Why don't you sit up here for a while?"

He turned to find Shea watching him from the leather couch that faced the fireplace, her eyes wide and concerned.

With good reason. This screwed up everything.

He rose, grimacing a little as his leg muscles protested the movement, and sat next to her on the couch.

"Is he going to be okay?"

"Yeah." Gabriel would make sure of that, even if he had to carry the damn mongrel to a vet to have him stitched up. There had to be a *versipelli* vet around here somewhere. "He should heal pretty quickly. But he can't change until he's healed more."

"He's *lucani*."

"Yeah." Something in her tone drew his gaze away from Quinn.

"He's gorgeous."

Jealousy bit into his ass with sharp teeth. Idiot.

"Quinn will love to hear you say that. Just wait until he's awake. We can't leave until he's healed, though."

Another day, maybe two. It shouldn't be a problem, but he'd wanted to have Shea and Leo at the compound by tomorrow. Shit.

"Hey, tell me about Quinn. What does *legatus* mean?"

He heard her question but ignored it. Gods-be-damned, how the hell had Quinn gotten hurt?

"Gabriel?"

Shea's soft tone cut through his thoughts and he turned his gaze toward her.

"What's a *legatus*?"

He answered without thinking. "Legion commander. He's in charge of the Eastern Pack's soldiers."

"Like in the ancient Roman army?"

"Yeah. The *lucani* base their command structure on the old Roman legion."

"How did you and Quinn meet?"

"We were raised together after his mother tried to kill him when he was twelve." He nodded at Shea's gasp. "Barb was always a little unstable, but when he shifted the first time after he hit puberty, she locked him in his room and tried to burn the house down around him. She's got a padded cell at Wernersville State Hospital. He hasn't seen her since. His father was my dad's second cousin, so they came to live with us."

"Where?"

"About an hour outside of Philadelphia."

"What about your mom?"

"She didn't live with us."

"And you won't tell me who she is?"

He shook his head, his gaze drawn back to Quinn. If anything happened to Quinn, it might be the final straw that broke Serena's heart. "Can't. There's a difference."

"So you grew up in an all-male household. I can see how that warped your little mind."

He smiled, though it was weak. She was trying to take his mind off the situation, and he appreciated it. But he had too much to think about to be distracted.

They could stay here indefinitely. In the nearly two hundred years since it'd been built, this house had never been discovered. They were safe, unless Dario's men could somehow track Leo through the shields on the property. He wasn't ruling it out, which was why he'd wanted to head out today. But there was no way he'd leave Quinn behind.

And, truth be told, he didn't want to give Shea and Leo to another *grigorio*.

There were only three *grigori* he'd even consider, anyway. Franco was in Europe at the moment. Donal had his hands full with Furia and Madrona in Louisiana. And Matt...

Shit, he should have called Matt the second Shea had told him who she was. Matt deserved to know what was going on.

But Gabriel honestly hadn't thought about the guy until right now.

He'd should—

Shea's slender hand cupped his cheek, her skin soft against his two-day growth. His eyelids fell and he let the warmth of her skin soak into his. Damn it, he shouldn't like her touch this much. It was dangerous.

"Shea—"

"Shh. Just be quiet, Gabriel."

She sealed her mouth over his and he let her kiss him. Let her lips caress his until all he wanted was more of her mouth, hot and wet, her tongue slick against his.

He settled his hands on her waist and lifted her until she straddled his lap. She settled in, knees sinking into the cushions at his hips, bringing the heat between her legs closer to his aching cock. He wanted to press against her, rub against her softness, but that would require too much energy.

Goddess, he was tired. Too tired to move her away like he should. She was the one in charge. When she lifted her lips, he forced his eyes open to stare into hers.

"Did you get any sleep last night?" she whispered.

His eyelids felt so heavy. No, he hadn't slept last night, and he wouldn't get any tonight either...

"You need to rest, Gabriel. You're no good to us if you're not thinking straight."

Damn, she was working a spell, felt it brush against his *arus*, whispering to him to sleep. He couldn't afford to sleep now. He struggled against the sleeping spell she'd woven but he couldn't fight it and the world went dark.

***

When Gabriel's head dropped onto her shoulder, Shea let it stay there.

She could tell he'd been exhausted but wouldn't give in to natural sleep. So she'd woven one of the simple spells her mother had taught her so many years ago.

He'd be pissed when he woke, but he'd be rested. And since Quinn couldn't be moved immediately, he could afford the downtime.

Otherwise, he would have sat here and worried about...everything. About her, about Leo, and mostly about the gorgeous wolf lying on the floor.

She sat there another minute, enjoying the feel of him against her. His hair felt like silk against her cheek and before she could stop herself, she slid one hand into the black strands.

It took her a few minutes to realize the voices weren't buzzing any louder than normal. Whenever anyone except Leo touched her, the voices reacted. As if they were warning them away. They'd nearly screamed when Gabriel had grabbed her in the car but now, even though she was so close to Gabriel, they were almost quiet. Maybe they were getting used to him.

She didn't know how long she sat there, letting her fingers drift through his hair, winding it around her fingers. Turning her head, she let her lips brush against it, breathing in the spicy warm scent of him. Goddess, she would love to stay right here...

The wolf whined and she turned to find pale blue eyes staring up at her, pain evident in his gaze.

Careful not to jostle Gabriel, she got off the couch and knelt on the floor, unable to resist stroking Quinn's beautiful fur.

"I can help with the pain, if you want," she offered. "And with the healing. I didn't offer earlier because I wasn't sure how Gabriel would react to what I'm going to do. Just nod for okay."

The wolf snorted and shook his head.

"I'll take that as a yes. Okay, I haven't done this for a while, but I know what I'm doing."

She hoped. She took a deep breath and lifted her dress over her head.

* * *

Shea regained consciousness with a burning ache in her right leg that she knew would get worse before it got better and the feel of warm flesh against hers. Shifting, she tried to get more comfortable. And realized she was on the floor, her head pillowed on an equally naked, firmly muscled chest.

"Well, darlin'," a deep voice drawled in her ear. "This certainly beats the doggie doctor any—Holy shit, your eyes."

She bent her elbow to support her head and stared at the tawny-haired stranger gaping at her. Despite her nudity, his gaze stayed locked on her eyes.

"Jesus, who are you?"

"Shea Tedaldi."

His mouth opened and closed twice before he smiled and said, "Well, honey, I'm Quinn, and I'm damn glad to meet you."

Those blue, blue eyes would not look away.

"Nice to meet you, too. How are you feeling?"

"Well, now, I guess that depends."

She couldn't maintain that gaze anymore so she sat

up and ran her fingers through her tangled hair. "On what?"

"On whether or not Gabriel's going to kick my ass when he wakes up."

Reaching for her dress, she pulled it over her head before Quinn noticed the huge bruise on her leg. "And why would he do that?"

"Well, considering you and I just spent the better part of two hours naked and pressed together, I'd say he's gonna be pissed."

"Then you don't know shit," came a growl from the couch. "*Vaffanculo*, Shea. What the hell'd you do to me?"

Turning, she saw Gabriel rub a hand over his face as he sat up, a look on his face that could only be described as royally pissed off.

Time to pay the piper.

"You needed the rest." Standing, she shook the dress down her legs as she walked carefully to the couch, trying not to limp. "How do you feel?"

Gabriel shook his head, hair brushing his shoulders. Her fingers actually clenched with the desire to touch it, even through the increasing pain in her leg.

He looked up at her, his gaze hot. "Like I got run over by a truck."

She lifted her chin. No way would she apologize. "No, apparently that was Quinn. The disorientation will pass in a minute. You could have used a few more hours."

He scowled at her. "Yeah, well, I'll decide when I have them." He looked like he wanted to say more, his lips tightening. Finally, though, he looked down at Quinn. "What the hell are you doing in your skin already?"

"Your girl here worked some powerful mojo."

"She's not my girl."

"I'm not his girl."

Shea shot Gabriel a look, but Quinn stood, blocking her glare with his long, lean, naked body.

"Oh, yeah." Quinn laughed. "This is gonna be real fun."

"Don't be an asshole." Gabriel stood and got right in Quinn's face.

Jeez, she did not want to have to break up a fight. Then Gabriel smiled, and her breath caught in her chest. Damn him, he was way too handsome when he smiled.

"I'm glad you're here," Gabriel said.

Quinn nodded, his expression softening, as he reached out to grab Gabriel in a bear hug. "Me, too. Looks like you've got a tale to tell."

Gabriel hugged him back then held put his hands on his shoulders and nodded. "Yeah, we do. But first tell me how the hell you got hit?"

Quinn sighed. "Food first." His gaze shifted to Shea. "And maybe some clothes."

Gabriel shook his head, a wry smile on his face. "Shea'll tell you not to bother with the clothes, but you're so damn gorgeous, you're distracting me."

"*Vaffanculo*, Gabe." Quinn smacked Gabriel's shoulder so hard, it had to hurt. "I've missed you, *ceffo*."

Gabriel nodded his head and returned the affection. "Yeah, well, I missed you, too, Lassie." He shoved Quinn away. "Now get dressed and I'll make you a couple of steaks."

Quinn turned to her and flashed a playboy smile that surely made women's panties fall to their knees.

"Thanks again, honey." Then he wrapped his arms around her, lifted her off her feet and planted a kiss on her mouth.

And oh, could the man kiss. Funny, though, that he didn't make her burn like Gabriel.

When he gently placed her back on her feet and turned to walk through the door, she couldn't help as her gaze slipped to his naked backside. He had one of the finest butts she'd ever seen on a man. Almost as nice as Gabriel's. Almost.

"After you put your tongue back in your mouth, you can tell me what the hell you did."

Shea turned and caught Gabriel's unamused gaze. With his arms crossed over his broad chest and his black boots spread, he looked like a pissed-off Hell's Angel.

She mirrored his stance, ignoring the pain in her leg, and lifted her eyebrows. "He's going to be fine."

"Explain."

She huffed. "I inherited my mother's Gift for healing. Quinn needed help and I healed him. End of story."

She didn't add that she knew Gabriel had been so worried about Quinn he couldn't think straight. She tried but couldn't hold his gaze, especially when he stared at her with such intensity. She nodded toward the kitchen. "Why don't we get the food started? I'm starving."

She had to walk around him to get to the kitchen. She steeled herself against the pain. As she passed, he caught her arm, stopping her, but she refused to look up at him.

"Shea."

She tried to ease away but he had a firm grip on her. "I'm fine."

"No, you're not. How bad is it?"

She released a controlled sigh. "Come on, Gabriel. You must know how healing works."

"Yeah, I do." He tilted her chin up with one finger so she had to look into his dark, worried eyes. When she met his, she couldn't look away, even when he released her. "Are you alright?"

She nodded, though it made her head throb. "I'm fine."

That beautiful mouth of his flattened and he growled, the sound making her thighs clench in response. "Don't lie to me. How bad is it?"

She sensed genuine concern and a hint of anger in him. She didn't know where the anger was coming from and it confused the hell out of her.

"Not that bad."

"Shea." He sighed and shook his head, his eyes closing for a second. When he looked back into her eyes, his gaze had softened. "Let me see your leg."

"No."

"Shea."

With a huff, she lifted her skirt. Purple, blue and black bruises covered the entire thigh. Quinn's femur had been broken and, as a result, she couldn't put much pressure on her leg when she walked or the pain would make her knees buckle.

It hurt like hell but there was no way she'd tell him that.

Gabriel drew in short breath. "Son-of-a— Shea, that's—"

"I'll be fine. Honestly, it'll heal in a few hours."

Anger, fear and something she didn't recognized crossed his expression in waves. When he finally settled on pissed, he shook his head just once. "Thank you. For Quinn." His hand curved around her nape, massaging the muscles in her neck. Warmth spread, easing the throbbing pain in her head. But it was the look in his eyes that made her heart beat just a little faster.

Spell Bound

And when he bent to lay his lips on hers, it pounded like a drum against her ribs.

This kiss was nothing like any they'd shared before. This time, his lips moved on hers with a hunger that made her forget the ache in her head and her leg.

She hadn't kissed many guys, but none of them had had the skill Gabriel possessed. His lips caressed hers, his hand at the back of her neck urging her to tilt just a little so they could fit together even more tightly. His tongue touched the seam of her mouth, and she opened to let him in, welcomed him with a flick of her own tongue.

He answered with a groan and slid the hand at her nape into her hair, cupping the back of her head.

Dear Goddess, this was bad. She didn't want him to stop. That was very bad.

And when he wrapped one muscular arm around her waist to lift her off her feet and against his body, she wanted him to do more than kiss her.

Her arms banded around his shoulders, her fingers sinking into his hair. So soft, silky. Like his lips against hers.

She wanted more. More of his mouth, more of his hands all over her body. She wanted to be closer. She bent her leg to wrap it around his waist—and gasped as pain shot through her.

"Shit." Gabriel grimaced as he pulled away then carefully swung her into his arms. "Damn, I'm sorry."

Gabriel cursed himself silently as he carried her to the kitchen. He knew she was in pain but the second he'd touched her, he'd completely forgotten everything but her taste.

Gods be damned, she'd come to him for help and, so far, all he'd done was fuck up.

First, he'd turned her away. Then he'd almost lost them both at the club. And he'd literally fallen asleep on the job today while she'd healed Quinn and did untold damage to her legs.

"Gabriel, for the Goddess' sake, I'm fine. Put me down."

"Shea, just shut up."

He glanced down, saw her eyes widen and cursed the anger in his voice. Hell, he wasn't angry at her.

With a sigh, he eased her onto one of the dining room chairs and pulled another closer to elevate her leg. Her skirt fell away, exposing her thigh, and he caught his breath at the sight. The colors had gotten more brilliant in just a few minutes.

His dad would've kicked his ass.

Rising, he went to the freezer for ice packs then to the drawer for wraps. Kneeling by her side, he eased the ice onto the bruise and wrapped it tightly with the gauze.

She didn't make a sound, but he could tell how painful it was by the way her fingers curled into her palms. His gut tightened in sympathy.

Pushing up from the floor, he shut off his brain and set about making food. Steaks and bags of broccoli from the freezer, potatoes from the pantry.

When he had everything started, he turned to find Shea watching him, an unreadable expression on her face, pain in her eyes.

"You can't take anything, can you? Nothing'll help."

She shook her head and he felt the anger build. He was so fucking stupid.

"Hey, look what I found."

Quinn reentered the room, dressed in loose cargo pants and a t-shirt, Leo slung over his shoulder. The kid, who'd slept most of the day, must have woken when Quinn went to bathroom. Gabriel heard Shea's indrawn breath, knew she was worried about Leo's reaction to the newcomer.

But Leo had made up his mind about Quinn if his excited expression was anything to go by.

"Sissy! He has fur on the inside."

Seemed the kid had finally found his voice. Gabriel couldn't remember Leo saying more than a few words the entire time he'd known them.

Quinn set Leo on his feet and he ran for his sister. Gabriel knew the kid was gonna go straight for her bad leg and he wasn't fast enough to stop him.

Shea winced but picked up Leo and settled his weight on her good leg. She seemed just as surprised by Leo's exclamation.

"Yes, I know. But how did you know?"

"I can see it."

Oh, yeah. The kid would make a great trophy for Dario. Christ, could this get any worse?

Quinn stopped at his side. "He knew right away," he said under his breath. "And he wasn't afraid of me. Came right up and petted my hair. He was waiting to get into the bathroom. Scared the shit out of me."

"Sorry. Forgot to remind you."

Quinn's expression hardened. "Dario's not going to stop, is he?"

Gabriel shook his head. "No. At least they don't know about Shea."

"What about Sissy?" Leo turned to stare at them.

"Nothing you don't already know." Gabriel dug up a smile, walked to the table and lifted Leo off Shea. Then, he transferred Leo to his back, where the boy clung as if he knew exactly what to do.

"Come on, kid. You can help me with the food."

Setting Leo on the counter next to the stove, Gabriel cooked as the ache in his chest grew every second. The kid reminded him of Nino so much it was starting to mess with his mind. He hadn't been able to save Nino or Davis, what made him think he could save this child?

And Shea? What the hell was he going to do with her?

He knew what he wanted to do. He wanted to take her to bed.

Wanted to strip her naked and lay her out on a bed, wrap one hand in that dark hair and let the other roam that beautiful body she had no problem showing off.

He'd start at her lips, let himself drown in her taste before he worked his way down, let his mouth taste those dark nipples while his hand stroked along her stomach and between her thighs. To the short, dark curls he'd seen there. When he'd sucked her nipples until she could barely breathe then he'd drift down to her ribs, dip his tongue into her belly button then—

"Hey, Gabe. I'm starving over here."

Shit. His attention snapped back to what he should be thinking about. And away from what he couldn't have.

The steaks. Quinn liked his bloody, and so did he. "What about you, kid? How do you like your steak?"

"Oh, he's doesn't eat—" Shea started.

"Like yours." Leo cut off his sister's reply and Gabriel turned to see surprise on Shea's face as she quickly closed her mouth.

"Shea?"

"A little longer for mine, please."

When the food was finished, Quinn grabbed the kid off the counter and set him in a chair. Leo immediately dug in.

Gabriel slid a plate in front of Shea as he sat down next to her.

He let her eat in peace for a few minutes before he said, "I want to start Leo's training."

In his peripheral vision, he saw the kid's head pop up but his gaze remained on Shea. He watched as her brow furrowed and her suspicious gaze landed on his. Yeah, he'd known she wasn't going to like this but it couldn't be helped.

"What training?" she asked.

"The kid has power, Shea. A lot of it. He needs to know what to do with it."

Her mouth firmed as she shook her head. But she didn't say anything.

"Shea, you've got to consider—"

She stood, making Quinn and Leo transfer their attention to her. "Leo, I'll get you some milk. Quinn, you want anything?"

Quinn's sharp gaze darted between her and Gabriel. "Ah, no thanks. I'm good."

She nodded and limped to the refrigerator. Gabriel got up and followed her to the other side of the room, where she was slapping open doors to find glasses.

"Shea." He kept his voice low. "He's got to know how to handle it, how to use it."

Finding the glasses, she grabbed one and nearly shattered it when she slammed it on the counter. "He's six years old. You will not drag him into this."

"I was three, Shea. Your dad had probably already started with him. He's powerful and he needs to learn how to control it and what to do with it. Ultimately, this isn't your decision to make."

Now her splintered eyes turned hard, that fascinating

mix of colors hypnotizing in her fury. "Yes, it is. He's my brother, my responsibility. I will not drag him into this because I couldn't— Because I wasn't…"

She turned away to face the cabinet doors.

He wanted to put his arms around her, pull her back against him but didn't think she'd let him. "You weren't what?"

She shook her head, as if she could shake the thoughts out of it. "Nothing. Shit." He heard something crack and realized it was the glass in her hand. Hairline cracks filled the surface. "Damn it, he didn't ask for this."

"No one asked for any of this, Shea."

She took a few deep breaths and her gaze slipped to the kid, eyes wide, listening to Quinn, who wisely kept Leo engaged with some story.

Taking a deep breath, she lifted her gaze to his. "Can we just finish lunch? Please. I need… I need to think a little."

Because she looked liked she'd hit the end of her rope, he agreed.

But he knew it was only delaying the inevitable. Leo had to be trained. Not only would he be able to better protect himself, but he'd learn how to use his power without hurting anyone.

Himself included.

* * *

As the men proceeded to devour everything on the table and Leo clung to their every word, Shea knew Gabriel was right.

Leo needed something she couldn't give him. Something Gabriel could. It bugged the hell out of her, ate

Spell Bound

at her all through the meal, picking away at her brain.

One more failure to add to the list alongside her inability to work spells and her failure to make it into ballet school.

Leo looked more excited than he had the whole time he'd been with her. And who could blame him? The men were fascinating. Gabriel and Quinn so in tune, they finished each other's sentences as they talked about mutual friends. She'd never had that closeness, that sense of belonging, of understanding.

She and her mom had never been close. Celeste hadn't been one for kisses and hugs. That affection had come from her dad, who she'd worshiped. When she'd discovered the outside world her parents had hidden from her, she hadn't blamed her dad. Only her mom. It had driven the wedge deeper.

Later, working in strip clubs, she hadn't really socialized with the other women or met many nice guys. There'd been a couple of decent men who'd asked her out, employees at the *lucani* clubs she'd worked.

None of them made her burn the way Gabriel did. None of them could make her blood boil with a look or her thighs quiver with a touch.

None of them made her want more.

Of course, none of them had wanted to train her baby brother to be a killer, either.

Damn it, she knew that wasn't fair. She knew her father probably had started Leo's training. Leo had never mentioned it, but then maybe she hadn't asked the right questions. It had taken months for the shock of their parents' deaths to wear off, months where Leo woke screaming from a restless sleep and hadn't strung more than two words together at a time. She'd felt useless then.

And the feeling wasn't going away.

"Shea." Gabriel voice set her every nerve ending on alert. Her gaze met his head-on. "Are you finished?"

Dear Goddess, what she wouldn't give to be finished with all of this.

Anger began to bubble in her chest. She'd never asked to be born a Priestess of Menrva, had never wanted to give her life to the service of a Goddess who had deserted her people. She didn't want to be the answer to a five-hundred-year-old curse no one knew how to break. She didn't want to hear voices in her head. And she certainly didn't want her brother to be pursued by a madman or have Gifts he couldn't control.

How good would it feel to let that anger consume her? To give in to it? To have a meltdown, kicking and screaming until she couldn't scream anymore?

Then she looked at Leo, still listening to Quinn with wide eyes. So young. And she shoved all that anger back down into the little hole in her chest where she kept it buried.

She looked back up at Gabriel, his gaze knowing and compassionate, and took a deep breath.

"Yeah, I'm finished." She turned to Leo with a smile. "Hey, bud, I saw a Wii in the TV room off the atrium. You want to vege out for a while?"

Not even hanging out with Quinn and Gabriel could compare to the joys of the Wii, which he'd discovered at one of the strip clubs and had played every night for hours. Nodding eagerly, he headed down the hall. Out of hearing.

Both men stared at her.

No one said anything.

Chapter Eleven

"I want us to split up," Gabriel said.

"What?" Quinn barked.

"No way." Shea slashed a hand through the air for emphasis. "No. That's out of the question."

Gabriel leaned forward to look into Shea's eyes. "Hear me out before you dismiss this. I want to send Leo to the compound. And leave him there with Quinn."

Quinn shook his head, his expression horrified. "Oh, shit, Gabe—"

Gabriel held up one finger before Shea could break in as well. "We'll go together, but then I want to leave Quinn and Leo with Serena. You and I," he looked at Shea, "need to see someone who might be able to help you find out more about your…role in all of this. And I don't plan to leave Leo and Serena alone with Quinn."

Shea shook her head. "I don't care who you plan to call to protect Leo. There's no way I'll leave him behind."

Shea's fierce expression made Gabriel's chest tighten. She'd fight him tooth and nail over this and he knew exactly how she felt. But it didn't change the fact that they needed to do it.

"Who are you thinking of?" Quinn asked.

"I want to bring in Matt."

Quinn's eyes widened before he started to grin. "Oh, baby, you're not screwing around, are you?"

He didn't answer Quinn but looked straight into Shea's angry eyes. "No, I'm not. And I wouldn't do this if I didn't think it was necessary."

It had nothing to do with the fact that he was getting too close to the kid and he was scared he'd fail. Fail both of them.

After a deep breath, Shea asked, "Who's Matt?"

"He's the best *grigorio* there is."

"And he's a fucking lunatic." Quinn laughed, but the sound was hollow. "Dario's men think he's the anti-Christ. I'm still not sure they're not right."

"I want him to take over Leo's training."

Shea shook her head. "No—"

"Hell, Gabe. Do you think you'll even be able to get him out of that pit in Vegas?"

Gabriel nodded. "I think he'll come. For Kyle's sake."

"Shit." Quinn scrubbed a hand through his hair. "I didn't think of that. You're right."

Shea held up one hand. "Why would he do anything for my father?"

"Because he's Kyle's brother."

* * *

Shea felt his statement hit her like a blow to her chest. Blinking, she drew in a sharp gasp, her hands drawing into fists on the table.

"Brother?" They had an uncle? She'd thought they were alone, she and Leo. Goddess, did they have other family?

Gabriel must have read her mind. "Your mother had a sister."

"Is she still…"

He nodded. "Yeah, she is. She was cursed, too."

They had an aunt. Another member of the *boschetta*. More secrets. So much their parents had hidden.

She took a deep breath, trying not to hyperventilate. She let her gaze catch and hold Gabriel's. Like a lifeline. "I didn't know. Dad never said anything about other family. I never…never thought to ask."

Gabriel reached across the table, almost but not quite touching her hand. "No reason you would have. Like I said, *grigori* are trained from an early age not to discuss family connections. It can get…complicated."

She snorted. "Good word."

Gabriel sat back in his chair. "So we're going to see someone who might be able to uncomplicate things."

"Who?"

"Madrona. She's the historian. She and her sister, Furia, live in New Orleans."

"And what do you think she'll be able to tell me?"

Gabriel shook his head. "I'm hoping she'll be able to tell us what you need to know to break the curse."

She dropped her gaze. "Yeah, well, that's the big question, isn't it? Why the hell am I here?"

No one had an answer. She didn't have an answer. Maybe this Madrona would have an answer. But it would mean trusting an uncle she'd never met with her brother's life.

"So," she sighed, "if I agree to this, and I'm not saying yes, but if I do, what time frame are we looking at?"

Gabriel's expression didn't change at all. "It'll take probably a day to get hold of Matt and at least two days for him to drive. He doesn't fly. Until then, I want to start Leo's training."

Just the thought made her stomach roll. But she knew

Gabriel well enough by now to know he wouldn't let up. "And what does that include?"

"Self-defense, weapons, tactics, skills development. I need to find out what he can do before I'll know what else we'll need to teach him."

Quinn stood. "Hey, I'm gonna leave you two to hash this out. I'll go keep the kid company awhile."

Gabriel turned to grin at Quinn. And all the air left the room. How did Gabriel manage to make her hot with just a smile? "Maybe you can finally beat someone on that damn thing."

Quinn flipped him off with a smile. "I'd kick your ass, buddy." Then he turned to her and winked. "Don't let him bully you, Shea."

He turned and walked out of the room, leaving her alone with Gabriel. Strange things happened when she was alone with Gabriel. Emotions she had no time for, kisses she shouldn't want, desires she couldn't fulfill.

All wrapped up in a man she'd met only days before.

She stared into his steady brown eyes that never flinched. "You think Madrona will have answers?"

He nodded. "I think she's our best bet."

Not "your" best bet. "Our" best bet.

A simmering warmth began in her stomach, making her shift in her seat. Gabriel twisted her emotions in knots, an odd feeling for her.

"I still can't believe Celeste never said anything about the curse," he said.

"My mom wasn't big on heart-to-hearts." She shifted in the chair, trying to find a more comfortable position for her throbbing leg. "And I think my dad—"

Gabriel stood and carefully lifted her out of the chair. "Come on. Let's find a better place for this conversation."

She slid her arms around his neck without thought then tried to ignore the strength of his broad shoulders. And the warmth of his thick arms banded around her as he carried her through the hall. And the spicy male scent of him that made her stomach tighten in knots.

She didn't look up at him. If he looked down, he'd see every one of her emotions.

And that would be a disaster.

So she stared at his jaw, at the black whiskers of his beard. And wondered what they'd feel like against her skin.

She barely noticed they'd walked back to the front of the house, past the room where Quinn and Leo played games to a backdrop of grinding metal and screeching guitars. She finally dragged her gaze away when he pushed open a door and carried her into a dark space. Setting her on a soft surface, he walked away. A few seconds later, the door clicked shut and light flooded the room.

She gasped. "Oh wow."

From her seat on a soft leather club chair, Shea didn't know where to look first.

The library was open to the second floor and its four walls were covered in books. A spiral staircase to the left of the door led to a small landing above. Two ladders ran on a rail system around the entire room, tall enough to the reach the top shelves under the ceiling.

"Cool, huh?" Gabriel's smile reappeared as he sat in the matching chair across from her. He didn't settle in, though. He rested on the edge, feet on the floor, elbows on knees.

Ready for action.

"What are they all?"

Her gaze continued to roam the walls, picking out what looked to be ancient stone tablets on a shelf between the floor and the first landing, and whole sections of books by some of the most famous fantasy writers in the world. An avid reader growing up, Shea had always imagined this was what heaven looked like.

"A lot of everything." Gabriel's voice echoed slightly. "The *versipelli* started this collection centuries ago. Some are grimoires, some are journals. There are whole sections devoted to different histories."

"I could spend hours in here and never be bored."

"This was where I spent most of my time when my dad and I would lay over here. The *versipelli* are rabid about history. I think you'll be able to find better answers to some of your questions here than I can give you. Serena has the women's journals at the compound, but the *grigori* histories are kept here. I never met your father but I heard he spent a lot of time here before he and Celeste disappeared."

She nodded, smiling. "I can believe it. He had a story for everything. When I left…"

Her heart tightened in her chest, unable to finish. A memory of her parents flashed into her head. Her mom's quiet laughter as her dad told Shea some outlandish story. He'd been good at stories, especially the ones about beautiful folletti with butterfly wings and foolish boys who swiped gold from mean Etruscan orciuli.

Would the pain of losing them ever diminish? And could she ever forgive them or understand why they'd never told her about the curse?

Gabriel didn't say anything. She knew he wanted to ask more questions, but he didn't and, for that, she was grateful. She looked at him and found him watching her. So intently, she felt heat bubble in her stomach. "So, did you bring me in here just to let me look or do you have something to show me?"

Spell Bound

His grin reappeared, the one that made her stomach drop to her knees. "Let me get your grandfather's journal. Maybe he'll have some answers for you."

He walked to the wall behind them and climbed the library ladder nearly all the way to the ceiling. He stood there for at least thirty seconds looking at the spines before grabbing one and climbing back down.

The book he held would have made Buffy's Rupert Giles giggle with glee—a thick, leather-bound manuscript. But Buffy was fiction. This was the real deal.

And this one had been written by her grandfather.

"I've never read this," Gabriel said. "Not sure anyone else has, either. The *grigori* aren't required to keep journals. And if they do, they're not supposed to mention the cursed *streghe* by name. But if Marcus wrote like he told stories, it'll be a hell of a read."

She ran her hands over the cover, not opening it yet. She wanted Gabriel to talk more. Just the sound of his voice eased something inside her. "You knew him?"

"Yeah, I got to meet him a few times. He died when I was around ten."

Which meant he'd been alive at her birth. She'd always assumed her grandparents were dead. Her parents had always talked as if they were. Still so much she didn't know. "What was he like?"

"He trained as a *grigorio*, but because his father was still alive and caring for his *strega*, Marcus became a soldier. He was Special Ops for the U.S. government for years. Fought in World War II. Then he raised two of the best *grigori* there have ever been."

She held onto the book but didn't want Gabriel to stop talking just yet. "So my grandfather's mother was a cursed *strega*?"

"Yes."

"And my mother has a sister."

"Yep."

She sighed, feeling lost, as if she'd forgotten something she'd never known she needed and now couldn't live without. "I feel like I'm trying to build a house without the blueprints."

Gabriel settled back in the chair and she relaxed. He wasn't going anywhere yet. She wasn't about to acknowledge, even to herself, how comforting that was. "Maybe your grandfather knows something about the curse."

She sighed. "That would be almost too easy, wouldn't it?"

He nodded, the black strands of his hair falling over his shoulder and drawing her gaze. The guy was just too damn gorgeous.

"Yeah, probably," Gabriel said.

Shaking her head, she decided on another line of questioning. "So, how can you tell if you're born *grigori*?"

"If he's born to one of the thirteen, it just comes with the deal," Gabriel said. "If he's born to a *grigorio* and a woman who isn't one of the *streghe*, there are ways to tell. Enhanced strength, hearing and sight, the ability to manipulate metal. Your brother has the sight, a shitload of *arus* and the tocadura. Probably more powers we don't yet know about. That's why he needs to be trained."

She dropped her gaze to her grandfather's journal as a chill whispered up her spine.

Leo was only six.

And I was four when Mom started my training.

"Hey. Shea." His quiet tone made her eyelids fall. "He needs to know."

She didn't really have a choice, did she? She was

unprepared for all of this, so in the dark. Even with all her dad had taught her, obviously it hadn't been enough. And now she was responsible for Leo, too.

Did she want Leo to grow up as oblivious as she had? She realized her parents had thought they were protecting her by not telling her about the curse. But she knew they'd made the wrong choice.

She didn't want Leo to be as clueless. Or hate her for withholding information.

Didn't want to lose him to Dario because he couldn't defend himself.

She raised her gaze to meet Gabriel's and nodded. "Then I guess you should start."

* * *

Gabriel left Shea in the library, nose stuck in her grandfather's journal.

He left because, if he didn't, he would've sat there and watched her read.

Ceffo.

Instead, he walked over to the TV room and stood in the doorway, waiting until Leo and Quinn, side-by-side on the floor, finished their race.

"Hey, kid. You kick Quinn's a—butt?"

Leo looked up at him with big, dark eyes, so much like Nino's he couldn't stifle the slash of pain before it managed to nick him in the heart. He covered his expression well enough, though, because Leo didn't seem to notice.

"He's good." Leo didn't smile but his eyes brightened. "I'm better."

"You just wait." Quinn dropped the controller and leaned back against the sofa. "I'll get you next time."

Leo held out his controller to Gabriel. "Do you want to play?"

Damn, the kid was too good to be true. Gabriel didn't want to like him so much, but it was hard not to.

"No, thanks. I've got another game we can play, though, if you want."

Leo's expression turned eager and he scrambled to his feet, the top of his head barely reaching the bottom of Gabriel's rib cage. "Did Sissy say it was okay?"

Gabriel dismantled his smile in mid-formation. She'd taught the kid well. "Yeah, she did. Come on."

Leo padded after him like a puppy, Quinn bringing up the rear as they headed to a stairway hidden behind a door in the dining room. Flipping the switch for the lights at the bottom of the stairs, Gabriel led them up, smiling at Leo's gasp as the room came into sight.

"Wow. What is this?" he asked in a hushed whisper.

Gabriel stood aside so Leo could walk into the open space. "This is a training room."

"For what?"

"Guys like us."

Leo tore his gaze away from the sights to look at him. "Cool."

Quinn laughed as Gabriel nodded. "Very cool."

Overhead, skylights revealed the clear blue sky and illuminated the weapons lining the walls. Gabriel knew all their names, had been trained on all of them. Some were thousands of years old, like the double-edged gladius. Some were ceremonial, and some were experimental prototypes created by Digger and his father and grandfather.

Leo started at the closest wall, examining the cinquedea, the short sword of the Roman gladiators; ran his finger over the shafts of the hasta and pilum. He spent some time staring at the round, razor-sharp chakram before moving onto the Indian tiger-claw blades.

He walked halfway around the room before he stopped and reached for a matched pair of Malay kris. His hands already on the hilts of the blades, Leo turned to look at Gabriel. He never questioned instinct so he nodded.

He let the kid remove them from the wall and hold them in his hands, getting a feel for them.

"They're called kris," Gabriel said. "You want to learn how to use them?"

Leo's eyes widened. "Can I?"

"Yeah, you can." Gabriel squatted so he and Leo were eye-to-eye. "It's time to find out what you can do, Leo. You up for it?"

He nodded, his expression becoming serious. "Daddy said I had to be ready."

"Ready for what?"

"To protect Shea."

Christ, that was a hell of a lot of responsibility to put on a child's shoulders, even one as powerful as Leo. But then, Shea was a special case.

"Did he tell you anything else, Leo? About your powers?"

Leo shrugged, his gaze dropping to the weapons in his hands. "Sometimes they scare me."

Gabriel put his arms around the kid's shoulders before he even thought about what he was doing. "You don't have to be scared anymore, Leo. I'm gonna teach you how to control them. Okay?"

The little boy nodded but didn't lift his gaze.

"Did your dad tell you anything else? About what you can do?"

Now Leo looked up and Gabriel saw something hard flash through the boy's eyes. "He said Sissy would come for me and we'd have to take care of each other."

"Well, Quinn and I are here to help you with that now. So...you want to get started?"

When Leo nodded, Gabriel set him on his feet and waved Leo onto the mats in the center of the room. "Quinn'll get you going. I've got a call to make first."

He had Quinn start Leo on stretches before taking him through some simple moves with the blades. Gabriel made sure they were okay before he headed for an alcove at the rear. He picked up the old-fashioned black receiver, turned a few numbers on the rotary dial and waited until he heard Phil ask, "Party, please?"

"Matteo Michael Tedaldi, Las Vegas."

Phil paused before answering. "That may take a few hours, Gabriel. I will call you back at this extension when I've reached your party."

He caught her just before she disconnected him. "I need another connection. Crimson Moon Productions."

"Please hold and I'll connect you."

Serena answered on the fourth ring.

"Gabriel, is everything all right?"

He paused, hearing the careful way she tried to hide the slur in her voice. Shit, his mom was drunk. And according to his sisters, that was never a good sign. "Yeah, we're all fine. Quinn got here this morning." He decided against telling her about Quinn's accident. She'd be able to handle that better when she was sober. "But I've decided we need to split up. I want to take Shea to Maddie after we bring the boy up to you. I'm going to call Matt in from Vegas for Leo. The kid's strong. Really strong."

Serena fell silent and he knew she was biting her

bottom lip, thinking it over, trying to look at it from all angles. *Damn, Mom...*

After at least thirty seconds, she said, "I'll speak to Maddie, tell her to expect your call."

"We're going to move out after I hear from Matt, hopefully later today. We'll wait for Matt to arrive before Shea and I head to Louisiana."

"You appear to have this all figured out."

"Yeah well, I learned from the best."

She chuckled, but it had a shaky sound to it. "Stay safe, Gabriel."

"Hey. You okay?"

"Yes. I'm fine. I didn't sleep well. Stay safe."

* * *

Serena's head throbbed with a hangover and a vague sense of impending doom.

Looking at the bedside clock, she realized it was three in the afternoon. Dribbles of light seeped through the cracks where the curtains met the sill. Her mouth tasted like she'd eaten a whole bag of sour cream and onion chips and her throat was parched.

Groaning, she sat up and eased her legs over the side of the bed. The room spun around her for a few seconds before she got her feet on the ground.

She couldn't remember coming back to bed. She hadn't had a binge like that in years—

Quinn. She'd talked to Quinn last night.

Her temples pounded and her stomach rolled as their conversation came rushing back. Served her right. She'd said things to Quinn she'd never meant to say. Things he'd make her pay for the next time she saw him.

Because nothing had changed. Even though she'd told him how she felt, it didn't change the facts.

She couldn't be with him.

Losing her husband Nicolo five-hundred years ago had devastated her. But she'd had two teenage daughters to care for and they'd been on the run.

She still remembered that awful night in vivid detail, sometimes relived it in her dreams. After they'd burned Dafne, the villagers—men and women they'd grown up with and cared for for years—had stolen into their homes, slit the throats of the *streghe* and every member of their families then had carried the bodies to a mass grave.

She'd never forget the terror of her daughters' muffled screams, the sensation of the dirt pouring down on their bodies. The blackness in the pit, buried alive.

Her lungs starved for air as she clawed her way out from under the dirt. Frantically digging for her daughters. Seeing the horror in her sixteen-year-old children's eyes.

She hadn't believed. Not until that moment, when their bodies healed what should have been Fatal wounds, that they had truly been cursed. She hadn't believed and her husband had paid with his life, along with all the other *streghe* husbands and children not of the *boschetta*.

Bending at the waist, she took deep breaths, waiting for the nausea to recede. For the sounds to fade from her memory.

But the pain of losing Niccolo would never fade.

The second time she'd found him, his soul had been reincarnated three hundred years later as Charles Smithson, a farmer in 1820s New England. Losing Charles had hurt just as much as losing Niccolo.

If she committed her heart and something happened to her beautiful Quinn... She knew her heart would not survive this time.

Spell Bound

Sliding off the bed without jarring her head or her stomach, she went to the kitchen and mixed a virgin Bloody Mary, adding mint for her stomach and rue for her head. She felt a little better after finishing the glass, enough to banish all thoughts of the physical and concentrate solely on the spiritual.

Down the hall, she knelt before her altar, the familiarity of the tools comforting. The wand from the walnut tree in Benevento, the black cauldron she hadn't used to cook food for centuries, the athame her father had made for her.

After lighting the candles she made from beeswax, she opened the circle.

"Great Mother Goddess Uni, from whom all gifts emanate. I give thanks for your blessings."

A whisper of power brushed against her *arus*, like a cat rubbing against her legs. It soothed her jangled nerves, gave her a sense of serenity she sorely needed.

With a tiny yank, she pulled the nail, in its key form, from around her neck and held it in her hands. Wrapping her fingers around it, she felt it transform, then placed it on the altar.

"Goddess Menrva, whose wisdom is all-knowing, I am humbled by your faith in me to watch your most precious gift. Accept my humble words as offerings, Great Mother Goddess Uni. Grant Your protection to my children and my loved ones. And give safe passage to those no longer with us."

Poor sweet Tullia. Why her?

It was a question she knew better than to ask the Goddesses because, sometimes, there were no answers.

And in her darkest moments, Serena thought maybe, just maybe there were no answers because the Involuti, the founding deities of the Etruscan pantheon, had deserted them.

After she finished the prayer and banished the circle, Serena fell to the floor and let herself weep for Tullia's death, her tears pooling in front of the altar. Another offering.

Several minutes later, after she'd worn herself out, she dried her tears and took a deep breath. She had work to do. She couldn't put it off any longer.

In the office, she picked up the heavy black phone on the desk and called Madrona and Furia first. Her daughters would have only a vague notion of what had happened. Their Gifts, arrested at the time of the curse, were spotty.

The phone rang once before Maddie picked it up, her brisk hello erasing the lingering memories of her daughters' screams.

"Hello, sweetheart, how are you today?"

"Mama! I was going to call you today. We haven't heard from you for so long and we both felt something last night. How are you? Are you okay? What's going on?"

Goddess, Maddie could heap the guilt thicker with just a few words than Serena could ever hope to. Of course, they'd had five-hundred years to perfect their technique. But she wasn't ready to answer her daughter's last question yet.

"I've missed you, Maddie. What trouble are you and your sister getting into now?"

"Nothing much lately. Donal is a more-effective watchdog than the others you've sicced on us before. The bookstore is doing well, and Furia's finally agreed to close that burlesque club and open a respectable business. How is everything up there?"

She couldn't avoid it any longer. "Tullia's gone, honey. Last night. I don't have details yet, but..."

The silence from the other end of the phone throbbed

with unspoken questions. Maddie always thought things through before she spoke, looked at all the angles.

"Brian, too?"

"I don't know, sweetheart." *So much I don't know.*

"Do you want us to come?"

Oh, Goddess, yes. She missed her children. "Not yet. Soon. And Gabriel will be calling you. He'll explain why."

"Mama, is there something going on that we need to know?"

"I miss you, Maddie. You and Furia. I'll see you soon."

She hung up before she broke down again. She had other calls to make, calls that wouldn't be as easy.

Sophia and Nerina would need to be contacted wherever they happened to be in Europe at the moment. She wouldn't be able to notify Amalia. She had no idea where that girl was, though she'd tried for years to find her. She'd been the strongest after Dafne. She should have been the one to lead, not Serena. Serena didn't have the strength.

But Amalia had deserted them almost immediately.

Serena would have to find her this time. Amalia needed to be told about Shea. The rest of the *boschetta* needed to be told about Shea.

But not yet. Not until she'd met the girl.

Then hopefully, together they could figure out how to break this miserable curse.

* * *

It took Shea a few minutes to open her grandfather's journal.

She had the ridiculous sense that her life was about to change. The knowledge lay so heavy on her chest, she could barely breathe.

Get a grip, it's just a book. No harm ever came from reading a book. At least not in real life.

"Just open it already," she chided. "Do you really think you're going to find a page titled 'How to Break the Curse'?"

Forcing her fingers to obey, she cracked open the cover, nose wrinkling at the musty smell. Probably hadn't been opened in decades.

She gasped as the first few pages slid away from the rest of the book, thinking the damn thing was going to crumble before she got to read it. Then she realized the journal was more of a folio. The outer leather covers enclosed several paper notebooks, each labeled with a range of years. The first was 1941-1950.

She read every word of the first few pages, brief entries that talked about his days in boot camp, preparing for World War II. Those pages were fascinating glimpses of a time long gone but not what she needed.

After a while, she started skimming pages, looking for key words—Kyle, Celeste, son, curse.

Her grandfather hadn't been a real dedicated writer. He'd skipped whole years completely, wrote only a few passages for several years in the late '40s and early '50s.

Her dad's birth in 1960 started a slew of entries that continued through the last journal, dated 1990.

Just the sight of her dad's name made her chest tighten. Damn, she missed him.

Taking a deep breath, she wanted to read everything her grandfather had to say about her dad, but knew it would have to wait until she had more time. Now, she was supposed to look for answers.

She forced herself to skim her dad's early years, his training as a *grigorio*, searching for anything that might have something to do with the curse. And then she found an entry from 1972.

Kyle had the dream again last night. Woke up screaming so loud, thought he'd wake the neighbors. Third time this week.

Rina and I haven't talked about it, but she's probably thinking the same thing I am. It's been almost five hundred years since Paganelli's curse took the streghe out of the natural order of life.

Still no sign of the daughter foretold by D before her death. The daughter to break the curse.

Unless K's dream is a vision.

He described Dario perfectly, down to the mole on his cheek. K says he sees Dario stick a knife into his chest then into the chest of a dark-haired girl. The girl screams in agony and K wants to stop it but he can't. It's like he's watching it on television. He can see what's happening but he's not there.

He says he doesn't recognize the girl but I don't believe him. Asked him to describe her, but it made him cry. Figured it wasn't worth it. There's so much pain in his eyes. He's hiding something.

Was it at dream? Or a vision of things to come?

Maybe I don't want know.

Flipping through the pages with shaking fingers, she searched for any more references to the dreams, anything else her dad might have told his father.

Was it her mother he'd been dreaming about?

Or her?

She found her answer several pages later.

C&K stopped to say goodbye. They're disappearing. They want the girl to have a life before K's dream comes to pass. Before the curse is ended.

A low drone buzzed in her ears and her temples throbbed, the start of a headache imminent.

Setting the journal on the table in front of her, she swallowed a few times, trying to keep her stomach from revolting.

That was her destiny? To die with a knife in her heart? At the hands of the monster who wanted her brother?

No. That couldn't be it. It was too…gruesome.

But if that wasn't how to break the curse then why had her parents run?

And why hadn't they told her about the curse? Had they been trying to protect her? Or had her parents been biding their time until she was old enough to be sacrificed?

Her breath started to come in shallow pants, and her gaze fixed on the book in front of her.

No. It's not fair. It's not…

Vaffanculo. She couldn't breathe.

She sat there, trying to calm down, trying not to panic. Not to give in to the feeling that she was fighting a losing battle.

So many questions. Too many questions. But she knew one thing for certain—her parents had believed she could break the curse.

And they'd knowingly hidden her from the rest of the *boschetta*.

The drone in her head grew, the voices buzzing. But they weren't angry. No, they were upset.

Damn, her head hurt. She rubbed her temples, trying to massage away the pain.

Spell Bound

She knew what the voices were trying to tell her. They wanted her to know her parents had loved her. Her dad had told her every night before he tucked her in bed. Her mom... Had her mom ever said it?

She couldn't remember her mom saying the words. Not once.

Rising from the couch, she started to pace, accepting the still-sharp pain in her leg to bring a little clarity to her brain.

Had her mom just been biding the time until she could sacrifice her daughter to end the curse?

The voices responded with a surge of denial that stopped her in her tracks.

No, she didn't believe that, either. Her mom might have been aloof most of her life, but she hadn't been plotting her own daughter's death.

Come to think of it, aloof wasn't the right word. As a child, she remembered asking her dad why her mom was always so sad. She didn't remember his exact response. Couldn't remember if he'd actually answered her.

As she'd gotten older, she'd translated sad into aloof. So many years she'd spent pissed off at her mom. At her distance, her unwillingness to connect. Her disapproval.

Had her mom just been overwhelmed at the thought that her daughter would have to have a knife stuck in her heart to break the curse?

"Shit, Mom. What the hell am I supposed to do?"

Was she supposed to let a madman kill her to break a magical curse on five-hundred-year-old women she'd never met?

She laughed but slapped a hand over her mouth when the sound escaped. She sounded crazy.

Or course, she might be crazy. That would actually make more sense than believing her death could break a curse.

But she wasn't crazy and she knew it.

If she broke the curse, would Dario stop pursuing Leo?

Could she save her brother by letting Dario kill her?

Fear made her shiver and she rubbed at the goosebumps breaking out all over her arms and legs. It made her stomach roll.

Not fair. So not fair.

"Yeah, like anything in life is fair," she muttered. "What if…"

She didn't finish. She had too many questions and no answers. Would Serena or Madrona have answers? And to which questions?

"Stop, just stop. You don't have the answers and you're going to make yourself sick with worry."

And she couldn't afford that. They couldn't afford that. She had to think about Leo.

And Gabriel. Actually, she was probably thinking too much about that man. About his dark, steady eyes. Broad shoulders, wide chest and slim hips. She allowed herself one brief minute to fantasize about what she might do with Gabriel and a few uninterrupted hours. The feel of his body covering hers, his hair trailing along her skin…

She stepped forward—and the throb of pain in her leg killed that daydream. Still, it didn't hurt as badly as it had, and she bent her leg at the knee a few times, testing her mobility. She'd healed fairly quickly. That was a good sign.

Walking out of the library, she heard the ping of metal on metal and followed the sound to the stairs in the dining room. In the stairwell, she heard their voices perfectly.

"You're doing fine, Leo." Gabriel sounded pleased.

"Just remember to move your feet when you parry. Try that move again. Keep your arms loose, drop your shoulders. There, like that. It makes it easier to maneuver the blades."

"Did you use these, Gabriel?" Leo's sweet voice carried down to her.

"No, I started with a bo staff. It's not something you can carry around, but you can take that training and apply it to most anything you can pick up on the street."

She could practically hear Leo turning that one over in his brain in the short silence that followed. "You mean like sticks?"

"Yeah and other stuff."

"Show me?"

"Sure. Hang on a sec."

Not wanting to miss the show, but not wanting to distract them, she drew on her *arus* and whispered the spell to pull a glamour over her body, ignoring the slight throb in her temples. She crept up a few more stairs until she could see the room. And the two hot men and one little boy.

Leo sat cross-legged on a corner of the huge mat covering half the floor space, his wide-eyed gaze glued to Gabriel. Quinn rested against the opposite wall, using his discarded shirt as a pillow. He looked tired, a sheen of sweat on his lean body. Quite the sight for any red-blooded female.

But it was Gabriel who made her hormones dance the happy dance as he walked into the middle of the circle, shirtless, holding a long wooden pole. That chest should be classified a deadly weapon. Deadly to her common sense because she wanted to lick the beaded sweat off his skin.

He'd taste amazing, she decided. Salty and hot and...

Well, shit. She dragged her gaze away from his chest and checked out his weapon. And she didn't mean the one in his pants, though, she decided after a quick check, maybe she—

Bad Shea.

Regretfully, she focused her gaze on the bo staff, looking almost delicate in his large hands, but, she knew from watching her dad train that the pole could be just as deadly as any gun.

Gabriel started slow, the weapon slicing the air with a gentle whoosh. As he picked up speed, she could tell he'd logged many hours with the instrument.

His movements were as graceful as any ballet and just as hypnotizing. Concentration shone in his eyes as he dipped and swayed and swung the staff, gaining momentum.

Gabriel's body moved in a dance of strength and power, and soon she wasn't watching the staff. Instead, she watched the play of muscles in his broad shoulders as he swung the weapon over his head, let her gaze glide to his strong forearms as he brought the staff down hard, stopping just before it hit the ground.

Then he crouched, drawing her gaze to the black cargo pants molded over his bulging thighs.

She didn't notice Quinn had moved until he was in the ring. He'd picked up another staff and now swung it at Gabriel's head from behind. She managed to stifle her gasp just as Gabriel turned and blocked the swing.

Grinning, Gabriel stood and the fight began in earnest. It looked almost choreographed, like something they'd worked on for years. But she knew by the amount of effort they put into it that this was no memorized routine.

They fought each other with a ferocity that would have been frightening if she hadn't known how much they cared for each other. Their staffs met with solid snaps as they tried to find the other's weakness, moving all over the mat. They never came close to Leo, though, and Shea knew that took a high level of skill.

They must have fought for close to ten minutes, neither of them gaining the advantage for long.

When it seemed like Gabriel had Quinn on the defensive, Quinn would retreat then attack with a burst of speed. Gabriel never faltered, no matter what Quinn threw at him. He wore the other man down, letting Quinn get close then beating him back.

And when Quinn finally made one wrong move, Gabriel took out his legs with one swipe. Quinn hit the mat with a hard smack and Gabriel had the tip of the staff pointed at his neck in half a second.

Quinn started to laugh and Gabriel's intent expression faded into a smile that wasn't any less fierce. He tossed the staff to the side and extended his hand to Quinn, who promptly tried to throw Gabriel over his head. But Gabriel must have known what Quinn had in mind because he braced and flipped Quinn away. Still laughing.

"I never could get you to fall for that one." Quinn stood and brushed himself off. "Good to know you haven't lost your edge with age, buddy."

"You're still telling, Quinn. Those cub eyes do you in every time."

"Yeah, but only because you know me too well. My enemies fear me, kid." Quinn turned to wink at Leo then looked straight at Shea. "And the ladies love me."

She should have known the glamour wouldn't work with these two, and she dispelled it with a huff. Jeez, Leo could probably see through it now.

"Sissy, did you see? I'm going to fight like that."

Bittersweet emotion filled her chest at the excitement in Leo's voice. Seemed he'd finally found something to talk about. Standing, she walked up the stairs, aware that Gabriel watched her every move.

"That was beautiful." She stopped at the top of the stairs, knowing if she got any closer she wouldn't be able to resist sniffing the sweat on Gabriel's body, his olive-toned skin shimmering in the bright sunlight from the skylights. The only other outward sign of his physical exertion was the faster pace of his breathing. She had to tear her gaze away before she drooled. "Did you and Quinn train together?"

Gabriel nodded. "For a few years, yeah. Of course, Quinn liked to play dirty."

"Hey, I had no control over my change back then." He tried to sound pissed off, but she didn't think Quinn did anger. She didn't think he was made for it. "Whenever I got excited or frightened, I'd grow claws. One of the *lucani* defense mechanisms. We learn how to control it as we get older, but Gabe has a few scars to show for it."

"So do you." Gabriel turned to replace the staff on the wall and she noticed the faint scar of claw marks near the waistband of his jeans.

"Yeah, but you never gave me a hassle about yours."

"Then I guess I was too easy on you." Gabriel stopped in front of Leo and held out his hand, which Leo didn't hesitate to take, letting Gabriel pull him to his feet. And he didn't let go.

Jealousy rose, leaving a bitter taste in her mouth. Goddess, how stupid was she? Forcing a smile, she reached out to ruffle Leo's too-long bangs.

"Did you learn a lot, bud?"

Leo nodded, looking a little unsure now that he was standing in front of her, unsure how she would respond. "It was cool."

Her smile softened at the excitement in his tone. "Then you'll have to show me. But how about after we get something to eat? I bet you're hungry."

Now he gave her the tiniest bit of a smile, as if trying to remember how to do it, and the jealousy abated. A little.

"How about a snack?" she said. "I'm in the mood for chocolate."

Gabriel laid his hand on her forearm as she turned to go, stopping her in her tracks. His hand felt slick and warm against her skin, making her heart pound. "Shea, give me a minute. Leo, go with Quinn, okay?"

Leo didn't even hesitate. Just nodded and followed Quinn down the stairs.

"Did you find anything?"

She dropped her gaze and she knew Gabriel would know she was lying. But she wasn't ready.

Not yet.

"I need more time to go through the rest of journals. There's a lot of information. I just…need some time."

When she fell silent, she held her breath, knowing he wouldn't let her off the hook that easily. Of course, he wanted to hear what she'd learned. But she couldn't. Not yet.

"Fine." Surprise made her gaze jump back to his, staring down at her with compassion. "I've got a question for you."

Gabriel dropped his hand and she nearly grabbed for him, restraining herself at the last minute. She needed something to hold onto and he was fast becoming her rock.

"If I tell you to shoot me, will you do it?"

Her mouth dropped open. "What the hell are you talking about?"

He walked to a large chest on the back wall and pulled out one of the drawers. "Just what I said. If I tell you to shoot me, will you do it?"

Had he lost his mind? "Why would you tell me to do that?"

He turned to face her again, a small revolver in his hand. It looked downright silly there, feminine. Walking back to her, he held out the gun, butt first, determination etched on his face. "I won't be taken by Dario's men. If it looks like I will be, I want you to kill me. I won't let them have that pleasure. So, can you do it? Will you shoot me if I tell you to?"

Could she? Gabriel stared at her with his steady dark gaze, hair loose around his shoulders.

The man was gorgeous. He had the body of an Etruscan god—broad shoulders, wide chest, narrow waist and muscular legs. But it wasn't just the size of his body, so much as the way he held himself. His confidence.

She transferred her gaze to the gun in his hand, a Beretta Px4 Storm. Like the one she'd had to leave behind in their apartment in the city.

Grasping the weapon by the butt, she pointed the muzzle down and away. She checked to make sure the safety was on then checked to see if it was loaded. Yes to both questions.

She wasn't afraid of guns. Her father had trained her well, and she'd become proficient over the years, though the only thing she'd ever shot had been targets.

She would shoot anyone who tried to take Leo. But could she shoot Gabriel?

She shook her head and looked away. "I don't know. I don't know if I could pull the trigger."

"Come on, baby, you know you want to hurt me."

His tone teased a reluctant smile out of her. "Yeah, you're a bastard, but I still don't know if I could do it."

"Let's hope you don't have to find out."

He turned and walked down the stairs.

She took the gun to her room and hid it in her backpack then returned to the kitchen where the guys had a smorgasbord of junk food laid out on the table. Quinn had made sandwiches, enough for all of them. But chips, pretzels, cookies, candy and soda littered the table as well. All the things she'd tried so hard not to let Leo get hooked on. A habit she'd picked up from her mom. The first time she'd tasted chocolate, she'd been fifteen. Her dad had given her a Godiva chocolate bar as a birthday present.

Of course, she'd been hooked after that and, when she'd started to make secret forays into the nearest town, chocolate was always the first thing she'd buy.

The males congregated at the table, talking about weapons and fighting, guy stuff. She pulled herself onto the counter to munch Double Stuff Oreos and watch the testosterone show. Men were interesting creatures, particularly in the way they dealt with each other.

Quinn and Gabriel appeared to be on their best behavior, she assumed because of Leo and, for that, she wanted to kiss them. Both of them. Okay, maybe she'd give Quinn a hug, but Gabriel she wanted to keep in her arms for a while.

And that was probably the worst thing that could happen. But damn, he was fascinating.

"When did you know what you are, Gabriel?"

Leo's boyish voice rang out through the rustle of

bags and the background music of AC/DC coming from a small CD player on the counter.

Gabriel didn't hesitate. "My dad started my training at birth, I think. I don't remember a time when I didn't know what I am."

Must have been nice, she thought, to have a purpose in life from the time you were born. She'd grown up without one, never knowing from one day to the next what life held for her. She hadn't cared until she'd realized there was more to the world than their house and the forest. Then she'd discovered ballet and thought she'd found her reason for living.

"Where'd you grow up?" Leo asked.

"Mostly southeastern Pennsylvania."

"What about your mom?"

Gabriel paused before answering. "I didn't see my mom much."

"Why?"

"Because it wasn't safe."

"Why?"

Shea was sure Gabriel would redirect Leo's question. He surprised her.

"Because those men that are after you, they're after my mom, too. She didn't want anything to happen to me until I could defend myself."

Leo's expression hardened into one she'd never seen. It was mean with determination, anguish and fury. "They killed my parents."

Grief, biting and terrible, knifed through her.

Gabriel nodded. "Yeah, they did. And that's why we're here. The women need us to protect them. They have power, but they're not fighters. We fight for them."

Leo looked over at her. "I'll never let anything happen to you, Shea."

Tears she couldn't control sprang to her eyes but she blinked them back and smiled at her brother, forty pounds of skin and bones with too-long dark hair, big brown eyes and a solemn expression.

"I know, bud."

"Hey, Shea."

Gabriel's voice drew her attention. She couldn't read his expression. There was something in his eyes, something she wanted so badly to decipher.

"What?" she asked, but didn't get answered.

The phone rang.

Chapter Twelve

Quinn waited for Gabe to get the phone but the guy never acknowledged its ringing.

Hell, his gaze didn't stray from Shea for the slightest second. Probably didn't even hear the phone, if his expression was anything to go by. He'd never seen Gabe so fixated on a woman before. Any other time, Quinn would jump for joy. Now...

With a sigh, Quinn snagged the receiver off the wall.

"Speak fast."

"Quinn? Quinn, is that you?"

The voice on the other end of the phone froze him in place.

Shit, not now.

He had to swallow to loosen his tongue. "Hey, Tammi. How's it going?"

Gabriel turned to stare at him.

Oh, sure, now he had the guy's attention.

"Quinn, it is you." The young woman sounded so happy, guilt practically knocked him on his ass. "I thought you fell off the face of the earth. I had to badger your boss all day to get this number. Where are you?"

"Sorry, I...had to go out of town on the spur of the moment. We got notice of an audit at one of the clubs in Maryland. Is something wrong?"

Tammi huffed and, in Quinn's mind, he could see the woman the outside world believed to be his girlfriend. A twenty-two-year-old Villanova master's student in theater policy, Tammi Graves was blond, blue-eyed and brilliant. Except for the fact that she considered him the perfect boyfriend. She thought he was a normal guy with a normal life, a steady CPA for a chain of clubs and restaurants.

It was scary how much she didn't know. Would never know.

Quinn closed his eyes and turned away from Gabriel's intent stare and Shea's unspoken questions.

On the phone, Tammi laughed, a sexy little trill that didn't do a damn thing for him. "No, sweetie, there's nothing wrong. I just wanted to talk. Are you busy? You didn't call last night and I got a little worried."

Christ, he didn't need this now. Not now. He hated this fucking charade. It wasn't fair to Tammi, but Cole Luporeale, Legate of the American *Legio*, the *lucani* army, insisted he put on the show of a normal life, including a human girlfriend.

"I'm fine, Tam. Just busy. Didn't get back to the hotel room until early this morning."

"Where are you staying? The receptionist sounded really strange."

Stifling a slightly hysterical laugh, he took a deep breath. "A dive. Couldn't find a real room. There's some convention in town."

"So when are you coming home? I miss you already."

The pain in his chest tightened and he found himself trying to massage it away. Christ, could this get any worse? "Soon. Listen, I've got to get moving but I'll call you later, okay? We'll make plans for dinner when I get back."

"Okay. Don't work too hard, Quinn."

"Never. See you soon."

By the time he hung up the phone, the weight on his chest had morphed into a blinding pain behind his eyeballs.

Silence reigned in the room. Even Leo seemed to know not to intrude.

Quinn drew back his fist and hit the wall as hard as he could. Fire shot through his arm and shoulder and down his spine. It cleared his mind of everything but the pain. At least this pain would heal.

"Quinn." Gabriel's voice sliced through the tension. He ignored Gabe and pulled back again. Before he connected, Gabriel grabbed his wrist.

"Quinn, you'll break your hand and we don't have the time."

"I hate this, Gabe. I fu—" He caught himself before he singed Leo's ears. "I just hate it."

He looked up, found Gabe nodding in agreement. "I know. It sucks. But the alternative, if you're discovered—if any of us are—is worse. That can't happen."

"I know." He took in a deep breath, held it then let it out again. "I know. But I don't have to like it. She's a nice girl. I don't love her. I'll never love her. She deserves more than that. And so do I."

Gabriel heard the frustration in Quinn's voice, saw the pain in his eyes. He knew where it came from and ached for his best friend. Still, he understood Serena's reasoning. He couldn't resist a quick look at Shea. He understood those reasons too well.

He released Quinn's wrist. "It's been a long day. For all of us. Why don't we chill out for a while, get some rest. I'm hoping Matt will get back to me tonight so we can leave. If that's three in the morning, all the better. Shea." He turned, found her gaze glued to his, questions he didn't want to answer right now in her eyes. "Take Leo back to bed, try to get some sleep. I don't know when we'll go, but when it's time, we'll move fast."

She paused then nodded, and he was almost sorry she didn't fight him. He'd given her an order and typically she didn't take them well. Instead, she nodded at Leo and they left.

His gaze followed them all the way out the door.

When he turned back, Quinn's grin was shaky but there.

Gabriel glared at him. "Don't start, furball. Come on. I want to do a little recon."

* * *

Shea lay with Leo on the bed he'd slept in last night.

He'd fallen asleep the second his head hit the pillow. His sleep patterns were going to be completely screwed up.

Listening to his deep, even breathing in the dark, her hand stroking his back, Shea wasn't tired at all.

Her heart ached for Quinn. She wasn't exactly sure what had happened, but she could piece together enough to make sense. Quinn had a girlfriend who knew nothing about his real life. A life he couldn't disclose without putting a lot of people in danger.

Shea had grown up knowing there were other races in the world besides humans, races like the *lucani* and the winged folletti and the half-hided *salbinelli*.

What would Quinn's girlfriend do if he told her the truth? If he told her he could grow fur and become a wolf?

Would she laugh and think he was joking? Think he was crazy? Would she run screaming if he showed her?

Would she still want him?

She wondered, for like the millionth time, what a normal life would have been like. To grow up in the suburbs with parents who were school teachers or accountants. To believe magic meant pulling a rabbit out of a hat and that people who could scramble your brains with a muttered spell or children who could make things burn with the touch of their hands only existed in the movies.

Would she want to be so clueless?

Blessed Goddess, no.

Sure, there were scary things in the world, but being clueless didn't mean they wouldn't get you. She'd much rather know what was coming.

Which was where her parents had gone wrong. They had withheld information and, somehow, she'd known. She'd run away, thinking she could find answers to all her questions in the outside world.

She hadn't found a damn thing. And her parents had died.

Heavy footsteps stopped outside their door. She forced herself to close her eyes and breathe slowly when Gabriel pushed open the door to the bedroom.

He had to be able to tell she wasn't asleep but he didn't say anything. Seconds later, he pulled the door closed. Seconds after that, she heard them enter a room down the hall.

Might as well forget sleep. She needed a cup of tea.

In the kitchen, waiting for the microwave to finish her water, she stood in the open doorway that led to the garden at the back of the house, barely visible in the deepening shadows of early evening. The scents of oregano, basil, thyme and rose calmed her, reminded her of her mom's greenhouse, where she'd grown her flowers and herbs used in spell-casting.

Stepping out into the garden, she ran her hands over the herbs, plucking a lemon thyme leaf to crush and hold to her nose. The sound of running water caught her ear and she let her gaze run over the garden until she found the small waterfall burbling from a rocky outcrop at the edge of the tree line.

The water flowed in a steady stream out of the earth, down the fall and into a rock pile before seeping back into the ground. Even in the dusk, Shea saw the runes covering each rock. A shrine to the Moon God Tivr. Made sense considering this was a *lucani* safe house and the wolves worshipped the Moon God in particular.

She should make an offering. Even though she wasn't *lucani*, it couldn't hurt to have another god on her side. But she didn't have a traditional votive—a small statue or vase used as an offering.

Looking around, she spied the pale glow of white moon flowers. Perfect.

After snapping off a few blooms, she stood in front of the shrine and pricked her thumb on a sharp rock. Rubbing a few drops of blood on the petals, she tossed the flowers into the water.

"With my blood and this offering, I ask for your protection, Tivr. Lend me your strength to battle those who would harm my brother."

As the flowers hit the water and nestled in among the rocks, a howl split the air. Startled, she took a step away from the spring. Were there real wolves in these forests? Or had Quinn decided to take a stroll?

A gray wolf emerged from the trees, its loping gait steady but not threatening. Stopping at the top of the fall, the animal sat, staring down at her. He was huge and should have made her fear for her life. But Gods, he was gorgeous, sleek and muscular. And there was something about the way he looked at her, something about his eyes…

Oh, wow.

She dropped into a curtsy, the action a completely spontaneous response to the presence of a god.

"Tivr, Lord of the Silver Light. I am honored by your presence."

The wolf didn't come any closer, just stared at her for several moments before inclining his head and letting loose another howl.

Power emanated from him and his beauty amazed her. She wanted to run her fingers through his fur, which looked more luxurious than any mink or sable ever could.

Could you pet a god? Probably not.

So she held her curtsy, even though it hurt her leg to do so, and waited for him to move first.

After a few seconds, he hopped down from the top of the fall to sniff at the flowers she'd offered, then sat at her side, caught her fingers lightly in his teeth and tugged on them. It took her a few seconds to figure out that he wanted her to sit. So she did, cross-legged on the ground in front of the shrine.

Though she knew the Etruscan deities, with the exception of the Involuti, lived among them, she'd never knowingly met one. Should she look him in those silver eyes and tell him what she wanted?

"Yeah, that would probably be a good place to start."

She gasped as the wolf spoke in a perfectly human voice.

Spell Bound

And when he laughed, her mouth dropped open.

"Kinda weird, huh? Wolf talking. You'll get used to it." Tivr sat on his haunches and tilted his head to the side. "So, sweetheart. You got yourself a damn fine mess, don't you?"

For a few brief seconds, Shea considered the possibility that she'd fallen asleep next to Leo and this was all a dream.

"Nope, this is no dream, kid, so just spit it out."

And what could she say that wouldn't sound like whining? She so did not want to whine to a god.

"I'm worried about my brother," she said finally. "I'm afraid I won't be able to protect him. That I'll fail my parents and let something happen to him." She paused, looking up to meet the god's silver gaze. "Do you... Can you..."

She bit her lip. Could she ask a god a question? Was it allowed? Oh, what the hell. "Do you know how to break the curse?"

The wolf shook his head. "Sorry, sweets, I don't. That's between Uni and Menrva and Veive. None of the other gods know either. Believe me, it's not the first time someone's asked."

Despair hit her with the weight of a ton of bricks. If the deities didn't have a clue, then her father's vision was all she had to go on. And that just sucked.

"Hey, now, don't fall apart on me." Tivr nudged her shoulder with his snout, his soft warm fur brushing against her arm. "There's always more than one way to eat a cat, babe. Just because you think you have an idea, doesn't mean it's the right one. Sometimes you need to think outside the box. Besides, change is coming, sweets, and you need to be ready."

The intensity in his tone sent shivers down her back. "Ready for what?"

His fur bristled. "Battle. Gonna be a doozy, too. But then, the *Mal* never did go in for half measures. You need to be ready, babe. You and the kid."

The *Mal*? Battle? Her and Leo in a battle against the *Mal*? Didn't they have enough trouble with Dario?

She shook her head, wondering if she'd fallen and hit her head. Was she hallucinating? Goddess save her, she wished she were because Tivr was starting to freak her out. But she really didn't want to piss off a god by asking too many questions.

"I don't understand."

Tivr sighed, a weird sound coming from a wolf. "No reason you would, huh? Not many do anymore. Used to be, we had temples full of priests and priestesses deciphering our every word." He snorted. "Today, most don't make it to temple once a month. They don't practice the old ways. They turn to the Weather Channel to see if it's going to be a good growing season or watch CNN to know if there's trouble brewing in the world.

"No one studies the skies, the flights of the birds for omens. Those damn PETA people would be all over us if we started slicing up sheep for entrails. Hell, people aren't even afraid of lightning any more, which would really frost Tinia's cookies, if the bastard ever decides to show his face on Earth again."

Her eyes widened at Tivr's blasphemy but he didn't take notice.

"The old ways are ignored but we need them, sweets. We knew when we followed our people to the new world...we knew change was on the way."

He turned and his mouth curved in a toothy grin.

"And you're the front guard. You and your brother. The kid's strong. So are you. Gabriel's a good man to have at your back and so is Quinn. Things'll work out. You'll see. They have to. Just don't make any rash decisions."

As the wolf rose to his paws, Shea remained seated and bowed her spinning head. "Thank you for your counsel, Lord Tivr."

"Don't mention it. And I mean that seriously. This little section of woods has become my sanctuary. I'd like to keep it that way. See you around, sweets."

With a final howl, the wolf turned and disappearing back into the forest.

Holy crap. She'd just had a conversation with a god.

She needed to talk to Gabriel.

* * *

Wrapped in the power of the spell he and Quinn were working, Gabriel wasn't aware of Shea's presence until he heard her step into the second-floor map room behind them.

He'd known she wasn't asleep when he'd stuck his head in the bedroom, but he hadn't disturbed her. They could all do with down time.

Besides, he needed to get her off his mind. He'd been thinking about her way too damn much. And there was too much at stake for him to forgo common sense and lose himself in her body for one night.

But, damn, he wanted to.

His tongue tripped over a word and he felt the power around him shift. Shit. He needed to concentrate. He was searching for signatures, life signatures that would pinpoint any persons of Etruscan descent in a fifty-mile radius. His father could have done a hundred miles, but he wasn't that good. Quinn's connection to the forces that had built this safe house boosted his powers slightly. It would have to be enough. He couldn't allow anything—

"Shit!"

He broke the connection with Quinn and the spell when he realized the stupid mistake he'd just made.

He turned to find Shea's eyes had rolled back into her head and she remained upright only because her knees had locked.

"Shea, downstairs. Now."

"Gabriel, I can hear them. The voices. They're—"

He didn't wait for her to finish. He ran for her, catching her just as her legs buckled. Holding her against his chest, he took the stairs two at a time back to the first floor.

She was incoherent by the time he got her into the first bedroom he came to.

"Damn, I'm sorry, babe." He placed her on the bed, completely pissed. "Fuck."

"Christ, Gabe. Is she okay?" Quinn asked from behind him.

He shook his head, his gaze glued to Shea. "I don't know. Hey, babe, can you hear me?"

She didn't answer. She had her eyes squeezed tightly shut but two tears ran from the corners. He wanted to kick something. How could he have been so stupid not to realize what that room would do to her?

When the hell was he going to stop failing those who needed him?

* * *

Spell Bound

Shea never really passed out.

She knew what was going on around her, could hear Gabriel and Quinn talking, heard Quinn leave. She couldn't speak to tell them she was okay, but she thought she was.

She just couldn't make her body obey her commands because she was listening to the voices in her head. For the first time in her life, she heard them clearly. Distinct voices, all speaking at the same time.

She knew what those voices were now.

When they started to fade, she opened her eyes and looked directly into Gabriel's dark, worried gaze.

"Déjà vu, huh?" She smiled, thankful there were no painful side effects from...whatever had happened.

He shook his head and the grooves on his forehead deepened. "I screwed up and you paid. How do you feel?"

"Actually," she swung her legs over the side of the bed so she could sit up, "I feel fine."

Gabriel's hands settled with a warm, steady weight on her shoulders. "Don't move around too much. You might feel okay lying down, but—"

"I'm okay, Gabriel. Really." She couldn't help but smile up at him. "I heard them. The voices. Really heard them. I could understand what they were saying, what they've been trying to tell me for so long."

He released her shoulders and sat back on the chair he'd pulled to the side of the bed. "What do you mean?"

She grimaced as she held up a hand. "Don't look at me like that. I'm not going crazy. I heard them. They're not figments of my imagination or schizophrenia."

Gabriel's arms crossed over his chest, and his eyebrows lifted, his expression skeptical. "Oh yeah? So what are they?"

Without thinking, she reached out to cup his jaw with her hands, the rough scrape of his whiskers dazzling her skin. "It's the women. The cursed *streghe*."

His expression shifted, became wary. "How do you know?"

"Because I heard my mother."

He froze for a split second and she saw astonishment quickly followed by doubt flash through his eyes.

Her chest tightened, and she blinked back sudden tears. Damn it, that shouldn't hurt. She drew back but not fast enough. He caught her hands before she could get far. Still, the damage had been done.

He didn't believe her. And she cursed him for making her doubt herself.

"Shea, wait."

"Fuck you, Gabriel." She lashed out before she could help herself then shook her head, trying to tug her hands away from his. He held on, not enough to hurt, just enough to let her know he wasn't going to let go.

"Okay, sure." He nodded as if she'd asked him to clean out her car or feed the dog. "If that's what you want, no problem."

She knew he was just trying to get a rise out of her but her breath stuttered in her lungs at the image that popped into her head of Gabriel and her and a bed—

Shit. "Gabriel—"

"Shea, just give me a minute here, okay? I'm not saying I don't believe you."

That brought her chin up. "I don't need you to believe me. I know what I know. I have to go back and try to understand—"

He nodded, his jaw losing the stubborn edge it nearly always wore. "Fine. Great." He tugged on her hands, wanting her to look up. But she knew if she did, she'd get more pissed off and take a swing at that strong jaw. Or kiss it. "I'm glad you know what's going on. But you're not going back up there."

"What? Why?" Now she did meet his gaze and hers was blazing. "Who the hell do you think you are to tell me what to do?"

"Shea, listen to me. That room will drain you dry. It might even kill you."

"What are you talking about?" She pulled away, and this time he let her go. Damn him, she did not miss the warmth of his hands. She scowled that much harder.

"*Versipelli* energy is drawn from nature," he said. "It's not inherent, like in the *streghe*. The *versipelli* built that room to funnel power. It intensified your innate power before funneling it right out of you. If you'd stayed much longer, it would have killed you."

His expression twisted again, and he shook his head, drawing her gaze to his dark hair. He'd lost the leather band that had been holding it back and it waved over his shoulders. He had beautiful hair, almost too pretty to be a guy's.

"I wasn't thinking." He rose and started to pace. "I should have told you to go when I realized you were there. God damn it, you could have been really hurt, Shea."

He was pissed. She saw it in the way he stalked around the room.

"Gabriel—"

"You're not going back in there." He slashed a hand in front of him with so much force she swore she heard it slap the air. "So don't even think about it."

She sucked in a sharp breath, ready to let him have it, the stubborn, overbearing, pompous—

He slammed his fist into the wall by the door, exactly as Quinn had earlier today. She swore she heard bones crunch.

"Gabriel!" She jumped off the bed and ran to him, grabbed his hand before he could do it again. "You idiot. What the hell are you doing?"

"*Vaffanculo*, Shea, you could have been killed."

She looked up and found him staring at her, fear and anger making his dark eyes wild. He was mad at himself, she realized, not with her. It was a strange, warm feeling, to have someone worry about her. It'd been so long.

She took a deep breath and reached for calm. Gabriel had enough mad for the both of them right now. "I'm fine. Gabriel, really. I'm better than fine. Let me see your hand."

He didn't move, didn't speak, just stared at her. She couldn't handle that intensity for long and dropped her gaze to their hands. His knuckles were raw and bleeding. She felt his pain as if it were his own, felt it in her gut. Her Gift reached out to fix him, to make him better.

Or maybe it was the woman who wanted to take him in her arms and—

He flipped his hand and laced his fingers through hers.

She watched their fingers slide together, felt the roughness of his skin against hers. She blinked when he raised his free hand and tilted her chin up so he could look into her eyes.

He drew in a breath and she knew, before he lowered his mouth, that he wanted to kiss her.

Oh, please, yes.

She wanted him to kiss her, wanted that connection, to taste him again…

Spell Bound

At the last second, he closed his eyes and let his head drop back.

"We need to get the hell out of here." He drew in a deep breath and released her hand. "You're screwing with my head. It's not your fault. It's mine."

"I'm not—"

Gabriel exhaled one short, hard breath. "Shea. Please. Just…give it a rest."

She opened her mouth to give him a piece of her mind, but his expression made her pause. Worry showed in the furrows of his forehead and the flat line of his mouth. And that made her swallow anything she might have said.

Taking a deep breath, Gabriel released her hands. "We're leaving, as soon as we can get the hell away from here. Get your stuff together and wake Leo. I'm going back upstairs to finish what I started."

He looked straight into her eyes, worry firmly entrenched there, as well. "I don't want you anywhere near that room. Do you understand?"

It took everything she had to keep quiet when she simultaneously wanted to beat him over the head and kiss him. Instead, she managed a short nod, jaw clamped tight. He responded with a nod of his own and walked out.

Chapter Thirteen

The trip was uneventful.

And deadly silent.

Gabriel sat at the wheel of the Jeep Wrangler he'd traded for the Audi at the safe house, still berating himself.

Shea and Leo huddled in the backseat, while an unusually silent Quinn sat in the front. They were headed to Crimson Moon, Serena's compound outside Reading, and Quinn was probably trying to figure out what to say to her.

And he sat here, trying not to think about the female in the back seat. She'd finally fallen asleep about fifteen minutes ago, Leo's head on her shoulder. She hadn't spoken to him since they'd left the safe house.

It bugged the crap out of him.

It shouldn't. He shouldn't even be thinking about her. But he couldn't stop.

And he had a lot of damn time to think. He knew the way to the compound on the northeastern side of the city as well as he knew his own name. Located in the forest that covered Mt. Penn, on a narrow path that wound up the mountain, the house was disguised by a complex series of spells and wards that no one who didn't know the correct procedure to bypass them would ever get through.

Quinn shifted on the seat beside him, and Gabriel heard him take a deep breath then release it. These woods had always called to Quinn, just as they called to Serena.

Which made sense, considering Serena and Niccolo, her husband at the time of the curse, had been blood-bound, their souls tied together throughout eternity.

And Quinn, according to Serena, held Niccolo's soul.

Hell, if being blood-bound to another person made you as miserable as Quinn and Serena... Yeah, he'd take a pass.

Gabriel slowed then brought the car to a stop. "You want to get out and stretch your legs before we get up there?"

A weak grin surfaced on Quinn's face as he stared out the front window. "Want a little time alone with Shea, huh?"

Gabriel rolled his eyes. "*Vaffanculo, ceffo.*"

"Dude, I got eyes. Not that I blame you. She's great. And she looks at you like you hung the moon."

Gabriel flashed a look in the rearview, making sure Shea was still asleep. "*Baciami il culo*, Quinn. She's a job."

But even as he said it, he knew it was a lie.

And he knew Quinn wasn't buying it, if his shit-eating grin was anything to go by. "She's smart and strong and she doesn't take your shit. She's not too hard on the eyes, either."

Gabriel shook his head but couldn't dispute a word of it.

Still, he knew why Quinn was picking at him. "Maybe now, with Shea... Maybe Serena will—"

Quinn's snort cut him off. "You know her better than that, Gabriel. She's even more stubborn than you. And it's eating me alive. I've been sitting here dreading this but so damn excited to see her I'm shaking. She's never going to give in. And for my own sanity, I've gotta hear her tell me to get lost, so I can get on with my life." Quinn turned to face him, his expression set in hard lines. "You know I took the Bullet to get through college, right?"

Gabriel nodded. The Bullet was a dangerous cocktail of drugs laced with silver nitrate. It allowed *versipelli* to control their change during full moons when the urge is most powerful, especially for the younger males.

"I hated it," Quinn continued. "Hated that it made me feel dead. You have a switch inside, Gabe, that helps you do what the Bullet does for me. I used to think you were a cold bastard, the way you could turn off your emotions. Now, I think you're the luckiest man in the world."

"No, Quinn—"

Quinn talked right over him, his eyes staring blankly out the front window. "Did I ever tell you what they used to call me at college? The Monk. So, not only was I an honest-to-God freak with a secret I couldn't tell anyone, but the guys I lived with thought I was a completely different kind of freak."

The pain in his friend's voice made Gabriel flinch. He'd known Quinn had been unhappy at Penn State, but he hadn't realized how miserable he'd really been. "Hey, man, we're all freaks in some way. You grow fur. I can stop a bullet in midair."

Quinn frowned, drawing lines between his eyes. "You know I went out with a couple of girls in college, right? I never wanted one of them. Not Tammi, either. How freaky is that? I can't live like this anymore. The past six years have been hell, knowing I can't have the one person destined for me. How bad's it going to be if I let it go on another ten or fifteen years?"

Quinn turned away to open the door, but Gabriel caught his arm before he could get out. "Serena loves you. Maybe you just need to show her how much."

Blue eyes considerably dimmed, Quinn shook his head. "I wish I had your switch, Gabe. I brought a couple doses of Bullet. They're in my bag. Just wanted you to know, so if I start acting weird, you'll know why. I'll see you up there."

Quinn opened the door and stood then shed his clothes and dropped them on the front seat.

"Hey," Gabriel called to him before he took off. "Don't be too long."

"Yes, Mother." Quinn flipped him off, shook his hair back from his face and let the change roll.

The movies had gotten it more or less right about werewolves, the thought passed fleetingly through Gabriel's mind. It was painful but worth the grace of the animal.

Quinn rarely talked about the pain, but the howl that erupted from his throat as his spine contorted, his muscles lengthened and his bones reformed said it all.

A soft gasp from the backseat made him look in the rearview mirror. He saw Leo staring out the window with wide eyes. Shea remained asleep, one arm still around Leo's shoulders.

"Is Quinn okay?" Leo's voice quivered in the grayish-pink light of dawn.

"Yeah, he's fine. He's almost done."

Quinn was on all fours now, his back humped as his hands and feet curled into paws and his skin erupted with fur.

With a final shake, Quinn's tail unfurled behind him and he turned to look at them with his human eyes. With a howl, he shot off into the forest without looking back. Gabriel figured Quinn would need at least an hour before he showed up at Serena's door.

"Does it hurt?" Leo asked in a quiet voice.

Gabriel put the car in gear and started up the hill again. "Yeah, but Quinn says it's a fair trade, the pain for the pelt."

"What's the pelt?"

"His fur." He hit the edge of a nasty pothole and the car bucked. "Shit. Hold on, kid. This lane's a bitch."

"Gabriel, watch your language."

Shea had woken and, of course, the first thing she heard was his foul mouth. Just add it to the list.

He didn't bother to answer because it took all of his concentration to stay on what little there was of a road. Neither Shea nor Leo complained about the ride, although he heard them hit the sides of the car more than a few times.

When they reached the end of the line, and he turned off the engine, Leo was the first to see the house. Gabriel could tell by his hushed, "Wow."

If you didn't know what you were looking for, you could walk right by and not know you'd passed it. Built entirely of wood, with no windows in the walls but plenty of skylights, the one-story house rambled for close to a city block. Bark lined the outer walls, blending the building into the trees. Though the house was fully electrified and plumbed, you'd never know it from the outside.

Even the stone chimney was camouflaged, due in large part to a heavy network of spells.

"We'll park in the underground garage then meet Serena."

None of them said a word as he drove around to the side of the building. After he'd muttered a spell and clicked a remote he pulled from his pants pocket, the wall split open to reveal a descending ramp.

The sun had finally dawned and the light held a hazy blue hue. Then the garage door closed and the overhead lights flickered on, shutting off the outside world completely.

The power, the magic, in the structure of the building shimmered like a low-frequency hum in the air. If you stayed long enough, you got used to it. He hoped like hell it didn't trigger another one of Shea's migraines.

Gabriel had the bags out of the car before Shea and Leo climbed from the backseat. The kid hung close to her side, eyes wide. Her mouth set in a straight line, Shea took Leo's hand and tugged him even closer.

Gabriel fought the urge to pull them both into his arms and ease the fear on their faces. In the short time he'd had them, they'd gotten under his skin. And that, he knew from first-hand experience, could be deadly.

If he wanted to keep them safe, he shouldn't let them get close.

But isolation sucked and he was sick of living in a vacuum.

"Come on, let's get inside." He waved them up the stairs to a door at the top. "Serena's waiting."

* * *

Watching Gabriel open the door, Shea had the irrational urge to run. To take Leo and go somewhere no one would find them.

Which is what you tried to do for a year and look how that had turned out.

An insidious fear had started to creep up on Shea since they'd left the safe house, a panicky weight that settled on her chest and constricted her breathing.

Would Serena, a five-hundred-year-old *strega*, want to offer Shea up on a plate to Dario if Shea revealed what her grandfather had written in his journal?

Or would Serena have another theory on breaking the curse, one that didn't end with a knife in Shea's chest?

Hope and fear made her chest tight. Damn it, she was no coward. She wanted answers. If she wanted to get Dario off Leo's back, she needed to be strong.

Leo's thin arm snaked around her back, hugged her closer. She looked down, expecting to see fear in his eyes.

"It'll be okay," he whispered.

So young to be so solemn. She blinked back tears and forced steel into her spine. "I know, bud. Come on, let's get this done. You and me, just like it's been for the past year."

"And Gabriel and Quinn."

Her smile faltered for just a second. "Yeah. Them, too."

With one last hug, she took Leo's hand and forced air into her lungs before she walked through the door into a homey, cottage-style kitchen.

Just in time to see a beautiful, dark-haired woman run one, slim-fingered hand down Gabriel's cheek while the blasted man smiled at her. Something sharp and mean cut across her chest, some emotion that made Shea want to run her nails across the woman's perfect cheekbones.

The voices immediately rose up in opposition. They wanted her to get closer, to embrace the woman. They missed her. Shea felt their longing as an almost physical ache.

Shit.

Spell Bound

Her entire body stiffened, muscles quivering, ready to run. Away or straight into Gabriel's arms? Hell, she couldn't do either.

Finally, the woman, who couldn't have been more than thirty, turned to her with a sad smile that looked remarkably like Gabriel's.

"Shea. Leo." She stepped toward them, her arms lifting just a bit before falling back to her side as Gabriel moved around her to stand next to Shea. "I'm so pleased to meet you. And so very sorry about your parents. Your mother was my best friend. I miss her everyday."

God, the woman's voice. Her accent was just the same as her mom's. The one that came from English being her third language.

"Yeah, well, she never talked about you other than to say you were one of the priestesses."

Damn. She wanted to take the words back the second they left her mouth. She was being petty but her default setting lately was smart ass.

Banding her arms around Leo's shoulders, she pulled him back against her, drawing strength from his warm body. She flicked a glance at Gabriel, now leaning against the wall at her side, arms folded across his chest. Watching her.

He'd been ready to kiss this woman.

And that matters why?

Serena's expression didn't change. "No, dear, and I understand why. She and your father disappeared soon after you were conceived, as far as I can calculate. If I'd known what was going to happen…"

Despair hit Shea low in the stomach, as if she'd been sucker-punched. A reaction to the same emotion in Serena's voice.

"Not your fault." And it wasn't, not any of it. "I'm sorry, it's been…"

Shit, how did she finish that? Shea stared straight into the other woman's odd, shattered eyes—that exactly mirrored her own. The exact same eyes as her mother.

Serena just shook her head. "Shea, please. You have no need for apologies."

Serena turned to Leo then, and her smile returned. "Welcome, Leo. I must say you look very much like your father. He was such a handsome man."

"Was" being the operative word, Shea thought with a painful lurch of her heart.

Serena's smile faded as she met Shea's gaze again. "I know we have a lot to talk about, but maybe you'd like to have something to eat or take a shower? Maybe Leo would like a nap?"

Leo shook his head, but didn't speak.

Serena nodded. "That's fine, too. I understand Gabriel has started your training and that you're doing very well." Serena looked to the door then looked at Gabriel. "Is…Quinn still in the garage?"

"He needed to stretch his legs," Gabriel said.

Serena nodded slowly and sighed, a hint of a shake in it. "Good. That's good. Then why don't you show Shea and Leo their rooms and, when you return, we'll figure out what happens next. I'll be in the kitchen. I'm sure you're all hungry…and Quinn will need to eat."

Serena moved toward Gabriel with a loose-limbed and utterly confident gait. Her old-fashioned peasant dress swirled around her bare legs and she wore no shoes. She appeared utterly comfortable in her skin.

Guess that's to be expected after five-hundred years.

Raising both hands to his cheeks in a gentle caress,

Spell Bound

Serena then slid her fingers into the softness of his hair, letting the strands slip across her skin.

Shea's fingers curled into her palms at the intimacy of the action. Serena smiled, and Shea knew why. Gabriel's hair felt like silk. She knew the pleasure to be had from running her fingers through it. She would never admit it to Gabriel, but she loved his hair.

And another woman had her hands in it.

Her fingers itched to scratch Serena's eyes out, which really would've been a stupid-ass move. But, Goddess, she wanted to. And when Serena stood on tiptoes to press a kiss to each cheek, Shea felt her nails break through the skin on her palms and forced herself to unclench her fists.

Shit, this was so not good.

When the other woman walked out of the room, Gabriel turned back to Shea.

His hair a little mussed from the other woman's fingers, he looked sexy and kissable. And she wanted to smack the man.

What was his relationship with Serena? And why the hell had he kissed her back at the safe house if he had a relationship with Serena? Bastard.

His eyes caught hers, and she tried to unclench her jaw, to force the tension from her body. To hide her jealous reaction. Which just pissed her off more.

Of course, she didn't fool him, not if the hint of a smirk on his lips was any indication.

"Come on," he said. "I'll show you your room. I figure you'll want to stay with Leo."

He led them through the house but Shea had too much on her mind to notice her surroundings. Leo had a death grip on her hand, and she wasn't about to let him go.

Halfway down a hall full of doors, Gabriel opened

one, stepped in and took a quick look then waved them through.

Shea registered four walls, two beds, a large armoire and an attached bath. No pictures, no TV, no personality.

Leo headed straight for the attached bathroom, closing the door behind him, leaving Shea standing in the middle of the room.

Gabriel walked up behind her and put his arms around her shoulders, pulling her back against his hard chest.

She stiffened even as she soaked in the warmth of his large body. Damn, she really shouldn't like the sense of being enclosed by him as much as she did. Everything was so complicated right now and adding her feelings for Gabriel to the mix just made everything seem like a powder keg doused in gasoline.

Still…was it so wrong to want to be safe?

"Take a deep breath."

His words slid past her ear on a warm breath, stoking the fire in her blood. She'd been so cold only a moment ago and now her skin burned where he held her against him. But it wasn't only her skin that burned. It was a place deep inside that burned as well.

"And drop the attitude," he murmured in her ear.

His hands shifted around her shoulders as she turned to meet his gaze. "Is she your lover?"

The full-blown smile she'd longed for days to see on his face made her stomach flip.

"She's my mother."

Chapter Fourteen

Gabriel's grin spread as Shea's jaw unhinged.
"Your mother?"
"Yeah."
"But...but she's..." She broke off and looked down, her mouth beginning to tremble at the corners. "Oh, hell. I'm completely lost here, Gabriel. I don't know what to think anymore. There's just too much...too much I don't understand, too... How old are you?"

He took the non sequitor in stride, his hands firm on her shoulders in case she fainted. She had that look. "Twenty-eight."

"If you're her son, then you have two sisters who were cursed at the same time as your mom, according to the history."

He nodded. "Maddie and Furia. You'll like them. They're a lot like you. Stubborn, strong. Mouthy. I love them both, but Furia's got issues."

Something else I'll make Dario pay for.

Shea nodded and, for a second, he thought she might lean into him. He wanted her to lean on him, wanted her to need him and damn the consequences.

The door to the bathroom opened and Leo walked out. Shea pulled away, making his hands drop, and turned to smile at the kid. "Think you can eat something, bud?"

Leo looked from Shea to him, his gaze considering. Gabriel stood a little taller and looked the boy right in the eyes.

"Are you gonna take Shea away?"

Smart kid. No one had said anything, but somehow Leo had picked up on the plans. "Yeah. Shea and I have someone we need to see."

"Will Quinn stay?"

"I don't know." He hoped so, for Quinn's sake and for Serena's and Leo's. "He will, if he can. And there's someone coming to take over your training, someone I think you're going to like."

Leo's mouth quivered. "But...I like you."

His heart twisted in his chest. This shouldn't hurt so damn much but he was already in deep with these two. "I like you, too. But your sister and I have something to do."

Leo blinked, as if trying to hold back tears. "I'm not supposed to leave Sissy, not ever. And I could help."

Gabriel kneeled down to look into Leo's eyes. "I'm sure you could help. But you need to train, too. And we won't be gone long."

Leo just stared and Gabriel could tell the kid was about to lose it.

The tightness in his throat told Gabriel he was, too. He stood, not all that steady himself. He didn't want to leave the kid behind. But it was the right thing to do. "Don't worry about it now, bud. Come on. Let's find something to eat."

* * *

Another pot slipped from her hand, making a jarring clatter as Serena tried to put a meal together. That was the

Spell Bound

second pot she'd dropped. If she wasn't careful, she'd break something. She'd nearly cut her finger off slicing the ham—

"Serena."

Gasping, she dropped that pot one more time.

Sweet Mother Goddess, she hadn't heard Quinn enter the kitchen. That was dangerous. The boy slipped through her defenses in more ways than one.

And that voice. Goddess bless her, his voice tugged at her very soul.

She caught herself just before she turned and threw herself at him, which would have been completely embarrassing for a woman of her age. She drew in a deep breath, trying to calm her racing heart before she faced him.

Oh...Goddess. This was why she stayed locked in her house on a hill.

He stood in the doorway, sweaty, intense and, Goddess help her, completely naked.

And no longer a boy.

If she was honest with herself, Quinn hadn't been a boy for six years. Still, he was young. And so damn mortal.

"Are you hungry?" She refused to back down from his stare. "I've got pancakes, eggs, bacon, ham, home fries." Because she knew he loved all of them.

Jaw set, he nodded. "You know I am. I need a shower first, but after I eat, I'm leaving. Gabriel called Matt, so they won't need me. I'm not staying."

Her heart contracted in her chest until she was sure she was having a heart attack. "Where are you going?"

He looked at her with weary blue eyes, his beautiful face set in stern lines that looked so out of place there. Those lines were her fault.

"I'm tired of this game, Serena. Tired of waiting. You won." He moved toward her and she struggled to keep her gaze from slipping lower than his chin as he got right in her face. "But here's something to think about, babe. Until you decide to take another lover who isn't me."

She should have seen it coming. Should have known he was going to kiss her. Maybe she had. Maybe she didn't care. She closed her eyes and shut off her brain.

Quinn wrapped wiry-strong arms around her shoulders, brought her body flush against his and took her mouth in one perfect motion. His lips, hot and firm, devoured and devastated. The heat of his naked body blasted through the thin cotton of her dress, and the musky scent of his sweat made her sex clench in response.

Quinn groaned deep in his throat, and his body surged against hers. His erection hardened against her stomach and his kiss became more powerful, more desperate.

His lips ate at hers with a hunger she echoed, and her mouth opened to allow his tongue in. His taste seeped into her blood-stream like a fast-acting drug, tantalizing her nerve endings and making her head spin.

She shouldn't respond, for both their sakes. But she couldn't help herself. This was her man, the man she'd always loved, would always love. Couldn't live without. Couldn't bear to lose him again.

Her arms rose to snake around his waist—and he shoved away from her.

Eyes wide, bare chest heaving, Quinn looked as shocked as she felt. She didn't know how long they stood there, staring at each other. She couldn't help but hope he wasn't done. That he didn't have the strength to walk away from her. Because she knew if he took her in his arms again, it would be the end of her resistance. She would give herself to him because she wouldn't be able to stop, wouldn't want to stop.

Then his eyes closed and he groaned, just a small sound at the back of his throat.

"Gods-be-damned, I love you, Serena. It's in my genes, for fuck's sake. But I can't live like this. If you don't want me, then tell me. I'll find someone who does, someone who won't turn me away."

Without looking at her again, he walked out of the room.

Despair tore through her body with poisonous agony. Images of Quinn with faceless women bombarded her brain. She didn't want to imagine him with anyone else, couldn't bear to think of some other woman's hands on his lean body or sinking into his shaggy blond hair.

Though Quinn had the soul of her mate, she also knew he was just Quinn. Niccolo had rarely smiled and his mood had scarcely wavered. Quinn's smile appeared at the slightest provocation and his mood could change in a blink. His fierce loyalty to his family and friends was legendary, but Goddess forbid if you got on his bad side. He could be intractable.

Like now. He wanted all or nothing.

And either would tear her heart out of her chest.

* * *

They sat down to eat in the kitchen around eight. Tension hung in the air like smoke, and Gabriel had had just about as much as he could take.

The kid was too tired to talk so he just shoveled food.

Shea looked shell-shocked and only managed a couple of mouthfuls before she started pushing food around her plate.

Quinn couldn't take his eyes off Serena, and Serena didn't look at anyone as she floated between the stove and the table, refilling bowls and picking at a few pieces of melon. She never could eat when she was worried. Stress showed in the furrows on her forehead and the ashen pallor beneath her skin.

Gabriel knew his mother. He knew she was worried about Quinn, worried about Shea. But it was Leo that had her tied in knots at the moment.

He'd caught the look of absolute desolation in her eyes when she'd first seen him. The same look Gabriel probably had the night Shea came to his door in Reading.

Leo looked so much like Nino. Her dead son. The brother Gabriel hadn't been able to save.

Christ, they were lucky the house didn't explode from the tension.

"So, Quinn," Gabriel asked the first question that came to mind that didn't deal with a touchy subject. "How's the new club in Jersey?"

Quinn jerked then shook his head as if to clear it. "Good. We're almost ready to open."

"You gonna work there for a while?"

"Yeah, then I thought I'd head out to Vegas, see how the casino's holding up."

At the sink, Serena dropped the plates she'd been holding, pottery clattering on porcelain.

Quinn's eyes narrowed as he continued. "After that, I don't know. Maybe I'll head overseas for a vacation. A few months away might do me some good."

Serena stiffened but continued to stack dishes in the sink.

Gabriel knew what Quinn was up to, knew he was pushing her. At any other time, he'd be okay with it. But not now. Not—

"That sounds great," Shea said. "A vacation sounds great right about now."

She said it in a teasing tone but the longing in her voice made Gabriel's stomach twist. He wished he could take her and Leo away. Make it safe for them to go to Disney World or the Grand Canyon or hell, even the Jersey shore for a weekend.

"Somewhere with a beach," Leo added, his little-boy enthusiasm digging the knife just a little deeper in Gabriel's gut.

"Sure, bud," Shea answered. "Somewhere with a beach."

The sorrow in Shea's voice sent that knife straight up into his heart. He knew she thought that trip would never happen.

And Gabriel's hatred for Dario burned through his blood like acid.

Carefully, he put down his utensils before he bent them like matchsticks.

Luckily, the kid's mouth cracked open with a huge yawn and Shea smiled.

And the dagger in his heart became an ache in his groin. Damn, he did not want to be sporting an erection right now.

"Time for bed, isn't it?" Shea said.

Serena frowned, flashing a look at Gabriel.

"Shea worked nights, so she and Leo slept during the day," Gabriel answered Serena's unspoken question.

"Oh, really," Serena said. "What did you do, Shea?"

"I was a dancer."

"Really? I love the ballet—"

"I worked for Harry." She never lowered her gaze, but Gabriel knew she was waiting for Serena's condescension. "It paid the bills. I had aspirations of being a ballerina, but they never panned out."

"Sissy's a great dancer," Leo piped in.

"I'm sure she is." Serena smiled at the boy, meeting his eyes for only a brief second before looking back at Shea. "There's a studio in the house. My daughter Madrona had it built years ago so she could practice her yoga. It doesn't get much use now, but the floor's wooden and there are mirrors. You could practice if you like."

Shea's expression eased a little. "Thanks, I might take you up on it. It's been a few days since I stretched and my muscles are starting to tighten."

"What about you, Leo?" Serena's eyes skimmed the boy before going back to the dishes she was washing in the sink. "What do you like to do?"

Quinn's sharply indrawn breath drew Gabriel's attention. His golden skin went pale beneath his tan and his fingers tightened around the fork in his hand.

Quinn looked like he'd taken a blow to the head. Seemed he'd finally realized why Serena was so upset. Christ, he could practically see Quinn berating himself for his insensitivity earlier, watched his gaze shift back to Serena. Quinn's desire to take Serena in his arms was written all over his face.

Did he look at Shea like that?

Vaffanculo. He hoped he wasn't that transparent.

Leo's second yawn cut through the tension as Shea gave a shaky laugh.

"Come on, bud." She held out her hand to the boy. "Let's get some sleep."

Spell Bound

Leo hopped off his chair but stopped at Gabriel's side, wide eyes looking straight into his. "Will you come, too?"

He didn't even have to think about his answer. "Sure, kid."

But he paused before he got up as his gaze caught Shea's. He saw warmth there and something he couldn't interpret. Didn't she want him to come? Hell, she'd just have to get used to him being around because...Oh, hell, he couldn't even finish the thought.

Idiot. You're such an idiot.

He stood, watching Shea's expression. When she smiled, the knot in his stomach loosened.

After a quick glance at Quinn, staring at the table, and his mom, staring into the sink, he took Leo's hand and walked him and Shea back to their room.

The kid was fading fast, and Shea looked like she needed a break. Hell, they all needed a break. He knew he needed to get back to the kitchen before Serena and Quinn started in on each other and said things they couldn't take back.

Leo went straight to the bed, kicking off his shoes and jeans before pulling down the covers and crawling beneath. Shea toed off her shoes, leaving her clothes in place, then lay on top on the comforter, drawing the kid into the curve of her body.

Gabriel wanted to lie behind her, wrap his arms around both of them and ignore the rest of the world for a while.

Since the deaths of his dad and brother, his need to shed Dario's blood had buried any tender feelings he might have had for anyone. He'd let anger and despair dictate his life. Shea and Leo made him realize what he'd been missing.

His feet moved, taking him closer to the bed. His knees bent and he sat on the edge.

Shea's hair lay like dark silk on the pale blue comforter and he sank one hand into its softness, weaving his fingers through the strands.

Those shattered-glass eyes caught and held his. Heat pooled in his groin, making his cock thicken in anticipation.

Did Shea want him just as much?

He refused to examine her aura, afraid he wouldn't see her answering desire for him.

Instead, he forced himself to look at the kid, staring up at him, as well.

"You okay, Leo?"

The kid nodded, his eyes already half closed. "Don't leave, 'kay?"

Gabriel's heart contracted. "I'll be in the house the whole time, Leo. I'm not going anywhere." Not yet, anyway.

"'kay."

Leo's eyes closed, and Gabriel swore the kid was asleep already.

His gaze returned to Shea's, watching him closely. "You up for talking to Serena or you want some time?"

She didn't answer him right away, her hand rubbing Leo's back in small circles. "I think your mom's probably anxious to talk, don't you?"

"She's waited five-hundred years, Shea. Another few hours aren't gonna matter."

Nodding, Shea's lips lifted in a slight smile. That smile lit his libido like a match to a firecracker. Time to get out of here. Still…

He leaned over and laid his lips on his hers. He didn't

linger and it wasn't sweet. There was no tongue and he didn't touch her anywhere else. But he needed that connection, no matter how brief.

Their eyes met and held for a brief second before hers closed, and he felt her lips soften, conform. Yield.

Lust roared up but he shut it down in heartbeat. This wasn't the time.

But later…

When he straightened, she looked a little less pale.

"Come out when you're ready," he said. "Take all the time you need."

Then he headed back to the kitchen to put out the fire there.

* * *

As soon as Gabriel left the room with Shea and Leo, Quinn started to apologize.

"Jesus, Serena, I'm an idiot. I'm so sorry for acting like an ass."

He'd been so caught up in his own drama that he'd failed to realize the memories Leo would trigger in Serena. Christ, the kid looked so much Nino with his dark hair and eyes.

Serena stood at the sink, her back to him. "There's nothing to be sorry for." She turned on the water and started washing dishes. "Are you finished?"

He stood and walked to her side, dishes in hand. He wanted her to turn to him for comfort, wanted to wrap his arms around her and ease the loss he saw in her eyes. "Yeah, I'm finished. You never talk about him. Maybe you should."

Serena shook her head but wouldn't look up.

"There's nothing to talk about. I have to live with his death. Not you."

His arms ached to hold her but knew she wouldn't allow it. And he didn't think he could stand to be refused again. "I'm still sorry." As he put his dishes in the sink, he heard Gabriel leave Leo's room and head toward them. "I'll leave you and Gabriel alone to talk strategy."

"Quinn." Serena finally looked at him. "Please."

His heart dropped into his stomach then flew back up to his throat. He didn't know what she was trying to say, didn't know how to read her expression.

This whole situation was completely screwed up.

"Quinn, I…"

Gabriel walked into the room.

"Hey. Everything okay?"

Quinn could have cheerfully strangled him. But Shea and Leo needed him too much.

Serena released his gaze to turn to her son. "We're fine. Have you heard from Matt?"

Gabe put his arm around his mother's shoulders and drew her close. Serena slid her arms around his waist and held on for a few moments before stepping away. It made him feel like an ass for being jealous of his best friend, but Quinn wanted to be the one Serena needed.

"No, not yet. But he'll call. And when he gets here, Shea and I'll leave for New Orleans. Right now, I want to make sure we weren't followed." Gabe's gaze locked onto Quinn. "I need you to give me a hand."

Quinn shook his head, needing to be gone. He'd done enough damage already. "You don't need me. Let Shea—"

Gabe cut him off. "No. It'll go faster if we do this together."

And it would keep him here longer.

"Gabe—"

"Quinn." Gabe's voice lowered but took on intensity. "I need you."

Quinn didn't say anything. Gabriel was his brother in all ways but blood and the one person Quinn knew he could count on unconditionally.

He took a deep breath and let it out with a muttered, "Fuck." Then he shook his head and set his jaw. "Fine. Let's do this."

Chapter Fifteen

Shea sat on the bed next to Leo, rubbing his back, even though she knew he was asleep.

Poor guy was completely worn out from stress, excitement and fear.

Not a good combination for anyone, much less a six-year-old boy whose parents had been murdered and who could make grown men scream just by touching them.

Staring down at him, she saw her parents in his every feature. The ever-present guilt settled on her chest.

If she hadn't left, would her parents still be alive? Had she made a mistake, left a trail back to them? Had she... What?

She had no answers to those questions. And she shouldn't be thinking about that now. Right now, she had to figure out what to do. About Leo. About the curse.

About Gabriel.

Simple answer to that last one. Not a damn thing.

Because if what her grandfather had written in his journal was true, there was no point in starting anything with Gabriel. She wouldn't be around to finish it. She was pretty damn sure that she wasn't going to be breathing when the fat lady sang.

She swallowed back a sob, not wanting to wake Leo.

Not fair. So not fair.

Would Serena have any answers?

Please, Great Mother Goddess, let her have some answers.

She bent and pressed a kiss to Leo's baby-soft hair then left the room after lighting the small lamp in the corner.

In the hall, she headed back the way they'd come. Paintings of landscapes covered the plastered walls, which had mellowed with age to a gorgeous sunset gold that most people paid big bucks to have faux-painted that way. According to Gabriel, his mother had lived here for two centuries.

She'd passed several rooms when she heard chanting—male voices, faint but clear—and followed the sound to a small altar room. She stopped well away from the door so she didn't disturb Quinn and Gabriel, sitting on the floor in the middle of a ritual circle, heads bent over a moon bowl.

They didn't notice her. They were too immersed in the spell they were weaving. A powerful spell. She felt it undulate out of the room, washing over her then moving on. They were searching, checking to see if anyone had followed them.

So much power. Most of it coming from one man.

Her gaze lit on Gabriel and stuck. The heat that snuck up on her every time she was with him began to pool low in her stomach. It made her wet, made her want to kiss him and have him put his hands on her.

But it was the ache in her chest that was the real problem.

She'd fallen for the guy.

Which was such a dumb-ass move on her part. It ranked right up there with leaving home to become a ballerina. And thinking that a girl who'd been raised to become the priestess of an ancient goddess could ever have what the *eteri* considered a normal life.

A light tap on her shoulder made her turn with a start. Serena stood behind her, her smile gone now, her eyes deadly serious.

For some inane reason, the "Jeopardy" theme music started to run through her head. Funny, she'd never found it ominous before.

Serena led her through the maze of hallways to a sitting room on the other side of the house, far enough away that they couldn't hear the men and, more importantly, Shea thought, the men couldn't hear them.

"Is Leo asleep?" Serena asked as she sank into a deep, comfortable-looking leather chair, curling her legs under her and waving Shea into the matching one across from her.

"Yeah, he's wiped out."

"He looks very much like your father, but then you know that. And you look so much like your mother, it's almost startling. But that's not what you want to hear, is it?"

Shea took a deep breath. "I'm not really sure what I want to hear."

Serena smiled. "What is it you don't want to hear first?"

"How old are you?"

Serena lifted her delicately pointed chin. "I was born in 1457 in a small village in the hills of Toscana. I was thirty-three when Fabrizio Paganelli cursed my *boschetta* for failing to save his son. If we had known the bastard was *Mal*, we never would have agreed to help.

"Your mother argued against it from the beginning.

She said later she knew there was something wrong with Paganelli but never realized just how evil he was. After the curse, after—" Serena shook her head, as if to get rid of a bad image. Then she glanced down at the leather thong visible around Shea's neck and pointed to it. "Did your mother... Do you have the nail?"

Shea's hand automatically lifted to touch the key. "Yes. She hid it with Leo."

"And you know what it is?"

Shea nodded. "I was trained to take my place among the Priestesses of Menrva. I know the history and the rituals. I know we wait for Menrva to recall us to our duty, and when She does, I know that we will once again use the nails for their true purpose—to sever fate by hammering the nails into the wall of Menrva's temple, letting our people begin a new year unencumbered by the problems of the past."

Serena nodded as if she were a star pupil. "Your mother taught you well. But she never mentioned anything about the curse?"

Shea shook her head.

The other woman's smile softened. "And you don't understand why she never told you, do you?"

"Not a clue."

"Did you know that in all the long years of her life, your mother never had another child? Not with her first mate, Antonio. Or with Franco, Antonio's first reincarnation."

Shock made her mouth open then close. Well, damn. She'd never even considered that there were other men before her father, much less other children. She barely forced herself to shake her head again. Much more of that and she was going to be dizzy. Screw that, she already was.

"For so many years, your mom prayed for a child. And I know she cherished you with all her heart."

Shea's heart pounded with the force of how much she wanted to believe Serena. Pitiful, really, how much she yearned for something that no longer mattered. Her mom was gone.

"Your name is beautiful," Serena continued. "Did your mother tell you where it came from?"

The question took her off guard. "I looked it up in a baby book once. It means 'from the fairy fort.'" She shrugged. "I guess that's self-explanatory. Except, it's Celtic."

"Yes, it is. But Celeste didn't give you the name because of its meaning. Have you ever read 'The Sword of Shannara' by Terry Brooks?"

Shea felt her eyebrows lift. "I'm named after a character in a book?" She couldn't believe it. Her mother had never been frivolous. She'd rarely smiled. And when she had, it had usually been directed at her dad.

"Actually, it was a series of books. Your mother loved them. She particularly liked the character of Shea."

"Why?"

"Because he had a quest to undertake and when he completed it, all was right in the world. She knew you would have a hard road. One you would have to travel alone." Serena sighed, her expression sobering. "I wish I could tell you all you had to do was perform a spell and this would all be over.

"But this is a blood curse and blood demands blood."

A vicious chill cut through Shea's body. Oh God. Serena knew. She had to know about her father's visions. What should she say? Should she confess—

Serena grimaced and turned away. "I'm sorry. I've been locked away in this house for so many years, I forget myself." After taking a deep breath, Serena returned her gaze. "Though we know how Fabrizio performed the curse, we've never been able to break it. Our seer, Dafne, foretold the end but died before she could tell us more."

"Burned at the stake." Shea forced the words through the knot in her throat.

Serena's eyes filled with tears. "Fabrizio's eldest son, Remo, had her burned at the stake in 1509, when it became obvious we were no longer aging. Then he incited the villagers against those of us who remained. They killed our families and tried to kill us, too. But instead of burning our bodies or our hearts, which we cannot survive, they merely slit our throats. When we dragged ourselves out of the shallow grave they'd buried us in, we realized we could not die by normal methods."

Horror made Shea's stomach seize in on itself, multiplied by the stark agony on Serena's face. Her grandfather's journal had made no mention of this. How had they survived?

Blessed Goddess, Mom...

"My daughters, Madrona and Furia, both members of the *boschetta*, had been cursed as well, but my beloved Niccolo and your mother's Antonio were lost that night. After..." Serena closed her eyes and took a deep breath, as if willing away the images in her brain. "Those of us who remained scattered across Europe.

"What we didn't realize at the time was that Fabrizio's curse had returned on his sons. We don't know what happened to Remo and Parente. But Dario made it his duty to hunt us down and kill us."

It sounded like some fictional horror story to Shea, better suited to a Stephen King novel. But Shea had seen Dario's methods up close and personal.

"Dario wants your brother because he has power, power he would force him to use against us. He's managed to take other children before. I don't know how he managed to find your brother or your parents but—"

"It was my fault." The words tried to stick in her throat but she forced them out, forced herself to say them.

Serena's brow furrowed. "What?"

Shea dropped her gaze to the floor, not wanting to see the condemnation in the other woman's eyes. "I left six years ago. Left Wisconsin for Philadelphia and never went back. I didn't see them before…" She shook her head. "I must have left a trail, something… I don't know. That must've been how he found them."

Serena shook her head. "Shea, I was your mother's best friend, and I knew nothing about you. Believe me, Dario doesn't know you exist. You are not to blame for your parents' deaths."

Bullshit. She was responsible. She knew it. But instead of allowing Serena to try and change her mind, Shea moved on.

"Was my dad really my mother's reincarnated bloodbound mate?"

Serena's laugh wasn't faked, though it sounded rusty. "Yes, he was. They were very much in love, no matter what century."

Shea had never doubted her mom's love for her dad. It had been evident in every look, every touch. "Were you blood bound?"

Serena's amusement vanished and, in its place, Shea saw pain. Centuries of it. "Yes."

She should stop. She knew it was none of her business. Still… "Do you know where he is now?"

"Yes."

Spell Bound

"But he's not with you?"

"No." Serena sighed. "It's been more than two-hundred years since his last reincarnation. You learn not to wish for what you can't have. And you learn that loving is much worse when you know you're eventually going to lose it."

Shea's breath caught in her throat and her chest closed in on itself with pain. And not just her own. Serena's pain went so deep, it felt cold against her skin, like a bitter fog.

Shea started to reach for Serena, but stopped, curling her hands into fists. Afraid if she touched her, Serena's despair might drown her.

All five hundred years of it.

"I'm so sorry." Sorry she hadn't broken the curse, sorry she didn't know how.

Yes, you do. Your father's vision...

Serena's mouth twisted but not in anger. "Sweetheart, none of this is your fault. My shortcomings cannot be laid at your feet. Yes, I love him with all my heart but...there are complications."

"Only in your mind, Serena."

Quinn spoke from behind her and Shea turned to find both Quinn and Gabriel in the doorway.

Quinn's angry, anguished expression cleared up any question of who Serena's mate was.

"Did you find anyone?" Serena directed her question to Gabriel, ignoring Quinn.

Gabriel's jaw set as he glanced from Quinn back to Serena, but he shook his head. "As far as I can tell, no one followed us. We're safe."

Serena nodded. "Good. That's good." Serena glanced back at Shea. "I was hoping you and Leo would join me tomorrow for the summer solstice treguenda. It's been a while since I've had guests for a ritual. Now, if you don't mind, I have some work I need to do."

Shea watched Quinn stiffen as Serena dismissed them, watched Gabriel glance at his mom and his best friend with sympathy in his eyes. Then Quinn turned and headed down the hallway without another word.

After a look from Gabriel, Shea swallowed the rest of her questions and walked out. Gabriel shut the door behind her, closing him in with his mother.

Shea stared at the door for a second. Guilt, fear, sorrow felt like a boulder tied around her neck. She wanted to sink to the floor and crawl up in a little ball.

The voices buzzed, soothing her somewhat. Weird how, for so long, she'd thought them an annoyance. Now…now they were a comfort. Something familiar to hold on to when everything else had turned to shit.

She started to head back to Leo, but the sound of something smashing against the wall in a room behind her stopped her in her tracks.

Quinn. She heard him pacing, like a caged animal. Heard something else break, something crunch. Then…nothing.

She didn't want to intrude, but Quinn's agony was palpable. She could feel it, like smoke in the air.

Turning, she stuck her head through the slight open door and into a tiny bedroom. Quinn sat on the bed, elbows on his knees, head in his hands.

He didn't look up. "I'm not really up for visitors."

"I know. I just…It's your pain. I can feel it."

He blew out a gusty sigh and, when he raised his head, Shea saw tears in his eyes. "Yeah, sorry. I'm not that good at burying my emotions. But I'm heading out soon so that won't be a problem. Tell the kid goodbye for me, okay?"

"Do you have to go?" She still wasn't sure she could leave Leo behind, even if it was for the best. But to leave him in the care of a woman they'd just met, without anyone he considered a friend? "Gabriel wants to leave Leo here but I don't think he'll be comfortable without someone he knows."

Not that they'd known each other long, but it was funny how you could become so close to someone in so short a time, yet live with someone for seventeen years and not know the most important things about them.

"Shea—"

"Quinn, please. Please stay. For Leo's sake."

Quinn didn't lift his head, just shook it. "Serena will be okay with the kid. She loves kids."

"But he doesn't know her. He knows you. He trusts you."

"Shea—"

"Quinn—"

"I can't, Shea. I'm sorry." Quinn cut her off then drew a deep breath as he wiped his wet eyes. "Look, there's stuff...I can't..." He huffed and stood to grab a duffel bag off the bed. "I guess you figured out whose mate I am, huh? Let me tell you something about love, babe. It sucks. And I can't stick around anymore without having my heart torn out of my chest."

His anger and hurt brushed against her senses like sandpaper, raspy and harsh. She knew he was in pain, but she had to make him stay.

"Quinn, please. I'll beg if I have to."

He was halfway to the door when he stopped, his head hanging. "You don't know what you're asking."

Oh, she had a bit of an idea, but Leo was her priority. "Probably not, but I have to ask anyway. Please stay. For Leo. He's just a little boy."

He stood still as a stone, his breathing ragged, his back rigid. Finally he turned and she knew she'd won by the look on his face. But at what cost to him?

No, he was a grown man. He'd cope. Leo was just a baby. He needed someone with him. Someone he trusted, someone he knew. He'd taken an instant liking to Quinn therefore Quinn had to stay if she or Gabriel couldn't.

"*Shit*. Fine. I'll stay. For Leo."

She walked to him, kissed his cheek and hugged him tight. "Thank you."

"Yeah, yeah." He dropped his pack and hugged her back so she felt the slight tremble in his arms. "Just don't blame me when the house implodes."

* * *

"You going to put him out of his misery or do you really want him to leave?"

Gabriel watched Serena rise from her chair and head for the liquor cabinet, where she pulled out the Jack Daniels and a shot glass. She held up both and shook them at him.

With a sigh, he held up his index finger. One shot wouldn't kill him. And maybe a few would loosen up his mother to the point where they could talk.

"Mom." He watched her hand falter at the term. He used it sparingly and only when they were alone. He'd been taught early on not to call attention to their relationship. "This is killing him. And you're not too steady yourself. He loves you."

Spell Bound

"Love is painful, Gabriel." She poured herself a shot and downed it with practiced ease. "Haven't you learned that?"

Ooh-kay. It was going to be one of those nights. Usually when his mother started on the hard stuff, he headed the other way. He knew, only because his sisters had told him, that their mom sometimes had a problem with alcohol. The problem being she liked it too much.

He'd never seen her sloppy drunk but after what she'd been through, he couldn't say he blamed her for using liquor to dull her pain for a while. But he couldn't stand to see his mom or Quinn in so much pain.

"You taught me," he took the bottle out of her now shaking hand and poured his own shot, "that love is the most all-consuming emotion in the world and the only thing worth living for."

He downed his shot then put the bottle on top of the cabinet, out of his mother's reach.

"Well, then let me tell you something else." With the flick of one finger, Serena bespelled the bottle off the cabinet and into her outstretched hand, her back to Gabriel as she stared at the Jack. "In the immortal words of J. Geils, 'Love stinks.'"

He snorted in amusement. His mother was a complete contradiction, full of old-world and pop culture. She made her own clothes though she did it with the most up-to-date sewing machine on the market. She grew her own food but couldn't get enough Doritos. She made her own shampoos and soaps yet couldn't live without her satellite TV or radio.

But his amusement turned to frustration when she looked at him. Fat tears rolled down her face as her bottom lip trembled.

"Damn it, Mom, why do you do this to yourself?" He reached for her, pulled her into his arms and felt silent sobs rack her. "He loves you. Yeah, he's young and he's a pain in the ass and sometimes he's furry, but he would die for you."

She laughed, but it sounded more like a whimper. "And that's the problem, isn't it? He'll leave me eventually. You'll leave me, and I'll be alone again."

Shit. He didn't know how to answer that because it was true. Unless Shea...

He bent to whisper in her ear. "But we're here now. And there's hope. Finally."

A shudder rippled through her slender frame and she sighed. Then she backed away, the bottle still clutched in one fist. "I'm going to finish the bottle now, *il mio figlio caro*. You should get some rest."

"Mom—"

"Gabriel." Her voice held more than its normal hint of the old country, and Gabriel knew the conversation was finished. "I will see you at dinner."

With deliberate movements, Serena poured herself another drink.

Gabriel shook his head and left, closing the door behind him.

* * *

"Have you found it?"

"We believe so, yes."

Dario turned from the window, eyebrows raised. "You don't sound convinced."

Peter swallowed, blinking rapidly. "We've narrowed the area to a couple of square miles. We'll know for sure

Spell Bound

in a few hours. They're closing in on the site now. I sent five men—"

Dario cut off the other man by raising his hand. "I don't need to know details. Not yet. Report back when you do know for sure."

Then he waved the terrified man out of the room and turned back to his contemplation of the Gulf of Mexico across the street from his house.

This water was nothing like the murky Atlantic. It reminded him more of the soothing blue Mediterranean. He hadn't been to Italy in years, and he was starting to feel the irresistible pull of home.

Florida was so different, brown and flat where Tuscany was lushly green and hilly. He'd been living in Florida for the past fifty years, drawn to the proximity of the water and the relative quiet of the jut of land that was Pass-a-grille Beach. The community was secluded and the residents transient enough that he'd never had anyone become suspicious of his never-changing age.

But he wanted to go home, wanted to finish out his natural life in the land where he was born and go on to his reward. Whatever that may be.

His father had died nearly five hundred years ago. Freed from the constraints he'd condemned his remaining sons to bear.

Christo had been the lucky one. He had died—at the hand of the *streghe*, his father had believed. Dario didn't have an opinion on that. Frankly, he hadn't cared enough about Christo to miss him. His youngest brother had been a mean-spirited faccia di stronza.

He'd been closer to his older brothers, Remo and Parente. But they'd been given different directions for their lives. And while they had come to grips with their unnaturally long existence, only Dario continued to fight to release their souls.

Hell, the women should thank him. They should seek him out and ask him to take their lives. And when the last of them was dead, the curse would be broken. Blood for blood. His father had drilled that into his head.

Instead, the *streghe* continued to elude him, to bear male children he ruthlessly turned—when he could catch them young enough—to hunt the women and destroy them. It was for their own good, of course. They would thank him when this was over and they could return to the natural order of life, death and rebirth.

When he broke the curse.

Now Peter believed he'd found what had eluded Dario for centuries. He didn't know whether to hope the imbecile had really done what he'd said or laugh in the man's face.

How could he have found the women's American stronghold when Dario himself had searched for years? How had they finally given themselves away?

He'd find out soon enough. But God help Peter if he was wrong this time.

Chapter Sixteen

After wringing that hard-won promise from Quinn, Shea fell into the bed beside Leo's and forced herself to go to sleep.

When she woke, she opened her eyes and found her brother sitting by her side, his face inches from hers, staring straight at her.

She yelped and sat straight up, knocking Leo off the bed as he dissolved into laughter.

"Gotcha! I gotcha good, Sissy."

It took her a minute to orient herself, to remember where they were, why they were here. She drew in a breath to scold him—and then it hit her.

Leo was laughing.

In all the time she'd known him, she'd never heard him so much as a giggle. The sound was so joyful, so normal, that the words died on her tongue, and she could only stare at him. The kid hadn't said more than a hundred words to her before they'd met Gabriel. And now he was laughing so hard, he had to hold his stomach.

And she realized she didn't know how long it'd been since she'd laughed.

A year, maybe more?

Way too long.

She felt her smile widen, felt a chuckle begin in her

chest until it turned into an all-out belly laugh. It felt good... right. She let herself laugh until her stomach hurt.

Leo stopped long enough to gape at her then started laughing again.

He didn't expect her to slip off the bed next to him, grab him around the middle and tickle him for all she was worth.

He started to squirm, his little body wriggling as he tried, though not very hard, to get away.

"No, Sissy, stop!"

He didn't mean it and she knew it. She knew the game. She'd played it with her dad when she'd been Leo's age. She'd loved to have time all to herself with her dad, when he'd paid attention only to her. They'd talked and laughed like there was no one in the world except the two of them.

Leo lunged away and she let him go, knowing the game for what it was.

"You can't hold me, Sissy." He backed away to the other side of the room.

She smiled and lounged back against the bed. "Oh, I don't know about that. I'm faster than you think, bud."

"Nah, you're just old."

That lifted her eyebrows. "Old, huh?"

With a simple spell, she bound him to the floor, only long enough for her to grab him and start tickling him again.

Through his laughter, he yelled. "Hey, that's cheating!"

"All's fair in love and war, bud, and calling me old was an act of war."

"Okay, you're not old."

She stopped tickling him again, and, with a spell of his own, he bound her, long enough for him to scoot across the floor, out of reach again.

On the other side of the room, he continued to laugh. "Just slow."

She laughed along with him, but inside she was shaking her head. He'd copied that last spell directly from her. As far as she knew, he'd never learned it. Granted, it was an easy one, but he'd performed it perfectly.

He had so much power. He needed someone to show him how to use it and control it.

Someone who wasn't her. She stopped laughing with a sigh. "I'm going to have to leave you for a while, Leo. I don't want to, but there's somewhere I have to go."

He dropped his gaze to the floor and started to pick at the hole forming in the knee of his jeans. "With Gabriel."

"Yeah."

He bit his bottom lip, as if he were going to cry. "Daddy told me not to leave you, Sissy. Not ever."

"It won't be forever, bud. Just for a few days. I promise to come back as soon as I can."

He didn't look convinced. "Is Quinn going, too?"

She shook her head, fighting back her own tears. "No. Quinn's going to stay with you."

That perked him up. The corners of his mouth picked up a little, and he slid back to her side. "And you won't be gone long, right?"

"No, I promise. I'll be back in a few days." *I hope.* "I'd take you if I thought it was safe, Leo. I would. But I think you'll be better off here. Plus, someone else is coming to help."

"Who?"

"Our Uncle Matt. He's daddy's brother."

Leo nodded, thinking about that one. "Does he look like Daddy?"

Shea had never even thought about it. "I don't know. I've never met him."

"Do you miss Mommy and Daddy?"

The sharp slice of guilt slid through her chest again. "Every day."

"Me, too." He nodded, and she braced herself to see condemnation in this eyes. Instead his smile returned. "But I've got you."

Warmth replaced the guilt, and her eyes flooded with tears. She didn't let them fall, though, because he might not understand. "That's right. You do. And I," she grabbed for him while he wasn't expecting it, "have you."

He shrieked as she started to tickle him again, but he got his own licks in, digging his little fingers into her ribs and wiggling them until she had to laugh.

The door slammed open, bouncing off the wall, and Gabriel charged into the room, a short sword in his hand and a fierce scowl on his face.

The intrusion silenced them as they stared at Gabriel, who looked ready to kill something.

"What the hell's going on?"

After a few shocked seconds, they dissolved into laughter again, Leo curling into a little ball to hold his stomach.

Gabriel's gaze narrowed, and they laughed harder at his stupefied expression. "*Vaffanculo*, Shea. I thought you were being massacred."

"Don't," she had to stop and take a breath, "swear."

"Don't—" He paused, shot a glance Leo, who'd wound down to a giggle, then back to her. "You think this is funny?"

"Mm hmm." She finally subsided to a chuckle but that wouldn't last long if Gabriel didn't lighten up soon. She'd have to laugh at him. And then maybe she'd have to cry.

Spell Bound

With deliberate moves, Gabriel lowered the sword and leaned it against the wall before stalking over to Leo. "And you? You think it's funny, too?"

Leo stretched out, put his hands behind his head and nodded.

With lightning speed, Gabriel grabbed Leo by the ankle and dangled him from one hand. "So who's laughing now?"

Leo was, as Gabriel lifted him, with no visible effort, until they were almost eye-to-upside-down-eye. The little boy squiggled and squirmed, but Gabriel looked like he could hold him there all day.

"I was coming to wake you," he told her. "It's almost six. We usually eat around eight. I thought you and the little laughing hyena here," he gave Leo a shake that made the little boy laugh even harder, "would like to take a walk."

Then he grinned at her, nearly stealing her breath away. Didn't he know she'd follow him anywhere? "Sure. That'd be great. Just…give me a minute."

She headed for the bathroom as Gabriel lowered Leo onto the bed. She brushed her teeth and hair then stopped to look in the mirror, wondering if she should change her short black t-shirt and faded jeans.

Barely reaching the edge of her ass-hugging pants, the shirt showed off her flat stomach and molded to her decent breasts. With her hair down and without makeup, she looked younger than she was.

Maybe she should—

This isn't a date, you idiot.

Her reflection wouldn't stop grinning, though.

With a disgusted huff, she turned and walked back into the room. Leo had already donned his sneakers and climbed onto Gabriel's back. Their hair was the exact same shade, she noticed. Raven-black and silky. If Leo let his grow, it would probably look exactly like Gabriel's. Did Gabriel have any brothers? He'd never mentioned any but maybe that was some *grigorio* thing, like not telling anyone who your mother was.

Gabriel's gaze caught and held hers and desire hummed along her nerves, burning away everything in her brain but the urge to flirt with him. To tease him.

For just a few hours, she wanted to be a normal twenty-three-year old.

But since that wasn't going to happen, she wanted to have just a little fun before she had to—

No. Probably better not to think about that.

Forcing a smile, she stepped through the door, letting him close it behind her. Then she stopped. This place was a huge maze, and she had no idea where she was going.

She followed Gabriel through the house to a sturdy wooden door. When he opened it, the gray wolf sitting on the outside step turned his head toward them and yipped.

For a second, Shea recalled her encounter with Tivr, which she still hadn't told Gabriel about. There'd been no time. And she'd been pissed at him, which hadn't made her talkative.

But she knew this wasn't Tivr.

"Quinn?" Leo said as he slid off Gabriel's back to kneel beside the animal and stroke his fur. The wolf leaned back his head so Leo could scratch his throat.

"Yeah, it's Quinn." Gabriel sighed. "And he'll have you do that all day if you let him."

Quinn shot a growl at Gabriel then trotted off the step, looking back at Leo. Leo, in turn, looked back at Shea.

"Can I?"

Gabriel nodded when she looked to him for guidance. When had that happened, she wondered? When had she started looking to Gabriel for answers?

And when had he become more to her than just Leo's guardian?

Quinn took off like a bullet and Leo ran after him with a shout, his little feet flying, legs pumping. She lost sight of him almost immediately in the dense forest and she drew a quick breath, ready to call him back. What if—

Gabriel laid his hand on her shoulder and squeezed, the heat of him searing her through her shirt. "He'll be fine. We checked. There's no one around. Let him run a little, Shea. He needs it."

He was right. She knew he was right, but for the past year, they hadn't been able to go anywhere without looking over their shoulders.

Shaking off that thought, she let Gabriel lead her into the forest. They walked, side by side, not talking, not touching.

His long muscular legs ate up the ground, though he shortened his pace so she could keep up without having to hurry. The tight black t-shirt he wore bared most of his bulging biceps and she wanted to feel the strength of them under hands. The t-shirt clung to his broad chest and tight abs and…

She wanted to pull him down to the ground and make him kiss her, let that amazing body cover hers and block out the world.

As he stripped her, the air would cool her overheated skin and the fading sunlight would eventually give way to an all-consuming darkness that would hide them from prying eyes.

Alone in the dark.

As they headed in the same general direction as Leo and Quinn, the sound of Leo's laughter echoing through the trees brought a brief smile to her face.

Would there come a day when his laugh wouldn't be so amazing? When it'd become an everyday occurrence?

Or would they always be on the run?

And would she be here to hear it?

"When did you find out what your mother was?"

The question had been rolling around in her brain for a while, something she hadn't felt right asking. But out here, under the sky and surrounded by the encompassing forest, it seemed okay.

"I was eight."

Not much older than Leo. He'd need to know, too. Someday. "How'd you handle it?"

His snort was amused. "Disbelief, shock, denial. But after a while, I figured it wasn't all that strange, considering all the other shit I'd been dealing with since I was born."

"Did you go to school?"

Now, he laughed outright and her thighs clenched. "Hell, no. I would have blasted the teachers into walls the first couple of years after I came into my full powers. I did get my diploma. I had a tutor for school subjects, took the GED when I was sixteen. I would have blown it off but my parents insisted. My dad trained me in everything else."

Gabriel knew exactly what question Shea was going to ask next. He braced himself for it.

And, as fate would have it, they stepped into the clearing at that precise moment.

"What happened to him?"

Someone else might have tripped over the two small headstones before noticing them. Gabriel would be able to find them on a pitch-black night during a hurricane.

As always, the grass around them was neatly trimmed and the oaks Serena had planted the day of their burial more than a decade ago grew strong.

"Dario's men killed him." The familiar ache returned to his chest. "They'd come for my brother, Nino. They didn't want me. I was too old. But I was strong enough that they knew I had to be out of the way. I was stupid. I let them down, and they died."

Lowering himself onto the ground beneath his father's oak, he leaned back against the trunk, watched her stand next to the graves.

"I don't believe that."

He snorted. "Quinn and I were out screwing around, blowing off steam. I'd had a bad feeling all day. I couldn't explain it, but it was like…someone had my lungs in their hands and they were squeezing." He rubbed at his chest, remembering that ache. "I should have stayed home that night. I should have known."

She sat next to him on the ground, close enough to touch but not.

"How old were you?"

He shook his head. "Just shy of eighteen." Old enough to know better. "Doesn't matter how old I was. I wasn't there when they needed me. That won't happen again."

He wouldn't—couldn't let that happen again. Couldn't bear to think about another small headstone with Leo's name on it. Or Shea's. "Quinn was only fifteen. We killed our first men that day. And it was too late. By the time my dad knew what was happening, it was too late."

He still remembered every second of the phone call from his dad.

"Get the hell out of here, Gabriel. You and Quinn, go somewhere, anywhere. Dario's men are here and I don't want you anywhere near them. I'll call you when it's safe."

Gabriel had, of course, said fuck that. He and Quinn would be there. "Hold on. We're coming."

He'd believed his dad could hold them off. Davis Borelli was the best of the best. The strongest.

But the ten-minute drive from town had been excruciating.

And when they'd arrived, he'd seen Nino's lifeless body cradled in his father's arms as a dark-haired man pulled the trigger on the final shot through his dad's temple.

What he couldn't remember was exactly what happened after that. Quinn had filled in the gaps, but Gabriel only remembered bits and pieces. Blood, fists. The crunch of breaking bones. Quinn's growls. And the screams of grown men.

Magic that had seared through his skin like the flame of a butane torch.

Fueled by rage and grief, he and Quinn had killed the last two men his dad hadn't been able to. And when they were done, there hadn't been enough left for two body bags for the four men.

He had no regrets. They'd deserved it.

"Gabriel. I'm so sorry."

Shea's quiet, sorrowful voice ripped him out of the past.

"It was a long time ago." But he would never forget. Not one detail.

Spell Bound

She shifted closer, close enough for him to feel her, smell her, but still not touching. "Your mom must have been devastated."

"I think she wanted to die, too, but she had three other children. And Quinn."

"Who she won't allow close to her."

He looked into her eyes. "I can see her point. It's tough to love someone you're going to lose."

She nodded, her expression solemn. "But think of everything she'll have missed by denying herself. What about you, Gabriel? What are you denying yourself?"

Too damn much.

He managed to keep the words from escaping, but she had to be able to see them on his face.

He wanted her. Ached for her in ways he'd never ached for anyone.

But if he let his emotions get involved, he might slip. Might miss something because he was so focused on her that he couldn't see anything else.

He didn't want her and Leo to pay for his fuck-up.

He opened his mouth to say just that but before the words formed, she straddled his lap and sealed her mouth to his. It was lunacy, but the minute her mouth touched his, everything else slipped away.

The woman he wanted more than he wanted to breathe had her arms locked around his shoulders and her tongue in his mouth. His body reacted with a powerful rush of adrenaline, making his cock hard and his brain explode with sensation.

Wrapping his arms around her waist, he crushed her against him, smashing her breasts flat to his chest and bringing her crotch against the throbbing ridge in his jeans. He breathed in through his nose, her sweet, subtle scent screwing with his head while his hands flattened on her back and drew her even closer.

She moaned into his mouth, let her fingers slide into his hair and catch. Lust warred with reason, and, for the first time, lust won.

He kissed her, hard, slid his tongue into her mouth to tangle with hers. He kneaded her back like a cat then slid down to cup her ass, pushing her hips into him and rubbing her mound against his cock until he was primed to explode.

Hell, he wanted to, but he wanted to do it inside her.

Untangling her hands from his hair, she moved them to his shoulders in a light caress then stroked down his biceps and slid around his back. Her fingers dug in until she had his t-shirt bunched in her hands. He leaned forward so she could pull it over his head, releasing her mouth only long enough for her to do it.

He reclaimed her lips with a desperation that should have worried him. They were on borrowed time, and he didn't want to waste any. Leo was out there, running with Quinn, who he trusted to keep the kid safe and occupied for these few stolen moments.

Rolling her under him, soft grass at her back, he grabbed both of her wrists in one hand, drawing them above her head. She arched into him, breasts pressing against his chest, belly to belly, and he let his mouth trace down her neck to her collar bone. He licked the delicate bones there as he heard her breathing shallow out. Slipping his free hand under her t-shirt, already riding above her belly button, he splayed his fingers across her stomach then dragged them up to caress her bare breasts beneath her shirt.

Her nipples pebbled and his hand trembled as he

pulled her shirt up and bent his head to suck on her, the salty taste of her soft skin messing with his head, making him drunk. She arched even further, tugging her hands out of his grip to thread her fingers through his hair again and hold him to her.

As he suckled, his free hand moved to the waistband of her jeans. The smooth skin of her stomach quivered and he stopped. Until she lifted her hips, encouraging him to continue. She wasn't wearing underwear. Hell, maybe she didn't own any. Then his hand slid into her short, silky curls and he hoped she never did. He wanted unrestricted access to her at all times.

She froze, waiting, and he let his fingers rest there, soaking in her heat. He wanted to slide his fingers into her, feel how wet she was, feel her sex close around him. Wanted more than anything to rip away their clothes and take her, but they couldn't. There wasn't enough time or privacy.

Still, he couldn't leave her until the primal part of him that wanted satisfaction heard her cry out his name. He wanted that. Needed it because they could have nothing else right now.

Sliding his fingers further, he brushed against her clit. Slow and light, he played with her, taunted her, until he felt her body arched into his, her fingers biting into his biceps as she sought a harder touch.

He gave it to her, stroking that little nub of flesh with more pressure until she began to writhe beneath him. His mouth still locked on hers, he stabbed his tongue into her mouth in time with his strokes and ignored the punishing ache in his body as his fingers played over her silky flesh.

Goddess, she was hot and wet and so fucking responsive, his cock strained against his zipper, seeking home.

With a gasp, she broke their kiss, drawing in air as if she were drowning, and he shifted his mouth to her neck, opening on the skin below her ear and reveling in the taste of her.

She was close, so close to breaking, her hips moving against his fingers, her hands clenching and releasing. Her breathy cries felt like physical caresses on his cock, cranking his need to finish her.

He turned ruthless, mercilessly teasing her. Hard and fast then slow and light. Her body responded to his every move, twisting and craving what he could give her.

Until finally, he felt her break. Catching her cry in his mouth, he felt her body tense and arch into him, her hip catching against his raging erection and nearly pushing him over the edge with her.

Her sex clenched around his fingers, and he groaned thinking about how fucking good that would feel around his cock.

They lay there for minutes, his fingers embedded in her wet heat, face buried in her neck. When he'd decided he wasn't going to come in his pants, he slid his hand free and wrapped both arms around her, rearranging them until her head lay on his chest and her breath warmed his skin. He tortured himself for a few more minutes by just holding her.

If he failed again, this was what he'd lose.

Blessed Goddess, don't let me fail.

After a few minutes, her breathing returned to normal, and she sank into him, body draped across his, head burrowed into the curve of his shoulder.

It'd be relaxing if not for the almost overwhelming urge to thrust his still-aching erection against her.

Not the time. Not the place.

But, Christ, he wanted to. He wanted to strip her, spread her out on the ground and sink into her until he forgot his own name.

Shit, he had to relax. Focus inward and concentrate on breathing. Yeah, like that was gonna work. Especially when he felt her hand begin to rub against his chest.

And when she shifted slightly off of him, he opened his eyes and found himself staring directly into hers.

* * *

Shea had never had an orgasm by anyone else's hand before.

And damn... good thing she hadn't known what she was missing.

Then again, it might not have been as good with anyone who wasn't Gabriel.

And what would happen when they actually got their clothes off and he could take her completely?

She wanted to know.

Staring into his dark eyes, she let her hand slide down his hard chest to the defined ridges of his abs. His gaze stayed steady but his muscles contracted under her fingers. The corners of her mouth kicked up in a half smile, making a muscle tic in Gabriel's jaw.

Good. He wasn't as steady as he fronted. She slid her hand further until she reached the waistband of his jeans. For a few seconds, she let her hand lie there, not moving, letting him sweat just a little.

Then she cupped him through his jeans, the hard bulge twitching under her hand, straining against the placket until she was sure it'd burst through.

Her smile widened as his lips parted to draw in air. She loved how the touch of her hand affected him.

Gently at first, she stroked him through the fabric, watching his expression tighten into a fierce mask. But she wasn't afraid. Hell, no. It made her hot and a little more bold, letting her fingers undo the button at the top then pull down the zipper, careful not to pull it down too fast and possibly hurt that part of him she so wanted to ease.

With the zipper split, she maneuvered her hand into his pants, his soft cotton underwear tight and fighting her. Still, she was determined and finally got her hand exactly where she wanted it. Gripping him.

He was hot and hard and soft and huge. Goddess, the man truly had been blessed. Her fingers didn't meet when she wrapped them around his shaft and started a slow glide.

When his breath hissed in and his head kicked back against the tree, she thought she might have hurt him. But when she paused, he laid his hand over hers and wrapped her fingers more tightly around him.

She picked up the rhythm, working him with her hand, watching his face to see if he liked when she squeezed him at the tip before working her hand back to the base, then sliding farther to cup his heavy balls.

His moan fired her previously slaked desire, making her sex ache. When his eyes closed, she leaned in and sealed her mouth over his, sliding her tongue into his mouth, flicking at his until he responded in kind. When his hands slid into her hair to hold her to him, she slowed her hand, and only when he'd eased his hold on her did she grip him tighter.

Power. She liked it.

So much so, she wanted him to come on her command. She stroked him faster now, feeling his muscles strain toward release, his tongue a furious whip in her mouth.

Goddess, she ached, pressing her sex against his hip

Spell Bound

and rubbing hard as she rubbed him. She felt another climax build in her body, reached for it, just as his cock jerked in her hand and a warm wetness coated her fingers. Her body pulsed in time with his.

They lay there, breathing, her fingers still clutched around his softening shaft. Silence but for the soft rustle of the leaves above.

Shea didn't want to move, and she wasn't quite sure her body would obey if she did try to get up. Not that she could because Gabriel's arms were tight bands around her.

Which really wasn't a problem.

But he'd probably like to have his property back.

She released him but didn't realize she didn't know where to put her sticky hand. Gabriel solved the problem for her by sitting up and wiping her hand and his stomach with his shirt.

Then he zipped his pants and hers, his motions almost too controlled.

He didn't say anything, his gaze on whatever his hands were doing and, as she watched him take a long look at his shirt before he dropped it on the ground on his side away from her.

What the hell? Was he angry at her? Embarrassed by what they'd done? Did he regret this?

He looked up at that second and caught her gaze, his so dark, it was like looking into a pit of molten dark chocolate. Her breath caught at the banked emotion, and before she could draw in a needed breath, his mouth came down on hers with a determination she couldn't deny.

He broke off the kiss a few seconds later with a guttural moan.

"Later," he said.

She nodded, not sure she could speak.

Damn, she wished it were later.

Chapter Seventeen

Dinner was quiet and way too long for Shea's peace of mind.

Tonight, she and Gabriel would finish what they'd started in the woods.

Just thinking about it made her shift on the chair. She was almost as bad as Leo, who practically bounced on his seat and couldn't stop running at the mouth, which turned out to be a good thing because none of the adults could string more than three words together without stumbling over them.

Serena's eyes held a faint red tinge, as if she'd been crying and had done her best to clean up before she'd had to face the crowd. She smiled at Leo's continuous jabber and asked Gabriel an occasional question but that was it.

Quinn didn't speak to anyone but Leo. Gabriel kept sliding her hot glances that sizzled along her nerve endings and promised heaven later.

Goddess, she wanted him. Wanted it to be midnight, wanted Leo to be sleeping soundly and Quinn and Serena to be elsewhere so she could lock the door to his room and spend the night learning how to make love to him.

She didn't want to die a virgin.

Hell, she couldn't give a good reason why she'd never gone to bed with a guy before. It wasn't like she hadn't had offers.

Spell Bound

Something had always stopped her. Though it would sound crazy to anyone else, she knew the voices in her head would have disapproved. But they shut up when she kissed Gabriel. That had to mean something. Didn't it?

"Are you finished, Shea?"

Serena's voice broke into her thoughts, dousing her libido as her brain made the connection again between Serena and Gabriel. Mother and son.

They didn't look all that similar, though their smiles were identical. Gabriel must resemble his father, she decided.

"Can I help with the ritual tomorrow?" Leo broke in, practically bouncing off his chair. "I watch Shea all the time and my mom taught me a little. And my dad."

"I don't see why not, Leo." Serena smiled at him as she collected plates from the table. Quinn stood and put his own in the sink before she could get to him. Her smile faltered but she continued uninterrupted. "When Gabriel was a little boy, he loved to help, too."

"No offense, but I think I liked the rush afterward more than the actual helping." Gabriel's mouth lifted into a grin. "Kind of like a good sugar high."

Serena's glance was indulgent. "You always did have a sweet...tooth."

After putting his plates in the sink, Quinn walked out of the room without another word. Serena stared at the door then sighed.

"I'll be right back."

Shea watched her disappear through the same door, back straight and an air of determination that was nearly visible.

"Is Quinn in trouble?"

Leo's whisper made her smile and she shared that smile with Gabriel, who shook his head.

"No, he's not in trouble, bud," she said. "He's just, ah, kind of tired."

"No," Leo shook his head. "He's sad 'cause of Serena. And Serena's afraid of him. Why is she afraid of Quinn?"

Shea couldn't think of one damn thing to say. She hadn't realized how good Leo was at picking up on emotions. She felt Serena's exasperation like a whisper of cool fog against her skin. She wondered how Leo sensed emotions. She'd never thought to ask.

Gabriel answered before Shea could pull her thoughts together. "Serena's not afraid of Quinn, not like you used to be afraid of the dark. Serena's afraid of something bad happening to Quinn. Do you understand?"

Leo mulled it over for a second. "Yeah, but I still don't see why he wants to kiss her all the time."

She couldn't help it. She choked back a laugh as Gabriel's mouth twitched. He looked to her for guidance and she shook her head. "You're doing fine, big guy. Go for it."

Instead, Gabriel asked, "How do you know that?"

"I see it in my head when I pet him. He's so soft. Can I have fur when I get bigger?"

Shea thought her head should spin at the speed Leo switched subjects. Since Leo had rediscovered his desire to talk in the past few days, he seemed to be making up for lost time.

"No," Gabriel said. "You're not going to have fur when you get bigger. So you want to watch some movies before bed? I think Serena has more movies than a video store."

Effectively sidetracked, Leo bounced off his chair, ready to go and, intrigued, Shea followed Gabriel through

Spell Bound

the house by way of another hallway that led to a stairs leading down.

"Wow," Leo said as he got a look at the room. "Does Serena play with all this stuff?"

Gabriel grinned as Leo walked over to the pool table and ran his fingers along the carved wood before he headed for the DVDs flanking the huge television that covered almost half the wall.

"She can beat me in pool nearly every time but I remain the all-time pinball champ."

Shea smiled at the image of a young Gabriel spending hours at the pinball machine. But just as quickly, that image was replaced by one of a teenage Gabriel standing over his dead father.

So much pain.

Standing to the side, Shea watched Gabriel help Leo pick age-appropriate movies. Leo looked like a kid in a candy store. They'd seen one movie in the past year in a movie theater, a Disney release. So, of course, Leo chose "Monsters," "The Jungle Book" and "Peter Pan."

Then they settled on the curved couch, Leo between them, as Gabriel fiddled with a remote that looked like it could control the space shuttle. A second later, several pieces of equipment blinked to life on the cabinet below the television. He pushed another button and the lights dimmed.

And finally the movie started.

In the flickering light from the screen, Shea watched Leo's eyes widen in wonder. Lifting her arm, she settled it around his shoulders, drawing his warm little body into her side. He snuggled in without taking his eyes from the screen.

So small. So not fair.

"Shea." Gabriel sat on the other side of Leo, watching her. Their gazes met and held. "You want popcorn?"

Her lips curved into a grin even as her mouth began to water. And not just for popcorn. "Sure. Lots of butter."

"Only way to eat it."

* * *

Serena knew where she'd find Quinn.

In the one room of the house he knew she wouldn't go.

Unfortunately for Quinn, she'd decided it'd been way too long since she'd confronted this particular demon.

She hadn't opened the door to Nino's room since his death. The pain in her heart had subsided in recent years, but not enough. It would never be enough. Still, the situation with Quinn had reached its breaking point.

Down the south hall, past the secondary altar room, through the entrance to the west rooms.

The door was closed, but she knew exactly how the room would look. Exactly the way Nino had left it the last time he'd been here.

It took her nearly a minute to grab the doorknob.

She tried to prepare herself for the despair to hit her, the gnawing pain that lives with you when you lose a child. Gabriel had been her first in all the centuries since the curse. She'd loved him with the passion of a new mother, despite the circumstances of his birth.

Nino had been a joyful surprise. Where her daughters and Gabriel had been solemn children, as if they'd always known the weight of the world was on their shoulders, Nino had woken every day with a smile on his face. Davis' influence, she was sure.

Davis...

No, she couldn't think about Davis, not now. She had to concentrate on Quinn. And how best to break the hold she had on his heart.

She took a deep breath, twisted the knob and opened the door.

Quinn sat cross-legged in the middle of the floor as he meditated, looking so incongruous on the carpet printed to resemble a small town. Nino had played on that carpet for hours.

She took a deep breath and ignored the bed where Nino had slept, still made up with his Thomas the Tank Engine sheets and the toy truck in the corner, laying on its side, exactly how he'd left it.

"We need to talk," she said, her voice sounding horribly loud in the quiet space. "This has gone on long enough."

He didn't acknowledge her immediately, but after a few seconds, his eyelids fluttered and he lifted his mesmerizing blue gaze to meet hers. Those eyes always reminded her of the warm Mediterranean. But his mouth was set in a cool, straight line, only the muscle jumping in his cheek gave away his anger.

"Are you ready to admit you're wrong?"

Sweet heaven, he was gorgeous when he was pissed off. She wanted to smile at his youthful fire, but she knew it would only anger him more. And make her want him more.

She already wanted him more than she wanted to breathe.

To steady herself, she let her gaze roam around the room. To remind herself why she couldn't let herself love him.

"I'm not wrong, Quinn. I'm not going to change my mind. Find someone else. Take another lover." Just don't ever tell me. "Don't wait for me because it will not—"

He rose with a speed and agility she should have expected but hadn't. He had her up against the wall before she knew what he intended, mouth crushed against hers, kissing her with more passion than skill.

His lips forced hers open, his tongue stabbing into her, gliding against her tongue. The taste of him, unfamiliar and heady, made her moan.

She wanted to push him away but her body knew her mate, knew this was the only man for her. And had decided it'd been denied long enough.

Her knees weakened but his hands caught her under her arms, lifting her until her feet left the floor and she had to grip his shoulders to maintain her balance.

Balance she didn't have without her blood-bound mate in her life.

When he drew back, her stomach rolled at the frustration-love-hope-despair she saw in his face.

She couldn't stop herself. Her hands lifted to cup his tense jaw, letting the warmth of him soak into her skin. His eyelids flickered but didn't fall, lips parting to draw in air but he didn't move.

Touching her lips to the corner of his mouth, she drew in his musky scent, let it seep into her soul. Where it belonged. The rough stubble against her skin made her heart ache. She wanted him to rub his chin against her breasts, her stomach. Wanted him to brush it against the inside of her thighs when he put his mouth on her sex.

Her body shook with the strength of that image, just as it did when she dreamed in the middle of the night. Those dreams taunted her with what she couldn't have.

She shut her eyes.

"No," Quinn growled, shaking her just a little. "No, don't you dare close your eyes. God damn it, Serena, you look at me. How can you live without this? Without me?"

She didn't live. Not really. She existed. And not well. But if she allowed herself to look at him now, she'd be lost.

As lost as she'd been at Nino's death.

Despair, black and bitter and choking, bubbled up from her gut, from the hole she'd buried it in. It leaked from her body in her tears, silent and pouring down her face now.

"I can't." She couldn't breathe but that wasn't what she meant. "I can't. Quinn. So sorry. It hurts."

The tears she hadn't shed so many years ago rose like a hurricane-fueled wave, pouring from beneath her closed lids, drenching her face. She couldn't stop them, any more than she could force the grief and anger and dread back into the whole.

This is what she'd tried to avoid all these years. And all it had taken was one kiss.

She wept, her body wracked by sobs. Quinn swore, something foul and directed at himself, and wrapped her against his body. Which just made her cry harder.

She wanted him so badly, her body ached with it.

But, just as she couldn't bring back her beautiful Nino, she couldn't have Quinn. She didn't deserve him and he deserved better. Better than a woman who had failed so many, who had let down her *boschetta* by not being the leader they needed. By having another child when she knew how much danger he would be subjected to all his life.

She didn't know how long she cried or when Quinn

carried her out of the room. It took all of her dubious control to rein in her tears, to push back the grief enough to move on. But when she finally got herself under control, she realized she was sitting on Quinn's lap on another bed in another room.

His arms wrapped around her shoulders, hers wrapped around his waist. Her tears soaked his skin, now sticky and damp.

For a few brief seconds, as sanity returned, she rested her cheek against his chest, heard his heart beating steadily beneath her ear.

Then she forced herself to push away. To get to her feet and meet his sorrowful blue eyes.

"Don't you see, Quinn? It's for the best."

Then she turned and walked away.

* * *

Gabriel didn't watch the movie.

He watched Shea.

Watched her eat popcorn and suck the butter off her fingers. Had to stomp down the urge to do it for her.

Got a hard-on watching her lick the salt off her lips.

And lost it as he watched her watch Leo with such fear on her face he almost howled in frustration.

He almost got caught watching her when the first film ended, and they both looked at him to switch the film. And when the next one started, he went back to watching her.

And thinking. Tonight. He had to have her tonight. So he could get this lust, this burn, out of his system. He had to be sharp, and he couldn't be sharp when he wanted her this badly.

About halfway through the second film, he felt Leo's body relax completely into sleep. Shea's gaze dropped to Leo then lifted to his. The desire in her eyes made his blood pump hot and heavy.

No more waiting.

He slid off the couch, careful not to wake Leo when he picked the kid off the couch and cradled him against his chest. Shea close on his heels, he took the kid to the bedroom they'd shared last night and laid him on the bed.

Shea made short work of his clothes, never once waking the little boy, then tucked the covers around him and made sure the nightlight in the bathroom was lit and the door was open.

Then she stood and looked at him.

Extending his hand, he waited, breath held, until she took it. Her fingers trembled in his, but her expression held no fear. Only a reflection of the same lust he felt.

With her hand in his, he pulled her out of the room and across the hall. His mom had known he'd want to be close to them, to protect them, so she'd put them in the room across from his.

His mom couldn't have known how he felt about Shea. Probably better she didn't.

Without turning on the overhead light, he shut the door and whispered a spell to light the candles on the side table. He needed to see her but not in the harsh light from the electric bulbs. He wanted to see her skin gleam in the flicker of candlelight.

He wanted to take his time, savor every moment.

But Shea had other plans.

She leaped at him, wrapping her arms and legs around him and sealing her mouth over his with a desperation that burned through his control with the force of a dynamite blast.

He didn't stop her, didn't try to slow her down, because she wanted exactly what he did. With one arm around her waist, he used the other to strip her t-shirt over her head, baring her upper body to him. He couldn't do anything about her jeans with her legs around his waist, so he started walking backward toward the bed.

When he hit the mattress with the back of his legs, he turned and broke their kiss, stomach clenching at the whimper she made when they lost contact.

Pulling her body away from his, he set her on the bed on her knees and started work on her jeans even as his mouth lowered to her breasts. Her nipples peaked hard and tight, and his tongue flicked over them mercilessly. She arched her back and he reached for the button on her jeans, nearly ripping it off in his haste. When he had the zipper down, he gave her nipple one last nip before he pushed her back on the bed.

She landed with a little gasp and started to laugh, which she continued until he stripped the pants off her legs, fell to his knees and put his mouth over her sex.

"Gabriel..." she gasped his name, as if shocked, but he couldn't stop now. And she didn't push him away. Instead, her hands sank into his hair as his tongue began to lap at her with broad strokes. Her moan made him shudder even as her musky heat coated his tongue.

With her legs over his shoulders and her hands in his hair, he ate at her like a man starving. He couldn't get enough, not of her breathy moans or the sweet taste of her. Moving his hands up her body, he cupped her breasts, rubbing her nipples in rhythm with his tongue on her clit. Learned what made her sigh and squirm and groan.

He played her body with single-minded intent, and when her body went taut, her thighs clenching around his head as she came, his inner caveman beat his chest and roared.

While she lay there, trying to catch her breath, he dragged off his own clothes and stood. He stared at her for several seconds, just looking at her beautiful brown hair, wild and dark on his bed, and at her toned body, still shaking from her orgasm.

Then her eyes caught his and his cock throbbed with the heat still flaring there.

When she came up on her knees in front of him, he thought she'd take it slow now. Thought that with the first rush over, they'd have time to play.

But Shea had other ideas.

With a quick twist of her upper body, she had him flat on his back on the bed and had straddled his waist before he realized what she as doing.

His body knew what she wanted, even if his brain hadn't quite caught up, and his hips arched as she took his cock in her hand and began to lower herself onto him.

But when she tensed and bit her lip, he grabbed her hips and held her completely still.

"Shea. Slow down, babe. Wait a—"

"I've waited too damn long. I don't want to wait anymore." She looked down into his eyes and then to where they were almost joined. "Come on, Gabriel. Please."

His eyes widened as he read between the lines, which was damn hard to do considering how fucking much he wanted to thrust into her. The tip of his cock was already enclosed in her channel and he felt himself twitch in anticipation.

But she was tight, so tight, and he didn't want to hurt her.

"Are you a virgin?"

He had to know. It wasn't going to make a difference to the outcome, but it would make a difference with how they played this here and now.

He had his answer in her silence and the look in her eyes.

His inner caveman gave a few more beats on his chest.

His. Only his. Always his.

He thrust up as he brought her hips down, impaling her on his cock in one smooth, fast motion.

Her gasp made him freeze.

"Are you okay?" He could barely get the words out from behind his gritted teeth as he grabbed at the reins of his control. "Did I hurt you, honey?"

She shook her head, the movement making her hips wriggle, her sheath contracting around him. "No, but I'm going to explode if you don't finish this." Her half-smile was the most beautiful sight he'd ever seen. "Come on, Gabriel. I want to make you come this time."

His groan echoed in the room. "If we do this right, we both will."

Then he showed her how.

He lifted her hips, eyes closing at the burn of flesh on flesh, on the tightness of her flesh around his. On her sleek, wet heat. Then he let her sink down on him, watching her face for any sign of pain.

He didn't want her to have any, not this first time, not with him. But she didn't seem to have any discomfort at all. Instead, she looked ecstatic. With her eyes closed, she set her hands on his abdomen and let him control the motion. Her back arched, like a cat in the sun, shifting the angle of their bodies and making them both groan at the few centimeters more he sank.

After a few minutes, she must have decided he wasn't going fast enough, so she started to move. Using her legs and her hips, she began to ride him, faster and faster still until his eyes rolled back in his head and he couldn't see. Only feel.

He tried to hold back his release, tried to make it last, but he couldn't refuse her.

His hands tightened around her hips, holding her steady, grounding himself.

And when she finally cried out and clenched around him, he felt his own orgasm explode out of his cock and into her.

For several heartbeats, he just breathed. The smell of sex and Shea's subtle scent made his cock twitch again.

Hell, he might actually be able to get it up again in a few minutes.

Then Shea leaned forward, draping herself over his body, head on his chest.

Wrapping his arms around her, he made sure she wasn't going anywhere.

And after a few minutes, her breathing pattern indicated she'd fallen asleep.

With his cock still pulsing in her body.

He closed his eyes and followed her.

Chapter Eighteen

Gabriel slept more soundly beside Shea than he'd slept in years.

But when he woke, she was gone. After throwing on some clothes, he checked Leo's room and confirmed that she'd only moved across the hall.

The two of them slept in the same bed, though Shea was on top of the covers. As if she hadn't meant to fall asleep there.

He made sure he didn't wake them. She and Leo could both do with some more rest.

Instead he headed for the kitchen and found his mom and Quinn.

Both of them looked like they hadn't slept all night. But he knew, from the strained silence, that they hadn't spent the night the way he and Shea had.

"Everything okay?"

His question elicited a nod from his mom, sitting at the kitchen table drinking a cup of tea, and another from Quinn, standing as far from her as he could get without leaving the room.

"Where are Shea and Leo?" Serena asked.

Narrowed gaze shifting between the two of them, he briefly considered asking what had happened then decided against it. He didn't think either of them would answer.

Besides, everyone was entitled to a little privacy. And their secrets.

"They're still sleeping."

His mom nodded. "I thought you might want to show her the studio today."

He planned to, right after breakfast. "I will."

"Good." His mom nodded and slid him a short-lived smile. "It'll be nice to have someone make use of it."

Silence descended again as Gabriel headed for the coffeemaker. The tension hung in the air, almost thick enough to choke. He opened his mouth to say something, anything, and Quinn stood.

"I'm going for a run. Be back later."

Serena's eyes followed him down the hall until she couldn't see him anymore.

Gabriel sighed. "Mom—"

"Good morning, Leo. Shea," Serena said. "Did you sleep well?"

Gabriel turned to see a quick blush heat Shea's cheeks as she and Leo walked into the kitchen. Shea opened her mouth to answer but Leo started to chatter about the movie they'd watched last night.

He tensed, wondering how much more his mom could take. But amazingly, her tension eased as she talked to Leo. They kept up a steady conversation all through breakfast. The kid had more questions than an encyclopedia had answers but his mom and Shea spoke to him without a hint of impatience.

He hoped Shea's easy smile and more relaxed manner this morning was a result of their night together. He knew he sure as hell felt better.

When she glanced his way and the corners of her mouth curled up just enough to give the impression of a smile, he felt like he'd won the freaking lottery.

If his dad could see him now, he'd shake his head.

"You're complicating things, Gabriel. Don't lose focus. They need you to be the strong one."

Emotion made you weak.

He knew that. But he couldn't help himself.

Tomorrow, he'd be strong. Today…fuck it.

They sat there for the better part of an hour, talking about nothing. Carefully talking about nothing. Letting Leo guide the conversation. It felt like a truce between two parties who weren't sure they were fighting. But it was better than being at each other's throats.

Finally, his mother said, "So, Gabriel, are you going to show Shea the studio?"

Shea's gaze found his. "Studio?"

He smiled at her, just to see her reaction. And wasn't disappointed to see heat rush across her face again. "Come on."

* * *

Shea followed Gabriel and Leo down the hall, trying not to overheat as she recalled last night.

Gabriel had gone to the bathroom to get a towel to clean her up after they'd had sex then rolled her onto her side, curled around her and fell asleep. His arm lay heavy around her waist, his body giving off so much heat, she hadn't needed a blanket.

She should have slept like a baby. She'd felt completely safe and protected and she wanted to stay there all night. And most of today. But she'd stayed with Gabriel only a few hours, worried that Leo would wake and be worried because she wasn't there. Leo came first. He had to.

Spell Bound

Last night had been a stolen moment.

Today…back to reality.

But maybe not just yet, because the room Gabriel waved her into made her muscles quiver in anticipation.

Mirrors covered two facing walls and shiny wood covered the floor. The studio was perfect, complete with a small piano on one end and…a beautiful bar along the long front wall.

"Serena won't tell you but she's actually a decent dancer, though I've never known her to dance for an audience," Gabriel said. "I only know because I used to sneak down here and watch when I was kid."

She trailed her hand over the bar, drew in a deep breath of air scented with lemon oil. Her muscles twitched at the prospect of putting on a leotard.

"Sissy, look. A piano." Leo's voice was awed. "Hey, this box has your name on it."

Leo held out a white shirt box he'd picked up off the piano bench. She took it, with a quick glance at Gabriel. His expression revealed nothing. Taking off the lid, she lifted out a delicate pink leotard and white tights.

A smile kicked up the corners of her mouth and tears formed. She had no idea where he'd gotten the leotard. She didn't care.

She walked over to him, lifted onto her toes and kissed him on the cheek.

The heat in his eyes when she drew back scorched her to her bones and drew all the air out of the room.

"We've got time," Gabriel said. "If you want to work out for a while."

"Shea, can I play it?"

With an effort, she dragged her gaze to Leo, already sitting at the piano, looking at her with wide eyes.

She looked at Gabriel, who shrugged.

"Sure, kid," he said. "But there's a…"

Leo ran his small hands over the keys, getting a feel for the instrument. She knew nothing about music other than she liked to dance to it. But she did know Leo shouldn't be able to play an instrument he'd never touched before.

After a few minute of pressing keys in different combinations, he started to play a melody she vaguely recognized. It took her a second but she finally—

"My Chemical Romance."

Their second album. It had been a gift from another dancer in the last bar she'd worked at in Atlantic City. She and Leo both loved it. And he was playing it slow enough for her to dance to. The kid constantly amazed her.

She smiled back up at Gabriel.

"Where can I change?"

* * *

"I'm assuming this will be your first *treguenda* with the nail in your possession, Shea. Would you help me prepare for the ritual?"

Serena's question startled Shea out of the peaceful mood left over from her practice. She and Leo and Gabriel were in the kitchen, having lunch in companionable silence, though Gabriel's every glance made her body heat and her blood sizzle.

But Serena's soft words doused her in cold reality.

Holy crap. With everything else going on, she hadn't even thought about the fact that she would have to perform what would have been her mom's duties tonight. It made her brain stutter to a complete stop for a few

Spell Bound

seconds as she blinked at Serena, her hand going to key around her neck.

Her mouth opened but nothing came out. She couldn't form a coherent thought beyond the fact that her mom was truly gone for good.

Except... she wasn't. The voices murmured softly behind her mental shield.

"Shea."

Closing her eyes, she saw her mom giving her the key for the first time and teaching her how to make it transform into its natural shape as a nail. Saw her mom show her how to perform the yearly ritual that charged the nail on the summer solstice. Saw the nail clutched in Leo's hand as he slowly woke in that hidden room in the basement.

"Shea? Are you alright?" Serena asked.

Slowly, she shook her head. "Yeah. Yeah, I'm fine." She looked Serena in the eyes. "Of course, I'll help."

Shea felt Gabriel's gaze on her as she rose and she gave him what she hoped was a reassuring smile before she turned to Leo. "I'm going with Serena, bud. You stay with Gabriel, okay?"

Gabriel gave her a look before saying, "No problem. We'll go work with your knives, again."

Leo gave her a quick smile because Gabriel had said the magic word. Knives. He loved training with Gabriel. Which was good, because if anything happened—

"Shea?"

Serena stood in the doorway, looking back at her. Waiting.

She followed Serena through the house to her private altar room. A tree stump sat in the middle of the room, only about four feet in diameter and two feet high, but carved over every inch with pictures of the Goddesses and Gods and Etruscan writing. Someone had put many years of hard work and loving attention into the altar.

"This is beautiful," Shea said, running her fingers over the smooth top.

"Gabriel's father made that for me." Serena walked around to the other side of the altar. "Davis was a master craftsman."

Shea looked up, catching the look of utter devastation that crossed Serena's face.

"I'm sorry." Shea shook her head. "I didn't mean to upset you."

Serena quickly wiped the expression away with a forced smile and turned to gather her moon bowl and other tools from a table on the far wall. "I know. Please, don't feel you have to walk on eggshells around me. Davis and Nino have been gone a long time. Sometimes, I actually like to talk about them. To remember them."

Shea nodded. She knew exactly what Serena meant. "Is Gabriel a lot like his dad?"

Some other emotion crossed Serena's face now, something Shea would have sworn was fear. But that made no sense. "Gabriel idolized Davis. By the time Gabriel could talk, he was finishing Davis' sentences. They never fought, never butted heads. Not over anything."

Unlike Shea and her mom. They'd constantly been at odds. And when she met the hiker, it'd gotten so much worse. They'd barely been speaking when she'd finally left.

Tears rushed to her eyes, and she tried to blink them away. They'd only give her a headache.

"Shea?"

Spell Bound

"How do you think the curse will be broken, Serena?" Shea looked the other woman directly in the eyes. "Do you have any ideas?"

Serena sighed as she sat on the floor before the altar, waving Shea down opposite her. "I've had many ideas over the past centuries. Most of us believed the curse would be broken the second you took your first breath. Most of us wanted to believe that. Now that we know differently, I'd like to say I'm at a loss." Serena paused as she set the moon bowl on the altar. "But I won't lie to you, Shea. I think... I think it's going to require sacrifice. One that involves blood. Your blood. I think your parents knew that, and that's why they disappeared."

Yeah, she thought that too. But hearing someone else say it made it that much more real.

And, strangely, that much more acceptable.

She looked into the moon bowl, at the green liquid Serena had put there, then back up with raised eyebrows. "You want to induce a vision with vervaine juice? Didn't Gabriel tell you about my headaches?"

The spell Serena wanted to try would definitely bring on a migraine. Vervaine was a powerful herb in its natural leafy state, but distilled down to a juice, it was capable of producing a hallucinogenic state that could last for hours. Or days.

Serena nodded. "Yes, but you're not doing the spell. I am. I just need a bit of your blood."

Foolish hope made her hands clench into fists and still she had to ask. "Do you think you'll be able to see anything?"

"I honestly don't know." Serena held out her hand. "I'm not a foreseer. But we don't have many options, do we?"

Shea only hesitated a few seconds before placing her hand palm up in Serena's, wincing only a little when the other woman cut the tip of Shea's index finger with the sharp athame then dripped a few drops of blood into the bowl.

Rising and stepping away from the altar, Shea wrapped her cut finger in the hem of her t-shirt and watched as Serena took the blade and mixed the fluids together. Chanting in Etruscan, with an accent that reminded her so much of her mother, Serena made pleas to the Goddesses Menrva and Uni for their strength to see what would be.

Dipping her finger in the bowl, Serena closed her eyes then painted the mixed blood and vervaine on her cheeks and down the pulse points on her neck. Her head fell back and her hands dropped to her thighs. She continued to chant, the words deepening until they were little more than a rumble.

Shea felt the air thicken around her as the spell drew power up from the earth. Serena's muscles quivered with tension as her voice became a whisper. Shea's temples began to throb at the amount of power Serena drew to her. The first tinge of fear crept up Shea's spine. Fear that Serena might not see anything. Fear that she would.

Shea gasped as Serena's head suddenly snapped upright until she stared straight at Shea. Only she wasn't seeing Shea at all. Serena's eyes stared straight ahead, looking at something only she could see.

Her mouth continued to move, to chant, but Shea couldn't hear her at all now. Her ears strained for any recognizable words or phrases. Anything that would indicate what she saw.

What—

Suddenly, Serena started to shake, her body twitching

uncontrollably, her head whipping back and forth, as if she were fighting something. Or the spell was fighting her.

Shea rose, not sure if she should touch Serena to bring her out of it or if that would do more harm. But Serena was going to hurt herself if she didn't stop.

But what if the spell was working? What if she interrupted the spell before Serena was finished?

Just as the thought crossed her mind, Serena slumped to the floor as the power in the air dissipated.

Shea hurried to her side, not knowing if she should touch her. "Serena, can you hear me? Are you okay?"

Serena groaned, and her face scrunched into lines of pain. "I can hear you, dear. Very clearly. Just…give me a minute, okay?"

It took more than a minute for Serena to finally open her eyes. And when she finally did, the woman's expression told her everything she needed to know.

"I'm sorry, Shea. I saw nothing."

* * *

Serena watched the girl's shoulders drop even as she tried to smile.

"That's okay," Shea said. "It was pretty much a shot in the dark anyway."

Serena pulled herself back to a sitting position, closing her eyes so Shea couldn't see the lie she was telling.

Because she had seen something, something that made her cold to her bones.

Something it took every ounce of her control not to reveal to Shea. The girl had inherited her mother's Empathic Gift. If she wasn't careful, Shea would pick up on her feelings and demand to know what she'd seen.

But there was no way Serena would tell Shea how she was going to die.

* * *

A slight breeze rustled the leaves as Serena led them on an unmarked path through the forest.

It was close to midnight, but the full moon cast enough light that they didn't need flashlights.

Deer, raccoons and possums were the only life Gabriel sensed. He heard no car noise, no planes rumbling overheard.

Perfect night for the ritual. He hoped like hell it dispelled some of the tension that had built through the afternoon and evening. No one had said anything. Nothing inflammatory, anyway. But everyone had been on edge.

Even Leo had seemed to regress back to silence.

When they finally reached the circle in the clearing, Gabriel sighed as the power of the earth called out to him.

A sense of calm laced with anticipation seeped into his blood from the ground up and he smiled, knowing there would be more magic. And it would be good.

Almost as good as sex. He turned to see Shea speaking quietly with Serena. Almost.

And it would have been perfect if it all hadn't gone so wrong.

* * *

One minute Gabriel was watching Serena perform the blessing to the Goddess.

The next he was flat on his ass, blown out of the circle by a blast of power so intense, he blacked out for several seconds.

When he came to, he heard Quinn calling Serena's name, Serena calling to Leo and Shea moaning.

Leo remained in the center of the circle, eyes closed, holding tight to Shea's hand as he funneled power through his body and directly into Shea. She was already on her knees and would soon be flat on the ground. In a coma.

The force of the magic the kid channeled had taken him under, made him oblivious to anything but the power he controlled.

He didn't realize he was going to kill Shea if he didn't release her.

"Gabe!" Quinn yelled. "Serena won't let me in."

Damn, they'd underestimated the kid again.

He had to get Shea out of there before the kid killed her. Holding out his hands, he tested the wards Serena had set up around the circle. The *arus* in his blood reacted violently to the amount of power enclosing Serena, Shea and Leo in the circle. He couldn't break the wards in his current condition. They were too strong.

"Mom! Let me in."

Serena didn't spare him a glance. "Too dangerous. Leo, sweetheart, listen to me. You have to release the power. You're going to hurt Shea."

The little boy didn't move. Gabriel was pretty sure he hadn't heard Serena.

Leo had tapped into the power of the ley line pulsing straight through Serena's land. It was why she'd settled here, how she'd kept this house hidden all these years.

Magic, as all Etruscans knew, came from the earth. It flowed like blood through the soil in veins—ley lines. When anyone used magic, they tapped into that power to do so.

Leo, with too little training, must have felt like he'd just swallowed the biggest fucking happy pill in the world.

All that power gave him a high better than sex and drugs combined.

And he was channeling it all through Shea.

If Leo didn't stop…

Gabriel took the only option left. It was going to hurt, hurt like hell. And not just him, but Serena, too.

Fuck it. He drew power into himself, up from the ground and through his body. Then he lifted his hands toward the shield and released the power at the shield his mother had set up.

A lightning bolt of sheer agony slashed through his body, seizing his muscles and making his head feel like he'd gone five rounds with a heavyweight champion. Ears ringing, he locked his knees when they wanted to buckle as the barrier Serena had erected fell with an almost audible crash.

As it did, Gabriel grabbed for Leo and Shea at the same time Quinn lunged for Serena, who fell to the ground in a dead faint.

Too late. Too damn late.

Touching Leo was like grabbing a live electrical wire. Sharp pain surged through Gabriel as Leo tried to hold on to the energy Gabriel wanted to drain away.

"Leo!' he shouted. "Leo, you've got to stop. You're hurting Shea. Let her go."

Gabriel yanked at the boy's arm, trying to get his attention but Leo showed no sign of hearing him. Gabriel didn't want to hurt the kid, but if he didn't release Shea soon, he was going to have to knock him out. First, though, he reached for Shea and Leo's joined hands.

And gritted his teeth against the force of power running between them. It took him several minutes but finally, he managed to separate their fingers.

All that energy needed somewhere to go and it chose to bitch-slap Gabriel, driving him to his knees.

Even so, he tried to reach Shea before she fell to the ground, unconscious, but just missed her.

Leo blinked and looked around, as if coming out of a deep sleep

"What... happened? I don't feel good."

Gabriel pulled himself onto his hands and knees and crawled to Shea.

"Gabriel? What's—"

Leo cried out at the sight of Shea crumpled in a ball on the ground next to him. Gabriel grabbed for him and missed. His body screamed in residual agony as he fell back to his knees. He wanted to curl into a little ball and wait for the pain to recede but he couldn't.

Leo sobbed over Shea's unmoving body while Quinn held a slowly awakening Serena.

"Quinn." It hurt to speak, but he forced the words out as he dragged himself to his feet. "Take Serena back to the house."

"No," Serena said, her voice weak but calm. "Let Quinn get Shea. You and I can help each other. Leo, sweetheart. Stop crying. Come here."

"Didn't mean it." The little boy sobbed out the words. "I'm sorry."

Serena pulled away from Quinn and took a few steps toward Leo, nearly fell then pulled herself together to reach for him. "Come with me, baby. Shea will be fine. Quinn's going to take her back to the house and she'll be fine."

Serena sounded confident and loving as she soothed Leo then got him walking back to the house, leaning on him, making him feel like he was helping her. And maybe he was. She looked ready to drop over.

As Quinn lifted Shea in his arms, Gabriel heard her moan, and he released the breath he hadn't known he'd been holding.

"Shea." His voice sounded like sandpaper on wood. "Can you hear me?"

"Come on, Gabe." Quinn held Shea in both arms but used one hand to pull Gabriel to his feet. "Let's get back. I don't want to be stuck out here if someone got a hint of that power. It was enough to light up the entire eastern seaboard."

Shit. Quinn was right. Someone might have picked up on the disturbance they'd caused. The flow of magic in the earth had been disrupted. Leo had unknowingly gathered it to him and bent it to his will, something you didn't attempt unless you knew what you were doing. He'd caused the natural order to unbalance for those few minutes. And for someone looking for a signal, this area had just lit up like a neon sign.

Still, the wards on the property would hold. They had to. And as soon as they were feeling a little better, he and Serena would strengthen them. After they got Shea back to the house, he'd have Quinn take a run around the property.

First, he needed to get everyone settled. And quiet the fear gnawing a hole in his stomach.

* * *

Quinn stepped naked out the back door, closed it behind him and took a deep breath of the now-still air.

The house reeked with fear. Serena's. Gabriel's. Shea's. Leo's. Even his own.

That had been too fucking close. And it'd happened

so fast, he hadn't been able to do a damn thing to help. It sucked to feel that powerless, to know you could lose someone in the blink of an eye.

He could almost, almost, understand Serena's reluctance to love him. If only—

"Shit." He had no time to think about this. It was his turn to be the protector. Closing his eyes, he reached for the place in his soul where he kept his wolf and unlocked it.

If anyone ever asked how he went from human to wolf, the only thing he could tell them was, it was like opening a door and letting the animal walk through and into his body.

And, fuck, did it hurt.

That was the main reason there weren't a lot of biters running around. Most biters, people who became *versipelli* by being bitten by one, went crazy from the pain and sheer lunacy of what was happening to their bodies. And then they usually killed themselves.

Hereditary *versipelli* had years of training to handle their change before they hit puberty and actually went through it. Some got lucky, able to "flash" back and forth between their animal and their human skins without much pain.

Not him, though. He had to bear the full brunt of contorting his entire being into the body of a different animal.

Now on four paws, he headed toward the perimeter, the dark no hindrance. He'd never get lost in these woods. From the first moment he'd stepped on the property, he'd felt like he'd come home. That had been just after Davis and Nino had been killed. He'd helped Gabe bring their bodies here to be buried.

It was the only time he'd ever seen Gabe upset by anything since Quinn and his dad, now retired and living in North Carolina, had moved into Davis' rural Chester County home. Quinn had been twelve, sick with anger and despair. His mother had tried to kill him, to burn the house down around him as he'd slept. That wasn't something you got over right away.

Gabe had been fifteen and they'd bonded over a fistfight for some imagined slight. Nino had been six and idolized Quinn and his big brother. He'd died of a stray gunshot in Davis's arms.

He shook his head and caught a glimpse of full moon through the canopy. It'd been full the night Nino and Davis had died, too. He remembered because at fifteen, he'd only been able to change for about a year. That night, he still hadn't been able to control it. He'd been the one to kill the man who'd murdered Davis, had torn him to pieces and almost went to work on Gabe before he could control the blood lust.

When they'd arrived here with the bodies, Serena had stepped out of the house, intense sorrow on her face, but she'd thanked him for trying to save their lives.

He'd fallen in love immediately, as he'd been meant to, he'd figured out later. What he hadn't realized was that she'd known for years.

Quinn stopped, nose twitching at an unfamiliar scent.

It smelled like a car, but not one that burned fuel. He sniffed again. An electric car, small and nearly silent, idled at the bottom of the lane. Three men. He smelled magic on two of them. The one would be no threat at all. The other…magic leaked from his pores like cheap perfume. They stood on the edge of Serena's sanctuary, undiscovered for nearly two-hundred years.

Quinn took off at a dead run back to the house.

Chapter Nineteen

The women were out cold, each stretched on a couch in the peristyle.

Serena had assured Gabriel she would be okay, she just needed a little rest. Then she'd closed her eyes and either passed out or sunk into a deep sleep. He'd wake her in a few hours, just to be sure.

Leo sat on the floor next to his sister, holding her hand. She'd opened her eyes a few minutes ago, long enough to smile at Leo, nod to Gabriel and close her eyes again.

He was feeling a little better. A stiff shot of Jack Daniels had helped the shakes and he'd eaten one of the two power bars he'd grabbed from the kitchen.

"Leo, come here, bud."

The boy left Shea's side reluctantly, looking as if he were about to get his butt smacked for misbehaving. Gabriel wasn't sure how to make this better for him, didn't know the right things to say, but he had to try. The kid couldn't keep beating himself up over this.

Leo lifted himself onto the cushion next to Gabriel but kept his eyes glued to the floor. Allowing instinct to take over, Gabriel lifted the little boy onto his lap.

"I know you're going to blame yourself for a while, Leo, but it wasn't your fault. You've got to get over it, because I need you now."

Leo lifted his tear-stained gaze, mouth quivering. "I didn't mean it."

Gabriel knew he should hug the kid, show some affection, but he was so damn rusty at it. He put his arm around Leo and gave him an awkward hug. Leo threw his arms around his waist and held on, silent sobs wracking his body.

"I know you didn't mean to hurt Shea. It was our fault…my fault for not taking more precautions. You've got a lot of power, Leo. You just have to learn how to control it."

"That's what Daddy said." Leo sniffled and wiped at his tears with the back of his hands. "When I did it at home. I hurt them, too."

Well, shit. That was probably how Dario had found them. He hoped Leo never realized that.

"I'm sure they weren't mad at you, either," Gabriel said. "But that's why your Uncle Matt's coming." He hoped. He still hadn't heard from him. "He can teach you how to—"

"Gabe! We gotta get 'em out of here. Gabe, where the hell are you?"

His heart skipped a few beats as he stood, Leo in his arms. "Back here! What's going on?"

Quinn barreled through the doorway, naked and panting. "Three men, one with a shitload of power, bottom of the hill. It can't be coincidence. We gotta get 'em out now."

Adrenaline dropped into his bloodstream with a fiery burn. "Get Serena. I'll take Leo and Shea. Take her to the cave. Don't wait for us, just get Serena up there."

Vaffanculo. After all this time. Dario's men must have been closer than he'd thought. Even though they'd planned for this, Gabriel had never thought it would actually happen. The place was too well-shielded.

He didn't wait for Quinn. He shifted Leo to his back. "Hang on and don't let go." Then he picked up Shea, whose eyelids fluttered open for a second then closed.

Leo's voice shook as he whispered in his ear, "They want me?"

Gabriel felt the boy's fear like a punch low in his gut. "Yeah, well, they're not going to get you. I won't let that happen."

Leo's arms tightened around his neck, almost cutting off Gabriel's air. The kid couldn't weigh more than fifty pounds, but Gabriel still felt a little out of it from earlier, and he had to carry Shea. But he wouldn't fail.

He couldn't.

* * *

Shea's body registered motion and a change in temperature as she fought back nausea and the headache grinding in her temples.

She drew in a deep breath and smelled Gabriel all around her. Forcing her eyes open the tiniest bit, she realized they were back in the forest.

And they were running. Actually, Gabriel was running, with her in his strong arms.

"Leo—"

"Shh." Gabriel whispered in her ear. "He's right here. Someone's at the perimeter. Be quiet until we get to the cave."

Fear hit her broadside, making her stomach roll. They'd been found.

Wrapped in Gabriel's arms, she couldn't tell how

long it took them to get where they were going. She huddled in his arms the entire way—in pain, silent and terrified. When Gabriel stopped, she looked up to see a sheer rock wall. Did he mean to carry them up that?

"Either of you claustrophobic?"

Gabriel waited until she shook her head before he set her on her feet, one hand on her shoulder to steady her, and let Leo slide down his back.

"Careful, the opening's not that big."

Actually, the opening was little more than a slit in the rock face that emptied into a cave, high enough to stand in and large enough to hold a small party.

Quinn had lit a small lantern on the far side, near a ledge hewn into the stone walls. He'd laid Serena there and stood, staring at her.

Leo's gasp echoed through the chamber. "Oh wow."

She didn't have a chance to see what made Leo sound so fascinated because Gabriel stepped into her line of vision, his gaze burning even in the dark shadows of the cave. "Don't leave. Not for anything. Serena might be out for a while yet. I blasted her pretty hard to break the circle."

A muscle ticked in his jaw, the only outward sign that he was worried. And fear bit into her chest a little harder.

"Keep Leo quiet and turn the light off when we leave, unless Leo needs it. I'll replace the wards and they'll hold. But if Quinn or I aren't back by daybreak, assume we're not coming."

His matter-of-fact tone felt like a blow to her head. His stoic expression never changed.

"If we don't make it back, after the sun goes down tonight, go to your buddy, James Riley. He'll take care of you until Matt gets here."

"Gabriel, don't—"

"Make sure Serena doesn't try anything stupid. Don't you do anything stupid. For Leo's sake."

"Gabriel—"

"And if I do come back…"

He dragged her against him and kissed her. Hard. She hadn't been expecting it, but it didn't take long for her to return his passion with her own.

His kiss was an all-out assault on her senses. His scent nearly suffocated her, and when he swept his tongue past her lips, his taste exploded in her mouth. Throwing her arms around his neck, she clung and gave back as hard as she could.

All her fear, all her pain, all the emotions she'd bottled up inside threatened to sink her into a dark place. Instead, she kissed the living daylight out of him and held tight to the fact that he kissed her just as ruthlessly.

When he released her, his eyes remained closed, and his chest heaved like he'd just run a marathon. She liked knowing she had that power over him.

When he opened his eyes to stare into hers, she knew what he was going to say before he spoke.

"When I come back, we'll finish that."

She took a deep breath and nodded. He didn't move right away, staring into her eyes for a few brief seconds before brushing past her. But he didn't go for the door.

She watched as he squatted down beside Leo and looked him dead in the eyes.

"While I'm gone, you listen to Shea. But you're a *grigorio*, Leo, and we don't scare easily. We fight and we win. The women need you to be strong for them, just like they're going to protect you however they can."

Then Gabriel leaned close and whispered in Leo's

ear. And when Gabriel pulled back and his mouth quirked into a full-blown smile, Leo's face split in a weak grin.

"No problem." Leo held out his hand, and Gabriel shook it.

Gabriel nodded one more time then stood. "Quinn, let's move."

Quinn pulled his gaze away from Serena and shook his head like a man coming out of a daze. Moving to stand next to Gabriel, he nodded to Shea and mustered a smile for Leo.

"See you in a few." Then he turned to Gabriel and his smile seemed almost normal. "Let us hunt some Orc."

Gabriel rolled his eyes as they turned to leave. "You watch too many damn movies, you know that?"

Quinn grabbed at his chest, mimicking a heart attack. "Holy hell, did you actually see 'Lord of the Rings?' I thought you were above frivolous things like movies."

Shea couldn't hear anything more as they passed through the rock.

Leaving her alone with a six-year-old and an injured *strega*.

"Don't worry, Shea." Leo tugged on her hand, drawing her toward the small light next to Serena. "It'll be okay."

* * *

Gabriel and Quinn doubled back to the house, but the intruders hadn't reached it yet. They were making progress up the hill, though.

Gabriel kneeled and dug his hands into the soil. Closing his eyes, he released his senses into the dirt, let them blend with the energy in the earth and extend outward.

He sensed the animals in the forest and the living trees in the ground. Beyond that, he felt the definite signature of men. He honed in on their location. It took several seconds, but he finally got a bead on them.

They'd passed through the confusion spells ringing the outer reaches of the property, which meant they had a pretty damn powerful stregone with them. Or they were just damn lucky.

Gabriel didn't believe in that kind of luck.

He tried to focus on the one with the most power, but they were shielding. They knew what they were up against, and they'd come prepared. Well, he'd make sure they weren't prepared enough.

Beside him, Quinn drew out his wolf in silence.

It didn't take them long to find the men. Three of them, keeping to the shadows. Two had strong glamours. The other one held a Ruger, which should be no problem. Automatic weapons usually couldn't shoot iron bullets with any accuracy. And iron was the only metal the *grigori* had no defenses against.

Gabriel motioned for Quinn to get behind the trio. Between the two of them, these three clowns didn't stand a chance. He recognized one of the men from the strip club. The other two were new. That meant there were probably more of them somewhere, maybe down at the car. Still, not bad odds. Finish these three then deal with the others before they realized these were gone.

He never considered defeat. He'd do whatever it took to make sure his mother's sanctuary wasn't breached.

Because they knew each other so well, Quinn knew exactly what Gabriel wanted him to do. He attacked first from the rear, grabbing one man's leg and disorienting them so Gabriel could come at them from the front when they turned to see what was biting them in the ass.

The fight was short and vicious and the invaders barely had time to defend themselves before Gabriel had slashed the throats of two and Quinn had torn out the throat of the other.

"Too easy," he muttered. "Too fucking easy."

Quinn growled low in his throat and shook his head, fur bristling at his nape.

"Decoys. Sonovabitch, they were decoys."

The words were no sooner out of Gabriel's mouth than Quinn shot off in the direction of the house, Gabriel close on his heels. They didn't pass a soul, which meant there were no more…or whoever was in front of them was more powerful than he was.

The teen from the other day. It had to be him. Gabriel muttered a seeking spell as he ran, fitting an image of the boy into it. And damn if he didn't find him. Close to the house. Not there yet and heading away at the moment.

Gabriel slowed and Quinn, attuned to his every move, dropped back to his side. He could see blood lust in Quinn's eyes. He felt the same way, but they needed a plan before they could take this kid out.

Adrenaline pumping, Gabriel forced himself to stop and motioned for Quinn to do the same. He had to think, had to get around this kid, who probably already knew they were looking for him. Surprise wasn't an option.

Gabriel bared his teeth at Quinn, who returned the grin. They'd give the guy what he was expecting. And let him screw up.

* * *

Serena woke minutes after the men left.

Rubbing her eyes, she sat up and gasped. "Gabriel! What's going on?"

"Serena." Shea hurried to her side as Leo flicked on the lantern. "We're okay. Quinn found someone at the bottom of the hill. He and Gabriel went to check it out."

It took the other woman a few seconds to register the information, pain still blurring her eyes. Then her lids descended and she raised a hand to rub at her temples.

"I should have known." She shifted her legs over the edge of the rough bed, her green dress shimmering in the lamplight. "How could I not have known? I've got to get out there—"

Shea clamped a hand on Serena's arm. "You have to stay right here. Gabriel left specific instructions. You go nowhere."

Serena shot her a look designed to make her cower in fear. "Do not presume to tell me—"

"If you go out there, you could get them killed. I won't let you do that."

Her eyes widening, Serena looked ready to blast her and Shea hoped Leo wasn't listening too closely. But then the other woman took a deep breath, as if she'd read her mind. Maybe she had.

"When did they leave?" Serena asked.

"I think about twenty minutes ago."

"Where's Leo?"

"Here," he called from the other side of the room.

Serena smiled in Leo's general direction, but when she looked at Shea, her expression turned serious and she spoke barely above a whisper. "I need to see what's going on. Don't worry," Serena added when Shea opened her mouth to protest. "I can do it from here. I just need some water and a bowl. Leo, come here, dear."

She didn't raise her voice much above a whisper, but Leo padded over with the lantern.

"I'm going to turn off the light and, when our eyes are accustomed to the dark again, I'm going to show you a pretty cool trick, okay?"

Leo nodded and didn't even flinch when Serena plunged the cave into darkness again. It didn't take long to regain their night vision, helped along by a faint glow from above, probably an opening to the outside. Serena led them deeper into the cave, to what appeared to be a storeroom. Bottled water, packaged food and a few boxes of herbs and magical supplies. From one of the boxes, Serena withdrew a jug of water and a large bowl lined with abalone.

"Have you ever seen a magic mirror, Leo?"

Leo's teeth flashed in the dark. "My mom showed me hers once. She said she was checking on Shea."

Shea gasped. Her mother had kept tabs on her.

"Your mom was much better at using hers than I am, but I think I can make this work."

Pushing thoughts of her mom to the back of her brain, Shea watched Serena pour the liquid into the bowl and set the bowl on the floor. Then Serena knelt, holding her hands over the bowl as she intoned, "Blessed Goddess, I entreat thee to show us those who would harm an innocent."

At first, the water showed nothing but the darkness of the cave. Then slowly, shapes began to coalesce. Or rather, one shape, someone climbing the hill toward the house. Then the water clouded again and another shape formed in the glassy surface. This one was practically at the cave and headed straight for them. Shea recognized him as the teenager from the rest stop.

Shea heard Serena draw in a shaky breath.

Spinning on her heel, Shea headed for the stockroom

again. She'd seen exactly what she needed there. When she returned, Serena stood in the middle of the room, arms crossed over her chest.

"What are you planning?"

Shea buckled the pugio's sheath around her waist and positioned it on her hip. She liked the feel of the small blade in her hand, better for close fighting. "Take him out before he gets me." She strapped a matching weapon on her left upper arm. "If it's a physical fight, I should win. I'm hoping I can surprise him enough to get the upper hand and incapacitate him."

"And if you can't?"

Shea felt her lips curl back in a snarl. "Then I'll kill him."

She went to move past Serena, but the other woman stopped her with a hand on her shoulder.

"Are you sure you can do that? Teens have a lot of raw power and earlier tonight..."

She didn't have to finish. Shea knew what she meant. But Shea knew something about herself.

"My father trained me, just as he would any *grigorio*. I can take him. I know I can. Don't let anything happen to Leo."

Serena nodded, but Shea wasn't sure what she was agreeing to. Didn't matter, because she wasn't waiting for the other woman's permission. She wasn't Serena's child or her underling or her anything.

Except...possibly her savior.

No, don't think about that now. Don't think about anything but what you have to do.

She turned to Leo, who gave her a steady look.

Knowing he had faith in her helped her pass through the wall and into the night.

* * *

During the past twenty years, Dario had rarely left Florida. But when Peter had relayed the latest message from his men in Pennsylvania, he'd decided the time had come to get out more.

Besides, if Peter's men were right, he wanted to be there when they confronted the women. He told Peter to have the men wait for him before moving and to stay well away from the house until he arrived.

By the time his private plane landed at the tiny Reading Regional Airport, he knew Serena was close. Call it intuition.

Driving to the site, he didn't bother to ask how the men had found her. Kelsey was with them. The boy had uncanny powers.

Of course, it helped that the boy was one of theirs.

"Have you located the house yet?"

Kelsey shook his head. "But I've got the perimeter mapped. There's a web of spells and wards in place and the whole area seems to be sitting on a well of power."

Dario smiled at the boy, who wouldn't be a boy much longer. Already fifteen, Kelsey had the strength of five grown men. And a backbone beaten into him by Dario himself.

"You've done well. Come on then, son. Let's find your mother and get reacquainted."

* * *

Gabriel and Quinn caught up to one of their quarry just as he was about to discover the house.

Even though he couldn't see his face, Gabriel knew it

wasn't the teen from the day before. This was a grown man, shorter but powerfully built.

Motioning for Quinn to move around and herd the man back to Gabriel should he run, Gabriel planned to come at him from behind. There was something about this one...something that didn't feel right. Something evil...

Shit, the guy was *Mal*.

Gabriel tackled him, taking him to the ground and smashing the man's head on the hard earth with a blow that should have knocked him unconscious. It didn't. Instead, the man twisted to his feet and spun, landing a punch on Gabriel's chin.

Smiling now, though the dark hid it, Gabriel swung back. Adrenaline flowed, better than the rush working a spell gave him. He needed a fight right now.

He let the man land a few, absorbing the slight pain, then he jabbed his fist into the guy's stomach, encountering solid muscle.

It was a silent fight, except for the few exhalations of air when one or the other would land a good one, and for the most part, they were well matched.

The man was shorter than Gabriel, but he had the same build and packed a lot of muscle. And he was fast. Gabriel was no slouch, but this man moved with the ease of someone who had trained for years, decades even. Which didn't make sense, because the guy couldn't be much older than himself.

At that moment, the clouds obscuring the moon shifted and Gabriel finally caught a glimpse of the man's face.

Holy shit.

Stunned, Gabriel stepped sideways, practically stumbling over his feet to put some distance between himself and the other man.

Stephanie Julian

What the hell kind of trick was this?

The man froze and stared back, his mouth hanging open in shock.

"Who the hell are you?" The words flew out of Gabriel's mouth before he could curb them, tightening his clenched fists until his knuckles cracked.

Shit, maybe he didn't want to know.

No, there was no maybe about it. He wasn't going to like the answer. He felt it in his bones.

Jesus, their faces…They could have been brothers, their features mirrored each other so closely.

The man lowered his own hands and retreated two steps, never taking his eyes from Gabriel's face. "I believe that is the question I should be asking you. Who are you, boy? Who's your mother?"

Rage bubbled like acid in his gut. "*Vaffanculo*. I'm no boy and I don't know what kind of trick this—"

"Believe me, it's no trick." The man's voice turned harsher, colder and his lips pulled into a straight line as he continued to stare at Gabriel like he was a bug under a microscope. "Are you Amalia's? Serena's? Ah, yes," he said, as if Gabriel had answered his question. "Serena. How did she do it? How could she have done it?"

The other man moved closer a step and Gabriel threw an uppercut before he realized he'd done it. The bastard dodged it with the dexterity of a pro boxer. Unnaturally quick.

From behind him, Gabriel heard Quinn growl, a growl he recognized. Something was wrong here, something really, really wrong.

Gabriel raised his fists again. "I don't know what the hell you're playing at, but after I pound you into oblivion, you're going to explain."

"Oh, I don't think you'll need to do that." The other man raised his hands in surrender, which Gabriel didn't believe for a second. "But I think you better brace yourself for a shock, son."

No, no, no. "Believe me, you'd better brace for the shock, and I am definitely not your son."

To his surprise, the man smiled. "Well, you can take another swing at me, but I'm pretty damn sure I'm your father."

Chapter Twenty

Gabriel's stomach plummeted, though he knew the guy was lying. He had to be. It was a trick, designed to make him drop his guard.

But if that was the reason, why hadn't the other man struck?

"Who the hell are you?"

The man laughed, though there was no humor in the sound. "Ah, the more important question here is who are you? But answer this one first. How old are you?"

"I'm only gonna ask one more time, then I'm gonna take you out. What's your name?"

"Gabe." Quinn, in human form, appeared behind the man. Gabriel had missed Quinn's change completely, and it pissed him off. "Fuck, man, he's cursed. I can smell it on him."

Gabriel shook his head. There was no way he could believe that. No way. He couldn't…There wasn't…

But somewhere inside, he knew. He steadied his arms when they wanted to shake, firmed his resolve and refused to believe.

There was a reason for this. There had to be a reason…

"I'm only gonna ask once more," Gabriel said through gritted teeth. "What's your name?"

Spell Bound

The man laughed, though it was more like a choked growl. "Dario Paganelli." He held out his hand, as if Gabriel would even consider shaking it, then let it fall with a shrug. "I'm pleased to meet you...Son."

* * *

Shea paused before she left the safety of the cave. Scanning the surroundings, she saw no one, but that didn't mean the teen wasn't out there. She just needed to pinpoint his location before she moved.

Closing her eyes, she slowed her breathing until all she could hear was the forest. She didn't need magic to listen to the sounds of the earth. She only had to open her ears.

A raccoon scurried in the brush somewhere to her left and several bats flew through the trees overhead, their leathery wings caressing the night air. A herd of deer grazed higher in the hills and light footsteps approached from the south.

Slowly, she opened her eyes and picked apart shadows in the darkness, starting to lighten though it was still a few hours till dawn.

There, to the right of the entrance. Something moved, something bigger than a fawn and smaller than a bear. Something human.

She couldn't be sure, but since he was walking away from the entrance, she was fairly certain he didn't know it existed.

Slipping from the safety of the rock, Shea moved without a sound. She hadn't been kidding when she'd told Serena her father had trained her as a *grigorio*, even if she hadn't realized it at the time.

And she'd been a damn good study. The boy didn't realize she had him until she made her move. But even though she'd anticipated his strength and his speed, the burst of pure hatred that ran through him when she wrapped her arms around him from behind, made her falter.

He flooded her with hate, made her skin crawl. Snarled like a wild animal and tried to pivot. Locking her hands together at his chest, she wrapped her left leg around his and tried to take him to the ground.

He almost got away by twisting into the fall, but she anticipated and kept him flat on his stomach. She tried to wrestle his arms behind his back, but they were trapped under his body, so she needed another way to subdue him. Even though he was taller, they were evenly matched in weight.

It took everything she had to keep him down. He flopped like a landed fish, only a hundred times heavier and more determined. They fought silently for control, and at one point, he got an elbow free that he landed squarely on her cheek. Pain exploded behind her left eye, but she didn't fall for his ploy when he went limp.

Instead, she tightened her grip so he couldn't slip away…and he hit her with a blast of power so intense it made the voices in her head scream.

She crumpled, hands clasped to her head, the pain blinding her.

The boy jumped to his feet and prepared to strike again. But he froze when Serena walked out of the cave.

The pain stopped, the voices died, and the boy very plainly said, "Hello, Mother."

* * *

Spell Bound

Quinn rushed the guy from behind.

He wasn't expecting it and hit the ground hard, but the bastard rolled and came up swinging. The lightning-fast punch connected with Quinn's jaw, jarring him off his feet. The guy was strong, far stronger than he looked.

And, holy fuck, the man looked just like Gabriel.

Quinn gaped for a brief second, allowing Dario to lift his foot to kick. Quinn knew he wouldn't be able to get out of the way fast enough and braced for impact.

Which never came.

Gabriel tackled Dario with a roar, wrapped his arms around the man and took him down. They scrabbled there for a few seconds, each getting in a few solid punches before Dario stepped away so fast he almost didn't see him do it.

But as far as Quinn could tell, the guy didn't have much magic of his own. Except for the fact that he was cursed.

Gabriel and Dario stood, staring at each other, neither speaking. Only the sound of their breathing could be heard.

Quinn could smell the distrust, the anger, the betrayal emanating from both of them. He didn't want to believe, didn't want contemplate what it meant, who this man was.

Quinn didn't know how long they stood there. He stood as well, wanted to be ready to fight again if Gabe needed him.

And was completely unprepared for the pain that slid through his body.

* * *

Out of the corner of his eye, Gabriel saw Quinn's body jerk.

What the —

Gabriel nearly panicked as a man behind Quinn

grabbed his suddenly limp body and held onto him, a Taser at his throat.

He turned back to the man he wanted to kill more than anything. "If you hurt him, I'll hunt you down and make you beg me to cut your heart out."

"Bloodthirsty, aren't you?" Dario smiled, but the sight sent revulsion coursing through Gabriel's body. "Seems you inherited more from me than just your looks. Of course, this changes things a bit."

Gabriel tried not to rise to his taunts but couldn't help himself. "Let him go now or I'll draw out your death for days."

Dario shook his head, his expression becoming thoughtful. "Tell her I want to meet. It's time to end this. We have much to discuss. Apparently. Tell her I'll return her pet then."

"There's no way—"

"You don't have much of a choice, boy." Dario's expression had gone coolly blank. "Talk to your mother. I think you're going to be in for a rude awakening."

With a short nod, Dario motioned for the man carrying Quinn to precede him. Gabriel wanted to tear the guy apart, but that stun gun had to be on a high setting if it had knocked out Quinn. Another jolt could kill him.

Torn in too many directions, Gabriel let them go.

He'd fix this. He'd get Quinn back. He'd prove the demon Dario wrong about his assumptions, and then he'd kill the man, no matter that Serena had forbidden it. He deserved to die.

Turning, Gabriel ran for the cave.

* * *

The boy threw Serena for a moment.

He made her tongue twist around the protection spell she was working, causing a momentary imperfection, but not enough to make it unravel.

And she knew it wasn't true.

This child wasn't hers. Couldn't be. But someone had lied to the boy, because he believed it implicitly.

Without breaking her silent chant protecting her and Shea from anything the boy threw at them, she shook her head. "I'm sorry, but you're not my child."

The teen bared his teeth and struck back with a jolt of power meant to level her. "You are my mother. He told me you would lie to protect yourself."

"If this is how you treat your mother then it's no wonder she didn't acknowledge you."

There, that one got under his skin. And it hurt her heart to see him flinch. Goddess, he was only a child. Dario had much to answer for. She wanted to wring the man's neck. Actually, she wanted to do a lot worse for putting that combination of fear and loathing in this child's eyes.

It made her sick to realize the lengths to which Dario would go to wipe her *boschetta* from the earth.

Damn him for making her just as ruthless.

"I am not your mother, but I could help you find her. It doesn't have to be like this. What's your name?"

The teen sneered, and for a brief second Serena saw pure hatred on his face. Her blood ran cold.

"You don't need to know my name. You just need to know how much I hate you."

In her peripheral vision, Serena saw Shea, still on the ground, close her eyes, but couldn't tell if it was in pain or preparation. She wanted to warn Shea against trying anything, but couldn't take her concentration off the boy.

He was strong, and he was trying to beat down her shield. Righteous anger fed him, anger she had to encourage, had to cultivate until it forced him to make an ill-conceived move. She needed to incapacitate him, knock him unconscious. She refused to take his life. She'd never had to kill before, wouldn't be able to live with herself if she did.

"Your hatred is directed at the wrong person." She moved closer, tried to put herself between Shea and the boy. "Do you remember me, child? Do you have any memories of me at all?"

"You abandoned me right after I was born." He spat the words at her. "Why would I remember you?"

There! She felt a slight weakening of his mental shield. It had been like a brick wall but now there was a chink of mortar missing.

"You wouldn't, because the man who raised you lied to you. He stole you from your rightful parents and corrupted you for your power."

"You lie." With one flick of his finger, he shot a bolt of blue fire straight at her heart. It deflected off her protection spell and bounced off the nearest tree, leaving the scent of burning wood.

"No, I don't. I could find your parents. Your real parents. Tell me your name."

Whose could he be? She should be able to tell.

The teen smiled, an expression that looked hauntingly familiar but still unknown.

"Father told me you would try to twist things. But it won't work. I've waited years for this…"

Pain hit her low in the stomach, taking her to her knees. Shock and disbelief made her freeze. She'd never been bested before.

The teen's handsome face twisted with fierce glee, and he pressed his advantage with another bolt of pain to her head. He shouldn't be able to affect her like this. She was older, stronger, supposedly smarter than this boy, yet he was beating her.

And she couldn't lose. There was too much on the line, too many lives at stake, lives she was responsible for.

Struggling to her feet, she submerged the pain and tossed his power back at him. It took him off guard for only a second before he hit her with another blast.

"You're weak, old lady," he mocked. "Weak and scared. Why don't you just give up, and I'll make it easy on the rest of them. Even the boy."

"Like Dario made it easy on you?" She could barely get the words out. A burning pain had started to creep down from her head and up from her stomach. She knew he was trying to reach her heart, and though he couldn't kill her, he could incapacitate her.

"He made me strong when you would have turned me into a servant."

He tweaked the pain again. She shuddered but managed to reply.

"He's made you the servant, child." She used the word deliberately, trying to get his anger to reveal his weak spot again. She had to hold out until then. "Where is your so-called father now? Cowering far from here, I'm sure."

"Oh, he's here. Closer than you think."

There, she felt the pain lessen just a bit and she forced herself to press back with her own power. She felt every nerve in her body scream, but it was enough to make him break his concentration.

Without warning, Shea rose from the ground and

punched the boy in the jaw in one smooth move. It was so unexpected, Serena's mouth dropped open as he hit the ground with a thud, out cold.

"I need some rope to tie him up." Shea looked at Serena and raised an eyebrow, looking so much like her mother. "Before he wakes up would be good."

Serena nodded and forced herself to move into the cave and, after a quick word of reassurance to Leo, found a length of rope.

Outside, she handed the rope to Shea, who tied the boy's wrists behind his back, working the knots with skillful hands. Leo stepped forward, his gaze glued to the other boy.

When she was done, Shea looked at Serena, waiting for instructions.

First things first. "We need to find Gabriel and Quinn and get out of here. We need to get Leo and this boy somewhere safe. Dario won't stop until he finds them, either of them."

"Who is he?" Leo asked.

Serena shook her head. "I'm not sure. We'll need to do a little research on that." She forced a smile for Leo, his features drawn into tight lines of fear. He was only six, after all. And so vulnerable, even though he had power she couldn't comprehend. Powers he shouldn't possess yet.

There were so many things she needed to know, so much she'd let slide in the past years.

And they were all about to bite her on the ass, as Davis would have said.

Because Gabriel stepped into the clearing.

* * *

Spell Bound

"Serena."

Gabriel tried but he couldn't keep the bite out of his tone. So many questions crowded in his head, he wanted to roar with rage.

For a second, his gaze dropped to the teenager bound and out cold on the ground. Shea and Leo stood next to him.

"Are you okay?" He forced himself to ask that question first, before anything else spilled out. Everyone nodded. "Good, get your stuff. Now. We need to move."

"Where are we going?"

Leo's quiet, terrified tone forced him to take a deep breath. "We need to get you guys somewhere safe. Then I need to find Quinn." He sliced his gaze at his mother. "Dario took him."

He ruthlessly ignored Serena's stricken cry and turned to Shea. "Get weapons. Whatever you want. I'll take this one inside then I've got to make a phone call."

Leo tugged on his hand and Gabriel focused on his face, forcing everything but the little boy out of his mind. Trying not to crush him against his chest, he pulled the kid into his arms as he stood so they were eye to eye. "Everything's going to be okay, Leo. I swear."

He waited until Leo nodded then set him down and lifted the teen in his arms. After he placed him in a small side cave off the main one, he wove a series of binding spells that should hold him for a few hours.

When he was done, he turned to find Serena watching him.

Questions rose in his throat like bile. He didn't want to do this now.

"Gabriel—"

He slashed out with one hand. "No. Not now. Just answer one question. Is he?"

Serena knew what he was asking. Her eyes filled with tears and her mouth quivered until she firmed it.

He didn't need to hear her say the words.

Betrayal and anger ate at his stomach, at his heart, threatened to swamp his reasoning. He couldn't afford that now. He had to get them all away from here and figure out what to do.

"Quinn—" Serena started.

"I'll find him," he snapped. "Dario wants to end this. He wants to talk to you, but that's not going to happen." He bit down on other words that would flay her to the bone. "I'll get Diego up here to take care of this one. Then I need to call Matt, find out where the hell he is."

Turning his back on her, he whipped out his cell phone and pressed one key. He spoke as soon as Diego answered, not bothering to identify himself.

"I need you at the compound safe site to pick up a package. Take it to town."

Diego didn't miss a beat. "You want me to put it out of its misery?"

Gabriel didn't answer right away. He stared down at the kid that could have been Nino. Could still be Leo if he fucked up.

"No, take him to Laran. Let him deal."

"Alright, but if he gives me a hassle, all bets are off."

One of only three living *grigori* who'd been born *versipellis*, Diego was a deadly weapon. He'd handle—

The hair on his arms rose. Shea was coming. He turned to find her staring at him. The urge to go to her, wrap his arms around her and lose himself in her warmth for a few hours nearly overwhelmed him.

But the anger, the betrayal, still bit at him. He was afraid of what he'd say if he went to her, afraid he'd want to drown himself in her, and he couldn't afford to lose the crystal clear clarity rage gave him.

He shook his head, mutely telling her not to speak.

Then he picked up Leo, standing silent at Shea's side, and headed back down the hill, knowing the women would follow.

* * *

Shea knew Gabriel was hanging on to his control by a thread.

Something had happened back at Serena's, something that had turned Gabriel's world upside down then blown it apart.

He looked shell-shocked.

So she didn't ask where they were going. Besides, it was pretty obvious. Back into the city.

They drove into the northwest section, where every other brick row house looked run down, the cars were a mix of older-model American and late-model Japanese, and men—boys, really—stood on street corners, eyeing every car that drove by.

This wasn't a neighborhood Shea wanted to be caught in alone, at any time of the day, despite the several churches along Schuylkill Avenue.

Leo sat in the front seat staring out the window, occasionally sneaking glances at Gabriel, while Shea and Serena avoided each other in the back seat.

The inner turmoil eating at Gabriel and Serena ate at Shea's gut, too, their emotions more painful than physical wounds. Which, of course, made the voices buzz like angry bees.

A few blocks off Schuylkill, nearly to the city limit,

Gabriel turned into an alley behind what looked like an abandoned warehouse. Another alley split the building in two and Gabriel turned into that.

The alley appeared to dead end into the building, but Gabriel pulled out his cell, pressed a button and said, "I'm at the door. Let me in."

After a few seconds, the brick in front of them dissolved to reveal a metal door, which slid open without a sound.

Gabriel rammed the Jeep into gear and they shot into the dark.

Apparently he'd been here before because he knew when to turn and when to stop, before the lights had barely flickered.

Shea held her breath as Gabriel threw the Jeep into park, nearly snapped the key in the ignition as he turned it off and slammed the door shut behind him with enough force to rattle the frame.

"Let's go," he said, his voice low and dangerous, then stalked off toward a door at the far end of the huge open space they were in.

Her mouth tightening, Shea nearly bit her tongue in half. She wasn't afraid of him. She'd get in his face soon enough because she needed to know what had happened with Dario.

The monster had gotten too close to Leo. He'd taken Quinn.

And she needed to make a decision.

The passage from her grandfather's journal sprang into her mind, the one about her dad's dream.

Damn, it'd been so much easier when she hadn't known Serena or Quinn or Gabriel. When it had only been her and Leo and she'd been unaware of the curse.

Part of her wanted to take Leo and run. Another part knew she couldn't leave Gabriel. Couldn't leave without knowing Quinn was safe in Serena's arms. If Serena would allow him into her arms. If the curse was broken...

She watched as Gabriel tore open the door and disappeared through it.

"Shea, why don't you and Leo go in?" Serena said. "I...think I'll just sit for a few minutes."

Gabriel's mother stared out the window, focused on something on the opposite side of the garage. More likely staring at nothing at all. Worry emanated off her in waves. Worry and despair.

"Sure. Come on, bud." She dug up a smile for Leo, staring at them from the front seat. "Let's see where we are."

With Leo's hand in hers, she headed for the door Gabriel had walked through.

Above them, the building rose three stories, open to the ceiling, and was empty except for a few cardboard boxes here and there.

Reading had been a hub of railroad activity in the 1800s and early 1900s. Men had made their fortunes in steel here and this building seemed old enough to be left over from those boom days. Today, many of the old railroad warehouses remained vacant. Although she was pretty sure this one wasn't completely deserted.

She felt the hum of energy like electricity under her skin. Someone worked a hell of a lot of magic here.

They were almost to the door Gabriel had gone through when Leo whispered, "Are they mad?"

He didn't have to ask who he meant.

Yes, Gabriel was furious with Serena. And Serena...well, she was heartsick down to her marrow.

"They just had a bad day, hon. We know how those go, don't we?"

"Are they mad at me?"

She stopped and gave him a tight hug, tears forming at his uncertainty. "No, baby, not at all. Gabriel's angry at the world right now. And Serena's upset about Quinn."

And if Gabriel doesn't shape up soon, I'm going to give him something to be really angry about.

She didn't know what had happened back at the compound, but she intended to find out. Something had driven a wedge between Serena and her son. Something he couldn't allow to affect his judgment. Not with Quinn kidnapped and Leo still in danger. And Dario wanting Serena.

That situation would be stressful enough to make anyone lose it, but she knew that wasn't all. Something else was making Gabriel almost crazy.

They reached the door just as Gabriel ripped it open. His fierce expression made Leo draw in a quick breath. Shea opened her mouth to tell him to get his shit together, but Gabriel toned it down before she could.

"Leo, there's someone here I want you to meet." Then he glanced at Shea. "Where's Serena?"

By the Gods, he was in so much pain, all of it showing in his eyes. Why he wasn't paralyzed, she didn't know. She wanted to wrap her arms around him and hold him close but thought he might shatter if she did. "She's still in the car. She'll come along in a minute."

"Fine." He held out a hand for Leo, who didn't hesitate to take it. "Digger, this is Leo. Leo, Digger Alfiero. He makes cool things. You want to take a look?"

A slightly familiar, handsome guy with short brown hair, pale green eyes and a lopsided smile stood in front of them in what appeared to be an apartment. There was a bed, a couch, a TV and a kitchen area but not much else. And still, she felt *arus* in the room, in the floor, in the air. Everywhere.

"Hey, Leo. Gabriel's told me a lot about you." The guy transferred his gaze to Shea and nodded. "Can I give him the tour? We won't leave the building, and no one can get in without my knowledge."

Obviously Gabriel had told Digger he wanted to talk to her alone. Well, tough. If Leo didn't want to go with Digger—

"Can I go, Shea?"

Okay, Leo had already decided Digger was okay. "Sure, bud. I'll be right here if you need me."

Obviously, he didn't at the moment because he walked off with the new guy.

Turning, she found Gabriel staring at the door to the warehouse. He was pissed. She saw it in the way he held his hands in fists at his sides and heard it in his voice, in the edge on his words.

"What's going on, Gabriel?"

He didn't answer right away, still staring at the door. Finally, he said, "I called Matt to let him know to meet us here. He's close."

"You're going to leave us and go find Quinn alone, aren't you?"

"Yes."

"Leo doesn't want you to leave."

His body tightened and a muscle jumped in his jaw. "He'll be better off away from me right now."

"I don't want you to go," she added softly. "You're not steady right now—"

He held up one hand like a traffic cop. "Don't. I don't

think I can stop myself from hurting you if you're in the way when I blow."

She shrugged. "That's okay. I'm up for getting a little rough."

He groaned low in his throat—in pain or anger, she wasn't sure which.

"Gabriel, tell me. It might help."

"This doesn't concern you."

Okay, that shouldn't hurt, but it did. She wanted him to confide in her. Wanted him to need to talk to her. After everything they'd been through in the past few days, she'd thought maybe, maybe he'd open up to her.

Give it up, girl. Ain't gonna happen.

Trying to swallow down the lump in her throat, she started to follow Leo through the door Digger had closed behind them.

She'd only gone a few steps when Gabriel spun her around, lifted her off her feet and crushed her against him, burying his face against the skin of her neck.

"I'm sorry." His words sounded like a growl in her ear. "I'm so fucking sorry."

He didn't say anything else but she felt his heart trip heavily against hers, his chest rising and falling as if he couldn't get enough air. If the guy didn't watch it, he was going to hyperventilate.

Wrapping her arms around his shoulders, the voices quiet behind their wall, she held on. It was all she could do, because he didn't seem in a hurry to let her go. And she couldn't honestly say she wanted to be anywhere else.

"That man killed my brother." Gabriel's voice held a wealth of despair. "He killed my…my father. I should have killed him before now. But Serena forbid it. Now…I failed them and I failed you."

Spell Bound

The weight on her shoulders grew a little heavier. She had to find a way to end this and soon. Too many lives were at stake—Gabriel's, her brother's, Quinn's, Serena's. And nine other *streghe* who lived in constant fear for their lives.

"If anyone's failed, it's me."

She hadn't meant to say the words out loud, but there they were.

Gabriel drew back to look at her, shaking his head. "You can't be blamed for any of this."

"I'm supposed to break the curse. It's my destiny, my purpose for being. It's the only reason I was born. And I've failed."

Fast-rising misery choked her. Goddess, she'd failed at everything so far. She'd run away from home and left her parents open to attack. Leo had almost been taken from her twice, and the women were still cursed.

"No, Shea." His arms tightened around her. "You haven't failed. We'll figure it out."

Not we. I have to find the strength to finish this.

But first, she needed…

Gabriel stared at her, dark eyes still stained with a grief she didn't understand. Was he so worried about Quinn? Then he shook his head and pulled her tight against him again.

"You know we're both completely fucked up. How the hell'd we get his far?"

She laughed, as she was supposed to, and swallowed a sob. "Just lucky, I guess."

Which was a complete joke. It wasn't luck. The only reason she was still alive and Leo wasn't with Dario was because of Gabriel. She wanted to stay in his strong arms and never leave.

She just didn't think it was meant to be.

Tightening her arms around his waist, she turned to rest her lips against his neck and felt a shudder move through him.

She loved the way he responded to her. Loved that he wanted her just as much as she wanted him.

Loved him.

* * *

Gabriel felt his control give way at the touch of Shea's lips, and he sought her mouth with a savage groan.

He needed her, needed to kiss her until all the other shit in his head went away. The reality of Dario's relationship to him was something he couldn't think about or he might just fall off the brink.

With one arm wrapped around her waist, he used his free hand to grab her chin and angle her mouth so he could devour her. He was rough, grinding his mouth on hers until she opened to him. It didn't take much, but he couldn't stop.

He plunged his tongue between her lips the way he wanted to take her body, hard and strong and just a little violent. He wanted to feel something other than this rage, but the rage was bleeding over onto her and he couldn't stop.

She didn't seem to mind. Her fingers latched onto his hair, nails scraping across his scalp, sending shivers through him. Then she sank her nails into his shoulders and pressed her hips into his, drawing his attention lower.

Sliding his hand beneath her t-shirt, he cupped one silky bare breast, rubbing his thumb against the already taut peak until she moaned into his mouth and arched into him more fully.

With a groan, he set her away from him only long enough to rip his shirt over his head. She followed his lead, dropping her shirt at her feet and standing in front of him naked from the waist up.

The lust in her expression tightened his already throbbing cock into a painful, burning ache. As her gaze trailed from his chest to his stomach and finally to the bulge of his crotch, his hand shot out to cup her nape.

He drew her back to him, eyes drifting closed as he absorbed the feel of her skin against his, hands splayed across her back. Her breasts nestled against his chest, the tips hard and pointed.

Her warm hands on his hips, she urged him even closer, until his cock pressed hard against her lower stomach, left bare by her low-riding jeans.

He ground against her and felt her hands trail from his waist to his chest, where she covered his nipples with first her palms then plucked the erect points with her fingers.

Holy Goddess, she was going to make him combust. He wanted to take her to the floor, roll her under him and spread her legs. Cupping the back of her head, he positioned her to take his mouth again and sucked on her tongue when she snaked it between his lips.

His cock rubbed against his jeans, demanding release. He had to get his jeans off so he could take her. They both needed to be naked.

She already had her hands on the button at his waistband, trying to force the little metal disk through the hole. Her knuckles dug into his stomach and she whimpered when she didn't get them open on the first try.

He moved his hands to help her—

And someone cleared his throat behind them.

Chapter Twenty-One

Gabriel shot to his feet, pushing Shea behind him to shield her. Adrenaline tore through his veins with razor-sharp claws.

He turned to find Matt Tedaldi leaning against the door, a bland look on his face as he stared at him.

It took Gabriel several seconds to put words together. "You're late."

Matt snorted. "Apparently not late enough."

Gabriel's eyes narrowed and his fists curled at the implication in Matt's laconic drawl. Behind him, he heard Shea pull on her shirt then step to his side.

Matt didn't acknowledge her, just addressed Gabriel. "They need to be ready to move in five. We'll head for Louisiana, see Maddie. Then Texas. I'll let you know where we end up."

Shea's mouth firmed at Matt's deliberate snub, and her hands clenched into fists at her sides. For a second, he thought she might go straight for Matt's chin with her fist. She'd reached the end of her rope.

Then Matt turned to Shea and smiled. Gabriel's eyes nearly popped out of his head. He'd never seen Matt smile. Not once in the fifteen years he'd known him.

"I take it you're Shea."

She nodded, staring at Matt like he was a bug under a microscope.

Surprisingly, he stuck out his hand and leaned away from the door to shake. "You look just like your mama. Pretty woman. Where's the boy?"

Shea took a deep, shaky breath. "With Digger."

Matt nodded, his expression softening just a bit. "Then I suggest you get him and your stuff so we can go. Got a lot of miles to cover."

For a few seconds, she stared at Matt with her mouth set in a mutinous line. Then those pretty lips softened and quivered and, without another word or a look in his direction, she pushed through the door Digger and Leo had disappeared into.

He expected to hear the door slam. It didn't.

"Christ, Gabe." Matt's drawl thickened with disgust. "Didn't you learn anything from your daddy? He would have been the first to tell you not to get emotionally attached to any of them."

The words got out before he could stop them. "Davis wasn't my father."

Matt shocked the hell out of him with his next statement. "Well, no shit, Sherlock. Not by blood, anyway. Anyone who had half a brain could tell by looking at you. But most people don't look beyond what they're told. Some of us don't want to. But Davis loved you like you were his, and if you wanna shit on his memory, then you do it away from me."

Gabriel opened and closed his mouth twice before he could speak. "You knew?"

"Knew what? That Davis wasn't your biological father? Shit, yeah. Don't know if anyone else did. Can't help you with who the real deal is."

Gabriel didn't know what to say to that. He didn't need any help figuring out who his real father was. He knew. He just didn't want to believe, didn't want—No, he couldn't go there.

"Why the hell didn't you say anything?"

Matt shrugged. "Wasn't my place. Besides, I'm not much for getting involved."

"Then why are you here?"

Matt shook his head. "Well, that would be the million dollar question, now, wouldn't it?" He glanced over his shoulder at the door. "She's gonna be a problem, isn't she?"

Gabriel huffed. "She's tough. She'll deal."

"What about the boy?"

"He's the most powerful *grigorio* I've ever met."

"Yeah, well, that would figure, wouldn't it?" Matt released a heavy sigh and shook his head. "Damn Kyle for leaving this mess to me."

"I don't think he had a choice in the matter."

Matt nodded then dropped his head and stared at the ground. "Kyle called me just before he was killed, said something was up, needed me to come. I didn't get the message until it was too fucking late."

Well, that explained Matt's grimmer-than-usual mood, Gabriel decided. "If you'd been there, they might have killed you, too."

Matt rounded on him again, and Gabriel could actually see a sheen in the guy's eyes. Hard-ass Matt, who didn't have a sentimental bone in his body. "I still don't understand how they got to Kyle. My brother was one of the best."

Gabriel shook his head. "I'm pretty sure Leo's power got away from him, and Dario followed the trail. Then I think...I think Kyle and Celeste sacrificed themselves for the kids."

Shea opened the door at that moment, Leo clutching her free hand while she held her backpack in the other. Her gaze tripped over Gabriel before she stuck out her chin and looked straight into Matt's eyes.

"No swearing," she said. "I have to agree to wherever we're going. You look at me when I speak to you, and you don't ignore Leo. I agree to jump when you say jump and bite my tongue most of the time."

Matt didn't hesitate. "I'll try to tone down the swearing, for the kid's sake. You can say anything you damn well want to me. I will look at you when you're speaking, but I won't promise to hear what you're saying. You can try to ditch me but it doesn't mean you will." He turned to Gabriel. "I take it you're going after Quinn alone?"

Gabriel nodded, trying to ignore the plea on Leo's face and the way Shea wouldn't look at him.

"Think that's wise?" Matt asked.

"I work better alone."

Matt shrugged. "Your funeral, then." He turned back to Shea and Leo and did something Gabriel hadn't expected. He knelt in front of Leo and stuck out his hand.

"Matt Tedaldi. I'm your uncle."

Leo swallowed and took his hand. "I'm Leo. Do I call you Uncle Matt?"

Matt's head tilted to the side, considering. "You can, if you want. And I'm gonna apologize right now for being an ornery bas—jerk most of the time. It'll save a lot of grief later, 'kay?"

That made Leo brighten a bit. "Okay."

Matt nodded and stood. "Let's get outta here."

Pain ripped through Gabriel's chest, nearly taking him to his knees. *Vaffanculo*, this wasn't right. They shouldn't be leaving him. But he had to find Quinn.

And Dario.

And he couldn't watch them and do that.

Leo walked over and held out one little hand to shake. Instead, Gabriel picked him up so they were eye to eye. "Listen to Matt, okay? He's a good trainer."

"We could come with you, Gabriel," Leo whispered. "We could help."

The pain in his chest tripled. "I know you could, bud. But I couldn't concentrate with you and Shea around. I'd worry about you too much. This way, I won't worry."

Tears popped into the boy's eyes. "Will we see you again?"

Gabriel nodded, every movement an agony. "Count on it. And the next time I see you, I'll expect you to have mastered those knives."

Leo's tears never fell. He blinked them away as Gabriel set him on the ground. Fuck. This wasn't right. This wasn't supposed to go down like this.

He turned to find Shea staring at him through dry eyes. She was royally pissed, whether at him or Matt or life in general, he wasn't sure.

Grabbing her hand, he drew her to a corner of the room, far enough so the others couldn't hear. "I'll come for you and Leo. As soon as I'm done here. We're not finished, you and I."

That made her smile for a brief second but something flashed through her eyes. Something that scared the shit out of him. "Be careful, Gabriel. I need— You need to stay safe."

She leaned up, pressed her lips against his cheek.

Spell Bound

Then she walked to Leo, took his hand and let Matt lead them away.

* * *

Serena was gone.

Mentally, Gabriel kicked himself backwards, sideways, up and down as he stood in the garage staring at the empty space where the Jeep had been. He should have known she'd do this, should have seen it coming.

But he'd been so fucking furious at Serena and so damn heartsick at sending away Shea and Leo. He should have realized she'd been planning something like this.

"Jesus, Gabe, where the hell do you think she went?" Digger shook his head. "Why the hell didn't she wait for you?"

That second question he could answer. The first... He didn't have a clue where she was headed.

But he bet she knew exactly where to find Dario. Had probably been in contact with the bastard when Gabriel had been stupid enough to leave her alone in the garage.

Gods-be-damned. She was going to give herself up to Dario for Quinn, and Quinn would do something so fucking stupid to try to save her that he'd get himself killed.

Crushing weight dropped on his chest like a solid block of iron, the one metal *grigori* could not manipulate.

He had to find them all and he had to be prepared to kill Dario when he did.

* * *

Matt had an old Chrysler with a front seat the size of a church pew.

Shea and Leo sat in the front with Matt…because he had an arsenal in the back. A rifle, two handguns, a few boxes of ammunition, two sets of wrist sheathes and throwing knives, and a few miscellaneous blades. A custom-made carrier held it all steady on the backseat.

She studied their new *grigorio*, their uncle, in silence as Matt drove with an intensity only madmen have, though his handsome features and curly, golden brown hair made him look more like a California surfer than a powerful protector. The shadow of whiskers on his square jaw added to his air of danger.

He looked like their father, enough so that her heart ached as they left the building. Except for his eyes. Matt's were bright blue and sharp, able to see through lies and into all your secrets. He turned those eyes on her now, only briefly.

"What?"

A man of few words. So unlike Quinn. So much like Gabriel. She hated him for sending them off with someone else, even though she knew he was doing what he thought best.

"Nothing."

Matt's right eyebrow lifted slightly but he didn't say anything.

"You look like Daddy," Leo said, his tone subdued. "Are we going to live with you now?"

Shea drew in a short breath, ready to punch the man if he so much as looked at Leo the wrong way.

Matt surprised the hell out of her. "Yeah, I'd like you to. You two are all I have left in the way of family. And frankly, I miss your dad. He was some years older than me, and…" Matt took a deep breath, "your parents raised me when my mom and dad were killed."

He now had their undivided attention. Their father had never talked about his parents. In fact, he'd never talked about Matt, but Shea wasn't about to mention that now.

"What happened?" Leo voiced the words Shea couldn't get past the lump in her throat.

Matt's fingers tightened around the steering wheel, and his foot goosed the gas pedal before settling into a slower speed for the city streets. "Car accident, if you can believe that. Drunk driver ran 'em down on the side of the road. They were walking home from a dinner party. Mom was killed instantly. Dad hung on for a few days until we pulled the plug. I was twelve. Your mom and dad took me with them after that. Kyle trained me, even though I wasn't sure I was going to be a *grigorio*. I thought maybe I'd follow my dad into the service first.

"We traveled for a few years, until I decided I could take care of myself when I was seventeen and set off to see the world."

The look he shot Shea said something she couldn't understand, but there was something…

"How old are you?" she asked.

"Thirty-eight."

She gasped. "You knew. About me. You were there when I was born."

"Yeah, I was."

Her mouth dropped open. "Did Mom…did she tell you how…how I'm supposed to break the curse?"

His expression softened, and he released one hand from the steering wheel to squeeze her shoulder. "Sorry, hon, she didn't. She never said a word about it."

The hope that had flared briefly but so fiercely for those few seconds died with a sharp pain in her chest, and she silently cursed herself for being a fool. She knew what she had to do. Her grandfather's journal and Serena had made that so clear.

This was a blood curse and it would demand blood in payment. Her blood.

And it was going to be soon. She just needed to know that Leo would be safe when she was gone. Then she'd finish this.

"Where are we going?" Leo's voice broke into her morbid thoughts and she waited for Matt to brush him off. He didn't.

"New Orleans, see Gabe's sister, Maddie. Then Dallas. I got a house there, been in the family for nearly a century. We should be safe for a while. If not, then Mexico. I got a few spots tucked away."

As Leo continued to ask questions, the buzz in Shea's head grew louder. It had started the second Matt had pulled away from the warehouse. She hadn't worried about it. Now that she knew what that buzz was, what it meant, she'd accepted it and didn't try to block it. She still couldn't make out what the women were saying, though, and it was beginning to drive her a little crazy. She knew they wanted to tell her something, something important. About the curse.

And that they were going in the wrong direction.

Matt finally hit the ramp for Route 222 and took it at sixty miles an hour. He pressed his foot to the floor when they hit the straightaway and shot over the Schuylkill River.

The inarticulate buzz became louder, more annoying, until her head started to throb. A migraine wouldn't be far behind.

But she knew what she had to do.

Spell Bound

"Matt. Stop the car. I have to go back."

Matt's jaw dropped, and he took his intense concentration off the road for one brief second. "What the hell are you talking about?"

"I have to go back. There's something I have to do. Pull over and let me out."

"Shea, there's no way in hell—"

She grabbed the wheel and forced Matt to pull the car to the side of the road. A chorus of horns and raised fingers from the other drivers didn't faze Matt at all as he hit the brakes. She threw an arm out to stop Leo's forward motion.

"Jesus H. Christ, girl, do you wanna get us killed?"

Before he could stop her, she'd twisted the keys and pulled them from the ignition.

"What the hell are you doing?"

She ignored Matt and looked at Leo, pasting on a smile for him.

"I've gotta go, bud, but you need to stay with Matt, okay? I need you to promise."

Leo shook his head once, vehemently. "No. Daddy told me I couldn't leave you. Never."

Shea shook her head, unwilling to thinking about the implications of that statement. She refused to put Leo in danger with her.

Matt's hands stilled on the wheel and his tone got deadly serious. "What else did your dad say, Leo? Can you remember?"

Leo nodded. "He said I'd know what to do when I had to."

She continued to shake her head, but Matt sighed. "Shea, give me the keys."

"No!" Gods, no. Her heart hurt just thinking about it.

"There's no way I'm taking Leo back into this mess. You have to protect him. I want you to take him away from this."

Matt held out his hand. "Honey, sometimes you don't get to make the rules. Sometimes the rules are already laid out ahead of time. If Leo says Kyle told him to stay with you, then he stays with you."

No, no, no. This wasn't what she wanted. She wouldn't allow Leo to go with her. "He can't. What if something happens to him? I couldn't live with that."

"Shea." Matt's voice got soft, softer than anything she'd heard come out of his mouth. "Your dad, he had the sight. You know that, right?"

She refused to acknowledge anything he had to say, but she couldn't tear her gaze from Matt's blue eyes.

"If the kid says he has to stay with you then you need to listen."

Looking into Matt's eyes, she knew he wasn't going to budge. And she knew Leo well enough to know if she ran, he'd follow.

She took a deep, ragged breath. "Will you promise me you will give your life for his if it comes to it?"

Matt nodded. "Absolutely. I'll do whatever it takes to make sure he's safe. You, too."

With a sinking heart, she handed over the keys.

"Then we need to find Dario."

Chapter Twenty-Two

Serena sat on one of the benches in City Park facing the band shell.

She wondered if the *eteri* who gathered here for summer concerts ever looked closely at the markings around the pond, if they suspected that the decorative carvings were really runes blessing Egeria, Goddess of Fountains, and Nethuns, God of Springs.

Germans may have been the first Europeans to settle the area and the architecture of the older sections of the city reflected their influence.

But the Etruscans had made their mark in other ways. The city still held a powerful magic, fed by the Etruscan descendents who'd flocked here a century or more ago with Italians seeking a better life.

Today, Reading had all the problems of its larger counterparts, like Philadelphia, but the outlying areas of Berks County retained or had reclaimed some of its original wooded glory.

Her home on Mt. Penn was in one of those areas.

She hoped she got to see it again.

Taking a deep breath, she shook her head to clear it of the fear in her heart.

"You can do this. You can do this." She'd been repeating the words over and over in her head since she'd left Gabriel and the others at the warehouse. After she'd made a phone call to the one number she'd been afraid to write down anywhere.

After a few minutes of disbelieving minions, she'd been connected to the man she sought.

Dario had sounded almost sad to hear from her but had agreed to meet her here. With Quinn.

Fear gnawed at her, mocking her decision to come alone.

"No. No! This is your mess. Fix it."

But what if she couldn't? She'd tried once before and look how that had turned out. She'd been so sure that plan would work. Yet she'd created another mess. She loved Gabriel more than her life, but she'd hurt him by keeping the truth from him. She feared he would never speak to her again.

Closing her eyes, she shut out her surroundings and tried to put herself into the dream state where peace was found.

Only to open them when she felt a familiar presence.

Gabriel.

He stood in front of the pond, leaning against the split-rail fence, staring at her. She wanted to go to him, throw her arms around those broad shoulders and hug him to her, but wasn't sure he'd let her. And she wouldn't survive his rejection.

He looked calm enough, but her son could hide so much behind those dark eyes. At the moment, though, she was too glad to see him to wonder how he'd found her.

She loved him so much. "Do you want to hear my side?"

He sighed and moved toward her. "I think I've figured it out. You thought I'd be the one. The female."

Goddess, bless him. "Yes. I believed if I could produce a child with the blood of the *boschetta* mixed with the blood of the Paganellis, the curse would be broken."

He sat on the bench next to her and stared straight ahead. "Why didn't you tell me?"

That was easy. "You loved Davis. I never wanted you to know you weren't his son. Stupid, yes?"

He sighed, and she heard more of his anger slide away with the breath. "No, just ill-advised, given how Davis died."

"Yes, it was. Davis had been my *grigorio* since he'd turned twenty-one. He kept me safe, kept me hidden, and he helped me get to Dario. Then, I wiped his memory of that night, and I never spoke of it again. Davis believed you were his. But he and I were never together until after I had been with Dario. When I knew I was pregnant, I seduced Davis." She grimaced. "Not one of my better moments. But I did love Davis. You have to know that."

Gabriel nodded. "What about Dario? Didn't he know who you were? Why didn't he recognize you?"

"He'd been away at school much of his life so we didn't have much contact with one another in our village. I went to him as a prostitute, one of the many he's had over the years."

"So you've known where he's been this entire time?"

"Yes, but I couldn't let the *grigori* kill him, Gabriel. Not even after…" She couldn't bring herself to say their names. Not now. "Dario is one of the keys to breaking the curse. I know it in my heart. I just don't know how."

"But you didn't have a daughter. You had a son. Celeste had the girl. Why?"

She shook her head. "I don't have any idea."

Gabriel sighed, frustration in every molecule of air. "You know I love you, right?"

Her heart flipped as only a mother's could when her child says those three little words. "Yes, and I love you with all my heart."

"Dario will never be my father. I may have his genes, but he's nothing to me."

She nodded, aching for everything he'd lost, for all she'd put him through. "Davis was your father. He loved you more than his own life. You and Nino."

An invisible weight seem to lift from his shoulders. "What do you want me to do about Dario?"

Grabbing his arm, she squeezed. "You can't kill him, Gabriel. You can't. And I don't believe he'll harm you."

"No, but he'll cut off your head and tear out your heart in a second."

She shook her head. "I think…he's as tired of this game as we are. Maybe he'll be ready to talk."

"Let's hope." Gabriel threaded his fingers through hers and squeezed. "But I'll be ready just in case."

And she knew if Dario harmed Quinn, Gabriel would try to kill him. She couldn't let him do that.

But if Dario harmed Quinn, she would kill him herself.

* * *

Dario sat in the back of the BMW sedan, waiting for the driver of the van behind him to signal he was ready to go.

She would be waiting for him, had tracked him down to let him know where to meet. He felt an unlikely twinge of respect for the woman and had refrained from asking the question uppermost in his mind.

Spell Bound

How?

He had a son. Gabriel had to be his son, they looked too much alike to be anything but blood relation. An emotion he couldn't place burned in his chest. How the hell had she managed it? The boy looked to be in his mid-twenties, but after you've lived five-hundred years, you begin to lose perspective on age.

And he hadn't lived like a monk. There had been women. Beautiful women he ordered from a menu like an expensive dinner and never saw again. There were always more, always different. There are many escort services in Florida if you know where to look.

She had to have slipped in one of those times.

Damn it, he should have been able to tell. His magic had never been powerful, which is why he needed their children, but somehow, he should have known.

He'd been so careful never to make a woman pregnant, not wanting to curse his child with the life he lived and the danger he faced.

Old anger welled in him now, drowning out other emotions. Anger against his own father who'd only had enough love for one son, but who'd used his others like pawns in a chess match.

Christo, the bastard, had brought on their father's madness with his death. He was the only one their father had ever really loved.

Remo, the eldest, should have taken on this burden, but he'd already been doing his father's work. With the strongest magic of them all, Remo had been given to the *Mal* as a child. Dario had seen him only occasionally growing up.

Parente had escaped into the priesthood, though how he'd fared there, with the level of magic he possessed, was a matter of debate whenever they'd crossed paths in the last couple hundred years. Which hadn't been often.

And yet they had been close as children, he and Parente, closer than the others. They'd shared common goals and beliefs.

Dario sighed at how much those could change over the course of a few centuries. Parente still believed they could do good. Dario had no such illusions left.

The world in which they lived now was not so different from the world into which they'd been born five hundred years ago. Poverty, war, starvation, intolerance—they all remained. Only the gulf between the classes was more pronounced and the toys men used today to torture and kill were different. Shiny, new and no less effective.

Peter slid into the front seat, a grim look on his face. Dario felt tension move up his spine like a snake.

"Have you found Kelsey?"

Peter shook his head and Dario had to restrain himself from physically striking the terrified man. He would find Kelsey himself. Later.

"We need to leave for the rendezvous, sir."

"Yes. Let's get this over with."

* * *

"Matt, you have to go faster."

Shea cringed as soon as the words left her mouth, because it was the third time she'd said it. It wasn't helping anyone's stress levels, certainly not her own.

"We'll get there."

Even though Matt answered with the same calm tone as the last two times, she could tell he wanted her to shut up. Only his strong will kept him from yelling at her.

Spell Bound

She slid a glance at Leo, who gave her a tiny attempt at a smile. It nearly broke her heart.

Goddess, please give me the strength to do this.

If she couldn't go through with her plan, her brother would never live in peace. And the women she'd been born to release from their curse might never know freedom.

They were headed back to the city. Matt had called Gabriel under the pretense of making sure he didn't want backup and Gabriel had told him he was following Serena to City Park and that he didn't need a fucking babysitter. And to make sure Shea and Leo stayed far, far away.

Yeah, right. Shea clutched her backpack tighter. She couldn't forget to take it with her. She didn't think she would, but with her state of mind, she just might. She needed—rather, believed she needed—its contents.

And she'd already made sure Menrva's nail hung around Leo's neck.

"We're here." Matt's drawl broke into her thoughts. "It's show time, kid."

* * *

Dario instructed Peter to park the Mercedes on Constitution Street behind the band shell. Drivers used the street to cut through the park but there were no other cars in the vicinity.

He saw two people sitting on a bench facing the stage. Serena and his son. The word sounded foreign.

Behind the Mercedes, the white van holding the *versipellis* pulled to a stop.

He took a deep breath, anticipation making his heart race. Soon. This would soon be over. After he convinced

Serena that his plan for their release would work, this miserable existence would end.

* * *

Gabriel stiffened and turned to watch the brown Mercedes park at the curb, followed by a windowless white van.

Dario. The man who'd fathered him was here. He felt absolutely no emotion at the thought.

He was going to get rid of this bastard once and for all. Whatever it took.

Standing, he watched Dario leave the Mercedes along with two other men. Another man got out of the passenger side of the van.

Which probably meant there were another two men inside the van, at least. Not great odds, but not impossible. Not with his mother's power combined with his.

They could get out of this without losing anyone but first he had to get Quinn out of the van.

Dario motioned the two men to stay at the tree line near the cars as he continued to advance.

"I didn't know you would be here, son."

His mind screaming at the word coming from this man's lips, he managed to rein in his anger. He wouldn't give the bastard the satisfaction.

"Where's Quinn?"

"In the van. Restrained but unharmed. I thought we could sit and talk for a few minutes first."

Gabriel had nothing to say to the man. Nothing at all. He only wanted to fight, to hit something, feel bones break, anything to get rid of this building sense of foreboding.

He had to think, had to be ready for whatever came next.

Spell Bound

* * *

"Damn it," Shea cursed, breaking her own rule about swearing.

As soon as they'd turned off Eleventh Street and into the park, Shea had seen Serena, Gabriel and another man standing in middle of the seating area in front of a large stage.

"We're too late. Matt—"

"Sit tight," Matt said as he slammed the car into park. "Don't go—"

Shea had the door open before Matt brought the car to a complete stop. She had to get to Dario, had to make him see she was the one he wanted, not Serena.

"Dario Paganelli," she called.

The little group turned to stare at her, as did the three men standing guard at the rear of the seating area. They reached under their coats and withdrew guns the size of small bazookas.

"No, don't shoot!" she said. "I need to talk to Dario."

"Shea, get back to the car." Gabriel practically growled the words, his face a tight mask of tension.

She ignored him, concentrating on the man who...oh, Goddess, he looked so much like Gabriel.

"Dario, I'm the one you want. Not Serena. I'm the one. You want to break the curse. You need me. You agree to let everyone here leave and I'll go with you."

Again, silence.

She refused to fail. Stepping closer, she raised her arms to show she had no weapons in her hands.

Dario stared at her, seemingly unmoved by what she'd said. "And what would I need with you?"

"I'm the answer. I'm the one you need to break the curse."

She watched Dario's expression tighten as she drew closer, close enough for him to see her eyes. Close enough for her to feel Gabriel's anxiety like a force field around him.

Finally Dario's eyes widened. "What are you?"

"I'm the key." She had to make him see, had to make him believe. "Can't you tell?"

She held out her hand but, at that moment, a shot rang out. Not a normal gunshot, but a blast from an attonitum, like the one she had stuffed in the back of her shorts. She hadn't known Dario's people had the specialized weapons.

She screamed, but she was too late. Her heart stopped in her chest when she heard Leo cry out Matt's name. In her peripheral vision, she saw Matt fall to the ground, a spreading bloodstain on his shoulder.

"Peter, stand down at once." Dario paid no attention to Matt, kept his gaze focused on hers. "What kind of a trick is this?"

She wanted so badly to see if Matt was okay, but she couldn't fail at this. Not now. "It's no trick. I know how to end the curse."

He cocked his head as if considering his options, but she knew he wouldn't pass up this opportunity. "And what assurances do I have that they," he pointed in Gabriel's direction, "won't come after us? Though your one *grigorio* is injured, I know the boy has power and my son...my son is strong, as well."

His son? Oh, Gabriel, I'm so sorry. "I can assure that they won't come after us."

"Truly?"

"Yes."

* * *

Adrenaline pulsing through his veins like magic, Gabriel knew he wouldn't want to live if anything happened to her.

"Shea!" He yelled, not bothering to contain the fear in his voice. "Don't do this."

"Son, I think she's already made up her mind." Dario never took his gaze from hers. "But what makes you think I won't kill the men and take the boy anyway?"

Her chin tilted up just a fraction. She wasn't kidding when she said, "Because I'll kill myself if you do. And your life will continue."

Dario raised an eyebrow. "Then I guess we'd better leave. Peter, let's go." He waved a hand toward the car.

"Shea." Gabriel could barely get the word out around the knot in this throat. She would not leave with Dario, not if he had to kill every man between here and her to do it. As he made the slightest move toward Dario, the man who'd shot Matt trained the attonitum toward the other *grigorio* again.

No, not at Matt, at Leo, kneeling by his side in the grass under a huge old oak.

"Gabriel. Don't." Shea turned to him. He could see fear in her eyes, but it wasn't fear for herself. It was for him and Leo and Matt. "This is for the best. Don't follow. Please."

"No! Damn it, Shea, this isn't the way." It couldn't be.

She only shook her head, removed her attonitum from the holster on her back and trained it on him. He heard the blast of power a millisecond before the pain in his leg nearly blinded him, it was so intense. He heard Serena cry out and then nothing.

He struggled out of unconsciousness through sheer force of will, long enough to see Dario and his men pull Shea into the sedan and toss Quinn out the back of the van as it pulled away.

"It's going to be okay, sweetheart." Serena was at his side, talking through her tears and tying a tourniquet around his thigh. "It's going to be okay. Just let me check Quinn then we'll follow Shea."

Serena moved away as Matt walked unsteadily to his side and flopped onto the ground next to him. "I didn't have a clue. Shit, I should've known she'd pull something like this."

Gabriel grabbed Matt's shirt and pulled him closer. "He's gonna kill her. We've got to find her."

"Gabriel." Quinn appeared at his side and dropped to his knees beside him. "She shot you. She fucking shot you."

"Quinn."

"Goddamn, Gabe, there's a lot of blood."

Quinn pressed his hands against the wound, shooting agony up his spine. But Gabriel knew it would take more than pressure. She'd hit the artery. She hadn't meant to. It'd been a lucky shot. Or unlucky, in his case. He was going to bleed out if he didn't get help soon.

"Quinn."

"Shut up, Gabe. I've gotta do something about this. We gotta get you to a—"

"Quinn, don't lose her."

Quinn's startled blue eyes met his, and his mouth dropped open.

"No way—"

"Quinn, if you don't follow, we won't know where he's taking her."

Spell Bound

"No." Quinn's emphatic denial made him push harder on the wound and Gabriel groaned. "You can't ask me to leave you. Serena can't take care of both of you. You'll die and there's no way—"

"Quinn. Please."

"Fuck!" The profanity sounded close to a growl. Then Quinn pulled the belt off his jeans and threw it at Gabriel. "If you die, I'll follow you to Aitás and kill you again myself."

Serena knelt by his side, placing a hand on Quinn's arm. "Go. We'll be okay."

Wrapping the belt around the upper part of his thigh, Gabriel cinched it as tight as he could. And could still feel the blood seeping out of him.

Quinn stood in jerky motions. "You better fucking be alive when I fucking get back."

Gabriel glanced up, saw Leo looking down at him from the car window. "I'll be fine."

Quinn followed his gaze and shook his head, breathing heavily through his mouth. He sighed then shifted so fast it had to be worse agony than Gabriel's bullet wound.

The wolf took off without a glance back.

"Leo." Darkness had started to seep around the outer limits of his vision, but he knew he couldn't lose consciousness. He'd die if he did. "I need you down here, buddy."

He heard the car door open, and Leo fell on his knees by his side. "Shea shot you."

"Yeah, but she had a good reason." At least, she'd thought she had. "Listen. You're gonna have to help me now. You're all I've got. Then we're gonna go get Shea."

The boy's eyes began to fill. "What if I can't do it?

What if I can't help myself like before."

Serena placed her arm around the boy's shoulders and squeezed him tight to her side. "I'll be here to help you, Leo. I'm not a healer, but I can guide you. Everything will be fine."

"You can do this. Leo, look at me." He compelled the boy to stare into his eyes. "I trust you, buddy. And Shea knew you could do this. That's why she left you with me. I need you."

Leo looked at the wound in his leg, then back into his eyes.

And with the trust of a six-year-old for his unworthy hero, Leo smiled and placed both hands on Gabriel's leg.

Chapter Twenty-Three

It wasn't long before the Mercedes pulled into the entrance to an industrial complex near Reading Regional Airport.

Shea felt every nerve in her body jumping. Her stomach knotted, her head pounding with tension. Only the voices were silent as she sat in the back seat next to Dario.

Dario hadn't spoken to her since they'd gotten into the car. He'd spared one look out the back window as they'd pulled away then had stared out the side window, ignoring her completely.

She hadn't been able to look back.

Goddess, please let Gabriel be okay.

Just the thought of what she'd done made her eyes burn and her stomach shrivel into a ball. A few days ago, Gabriel had asked her if she could shoot him if he told her to. She'd given him her answer a few minutes ago.

Now she had to be strong for a little while longer and finish this.

"So, are you ready to tell me how to break the curse or are you going to keep me in suspense?" Dario asked.

They were the first words he'd spoken since they'd gotten in the car but there was no way she was answering his question.

Instead she countered, "Your men killed my parents."

He didn't flinch. "And your parents were…?"

"Kyle and Celeste Tedaldi."

He nodded, and his gaze ran over her face, examining her features. "Your mother was a beautiful woman. They were all beautiful women. But they've been released now."

"No, unfortunately, they haven't. They're in here." She tapped her temple. "You butchered them. Now they're in limbo."

He nodded and something resembling pain crossed his expression. "That was never my intention. But their lives were an abomination, as is mine. The curse must end. My brother Remo enjoys this existence. He does not want to end the curse. I do."

His brothers? There were more? Goddess, help her. "Did you know about me?"

"No." He laughed, as if they weren't mortal enemies. "I'm still amazed at your presence. How exactly did you come about?"

She shook her head. "I don't know. I only know that I'm here, and I'm supposed to break the curse."

"And you are going to do that…how?"

Blood for blood. She didn't say it out loud, but she knew what would have to happen.

She couldn't let her parents' deaths be in vain.

* * *

Gabriel got a call from Quinn twenty minutes after he'd left to follow Dario and Shea.

When he hung up, he turned to Matt and Leo. Matt had tossed his blood-soaked shirt into the back seat so

Serena could wrap his wound. The blast had smashed through his shoulder with enough force to knock him to the ground, but the wound wasn't Fatal.

He held Leo in his arms. The boy was tired but he was starting to come around. He'd maintained a control Gabriel couldn't have managed under the stress and didn't seem to be suffering any adverse affects.

"Where is she?" Serena asked.

"At the airport."

"If he gets her on a plane, we're screwed," Matt said. "Let's get a move on."

Fuck, no. Gabriel was going nowhere with his mother and Matt, who probably had a concussion in addition to the attonitum blast wound but wouldn't let Leo heal him. Said the boy had already expended too much energy. And he probably had.

Matt and Serena would be staying here. And Leo was coming with him.

As if she'd read his mind, Serena helped Matt up and back to the front seat of his Chrysler.

We'll be fine, dear." She reached up to kiss his cheek. "I'll take Matt back to the compound. Come back to us."

"I will. Stay safe, Mom. I love you."

Her eyes filled with tears but she smiled. "I love you, too, sweetheart."

His gut burned as if he'd swallowed a vat of acid as he and Leo drove away in the Jeep. Their destination turned out to be a deserted-looking warehouse in an industrial park near the airport.

Quinn, dressed only in a pair of baggy work pants he must have stolen, emerged from the shadows along the side of the building. Gabriel pulled up next to him and got out of the car, signaling Leo to follow.

"They're in there." Quinn pointed the building behind them. "What do you want to do?"

He wanted Shea back, however he could get her. He wanted to be rid of the constant fear that ate at his guts for his loved ones. He wanted the damn curse broken.

"Hell if I know."

Quinn's jaw dropped a second before he emitted a short harsh bark of laughter. "Well, then I say we just walk in the front door and take back your woman."

Gabriel shot him a look. "You know, you're not that funny."

Quinn smiled at him. "Yeah, but your girl thinks I'm cute."

Gabriel snorted as he felt the weight on his chest lighten just a little at Quinn's banter. It helped pull him back from the brink of…what? Despair? No, there was no reason to despair. Not yet.

"Leo." He glanced down and saw resolve in Leo's dark eyes. "Your knives are under the seat. Don't leave my side unless I tell you to run, and you use those blades if you have to."

He waited until the little boy nodded. Christ, he hoped he didn't need the kid, but he couldn't take any chances. Not with Shea.

Gabriel pulled open the sliding door to the warehouse without encountering a challenge and scanned the empty space with his eyes and senses.

When he didn't find anyone, they ran for the back where a solid steel door was set in the center of a brick wall.

Quinn sighed. "I don't like going in blind, Gabe."

Gabriel shook his head. "Me, either. But we don't have a choice."

Leo's small hand pushed at his waist, trying to move

Spell Bound

him. Gabriel allowed him to get by then watched as the kid pulled at a string around his neck and pulled Shea's nail, in its shape as a key, from beneath his shirt. With the nail in his hand, he placed both palms on the door and closed his eyes.

"I see four people with guns and I see that other guy," Leo said. "The one who took Shea."

Jesus, this kid was a treasure. Gabriel would have given him a hug if he could have spared the time.

"What about Shea, Leo? Where's Shea?"

It took him a few seconds but Gabriel knew exactly when he found her. Leo started pounding on the door and screaming.

"No! Shea! No!"

* * *

Shea had prepared herself as best she could for this, but she still couldn't stop the shakes. Her teeth chattered and her hands trembled so badly, she couldn't hold them together.

For the past few minutes, she and Dario had discussed the process of what was going to happen, what needed to be done, but her brain could only think about Leo and Gabriel.

She wanted to hold her brother one more time. She hadn't been able to say goodbye in all the mess. And she wanted one last kiss from Gabriel.

She didn't want to let a mad man stick a blade through her heart so he could mingle his life blood with hers.

But here she stood, her mother's athame in her hand. Ready to end this. For her parents' sake. For the women. For Leo.

"And you're sure this will work?"

Dario stared at her with an expression of childlike curiosity, looking so much like Gabriel, it was starting to give her the creeps.

She forced her spine straighter and nodded. "Yes. It will." It had to. "Are you afraid?"

Dario chuckled, and the sound sent chills down her spine. "No. I'm not afraid of dying. But if this doesn't work, I will heal when the knife is removed from my heart. You won't, will you?"

There was no way she wanted to think about that now. "It will work. And when the curse is broken and you stop your pursuit of my brother and the women, it'll have been worth it."

Dario nodded, his expression considering. "You're a brave girl. You would have been more than a match for my son, I believe."

Her lip quivered before she could stop it. He was torturing her, the bastard. Why? When everything he'd worked toward for centuries was about to happen?

And it would happen. She truly believed this was the only way to break the curse.

Blood for blood.

Plus, the constant hum of the voices in her head were gone completely. She believed it meant she was doing the right thing. Of course, it also meant her mother had deserted her when she'd needed a good kick in the ass to forge ahead. Didn't that figure?

She looked straight into Dario's eyes. "Just get it over with."

Goddess, please give me the strength. And let Gabriel understand.

She took a deep breath as she handed him the blade.

***

Gabriel pushed Leo away from the door so hard the kid fell to the floor. He didn't have time to apologize. Laying his hands on the solid steel, he shoved with every ounce of physical strength and *arus* he possessed and felt the metal give beneath his hands.

Not enough. The door remained closed.

He growled, a guttural sound of frustration that echoed the roar in his head. He had to get in there. Shea was in there with Dario, and he had to get her out. Nothing else mattered.

He continued to push, but the steel wouldn't budge.

Damn it, he refused to fail her. It just wasn't an option.

He threw everything he had at the door, and still couldn't get it to move.

And then, just when he was about to start wailing on it in sheer frustration, he felt Leo step up beside him and place his hands on the metal next to his.

Adrenaline surged as they blasted the door away from the frame, knocking out two of Dario's guards in the process.

They rushed into the room—and found Dario sinking a knife into Shea's chest.

Leo screamed, a high-pitched wail, drawing Dario's gaze as he pulled the knife from Shea's body. And Shea crumpled to the ground.

Quinn jumped the two remaining guards as Leo ran for Shea.

Gabriel tackled Dario with a roar.

They hit the floor and rolled. Dario managed to escape from Gabriel's hold and come up to his feet, but

Gabriel didn't give him time to get set in a fighting stance. He swung out with a roundhouse that caught Dario in the kidneys and made him stagger back a few steps.

Dario shook it off and landed an uppercut to Gabriel's jaw that made his ears ring and followed with a jab to his eye.

Gabriel felt a snarl twist his mouth as they traded blow for blow with equal skill.

But where Dario was cold and calculating, Gabriel fought with a dark fury. He wanted to flay the man's skin from his body, make his blood run in rivers.

He wanted him to die.

Gabriel landed blow after blow and absorbed just as many, his fury giving him strength and insulating him from pain.

Blinking sweat and blood from his eyes, he waited for an opening, for the moment Dario would think he had him. He stumbled back slightly, faking a weakness he didn't feel and baring his teeth when Dario took the bait and followed him.

Dario stepped closer, expecting Gabriel to back away. But Gabriel stepped in, wrapped his foot around Dario's ankle and pushed, letting them both fall to the ground. Dario tried to twist into the fall, but Gabriel got his hands on Dario's neck and held him down.

Without a second thought, he grabbed Dario's chin in one hand and the back of his head with the other and twisted his head until he heard bones crack and felt Dario go limp.

The sickening sound didn't stop him from throwing Dario into the far wall, where he made a crater in the cinderblock.

"Gabriel!"

Leo called his name, distracting him from going after Dario and ripping the man's head off. The boy knelt next to Shea, who stared at him with tears in her eyes. He rushed to her side, dread sinking into his stomach at the amount of blood pumping from the wound in her chest.

"You should have let him finish." Her voice was barely a whisper. "Now it's all for nothing."

Shutting off his brain, Gabriel lifted her into his arms as Dario's men groaned next to their fallen leader. Quinn held them at bay with a fierce stance and a menacing growl.

"Don't leave me, Shea." Gabriel heard tears in his voice and wasn't surprised to realize his face was wet as he ran for the door he'd kicked in only minutes ago, Leo close on his heels. "Just hold on until we can fix you. Please."

Instead, she slumped against him, her breathing shallow and faint.

By the time they left the building, Quinn had run ahead, shifted back to human form and had the Jeep idling at the door. Leo climbed in the back seat and Gabriel followed, holding Shea. Quinn peeled out before he had the door closed.

She was almost gone. He could feel the life leaking out of her with each beat of her heart.

He looked into Leo's eyes.

The little boy's hands shook as he laid them on his sister's bleeding chest.

Chapter Twenty-Four

Shea awoke with the knowledge that she was still alive.

She knew because her chest ached...and the voices were back, whispering, taunting.

Failure.

She opened her eyes and stared at a plain white ceiling.

She tried to move but couldn't, her hands caught in some type of vise, and one strong, warm band anchored her to the bed.

Panicking, she drew in a deep breath and caught his scent.

"Gabriel."

Her scratchy throat felt like it was lined with hay, her voice barely audible, but Gabriel's head snapped up from where he'd been resting it on her lap. He had both of her hands in one of his and his other arm wrapped around her waist. It couldn't have been a comfortable position, but his gaze was sharp and alert when he met hers. Assessing.

She couldn't hold his gaze for long.

One big hand reached out to feel her forehead then ran the length of her hair, as if petting her. "How do you feel?"

She wanted to curl into him, but that weight on her shoulders was back. Heavier now. She'd failed them all.

Spell Bound

"Thirsty," was the first thing that popped into her head.

He reached for the pitcher on the bedside table, poured water into a glass then held it to her lips for a few sips.

When he withdrew the glass, she moved a few body parts experimentally and found nothing hurt. Even the ache in her chest was fading.

She looked down and found she was naked under the clean white sheet. She appeared to be fine. Only the faintest hint of a scar where Dario had stuck the knife in her chest. She remembered exactly how it felt, the coldness, the sheer agony.

"You let Leo heal me." She reached for the t-shirt at the foot of the bed and pulled it on, for the first time uncomfortable in her nudity. The huge shirt covered her to her kneed and smelled like him. "Is he alright?"

Gabriel watched her every move like a hawk. "He's fine, asleep in the next room."

She moved to slide her legs over the side of the bed. Before her feet touched the floor, he slid his arms under her and lifted her against his chest.

Because it was exactly where she wanted to be, and where she didn't deserve to be, she shook her head. "I can walk."

"Shut up, Shea."

Her breath caught at the frustration in his tone. She felt his disappointment in the tightness of his broad shoulders as he carried her through the Spartan bedroom into the hall and to the doorway of the next room.

He pushed open the door with his foot...and, in the dim glow of a night light, she saw Matt sprawled in a chair by the bed where Leo was curled in a ball.

Tears sprang to her eyes as she returned Matt's lazy grin.

"You're okay," she whispered. "They shot you. I saw them shoot you."

He ran a hand through his mussed hair. "Yeah, well, believe it or not, I'm damn hard to kill." He looked at Leo with a mixture of bemused devotion and confusion. "The kid's had a busy day. Only fell asleep about a half hour ago. I told him you'd be here when he woke up. Glad you're not going to make me a liar."

It all sounded so normal. Too normal. Everything back to the way it was.

Nothing had changed.

She started to shake, tried to control it, but knew Gabriel felt it as his arms tightened around her. But he didn't say anything.

"The kid's fine, Shea." Matt nodded toward the wall dividing the bedrooms. "Get some more rest. You need it. We'll talk later."

Her gaze went to Leo, curled in the bed, his little face peaceful in sleep. In his clenched hand he held the nail she'd give him. Menrva's Nail. Had it kept him safe somehow?

She felt a bone-deep shudder move through her body, and Gabriel turned and walked out of the room without another word.

Burrowing close to his chest, she soaked in his warmth, that damn cold ache wanting to consume her.

When he reached her bed, she fought the urge to cling as he set her down and pulled the sheet and blanket over her.

"Where are we?" she asked, not wanting him to leave.

"A friend's house in the city. He's out of town."

"And...and Dario?"

Gabriel's jaw flexed, emotion darkening his eyes as he eased onto the bed to sit beside her. "I left him there. I was too worried about you. There was so much blood, too much blood. You nearly died in my arms."

"I'm sorry." The tears she'd been trying to hold back leaked out now. "I failed."

She looked up as Gabriel framed her face with his hands and forced her to look into his eyes. She saw anger and anguish. Those emotions made her heart stutter in her chest.

"You're damn right you did. That was so fucking stupid, Shea. Don't ever do that again." His eyes burned like lasers into hers. "Gods-be-damned, don't you know if you had died, I would've let Dario kill me, too? Don't you know that?"

Stunned by his vehemence, she didn't move when he groaned and lowered his lips to hers. He kissed her with feverish intensity, his mouth, hot and moist, opened on hers, his tongue bullying its way past her teeth to engage hers.

This was exactly what she wanted. She wanted him to overwhelm her, to make her forget. She wanted—

He pulled back and took a step away from the bed, leaving her alone. She very nearly didn't manage to squelch her small cry at his departure. She needed him here.

"Jesus, Shea, you nearly died." He ran one shaking hand through his hair.

She couldn't believe how fast she went from abject despair to a subversive happiness that outweighed all other emotions. It left her lightheaded. She grabbed for his arm but couldn't reach. He was too far away. "Don't leave me, Gabriel. Please."

She held her hand out and waited, barely breathing when he hesitated. He stared at her hand for several seconds until finally he slid his hand into her, lacing their fingers together. When she scooted over, he eased onto the bed to stretch out beside her. On their sides, they stared at each other, and the tension eased from her body with each breath.

"How are Quinn and your mother?" she asked.

He nodded, his breath escaping on a rough exhale. "They're fine. Quinn took her to one of the *lucani* safe houses in Philly since we don't know what happened to Dario." With a sigh, he pushed her onto her back, laying his dark head on her chest. Then he wrapped his arms around her, enclosing her in heat, making her feel safe. Protected. Loved. "I couldn't let you do it, Shea. Not even to break the curse. We'll find another way."

So many mixed emotions rushed through her, she could barely focus on one. Frankly, she didn't want to focus at all right now. She merely wanted to absorb his strength.

She didn't know how long they lay there, silent. Gabriel's large hands splayed across her back on her bare skin, warm and comforting. She felt each individual finger like a brand on her skin.

A sad contentment stole over her. Even the voices were silent. His chest rose and fell against her side with a rhythmic motion that led her to believe he'd fallen asleep. But just as the thought flitted through her mind, he raised his head and looked into her eyes.

"How do you feel?" he asked. "Truthfully."

"I'm fine, Gabriel." Physically she felt fine, anyway. "Honestly. Nothing hurts."

Nodding, he slid off the bed, his gaze sliding to the door.

"Don't go." The words were out before she realized he'd bent to unlace his boots and toe them off before pulling his t-shirt over his head.

Shaking his hair over his broad shoulders, his gaze met hers before dropping to trail over her body.

Heat followed, licking along her skin as if he trailed his fingers over the same path.

"I told you, at Digger's, we'd finish what we started. I'm not going anywhere."

That heat began to spread, sinking into her skin and down into her soul, warming her where she'd been cold and heartsick.

Rising to her knees, she placed her hands on his shoulders. He had a few bruises here and there, but they couldn't mar his otherwise perfect body. She slid her hands from his shoulders to his chest, brushing the hard tips of his nipples on the way. She heard him swallow and draw in a deep breath then his hands settled on her shoulders.

He didn't pull her closer. He let her hands continue their downward path until her fingers slid into the waistband of his black cargo pants. Turning her head slightly, she rested her ear against his chest so she could hear his heart beat. The rough, accelerated pace let her know he was in the moment with her. Then his hands slipped up into her hair and he let his fingers tangle in the length.

The button on his pants provided a slight tussle, but nothing she couldn't handle. And the only rough spot she encountered was when she pushed down his pants and found herself staring at his naked erection, hard and pulsing and right at her lips.

Looking up into his face, she found the heat in his eyes reassurance enough to continue.

With her hands on his hips, she kissed the tip before taking him in her mouth and swirling her tongue over him until he groaned. His skin tasted salty and musky, and she could have held him there all night, learning the flavors of his body, but when he groaned again and pulsed in her mouth, he gently tugged her head back until she stared up at him.

"Slow down, Shea. I'm not nearly ready to end this yet. Lie back."

She obeyed, not because he'd told her to but because the look in his eyes promised more pleasure to be had. And when he reached out and flipped her over, he startled a laugh out of her.

But she wasn't laughing when he began to lick a wet path from her left ankle to her knee then followed the same treatment on the other leg. She felt the bed dip, felt him straddle her and run his fingers down her back, quickly followed by the scrape of his beard against her skin.

It was the most erotic foreplay and she shuddered against him. Her fingers dug into the sheets and she moaned into the pillow beneath her head as he continued his sexual torment with his hands and mouth.

They were everywhere—trailing down her back, kneading her thighs, caressing the inside of her arms and palming her ass—until she felt ready to jump out of her skin.

Then he shifted, rolled her onto her back and let his hands drag from her shoulders to her waist and back up to cup her breasts.

She could barely keep her eyes open, her senses shifting into overload when he flicked one taut nipple with his thumb and moved his other hand between her legs. He rubbed the sensitive bundle of nerves there with his fingers, playing her until she was hot and wet.

Then he slid one finger into her sex and her muscles contracted around him. His groan mingled with hers as he felt her muscles pull him in. She cried out when he removed his hands.

It was only for a second, though, because he pulled back to spread her legs and settle his body between them.

Her eyes closed at the feel of his blunt, burning erection seeking entrance to her body and she shifted, trying to make him hurry and fill the ache he'd caused.

Instead he moved back and her inner muscles contracted around nothing.

"Gabriel, please."

"Shh, slow down, love." He leaned closer to capture her lips while she wrapped her arms around his shoulders. "I'm not going anywhere. Not for a damn long time."

Her heart flipped at his words and her lips tilted into a smile. "I do love you, Gabriel. And you couldn't run fast enough to get away from me."

His gaze darkened. "Are you sure about that, Shea? Because I love you more than I want to live. And if you're sure…about me…" he reached for the bedside table and grabbed the knife he'd laid there, "then be blood bound to me. I can't lose you again. It was hell, and I can't go through that again. We'll be tied. Always.

Heart pounding in her chest, Shea wondered if she'd ever been so happy and so unsure at the same time. She was still the only link to breaking the curse. And to be blood bound meant that Gabriel would live his life yearning for her if she died before him. And the way her life was going, that could be tomorrow.

But in the next life, it would ensure that they found each other, and if it meant she got to spend every life with this man, she was game.

She held out her hand for the knife. When he motioned for her to take it, she shook her head. With a faint tremble, Gabriel drew the knife along her palm, barely hard enough to draw blood. Then he handed the knife to her and she did the same to his opposite hand.

Without hesitation, they laced their cut hands together as he nudged her legs farther apart with his own and slid into her. Just enough to make her gasp. He pulled back and thrust again, this time sinking all the way.

"I won't let anything happen to you, Shea." He withdrew, delicious friction setting off shudders through her body. He slid home again, slow and gentle, setting a tantalizing rhythm.

She felt heat begin low in her stomach, felt the tension build until she sought his mouth with hers and slid her tongue into his mouth as he slid into her body below.

He refused to hurry, even when she dug her fingers into his ass and arched into him, moaning his name. His easy rhythm made her burn more than any furious motion could have.

But it cost him to take it so slow. His breath labored out of his lungs with the force of a steam engine, bathing her neck in moist heat. His skin dampened with sweat, intensifying his scent and making her hands glide over his back and shoulders as she sought to touch every inch of him.

When she reached his ass again and slid one hand between his legs to rub at the sensitive skin between his cheeks, he finally broke.

His hands tightened on hers, the blood smearing,

meshing. His hips swung hard and fast, his cock rubbing every erogenous zone in her sex, overloading her brain with ecstasy.

With a cry, she arched into him as she climaxed, her sex clenching around him and milking his cock until he groaned and released into her, his seed bathing her in warmth.

Her world narrowed down to the two of them, bound together in love and sweat and blood. And then she felt something else. Something magical, something that broke apart from them and crested, making them cry out at the absolute joy of it.

It burned in their veins and sizzled along nerve endings until they were spent, gasping and drenched.

Gabriel collapsed on top of her, surrounding her with his scent and strength, his face buried in her neck. He was heavy, but it felt good. Right.

It took her a few minutes, but finally she was able to muster enough strength to turn her head and whisper in his ear. "What was that?"

He shook his head and shifted so he wasn't covering her completely. Sliding his hand out of hers, he held it up for them both to see. When she saw nothing but a thin healed scar, she checked her own and saw the same.

A smile curved her lips and she looked up to find Gabriel staring at her with a ferocity that made her sex clench. "You're mine now. And I'm yours. Whatever comes at us, we'll deal with it together."

Her smile grew. "I wouldn't have it any other way."

Epilogue

Serena woke with a gasp, one hand pressed against the pain in her chest, the other going to her eyes.

They burned, as if someone had thrown acid into them.

Great Goddess, what now?

She drew in a deep breath—and the pain stopped.

"Serena, are you okay?"

Quinn's voice came out of the darkness of his apartment in Philadelphia. He'd insisted on bringing her here after the debacle in Reading. She should have said no. But she'd been weak.

Now... now something was wrong. No...not wrong. Different.

"Serena?"

Jumping out of bed, she ran for the attached bathroom, threw the light switch—

And stared into the mirror at her own golden-brown eyes that she hadn't seen in five-hundred years.

Still, she didn't want this to end too quickly. A slow, steady climax was always more desirable than quick gratification. She'd been alone for so many years now and human males never could last more than thirty minutes, at least in her experience. What was thirty minutes in the span of a six-hundred-year life?

With her hands braced on his chest, she slid her wet flesh against his cock until it was soaked with the moisture seeping from her body. For half an hour, she rubbed her flesh against his, coming close but not achieving orgasm.

She never allowed the tip of his cock to slip further than an inch inside her body. Instead, she used the swollen head to rub against her throbbing clitoris then slid forward to allow it to tease the plump, hot lips.

Eyes closed, she concentrated on sensation, ignoring the man, pleasuring herself with his body.

But as the minutes passed, she found herself staring down at him.

His face didn't contain the perfection of the folletti but it had a rugged beauty all of its own. Her hand found its way to his jaw. Her skin, dark olive against his golden tones, caught on the stubble of the beard he hadn't bothered to shave in several days. She wondered what his jaw would feel like rubbing against her skin. Between her legs.

She moaned and finally let herself slide onto his cock, seating herself to the hilt. The wiry hair at the base of his erection meshed with the fine silk of her mound and she reached down to spread her lips so that the hair could tickle her clitoris.

And then his eyes opened.

Also by Stephanie Julian

Darkly Enchanted
paranormal romance
Spell Bound
Moon Bound

Forgotten Goddesses
erotic paranormal romance
What A Goddess Wants
How To Worship A Goddess
Goddess in the Middle
Where A Goddess Belongs

Lucani Lovers
erotic paranormal romance
Kiss of Moonlight
Moonlight Ménage
Edge of Moonlight
Moonlight Temptation
Grace in Moonlight
Shades of Moonlight

Redtails Hockey
contemporary sports romance
The Brick Wall
The Grinder
The Enforcer
The Instigator

Salon Games
erotic contemporary romance
Invite Me
Reserve My Nights
Expose My Desire
Keep My Secrets
Rock My World

Indecent
erotic menage romance
An Indecent Proposition
An Indecent Affair
An Indecent Arrangement
An Indecent Longing
An Indecent Desire

www.StephanieJulian.com

CPSIA information can be obtained
at www.ICGtesting.com
Printed in the USA
LVHW021451170220
647193LV00012B/889